A M Devlin

A SEMI-DETACHED WOMAN

Thousands have already met Polly Graham in the weekly column she writes for *Woman's Own*. Now many more can savour the witty, wry, yet sympathetic way she looks at everyday problems.

This is the story of a time in her life when Polly, a marriage guidance counsellor, could have done with some of her own advice. We meet her husband, Alan, who seems worryingly preoccupied with life at the office; their three children, Lizzie, Charlie and Jane; her best friend Gwen, whose marriage is *definitely* rocky; Eddie, the distracting young student who coaches Charlie in French; and the various women, including the Awful B, on the fund-raising committee she has been co-opted to join.

Polly's most endearing quality is her self-confessed lack of perfection: she has black thoughts about her children, she makes catty remarks to people she knows she should feel sorry for, she is competitive and jealous. She is also secretly writing a romantic novel . . .

Suburban North London is a state of mind as much as a place and Polly Graham dissects it with a wicked and gleeful humour. Funny, honest, sensitive to the tensions and dramas of ordinary domestic life, and full of warmth, this novel is totally irresistible.

A SEMI-DETACHED WOMAN

Polly Graham

COLLINS
8 Grafton Street, London W1
1987

William Collins Sons & Co. Ltd
London · Glasgow · Sydney · Auckland
Toronto · Johannesburg

BRITISH LIBRARY CATALOGUING IN PUBLICATION DATA

Graham, Polly
A semi-detached woman.
I. Title
823'.914[F]   PR6057.R23/

ISBN 0-00-222949-8

First published 1987
Copyright © by Polly Graham 1987

Photoset in Linotron Galliard by
Rowland Phototypesetting Ltd
Bury St Edmunds, Suffolk
Made and printed in Great Britain
by Robert Hartnoll (1985) Ltd., Bodmin, Cornwall

For Graham, Jane, Sarah,
Alexander, Laura and, of course, Ma

Preface

Once upon a time I was a young wife and mother of three small children and I was very happy. In fact I was happier and more contented then than at any other time. Well, I had never been very good at being a single working woman. I don't think I was cut out for the regular hours and routine of an average working day. I dare say it might have been different if I had enjoyed the work I was employed to do, but I didn't.

I didn't feel like a cabbage, neither did I accept the possibility that I would ever feel like one, and when people asked me what I did, I didn't say apologetically, as so many women do, that I was 'only a housewife' as though being one was a sub-human occupation for women of very little brain. However, I became aware, and indeed who couldn't be, of the vague stirrings of discontent down amongst the sisterhood. The women's liberation movement was gathering momentum and we women were being told, nay, commanded, to rise up out of the kitchen, cast off our domestic shackles and take our rightful place beside our menfolk in the boardroom. Some of my friends, housewives and mothers all, obeyed the call to arms, felt guilty, envied those of us who chose to remain at home and treated us with defensive disdain. Those of us still at home also felt guilty. We envied those who had resumed their careers and, in turn, treated *them* with defensive disdain. It was, in the vernacular of the time, a 'no win' situation.

Personally I had no desire to change my situation which I thoroughly enjoyed for another situation which I was pretty sure I wouldn't. However, although my children still needed me, I had come to understand that child-bearing and rearing were not, after all, to be a life-time occupation. I had sophisticated machines to do many of the traditional women's chores and being simply someone's wife could hardly be called demanding and was certainly not particularly energizing. It carried little status and I recognized that, as time passed, it would do little for my self-esteem. My sister Babs, a committed career woman and feminist, nagged me to consider seeking full-time employment while my husband Alan reared like a frightened horse at the very idea. It was, I'm sure, a predicament that many women will recognize.

For myself I felt there had to be a happy compromise; one that would allow me to stay at home with my husband and children while taking a productive and profitable interest in the world outside my home. You may be able to imagine my delight, therefore, when *Woman's Own* approached me with the idea of a column written by a full-time housewife; a woman who lived the life she wrote about without the assistance of nannies, housekeepers, researchers and secretaries. It was a novel idea at that time (though many magazines for women have since copied this successful formula) and a very exciting one, for it was the compromise I had hoped might come my way one day.

'You've done a bit of writing, Polly,' they said, 'and we like your style, so if you're willing . . .' (Willing indeed. I'd have sold my soul for such an opportunity), 'we'd like you to write about your life and times in so far as they touch on the lives and times of the readers of *Woman's Own*. Just tell it as it is.' Which is what I hope I have been doing, every week, for more than a decade now, in a column aptly, if not very originally, called 'Me and Mine'. During that period I have written about the problems associated with bringing up three independent and spirited children; the feelings, both good and bad, that are generated by a stable but nevertheless spirited marriage; the traumas of death, divorce and moving house, of poverty and unemployment, through the experiences of myself, my family and my friends. I have tried to take a dispassionate view of our ever-changing morality as it relates to the lives of the ordinary people amongst whom I live, and sometimes I have allowed myself to be hurt and angry at the injustices of fate. At all times I try to maintain a sense of humour. I am not political and though others might try to pigeon-hole me, I feel classless.

Over the years I have received many letters from readers who identify with the problems and situations I write about. Some of them have been angry and abusive, for not everyone agrees with the way I and my friends and acquaintances handle our lives. But most of the letters have been gentle, caring missives from women who don't make a habit of writing to strangers who write columns in magazines. I have, for example, received a great deal of positive help with Alan's migraines and my continuing weight problem. When my mother died from cancer I received hundreds of letters from people, both men and women, who felt they had shared the experience with me. I was very moved by their help and compassion. Latterly, the plight of our sick, old dog Poppy (many readers remember her as a puppy) has caused considerable anxiety amongst my readers. My feelings on the subject of AIDS – compassion both for the sufferers and for those who react with fear and panic – are shared by many people, but by far the majority of letters are from women who identify with the joys and miseries I express when I write about my husband and my children. I have come to think of my readers as my friends so it is not really surprising that a kind and caring letter from just one of them can set me up for the day.

Everything I write about has happened, though not always to me, and the places I write about exist. During the early years I wrote about our part of suburban north London, now I write about the rural area in which I live in the North-East. Though I have to disguise the characters that appear in both my column and this book, they are generally born from a combination of distinctive qualities and features that make up the people I know now, or have once known at some time during my life.

In this, my first book, I have chosen to take a retrospective though admittedly fanciful look at a short period in the early life of the Graham family. It was the beginning of a period of change for me, shortly before I began writing for *Woman's Own* and just after I began my training to become a Marriage Guidance Counsellor. I suppose it could be seen as a sort of breathing space for me and my friends for decision-making, but while we made our decisions, we involved ourselves in voluntary work and continued to keep the home fires burning. Looking back, it seems to me that we were peculiarly innocent and naïve for a group of women in our late twenties and early thirties (with the exception of the Awful B, of course, who was born middle-aged and Miranda Cutler who wasn't born at all, but was fashioned from one of Adam's ribs). However, we were about to emerge from the cow-like state with which nature endows most women during their child-bearing years, and this made it a dangerous time for marriages. We women were coming up for air after years of tending to the urgent needs of babies and young children, and our menfolk, accustomed as they were to playing second fiddles in all that domestic felicity, found the new demands upon their time and attention bewildering, if not downright irritating. Marriages that had seemed so solid and permanent were found to be built on very shaky foundations. Indeed, of the eight couples who sat down to our annual New Year's Eve supper that year, only three remain.

So some of those women decided upon a change of partner and a new family, and even now, in middle age, they are still tending to the needs of young children. Others made a satisfying career out of voluntary work. Some went back into paid employment because they needed the money and others because they needed the status and the self-esteem. One or two remained at home, housewives for ever though their mothering days are almost over, and a very, very few managed to combine the two to everyone's satisfaction. I admit

I was one of the lucky ones. I am paid to do what I enjoy doing most, in the place I most enjoy doing it.

Roxburghshire, POLLY GRAHAM
April 1987

Chapter One

On the very same warm, early September morning that five-year-old Jane, the youngest of three, fearlessly began her full-time schooling and Alan, my husband, was about to induct a new secretary, my erstwhile friend Gwen was ringing round her most reliable friends and acquaintances in order to invite them to sit on her new committee.

'I'm ringing you first, Polly,' she said, 'because I need your creative skills.' Gwen, who understood me well in those days, knew that the most passing of flattering references to my creativity was almost certain to prompt a positive response.

'If I may say so, your timing is bad,' I replied sharpish. 'Five minutes earlier and I'd've been in bed and now I've got two eggs on to boil and a squealing kettle.' Alan came bounding down the stairs looking more than usually bandbox fresh. He was preceded by an overpowering smell of Eau Sauvage spiked with TCP. I noticed a small puff of lint on his chin and knew he had tried to wet shave again.

'I hope she appreciates it,' I muttered into the receiver.

'You hope who appreciates what?' Gwen asked.

'I hope the new secretary appreciates the effort Alan has put into his appearance this morning.'

'New secretary eh?' There was a meaningful edge to Gwen's voice. 'What's she like?'

'I haven't met her so I don't know. But she's obviously worth his new grey light-weight worsted and a wet shave.'

'Sounds ominous . . .'

'Well, he *says* she's elderly with a moustache, but then he would, wouldn't he?'

'For goodness' sake get off the phone, Polly!' Alan bellowed from the kitchen. 'Come and see to these eggs. They've both cracked and there's a horrible mess in the pan!'

'You can deal with the eggs!' I shouted back.

'What do I do with them?'

God give me patience, I thought. 'Do you really want me to tell you?'

Without deigning to reply, he started banging about the kitchen like a demented donkey. 'I think he's about to throw a wobbly, Gwen – I'll have to go. Will you be in later?' She'd be in till midday, she said, and I told her I'd ring back.

'Who the hell was that, ringing you at such a ridiculous time?' Alan confronted me across the table with the look of a man who felt himself to be ill-used.

'Only Gwen . . .' I could hear myself being cravenly apologetic.

'I should've guessed,' he grunted and he spooned an interestingly shaped egg into my egg cup. I removed the bulbous blister of white from one side and cut into the shell with my spoon. A quantity of scalding hot water flowed out on to the plate and I consumed what was left in one mouthful. 'I wish she wouldn't keep ringing you first thing in the morning.' I tried to remember when she had last done so, and failed.

Alan's egg was in better shape than mine and I watched him silently as he executed his time-honoured breakfast routine. Tap tap tap round the egg-shell with the knife edge; cleanly slice top off; dip spoon in salt and gouge egg from perfectly formed crescent; dip first soldier into soft-boiled yolk. At this point he frowned and stared at the egg accusingly.

'It's hard-boiled,' he grumbled. 'I can't dip my soldiers.' He stabbed viciously at the rubbery yolk.

'What there was of mine was hard-boiled too,' I countered defensively.

'Is that supposed to make it all right?'

'No, but it shows I've no favourites.' Alan grinned despite himself. When he had scraped out the shell so that not a scrap of egg remained, he turned it upsidedown and plunged his spoon through the hollow remains.

'There!' he exclaimed with satisfaction and I wondered who he was lobotomizing this morning. Then he buttered a piece of toast, spread it with a generous dollop of home-made marmalade, ate half of it and gave the other half to Poppy, our young Labrador bitch. Standing up, he drained the tea from his cup and washed his sticky hands in the sink. Finally he kissed the top of my head.

'I'll catch the 7.15 this evening. I'm having a quick drink with Ted Netherby.' He stood at the bottom of the stairs, looked up and called, 'Bye kids!' There was a distant ragged chorus of goodbyes and then Jane appeared and hung over the banister.

'You can't go till I've got dressed, Daddy,' she commanded. 'You've got to see me in my school nuniform.'

'I've seen it on you darling and you look very smart and grown-up.'

'But it'll look different today because I'm going to school in it,' she pleaded, scampering off along the landing to get dressed.

Alan wavered uncertainly between being an exemplary father and an exemplary boss. 'Look, I can't miss my train today, Polly,' he said, looking at me expectantly, no doubt hoping that I would relieve him of the burden of reaching a decision. I sighed inwardly.

'You go and catch your train and I'll explain to Jane.'

He gave me a grateful squeeze. 'Right. Yes. Thank you,' he said, hastily reaching for his briefcase and umbrella. 'I don't know what I'd do without you.' I walked with him to the door and watched him crunch smartly down the gravel path. He turned and waved at the gate and blew me a kiss. Then he disappeared behind the towering globe artichokes that grew like weeds along our front border.

When Lizzie started school she was very calm and composed. She was neither grief-stricken nor over-excited, but then she has always taken a fatalistic view of life. I'm certain that if she'd been drafted into the army at five years old she would simply have shrugged her small shoulders with philosophic resignation. Charlie, on the other hand, accepts very little without challenge and I remember his first day as a day of battle and belligerence. He fought a rear-guard action from the moment he woke up. He refused to wear his uniform, he threw his breakfast on the floor, he had to be carried to the car and then he declined to get out of it at the other end. He shouted abuse at me and then at the nursery teacher who tried to prize him loose from my skirts. His bellows of rage echoed along the corridors behind me and burst out of the open windows as I walked purposefully across the playground towards the green iron gates.

'He'll be all right as soon as he knows you've reached the point of no return,' the young woman had reassured me, and sure enough, when I picked him up that afternoon, she told me that he had thoroughly enjoyed himself. Famished, he had wolfed down his lunch and had already made one enemy and one friend.

Jane, for whom everything in life is a dizzy adventure, treated school as just one more. She looked forward to it as another child would look forward to Christmas. Naturally she was a little nervous that morning as I led her towards the mobile unit that housed the nursery class. She stared, wide-eyed, at the swarms of children that zig-zagged about the playground with apparent aimlessness and when a motherly looking ten-year-old bent down to smile into her face, she drew back and clung to me for protection.

'Ah, isn't she sweet,' the child said gently, 'and what a nice dolly you've got.' Jane hugged raggedy old Prudumps fiercely to her chest and looked up at me for guidance. I smiled at the cheerful little girl and explained that it was Jane's first day and she was a bit shy. The child nodded wisely.

'I remember what it's like,' she said, and then she ran off to join a group of friends. They all turned to look at Jane and smiled fondly like young matrons admiring a new baby.

Jane smiled back tentatively and then flung herself at me and buried her flushed face in my skirt.

Jane and I joined the queue of mothers waiting to deposit their children with one of the three members of staff assigned to the infants class that morning. When it was Jane's turn to be shown her very own clothes peg and locker, she trotted off with her hand tucked into that of the young teacher without looking back. I believe I was nearer to tears than she was.

The house was uncomfortably empty and silent when I arrived back, so after I had cleared away the breakfast things and bundled the first load into the washing machine, I made haste to return Gwen's call simply in order to resume contact with the outside world.

'What is the brief of this particular committee?' I asked her warily. I was, and still am, extremely suspicious of committees. In my opinion they are usually formed in order to discourage decisive people from taking decisions, and the number of decisions taken goes down in inverse proportion to the number of people sitting on the committee. If I *have* to sit on a committee, I like it to be made up of women. Women reach decisions quickly and get on with more important things. Men are too combative to function well on committees. They all have long-winded opinions that they feel should be aired in the interests of democracy and they disagree with one another on principle.

'Well, it looks as though the Cottage Hospital is threatened by closure again,' Gwen said. I heard her light a cigarette and take a sip of coffee. Cottage hospitals are an endangered species. Ours has been under threat since 1944. Every time there is a government cut-back the regional health board takes a long, hard look at the Cottage. Local residents protest vociferously and a few health board secretaries are made redundant instead. 'I want to get a few motivated and like-minded people together to raise money for a fighting fund so that we are prepared for battle should the axe be in danger of falling . . .'

I should say at this point that Gwen's civic concern was not entirely disinterested. At the time of which I speak, she had a part-time job at the Cottage. However, she was also a local resident, and like myself, she had many good reasons for being grateful for the existence of our cosy little hospital. It has only three wards, but the Graham family has, at some time or another, made use of them all. It is a comfortable, old-fashioned place. The staff are compassionate and courteous as well as efficient and well-trained, and given the choice, people for miles round choose it in preference to the new glass palace on the hill for their minor ops and treatments.

Yet still I hesitated. Gwen tutted her annoyance. 'Look Polly, I'm not asking you to rob a bank,' she said reasonably, 'I'm just asking you for a little of your free time and you'll have a lot more of that now that Jane's at school all day.' Gwen didn't really approve of free time. Being a Calvinist at heart she subscribed to the puritan work ethic with all the proselytizing zeal of a latterday John Knox. I remember she always got on well with Ma and my sister Babs, who were both similarly afflicted.

'I haven't said I *won't* do it, have I?'

'No, but you're looking for an excuse, I can tell.' Gwen was right, of course. What I intended to do with the long, childless days ahead was write my First Novel and I didn't want anything to come between me and the written word.

'Really Gwen, I would like to help, but you see I have this . . . er . . . this . . . well, this sort of project planned . . .' I was not prepared to tell anyone yet about my forthcoming bid for literary fame and fortune. There was a long, thoughtful pause. I could hear a distant crossed line. Two men were talking about the cost of something that they thought was over-priced and they thought someone called Aubrey could do something about. They sounded decidedly miffed.

'I think Aubrey should watch his back,' I said with a giggle.

'What?'

'I said, I think –' I stopped. 'Can't you hear them?'

'Who?'

'Two men talking.'

'No I can't, Polly,' Gwen said irritably. 'Look, do you see this . . . er . . . project, taking up *all* your free time?'

'Most of it.'

'Is it something you can tell me about?'

'I'd rather not . . . just yet . . .'

'Oh well, if you don't trust me.' I did trust Gwen, up to a point. She could keep a secret, but she tended to let people know that she had one to keep. Some people, once they know you are keeping a secret, won't rest until they have relieved you of it and that always made Gwen a bad risk.

'It's not that,' I said, 'it's just that it might not work out and I don't want to make a fool of myself.' I knew that anything I said would just make Gwen more curious.

'Oh, go on,' she burst out, 'I tell you everything.' And she did, that's true. There wasn't much I didn't know about Gwen, from her shoe size (she had broad white flat feet that she called her Dover soles because of their marked resemblance to that broad white flat fish) to the most intimate details of her romantic obsession with Kevin, the french polisher. He had arrived one morning to french polish a small drum table that had been left to her by her Auntie Candice-Marie and he was still french polishing it two months later, only, Gwen confessed, without quite so much enthusiasm.

'Well,' I began unwillingly, 'if you promise not to laugh or tell anyone or even hint . . .'

'I promise, I promise.'

'I want to do some serious writing.'

'What? Do you mean letters or something?' She sounded disappointed.

'No, you fool,' I laughed, 'I want to write a book.'

'You? Write a book?' she said scathingly. 'Don't be daft. You can't even write a shopping list. You haven't got the self-discipline.'

'Well, I intend to try anyway.' I felt even more determined in the face of Gwen's vote of no confidence.

'What's it about then?' Oh no Gwen, I thought, I'm not going to tell you that. I don't want you looking for hidden truths in my steamy fantasies.

'I don't know yet,' I lied, 'but when I've worked something out I'll try it out on you . . . okay?' Gwen grunted noncommittally. Curiosity more or less satisfied, she returned, with her customary relentless perseverance, to the subject in hand.

'Do you intend to write this book eight hours a day, seven days a week?'

'You know I don't. I mean, I've got three children, a husband, a dog and two cats that all require servicing from time to time.'

'Don't be silly Polly, you know what I mean.' Sometimes, I thought, you do remind me awfully of Ma.

'All right then, yes, I intend to spend most of my free time on it.'

'Ah, well, you know what they say about poor Jack.'

'No, what do they say about poor Jack?' I asked, genuinely puzzled.

'All work and no play . . .' she said sweetly.

'But it won't be like that,' I protested. 'I shall like doing it . . . and if I don't, I shall stop.'

'There you are, you see Polly, you just don't have the necessary application. You are, if I may say so, a bit of a lotus eater.' I could see that this was yet another convoluted argument with Gwen that I was not going to win. Before long I knew she would start on the 'you're wasting your talent' bit and then it wouldn't be long before she would talk about housewives and cabbages in the same breath.

'Polly . . . *Polly* . . . are you still there?'

I said, 'I'm thinking,' sulkily, and then I remembered that it was my phone-call and I couldn't afford to think for very long. 'All right . . . so tell me, who else is on this committee?'

Gwen, sensing triumph within her grasp, launched eagerly into a list of names. 'Well, there's me and Maggie and Hannah for a start, and then there's Miranda Cutler who you've probably heard of and Patsy Pennant who's a part-time nurse at the Cottage . . .'

'Have they all agreed?'

Gwen hesitated. 'Well, not yet . . . but they will,' she added hastily. 'And I've decided to ask the Awful B –' I groaned. 'Now before you say anything, B's a marvellous committee woman . . . an absolute work-horse, and she does all the nasty jobs that no one else wants to do.'

'I know all about that, but can't you ask some other work-horse? B can be such a pain.' It's odd really, because when I'm not with B, I feel very fond of her. When I am with her, though, I come nearer than at any other time to committing grievous bodily harm.

'Do you know anyone else better equipped to sell tickets to people who don't want to buy them?' Gwen wanted to know, and I had to agree that I didn't.

'It's just that no matter how much I do, she always manages to make me feel as though I'm not pulling my weight,' I said.

'Well, you don't very often!' Then before I could protest she said with a laugh, 'I'm only joking.' But I knew she wasn't because Gwen always saw me as a large pink blancmange that refused to set and had to be propped up with boudoir biscuits. 'Look,' she continued, 'if I'm Chairperson I'll be able to keep B off your back.'

'Is that all arranged too then?'

'More or less . . . I mean, after all, it's my idea.' Gwen paused. 'Look, can I take it that this sudden interest means that you *will* come on the Committee?' Decision time and all my lazy genes, inherited I have always believed from my maternal grandfather, launched themselves into battle with my dutiful genes, almost certainly inherited from my maternal grandmother (and what a pair they were). My dutiful genes won, and so did Grandma.

'Oh all right,' I said, none too enthusiastically, 'but please can I be the one who Has Ideas and is Creative because I loathe Licking and Sticking.'

'You can't just do all the nice bits.'

'But you're having B to do all the nasty bits aren't you? That's what you said.'

'Sometimes, Polly,' Gwen began irritably, 'you're worse than B, do you know that?' Then quickly, before I could think up a suitably crushing retort, she changed the subject. 'By the way, are you two going to the Uttleys' house-warming?'

'Yup. Why? Do you and Mike want a lift?' My value to the community lies not in my generous nature or in my wit and wisdom, but in my abstinence on demand. As a chauffeur my popularity is unrivalled. I usually fill our old station wagon to bursting before a party but this naturally has its disadvantages. My charges watch me closely throughout the party to make sure that not a drop of alcohol passes my lips. They remember vividly the occasion I got tiddly on Buck's Fizz because I thought it was fresh orange juice and met a lorry head-on going the wrong way round a roundabout. Also, it takes a long time to get home. Decanting drunks from station wagon to bedroom with only other drunks to help is a bit like clearing a battlefield with a one-legged stretcher bearer.

'No . . . actually we weren't invited. Do you suppose the invitation got lost in the post?' Gwen sounded hurt and bewildered. It's horrible, isn't it, when everyone you know is invited to a party but you aren't. It always brings out the rejected child in me.

I didn't know what to say to Gwen so I settled for a platitude. 'I expect it was just an oversight,' which I knew wasn't true. Joan Uttley had told me herself that she was getting pretty fed up with Mike's constant groping even though she knew it was just wishful thinking. He didn't have enough daring to be a real lech.

'That's what I said to Mike but do you know what he told me? He said that Joan's been making passes at him for yonks and he had to be very firm with her at the last PTA meeting . . . I mean, would you believe it!' Frankly I didn't. There really was no escaping from the unpleasant fact that Mike was a groper. Naturally, as is the way of things, Gwen was the only person who didn't know it. The really funny bit was that he always reversed the story. If you were to believe him, Harrow was full of women eager to get their hands on his body. 'Anyway, I guess it means we'll have to cross the Uttleys off our Christmas card list,' Gwen said, somewhat wistfully. 'Well, I'd better get on . . . enjoy the party,' by which she really meant that she hoped it was a bloody awful party and that we'd wish we had stayed home and watched the telly. 'I'll keep you posted *re* the Committee. Byeeeee!'

During the early afternoon, after I had finished all the unpleasant chores like the good little Calvinist that I try to be, I sat down at the kitchen table to start writing my book. In anticipation, weeks earlier, I had already bought a dozen cheap exercise books and half a dozen pencils which I sharpened to a fine point and these, together with two erasers and a six-inch ruler, I put into an old plastic roll-top pencil box that had been mine since I swapped it for six *Eagle* comics.

I took the first exercise book from the top of the slim pile and on its cover I wrote in capital letters:

LOVE WALKED RIGHT IN

by

POLLY GRAHAM

I opened it at the first page and sat gazing at it for some time without writing a single word, but thinking very deeply nevertheless.

'Mrs . . .' I wrote, and then crossed it out. I started again. 'The room should have been empty . . .' But this wasn't right either. 'Mrs Caroline Manson inserted her Yale key into the lock, turned it and . . .' I crossed it out. Surely Manson was the name of that brutal American mass murderer and therefore not at all suitable for my innocuous wife. 'Caroline Bishop turned the key in the lock and pushed open her front door . . .' I tried again, and then again. 'The room should have been empty, for Mrs Caroline Makepeace, whose drawing-room it was, was playing bridge at the home of her friend Mrs . . .' I was finding it difficult to think up suitable names for my fledgling characters. My heroine, for example, had to have a sympathetic name with romantic overtones. It had to be suitable for a middle-class housewife in her middle thirties and it had to be a fairly ordinary name, for my heroine was a fairly ordinary woman. It should be a discreet yet distinctive name as befitted a woman to whom dramatic things were about to happen. I quite liked Caroline, which I decided to abbreviate to Caro to make her more interesting, but Makepeace sounded like an unmarried, elderly librarian, so I changed it to Stansbury. 'Caro and . . . Arthur Stansbury . . .' I said aloud and it sounded right for an affluent couple living in a large, comfortable, Victorian house in a smart suburb of London.

'The room should have been empty, for Mrs Caro Stansbury was playing bridge at the house of her friend . . .' Hang on, I thought. A woman like Caro Stansbury wouldn't waste her time playing bridge in the afternoon. So what was she doing that afternoon to enable Gulley, the engaging sneak thief, to climb through the window of her drawing-room in order to steal the silver? She certainly couldn't have a lover because she wasn't that sort of woman. She could be shopping at Harrods – no, not Harrods. Sainsbury's perhaps, or John Lewis. No, I decided she wasn't shopping either. Caro Stansbury was the sort of woman who shopped, when she had to, early in the morning, and she shopped at her local shops to get it over with quickly. She didn't like shopping, I was certain of that. But she was a good, dutiful woman, so she might be visiting a friend in hospital. She was also a caring mother, so perhaps she was at her son's school sports. What would I be doing that afternoon if I were she, I wondered. I would probably be over in Wealdstone counselling an unhappily married couple. So, I'll let her do some voluntary work. Not fund-raising. She wouldn't enjoy that. It wasn't cerebral enough for her. Meals-on-wheels? No, too humdrum. Then it came to me – the Citizens' Advice Bureau.

'The room should have been empty, for Mrs Caro Stansbury, whose drawing-room it was, was sitting behind a desk at the local Citizens' Advice Bureau helping old Mr Potter to fill out his tax return . . .' Those few lines, I said to myself with some satisfaction, really catch the flavour of Mrs Caro Stansbury. Then I glanced at the oven clock and was startled to see that it was already approaching 3.30, the time for Jane to come out of school. At the rate of three lines every two hours, I thought glumly, I'll be collecting my pension before I finish the final chapter.

Jane saw me peering through the classroom window and was covered with confusion. She looked away quickly and pretended to be absorbed in the story that her new teacher, Mrs Lumley, was reading to the class. But her cheeks were bright pink and she kept glancing furtively in my direction and giving me shy little smiles. She was embarrassed by my presence. I had a time and place and it wasn't mid-afternoon outside her classroom.

I stepped back into the shadow and continued to watch my youngest daughter. Soon she had forgotten me and became genuinely engrossed in the tale that was being told. It was obviously familiar to her for she laughed momentarily before the others and clapped her hands with anticipatory delight. I tried to lip-read Mrs Lumley and thought that she might be reading the dramatic and melancholy history of *Chicken Licken*, which was always one of Jane's favourites.

How pretty she is, I thought. (Jane that is, not Mrs Lumley, though Mrs Lumley wasn't too bad.) So like Ma, yet with the Graham fine bones and lankiness. Suddenly I was swamped by one of those uncontrollable and unexpected tides of pure love that are almost sexual in their intensity.

This was followed by the usual overpowering urge to cry.

'You all right?' A very small, young woman whom I hadn't noticed before was standing at my elbow looking up into my face. I was thankful for my all-concealing dark glasses.

'Yes, I was just stifling a sneeze,' I lied.

The girl nodded knowingly. 'I get hayfever from spooring leaf-mould this time of the year,' she volunteered. 'That's mine . . .' She pointed to a tiny, thin child with long pale blonde curls. I said I thought she looked very sweet. 'She's a he actually,' she said without seeming to have taken offence. 'His name's Wayne but a lotta people think he's a girl . . . he's that tough though.'

'I expect it's his hair, being long and curly I mean.'

'Mmmm, 'spect you're right – but it's fashionable see.'

I nodded understandingly but I couldn't help feeling sorry for Wayne, being tough and looking like a pretty little girl. A bloke would have to be exceptional to live that down. I hoped Wayne was.

'Which is yours?'

I pointed towards Jane. 'The little girl with the plaits and spotted ribbons.' I waited for some small reaction but the young woman simply gazed impassively at Jane for a few moments and then said, 'Reminds me of my sister's kiddy.' For a totally inadmissible reason I was not flattered by this. 'She was killed,' the girl announced baldly as though she was telling me the time. 'She was knocked down by a car a month ago.' I wasn't sure whether she was talking about her sister or her niece. 'It was awful . . . right outside the house. My sister saw it all through the kitchen window . . . she's been on pills ever since.' I shivered and involuntarily edged away slightly. However the girl shuffled after me. 'It was in the local paper.' She looked at me questioningly. Even though I hadn't seen the article, I told her that I thought I remembered something about it and this seemed to give her some kind of satisfaction, for she smiled for the first time and said that she had supposed I would have done.

'Hello Diane.' The young woman turned and acknowledged the newcomer with a brief nod.

'This is my sister,' she told me. I looked at the woman who had so recently lost her little girl. I hoped she wouldn't see Jane and notice the likeness. I thought it would be most upsetting for her. 'This lady's little girl looks just like your Linda. Look!' Diane's tactlessness appalled me but I could think of nothing to say. The two women peered in through the classroom window. 'That one over there with the plaits and spotted ribbons . . . do you see her?'

'Oh my God, yes.' Diane's sister pressed the moist palms of her hands flat on the glass window-pane. 'She's the living spit of my Linda.' I looked on helplessly as the woman caught her breath and began to sob loudly.

'I don't think that was very kind, Diane, if I may say so,' I muttered to the young woman.

'You mayn't,' she replied succinctly. Then looking coldly over her shoulder at me she put her arms round her wailing sister and they both moved away.

Several of the other waiting mothers gathered round Diane and her sister. There was a lot of mumbling though I couldn't hear what was being said, then one or two looked in my direction with hostile, accusing eyes. Clearly it was a popular tragedy and just as clearly they thought that I was to blame for the tears. I began to feel that perhaps I was.

Suddenly the door burst open and small children scattered in all directions like Smarties bursting out of a tube. The children belonging to the group of sympathizing mothers gathered around the adult skirts and soon began to pull and whine. I relieved Jane of some of her essential first-day-at-school impedimenta – Teddy and Prudumps the rag doll; an old first-aid book that had belonged to my long-dead father and had some gruesome pictures in it that thoroughly enthralled each of my children in turn; and a plastic bag of cut-out paper dolls and their clothes.

'What's that lady staring at me for?' Jane whispered suddenly. I looked up. Diane's sister had pushed her way through the clucking women and was gazing at Jane with red, hungry eyes. I sensed the ripple of prurient anticipation as it thrilled round the little gathering. This is a particularly tragic and unpleasant confrontation, I thought angrily, and I want no part of it. I took Jane's hand and pulled her roughly across the playground. A disappointed sigh seemed to follow us out of the wire-mesh gates.

'What is the matter with that lady?' Jane asked as we walked quickly away from the school. I decided to be truthful.

'You reminded her of the little girl she lost,' I said gently.

'Poor lady. How did she lose her little girl?'

'Now tell me darling, did you have a smashing day today?'

'Mmmmm . . . Mrs Yum-yum is very nice and kind. Mummy, how did that lady lose her little girl?'

'Did you eat up all your lunch?'

'No, it was yukky. Did the little girl run away?' I sighed and stopped. I knew I would get no peace until I told Jane what she wanted to know. She would simply go on and on about it until I lost my temper and I would regret that.

'Her little girl was run over by a car.'

Jane's eyes widened. 'Is she dead?'

I nodded. Tears welled up and tipped over her long, straight, dark lashes on to her over-excited pink cheeks.

'Poor lady,' Jane whispered, awe-struck at the enormity of such a loss. 'What a poor lady.' If I had expected Jane to identify with the little girl, I was wrong. I think Jane knew even then that though the death of a little girl is tragic it is worse to be one of those left behind to mourn.

Jane claims that she has no recollection of this incident, but recently I overheard her talking about her early days at school to a friend. 'There was this little boy with long golden curls who looked like a pretty girl,' she recalled. 'And we teased him dreadfully, so to get his own back he said I looked like a dead girl who had been run over by a car or something. I remember this worried me quite a lot until I understood that I looked a lot like his cousin who had died under a car.' So although she may not remember the episode, it certainly had repercussions.

'What's she like?'

Alan looked at me over the top of his paper. 'Who?'

'Your new mistress,' Lizzie replied for me adopting a serious, disapproving expression. I laughed but Alan looked slightly puzzled. The conversation was getting away from him already.

'Your new secretary, stoopid.' Comprehension dawned.

'She seems efficient,' he said briefly and then he turned back to his paper which is always more interesting than I am.

Mostly Alan has quite different priorities from mine. I ask what his new secretary is like, and he replies that she seems quite efficient when it must be obvious to anyone with half an eye that this isn't what I want to know. The things I'm interested in he will probably have failed to notice because he is not the least bit interested in gossip or the ever-changing and fascinating minutiae of human relationships. I mean, he has drinks with my best friend's husband and fails to report that Mike was accompanied by a nubile young redhead who was certainly not his daughter, his niece, his secretary or his wife, and it wasn't discretion that kept his mouth shut, it was indifference.

'I don't want to know how efficient she is,' I said irritably.

'Well, what *do* you want to know?'

'Well, for instance, what's her name? How old is she? What does she look like? Is she married? Divorced? Any children?'

Alan thought about these things for a bit and then sighed his resignation.

'Her name's Mrs Rosen . . . Sheila Rosen. I think she's probably about forty-eight, but I'm not good at guessing ages. She looks Jewish, you know, fairly exotic. Plump, black hair in a sort of bun. Wears reading glasses which she hangs round her neck on a gold chain. Good legs.' He looked at me questioningly. I smiled my encouragement.

'I can't think of anything else to say about her.'

'Try a little harder.'

'She's smaller than you. Expensively dressed . . . wears lots of heavy gold chains. Oh, and she's a divorcee . . . I don't know if she has any children. She makes an excellent cup of coffee and she was wearing a very heavy scent this morning which gave me a headache. I shall have to mention it to her.'

'There, you see, you can do it if you try,' I said, patting him on the top of his head as though he'd been a good dog. He jerked his head away irritably.

'You don't seem to understand, Pol . . . I'm only interested in her work. It's nice to have an attractive woman around the office, but I don't choose a secretary for her looks, I choose her for her speeds.'

It's odd to think now that Alan ever had a secretary of his own. These days, with the new order of things, he has a part-share in the company's only secretary and in any case does most of his typing for himself. In those earlier, palmy days he not only had a secretary, but he had an assistant as well. Ah well, at least he has a job. Well, he had one this morning.

Chapter Two

The inaugural meeting of the fund-raising committee was not exactly a howling success. Well, it wasn't from my point of view anyway, nor from Gwen's, but I suspect that as committee meetings go it was fairly run-of-the mill. Nothing much was achieved, but then you would only be disappointed if you expected something to be achieved; and despite my generally jaundiced view of committees, I did.

To be truthful, my view of events was almost certainly coloured by the fact that I was not feeling altogether tickety-boo. Poppy, our black lab pup, had been bilious most of the night after swallowing (or attempting to swallow) a large toad and Alan and I had a quite serious altercation regarding demarcation lines and areas of responsibility. You know the sort of thing: I cook the meals if you wash up; I pay the bills and you keep house; and more to the point that night, I clean up after the children and you clean up after the animals.

'You promised me,' I whispered harshly at Alan as we stood either side of the poor dog, who was looking from one to the other of us with a woebegone expression on her face. 'You promised me! If I agreed to a *large* dog' (I had pleaded the case for a smaller, more manageable dog like a terrier or a Sheltie), 'you would look after it and that doesn't just mean taking it for nice walkies in the evening after work. "You look after the children," you said, "and I'll look after the animals." So why should it be me who has to stand over a bath full of cold water at three o'clock in the morning rinsing sick from a dog blanket? Tell me that!'

'You don't have to go to work at 7.30,' he replied reasonably. Although I know he will never admit it, Alan is one of the school of husbands who subscribe to the idea that wives spend their days in a state of pampered idleness. He even goes so far as to suspect that I go back to bed when he has left for work.

Then, before breakfast, Jane ran away again. We had a brief, but as I remember it, quite friendly discussion about the necessity for teeth-cleaning while I was in the shower and when I came down to breakfast, she had simply disappeared.

'Where's Jane?' I asked Charlie, the Graham son-and-heir.

'She's run away,' he replied without looking up from his comic. My heart sank. Jane attached great importance to the nuisance value of running away and her timing was always perfect.

'Oh Lord,' I exclaimed irritably, 'not again. And it's raining. Charlie, you go up Cherry Lane, she's probably on her way to Granny's.'

'Ohhh Mum, must I?' he wailed. 'I've got to finish some homework.'

'Since when has comic reading been on the school curriculum?' He gave me a sour look and snatched his anorak from the back of the door, tearing the hanging loop as he did so. 'Damn it!' he said with feeling.

'Lizzie!' I called up the stairs. 'Will you cycle along the High Road. She might be making for the bus.'

'She's not on the run *again*?' I nodded. 'That child's a pest and I can't stand her . . . She only does it to annoy you. If you ignored it she'd stop doing it.' I didn't have the time to explain to Lizzie that you couldn't simply ignore a five-year-old's annoying habit of taking off at the slightest provocation, as much as you might want to. In any case, it was wise to take Jane's threats seriously. She was not given to bluffing. Sometimes she would hide somewhere simple in the garden or under the dining-room table but usually she went much further afield. On one occasion she was whipped from the jaws of a 124 bus just as it was about to draw away from the bus-stop. Occasionally she crossed the dangerously busy road outside our house in order to hide somewhere in the strip of overgrown water meadow that runs alongside a little stream, a tributary of the great Thames, that is rather grandiosely called the River Pinn, but usually she would toil up Cherry Lane to Ma's small ground-floor flat where she was always sure of a warm, sympathetic welcome.

The phone rang just as I was getting into my raincoat to search the garden. It was Ma.

'Polly dear, Jane arrived a few minutes ago so stop panicking. I'll give her some breakfast and then you can collect her from me and deliver her to school.'

'Is she *very* wet?' Ma said she was. 'Then I'd better bring a change of clothing and *please*, Ma, make sure she doesn't feed her breakfast to Gladys.' Unlike Jane, who is an unenthusiastic eater, Ma's spoilt and elderly Yorkie had a voracious appetite and what she liked best was food meant primarily for human consumption. Come to think of it, what dog doesn't?

'So why did you run away *this* time?' I asked Jane as I pulled away from Ma's. 'Wave to Granny,' I instructed her automatically. We both turned and waved at the featureless blob behind the lace curtain. Jane stared stonily out at the rain, which was just beginning to ease off. 'I asked you a question, Jane.' She sniffed expressively and continued to ignore me. Jane sulking is worse than Jane having a temper tantrum. I can cope with anger and frustration when they are expressed in a florid, outgoing sort of way but I am disarmed by sulking.

I really can't handle sulky people. I like people to be like me. I have a flash temper. I blow hot and then cold again within a matter of minutes and everything is quickly forgotten and back to normal before you can say 'Watch your blood-pressure'. On the other hand, a good sulk can go on for weeks and people who sulk rarely admit to it. 'I am not sulking,' my sister Babs once said to me after she had not spoken to me for three days, 'I am simply taking a long time to recover from being hurt by you during one of your famous flash tempers.' I admit it, I do say hurtful things when I am really angry and often they are truths which would have been better left unsaid. However, as I pointed out to her, I didn't sulk when she lacerated me with her cool, sharp tongue, even though it hurt like hell. 'Then that's where we're different,' she said icily and didn't talk to me for another day and a half.

Sulking is a very powerful expression of negative emotions such as disapproval or jealousy or hurt. Sulkers want us to know they're displeased with us without the hassle of eyeball to eyeball confrontation. They also relish their victims' confusion and exasperation in the face of silent and often protracted hostility.

Indeed, I was regularly brought to my knees by Ma's prolonged sulks. The trouble was, she was dreadfully inconsistent. I never knew from one day to the next what was likely to set her off. One week she would remain calm and tolerant through the very worst of my excesses, the following week she would withdraw from me completely for days because I lay in too long one morning. I hated being sent to Coventry by her, especially at weekends, so in an effort to right matters I would follow a policy of craven appeasement.

'Cup of tea, Ma?' I would call winsomely from the kitchen to Ma, who was busy frantically digging up the vegetable patch. Digging was what she always did to work off low spirits or bad feelings. She would grunt something that might have been anything but I chose to interpret as 'yes', upon which I would trip down the garden with a delicately laid tray of tea and biscuits. Without looking up she would say something like, 'Did I say I wanted a cup of tea, Polly?' in a curt voice and I would take it back to the kitchen and empty the teapot into the sink hoping the tea-leaves would clog the plumbing.

'Anything particular you want to watch on telly tonight, Ma?' I would make a point of asking. She always accused Babs and me of watching rubbish.

'Good heavens, I don't have time to watch the television.' (Notice that 'television'.) Implying that if I did I was a lazy, ignorant good-for-nothing.

'I'll make supper tonight for a change,' I would offer humbly.

'You can make something for yourself if you want, Polly. I'm not hungry.' How noble and abstemious she could make that sound and how greedy and self-indulgent I felt.

Sometimes I would even try to joke her back to normal. I would tickle her under the chin, which sometimes worked, or pull funny faces, which never did so I don't know why I bothered. Most often she would look at me and shake her head in a puzzled, sorrowful sort of way and say something like, 'Oh Polly,' sadly, or coldly, 'Yes, Polly, did you want something?' Sometimes, if I was lucky, and her sulk was coming to its natural conclusion anyway, she might snort with suppressed laughter and say 'Oh Polly' in a quite different tone of voice and everything would be all right until the next time. 'I Do Not Sulk,' she maintained loftily until her dying day, 'I just don't like scenes.' Well, give me a scene any day, is what I say.

I think sulking must be an inherited trait like a tendency to baldness or thick ankles. My grandmother sulked, my mother sulked, Babs sulks and now Jane sulks. She discovered the power of sulking immediately after she discovered the weakness of temper tantrums. My impotence and fury delight her. Sometimes, when she is feeling neglected, she will sulk just for the hell of it. 'What's up *now*, Jane?' someone will unwisely ask her and they will have played straight into her hands. If I've got the time and can muster sufficient self-control, I pretend that I haven't noticed. This provokes her into a temper which I can handle and is over in a flash anyway.

Using this tactic I prattled on happily about this and that as we finished our short journey to school.

'Bye bye darling,' I trilled and I gave her a big generous hug. Gripping my hand hard she glared up at me through venomous, slitty eyes. 'I ran away,' she hissed, 'because I don't like the taste of our toothpaste!'

Given Jane's obvious lack of commitment to hearth and home the signs do not augur well for any future long-term contractual relationships she may enter into – to wit, marriage.

In those days Gwen lived in half of an enormous Edwardian Gothic house and appropriately a relation of Mervyn Peake lived in the other half. It had once belonged to a rich and famous jam family and it still bore the traces of its former glory. It stood at the top of a high hill in my particular northern suburb of London and on a clear day you could see both Ruislip Lido glinting in the sun and planes taking off and landing at Heathrow. Because of its red brick gloom and its suffocating coat of uncontrolled dusty blackish-green ivy, we called it, affectionately, Hammer Horror House. But I loved the place. If Gwen hadn't seen it first and snapped it up I think I would have wanted it for myself. I still think of it with enormous affection even though Gwen and Mike have moved away. The families Bray and Graham had so many good times in that old house.

The early rain had stopped and the weak autumn sun was shining with surprising warmth by the time I arrived at Gwen's for the inaugural meeting, and Gwen had put some old wicker chairs from the conservatory out on to the vine-covered terrace. There were two women present I didn't know to speak to – Miranda Cutler and Patsy Pennant. Patsy I recognized as the mother of one of Charlie's school chums and from her greeting I knew she recognized me too. But Miranda was a more or less unknown quantity, although of course I knew of her – everyone did. From my distant shore I watched her progress round the group as Gwen introduced her. The first thing I noticed was the brevity of her mini-skirt. From there I couldn't help noticing the relative length of her legs. It was the year of the maxi and everyone over a certain age and shape had embraced the new fashion with relieved enthusiasm. But not so Miranda. She wore her white leather mini with a sort of brazen defensiveness. 'Comment if you dare,' she seemed to be saying to us, so of course we didn't. She was also far more relaxed and self-confident than any new committee member had a right to be. Although there was something slightly dated about her; her make-up was Elizabeth Taylor made up as Cleopatra and her mountainous, glistening coiffure relied for its bulk upon at least two hair-pieces and a tea-chest full of rollers. But she was younger and undeniably prettier than the rest of us.

'She's Bri Cutler's wife,' Hannah stage-whispered at me across the acres that separated us, 'and they say she's frightfully creative. That's why Gwen asked her to join us.' I felt the first faint stirring of unease. 'She's on loads of committees so she knows the ropes.' Bri Cutler was one of our local heroes at the time. You know, poor boy made good. After leaving school with a CSE in technical drawing he went on to found a large and rampantly successful chain of motor accessory shops. I read recently that his company has gone into voluntary liquidation, which oddly enough made me sad. We were proud of his success.

I knew, because people were always gossiping about the Cutlers, that they had recently moved into a small gem of a manor house in somewhere smart and urbanly rural like Sarratt or Amersham that had a tiled indoor swimming pool *and* a Jacuzzi, a sauna and a solarium. They ski'd every winter in St Moritz and they had a villa in Marbella, a Jensen Interceptor and a half-share in a colt that was tipped for stardom. They were the undisputed leaders of the Northwood and Pinner Jet Set and a lot of people hinted, without actually coming out and saying it, that he had a hand in the till. But then most people have a perverse desire to eat sour grapes, yours truly included.

'I know who she is,' I stage-whispered back. By this time Gwen had got round to me and I was being introduced to her latest acquisition. 'You two should get on,' Gwen said naïvely, 'you're both creative.' Put two creative people in competition with each other and invariably open warfare breaks out. For the time being however we settled for pinched smiles.

'What do you think of her?' Hannah asked after the delegation had moved on. I said that I thought it was a bit early to say, but I did add that I couldn't understand how anyone who still wore minis and false eyelashes could possibly be considered creative.

'Have you all got coffee, ladies?' Gwen asked. 'Well then, perhaps you will get seated so that we can get down to business.' The Awful B sat down next to Gwen and took a short-hand book and a very sharp new pencil out of her capacious handbag.

'Are you taking notes or something, B?' Maggie asked.

'I'm taking the minutes,' B replied importantly. Amused glances were exchanged and eyes were raised expressively to heaven.

'I asked her to,' Gwen explained, 'since her short-hand is still up to scratch.' She went on very quickly to outline our general aims and objectives and I couldn't help noticing the desperate look that was creeping into B's eyes.

'Could you slow down a bit please Gwen,' she pleaded eventually, 'and what came after "by Christmas"?'

'I only want rough notes, B . . . Just an *aide-mémoire* really.'

B, whose French is about as fluent as my Serbo-Croat, said, 'Ah, I see,' intelligently. She intercepted a meaningful look that flashed between Hannah and me which left me conscience-stricken for fully three minutes.

Having dealt at some length with our brief as a committee Gwen sketched out a few ideas that she said had occurred to her while she was doing mindless things like peeling the spuds and cleaning out the cat litter.

I struggled to keep my eyes open as she droned on endlessly about sherry mornings and sponsored slims. But eventually the combination of her voice and the warm midday sun proved too much for me. I had a brief, fragrant dream about me in a wonderful peppermint-green satin nightdress joyfully skipping up a wide, marble staircase. But before I could find out who I was skipping so joyfully to meet, I was woken abruptly by the sound of my name.

'Do you agree, Polly?' someone was asking me.

'Absolutely . . . yes,' I said rather over-emphatically. Gwen threw me a puzzled frown and I got the unmistakable impression that I had let her down in some way.

'Oh . . . all right then, if that's what everyone wants, we'll vote in a Chairperson.' Gwen, you will remember, was under the impression that the position would be hers by seniority. Clearly I had missed some exciting politicking. I tried to catch Hannah's eye but she was trying to catch Maggie's eye who was trying to catch B's eye who was busy busy busy with Gwen's *aide-mémoire*.

'Who wants to be Chairperson then?' Gwen asked us truculently.

'Well I don't,' I said positively and this earned me a small, grateful smile from Gwen. 'I want to be Creative Director.' Miranda Cutler, the unknown quantity, gave me a short, sharp look which I took as an indication of trouble to come, correctly as it turned out.

'I would like to propose Hannah for Chairman,' she said, stressing the word 'Chairman' rather unduly. Still, Chairperson is such a silly, contrived word isn't it? Maggie put her hand up and said in a small voice, 'I'd like to second that.'

'Well I'd like to propose Gwen.' B was bright red with suppressed rage. I knew she was taking Maggie's defection into the newcomer's camp as a personal affront. She frowned sternly at Maggie over the top of her National Health half-focals. 'And I've no doubt that either Hannah or Polly will second my suggestion.' Now to be truthful, although it hadn't occurred to me before, the idea of Hannah as Chairman suddenly seemed very attractive. Fond as I was of Gwen, she was not ideal Chairman material; too bossy and manipulative by half and a rotten delegator. She was, and probably still is, a very powerful woman and I knew she would impose her ideas upon us whether we liked them or not. On the other hand, it struck me quite forcibly that Hannah, with her calm, objective approach to life in general, would make an ideal Chairman. I knew I didn't want to second B's proposal.

'Well yes, of course I will,' Hannah said to B most obligingly. I breathed a sigh of relief which didn't go unremarked, for B was glaring at me expectantly at the time.

I put a heavily disguised tick by Hannah's name on the voting paper and B, our self-appointed scrutineer, finally announced that Hannah had been elected by a narrow margin of four votes to three. The painful silence that followed this announcement was awesome. I should have felt pleased at the result, but I felt like a traitor. I felt that I would never be able to look Gwen straight in the eye again. Maggie told me later that she felt the same.

Gwen pretended to an insouciance I'm sure she didn't feel but I awarded her A for effort anyway.

'Right, ladies,' she said briskly, 'now we've got that over perhaps someone would like to help me with the lunch?'

'What does she mean, lunch?' Maggie whispered anxiously. 'Did she say anything to you about lunch?' I tried to remember if there had been at any time any mention made of lunch.

'No, I don't think so,' I whispered back.

'Oh Lord, another black coming up.' She looked at me with raised eyebrows and shrugged. 'Er . . . Gwen!' She called after Gwen's retreating back. 'I . . . er . . . didn't realize you were offering us lunch.' Maggie's admission was followed by a chorus of worried voices.

'I didn't either.'

'Nor me.'

'I've got a hair appointment,' etc., etc. Gwen stopped abruptly and turned on her heel to face us.

'I said the meeting should finish at three p.m. Did you

assume I would let you go hungry?' Lining up beside Gwen, B adopted a reproachful expression. Struck dumb in the face of Gwen's magnificent disdain, we backed down and muttered things like 'So kind...' and 'Just didn't want you to go to any trouble...' and 'May I make a quick phone-call?'

Miranda was the first to express her feelings when Gwen and B had disappeared indoors.

'Well really,' she said. 'Is she always like this?' Hannah looked at her thoughtfully.

'She's had a disappointment, Miranda. After all it was her idea in the first place and she feels it is getting away from her.'

'I'm quite happy to give her credit for the idea if that's important to her. She just isn't the right person for Chairman.'

'Maybe not,' Hannah said, 'but we need her on the Committee. She's a tower of strength, full of ideas, enthusiastic and she works jolly hard. So please don't upset her unnecessarily.' It was at this point that I knew we had the right woman for Chairman. Hannah may look as though butter wouldn't melt in her mouth, but she has a back-bone of purest Sheffield steel.

Whilst we were toying with Gwen's slightly frozen pizzas and oily salad we tossed money-making ideas around in a desultory fashion. Gwen's earlier thoughts on sherry mornings and sponsored slims were very quickly discarded as old hat, which was just too much for Gwen who retired into a sulky silence from which she could not be roused. B suggested something called a chain coffee morning which sounded unbelievably complicated and boring.

'But it's such easy money,' she pleaded. 'I invite six people to coffee who pay fifty pence each. Those six invite a further six and so it goes on until you have hundreds and hundreds of pounds.' We felt this was something B could organize herself but it didn't need the help of the rest of us.

Miranda, who had been silent for some time, suddenly

said, 'Look, I know the point is to raise money quickly for the hospital fighting fund, but Bri's heard on the grapevine that there's going to be a stay of execution for another year at least. So it seems likely that the pressure is off for the moment.' Heads snapped up and all eyes turned towards her. Aware of the effect she was having she continued hurriedly, 'So that being the case, we have more time to plan something really big and jolly . . . And I must be honest, if I'm to put a lot of time and energy into this thing, I'd like to enjoy myself, and I don't happen to think that coffee mornings and jumble sales are much fun.'

'How does Bri know all this?' Gwen, who had at last roused herself out of her sulk, was quivering with emotion.

'He heard it from a good contact on the Council.' Bri will always be the sort of man to have good contacts on councils. 'And frankly Gwen, to begin with I thought you knew, and when I realized you didn't it was too late to just slip it into the conversation.' All of which was probably the truth but we knew Gwen would never believe that Miranda hadn't set out deliberately to sabotage *her* committee. I must admit I had doubts myself about Miranda's motives. She seemed to be playing her hand like an experienced poker player with an eye to the main chance. Just what the main chance would turn out to be had yet to be revealed.

The last thing I wanted to do was agree with anything Miranda Cutler had to say. Like Gwen I was beginning to feel usurped. Nevertheless, unwillingly I had to agree with her about coffee mornings and jumble sales. I find them boring to organize and just as boring to attend and I speak as one who has done both many times. Like her I fancied the idea of something big and jolly and already a rather exciting idea was taking nebulous shape.

'If what Miranda says is true,' I began thoughtfully, 'it means we have all the time in the world to organize something really big and unforgettable.' People began to look interested.

'You've got something in mind already, haven't you Polly,' Hannah said knowingly. 'Come on, let's have it.'

'Well, what about a fancy-dress dance with a theme, in a marquee on your tennis court, Maggie. *A Midsummer Night's Dream* on Midsummer Eve.' This was followed by a brief silence that was broken when Gwen clapped her hands and grinned round at everyone with pure delight.

'I think it's a fabulous idea. I can see it now . . .' She threw her head back and shut her eyes. 'Everyone dressed as characters from the play . . . the marquee got up like a fairy glade . . . we'll do all the food ourselves of course. Shall we be really daring and hire a disco?' It was the beginning of the end for three piece dance bands at that time, with the mobile discothèque taking over.

We all began to talk at once. Everyone seemed to have something to contribute and I was delighted that my embryonic idea had sparked off so much enthusiasm. I glanced at Miranda. She was watching me speculatively and I couldn't resist a small, triumphant smile. She waited for a lull in the discussion and then said, 'It's not a bad idea actually . . . of course it's been done before, but it's not bad all the same and it would give us plenty of time to raise the money we need for out-goings. If we organize something on this scale we're going to need some money in the bank before we start and we'll have to raise this with some awful coffee mornings I'm afraid, and some jumble sales. But we would make a big killing in the end, especially if we charge a realistic price for the tickets.'

I saw her point, everyone did, but we agreed we didn't mind some awful coffee mornings with such a grand finale in view.

'However, I have another idea you might like to think about,' she went on. Ah, how clever she is, I thought. Instead of giving my idea the thumbs down which would have made people suspicious, she makes a worthwhile and practical contribution towards it and only then launches her counterattack. 'What about a Box Barn Dance?'

'What's a Box Barn Dance?' someone asked.

'It's a Barn Dance Oklahoma style,' Miranda replied. 'I've already spoken to the Bloms and they're happy to loan us their Dutch barn. A stage designer friend of mine has already volunteered to transform it into Main Street, Silver Springs and he says he can get hold of a stagecoach for the night from a hire company that owes him a favour. We can charge less for the tickets because the idea is to auction off boxed picnic suppers. You'd be surprised how much money this makes. We prepare the boxes and no one knows what's inside them . . . great fun. And we all dress up as cowboys and Indians. A young chap who works for Bri has a country and western band. I'm sure he'll be happy to donate his services if Bri asks him.' She smiled knowingly and several people chuckled. As far as I was concerned the gauntlet was thrown.

There was an awkward silence before Gwen remarked acidly, 'Well, you have been a busy little bee, I must say.' Miranda caught the sarcasm in Gwen's voice and decided, quite wisely I think, that at this point discretion was the better part of valour. So if she had yet further plans for us, we clearly weren't about to hear them.

While the others discussed the pros and cons of the two equally splendid ideas that had been put before them, I considered the hidden motives behind Miranda's unforeseen and efficient forward planning. Who is this Miranda person anyway, I thought jealously, and I have to admit that jealousy is what I was feeling, to come muscling in on my territory. It's commonly acknowledged that if there is any creating to be done, I do it. I mean, who will ever forget the Hallowe'en party I master-minded in Gwen's massive cellars; the putrefying mummy in the front porch; the bloody hand-prints on the cloakroom wall; the ectoplasm on the stairs and the illuminated skeleton monk in the conservatory? Who will not recall with amazement and wonder the Vicars and Tarts Ball in aid of the church roof? Well, the Reverend Michaeljohn won't, that's for sure. 'Do you think it's entirely appropriate?' he kept asking me right up until the night and I kept reassuring him that it was its very inappropriateness that would bring them in in droves – and I was right. Poor old chap nearly fainted when he saw the church hall. Let me tell you, it is not an easy job to transform a prefabricated cowshed into a Victorian bordello. Though the Vicars looked sensational to a man, I'm afraid the same cannot truthfully be said of some of the tarts. The Awful B, who looks just a smidgeon like Mrs Whitehouse, could not manage without her glasses and insisted on wearing sensible shoes. 'Well dear,' she explained when I queried her brown Kay's, 'I'm going to be on my feet all night so I might as well be comfortable.' And Large Linda came as Lady Hamilton and looked more like a Madam than a Tart. However she had hired the costume for a previous occasion and said she was determined to get her money's worth. My self-congratulatory reverie was broken when Patsy gave a sudden, high-pitched squeal and jumped up from her chair as though she'd been stung.

'Cripes!' she exclaimed. 'Look at the time!' To my recollection this was the first time she had opened her mouth to speak. Because I had yet again forgotten to wind my watch, I could only guess at why everyone was shrieking and scurrying about like disturbed ants.

The guilt I feel when I am late picking up one of the children from school has always been out of all proportion. I am deeply moved by the sight of a small child waiting alone outside the school gates. I remember the terrible anxiety I felt on the odd occasions that Ma arrived late to pick me up and I assume, probably quite wrongly, that all children feel the same.

Jane hooked into my guilt right from the start and has played upon it, very successfully, ever since. 'Oh Mummy,' she would sob into my arms. 'I thought you were dead . . . didn't love me any more . . . had forgotten me,' etc., etc. and I would buy her off with ice lollies and Lion bars. Even now she maintains that the most positive sign of my love for her is when I pick her up from school unexpectedly. I mean, nothing else means a blink, but when I pick her up from school, she *knows* I love her. Silly, isn't it.

'Before we all disappear in a cloud of dust,' Hannah called after our fleeing backs, 'we must meet again very soon to make some final decisions.'

Later that evening, while we were eating our supper, she phoned with a proposed date for our next meeting. Why is it, do you suppose, that people who know perfectly well at what time you eat in the evening, always ring in the middle of it?

'Am I boring you?' I asked suddenly. Alan didn't reply, but continued to study the traffic formation ahead with the concentration of a man who feels himself to be in the middle of a minefield. 'I said, am I boring you?' I repeated in a loud voice.

It was the Saturday morning following the Committee meeting and having exhausted all the possible humour to be extracted from that, I had begun on a protracted outline of my forthcoming novel. Well, I felt that the time was right to amaze him with this hitherto hidden talent of mine. We were on our way to the John Lewis store at Brent Cross to order roller blinds for the kitchen. The traffic was heavy as usual – well, at least half of North London descends upon this huge shopping centre on a Saturday morning and the inevitable tail-back starts at Hendon Central.

He snapped to suddenly and shouted, 'What? What?' loud enough to be heard over a low-flying jumbo jet.

'I only asked if I was boring you,' I said mildly.

'You never bore me,' he replied, but this time his ritual response to that particular question somehow lacked conviction.

'What was I saying then?' I asked craftily. He thought about it for a while whilst negotiating the tricky exit from the A1(M) and the series of puzzling roundabouts that have sent many a would-be shopper off on to the lesser known stretches of the North Circular towards the Dartford Tunnel. Then he brightened.

'You were telling me all about the Committee.'

'That was earlier.'

'Something about your sister?' It was a good guess because I often do talk about Babs. I shook my head. He sighed, and said hopefully, 'Your mother?' I shook my head again. By this time we had joined the queue of cars that was slowly nosing its way round the service road towards the multi-storey car-park. A few cars peeled off in the probably vain hope of finding a hidden nook or cranny in one of the private car-parks, but we had learnt from bitter experience that, on a Saturday particularly, this could prove to be a colossal waste of time.

'I don't know,' he said finally, 'I give up.'

'I was telling you about the book I'm writing,' I said quietly in a voice that dripped neglect and long-sufferance and was guaranteed to squeeze the maximum amount of guilt from the situation. He gave me the sort of ingratiating grin that always reminds me of Tom the cat when he has been caught doing something unspeakable to poor Jerry by that red-neck bull-dog, Butch. Then he had the nerve to say,

'I knew all along really – I was only teasing you. It's autobiographical, isn't it?'

'Jesus, I hope not,' I said with a chuckle. 'It's about the break-up of a marriage in outer suburbia.'

Alan frowned doubtfully. 'Hasn't that been done before?'

'Dozens of time,' I replied, 'but the permutations are infinite and I think I've found a fairly unusual one . . .'

Alan braked suddenly while the car was resting at an impossible angle up a ramp behind an ancient Cortina that was belching black fumes from its dangling exhaust that found their way into our car via the cooling system. He leant impatiently on the horn, whereupon a hairy brown arm appeared from the Cortina driver's window and waggled two stubby fingers at us. All the passenger doors opened at once and an impossible number of adults and small children tumbled out. Folding pushchairs followed and finally a carry-cot, apparently complete with baby (though that can't have been so, can it?), emerged from the boot. When he had eventually dumped his load, the Cortina driver continued up the ramp and then parked in a 'NO PARKING' zone in front of a fire exit. We, on the other hand, found a spot on the top floor which was just about as far away from an exit as it could possibly be.

'Life would be much easier,' Alan mused dismally, 'if I wasn't such a law-abiding chap.' Inwardly I was forced to agree with him, having found out for myself, years before, how sweet life was if one didn't keep *all* the rules *all* of the time. 'They're a bit like the Ten Commandments,' I used to say to Alan when I thought there was a chance of relaxing his vigilance, 'you keep them in moderation.'

'Is this book of yours going to be a blockbuster?' Alan asked me as we began the long descent to ground level. 'You know, rags to riches and lots of sex and violence?'

'Well, not really. I mean, a broken marriage in Wimbledon is hardly the stuff of sex and violence.'

'Oh, I don't know, there was lots of sex and violence throughout the Smalls' divorce . . .'

'Ah yes, but the Smalls lived in Earls Court and before Clarissa was a make-up demonstrator at Selfridges, she was a Bluebell girl. That's quite a heady mix.'

'Well, my advice to you,' Alan said, as though I had asked for it, 'is to write something that sells, because we live in uncertain times.' And with that surprising assertion we made our way through the automatic portals and into the shopping centre.

Normally I don't like shopping, but Brent Cross always affected me in the same way as my childhood visits to Hamley's at Christmastime. Every shop display was like a magnet and I felt magically released from the constraints of my meagre bank balance. If I wanted something badly enough, I had a little oblong of plastic that said it could be mine. I might only be looking for a length of cheap dress fabric and a paper pattern, but within an hour or two I needed a tractor and trailer to haul away the loot.

Alan pulled me away from a display of new winter shoes and then strode off keeping the regulation six paces ahead of me until we reached John Lewis. I have often wondered about those six paces and have come to the conclusion that he must be ashamed of me. I really wouldn't blame him for we look an oddly assorted pair. Him, tall and slim and immaculate at all times, and me, firmly rooted for ever in the patchwork and Indian sandal quaintness of the hippy seventies. It's not that I particularly subscribe to the hippy philosophy, but I do have an earth mother shape that looks better and is more comfortable when shrouded in loose covers. The only other conclusion is that he believes a woman's place is quite naturally six paces behind her man.

'Why did you say that?' I puffed breathlessly when I eventually caught up with him.

'What?'

'That we live in uncertain times.' I know that in itself it wasn't a particularly odd thing for him to say, but there was something unsettling about the strange way he chose to say it. He made it sound like a warning and it had about it a ring of prophecy.

'Well, we do live in uncertain times,' he replied with a Gallic shrug. 'You never know, the company could fold tomorrow and I could be out of a job – or I could be contemplating running off with Mrs Rosen . . .'

'Is any of that likely?' I asked anxiously. He gave me a quick, peculiar, searching look and then grinned broadly and shook his head.

'No, of course not, silly,' he said, tucking his hand under my elbow and leading me into the store. 'I was just winding you up.' But I found his teasing uncomfortable nevertheless. It isn't difficult to unsettle me when my security is threatened and because he knows this, it is something he tries not to do – which is probably why I remembered this episode many times over the months that followed.

Chapter Three

At the moment, I thought, he looks a bit like Desperate Dan, but if I narrow his jaw and broaden his forehead . . . I squinted at the rough pencil sketch in front of me. I found the head that was slowly taking shape on the sketch pad, though it was nothing more than an idle doodle, oddly fascinating. What I have here, I thought with quivering, excited anticipation, is very nearly the face of Gulley, who was the young man who was surprisingly taking flesh as the hero of my First Novel.

'What you have there,' Gwen remarked drily (she had just popped round, she said, because she couldn't stand her kitchen windows with the sun behind them any longer), 'is a very good likeness of Eddie Taverne.' She looked at me thoughtfully. 'Why are you sketching Eddie Taverne?'

'That is *not* Eddie Taverne. It's just a doodle. Anyway, Gwen, I wish you wouldn't snoop. There,' I said, pencilling in bushy eyebrows and some extra chins, 'now it's Denis Healey.' But I could see she wasn't convinced. Neither was I for that matter. Gwen had put her finger unerringly on something I had been carefully avoiding ever since I had my Revelation.

I call it my Revelation because that's how my plot revealed itself to me. In a flash of blinding light, like St Paul on the road to Mandalay or wherever it was he was going at the time. I was on the road to Harrow Weald myself, sitting mindlessly, and no doubt tunelessly humming, in a queue at some traffic lights. The road was up and I suppose if I could be said to have been thinking about anything, it was the unnecessary number of men that were standing idly around leaning on shovels while they watched another bloke doing something technical with a complicated piece of machinery. The sun was beating down on them and most of them were stripped to the waist and oily with sweat and dirt. They came in all shapes, colours and sizes, but contrary to the popular, male-held belief, I was not, I repeat *not*, sitting there lusting. Occasionally I do, but mostly I don't.

Then the scene shifted. One of the men, a tall, bronzed youth of about nineteen with rippling muscles and a mane of tousled, tawny hair, turned with slow deliberation towards the waiting queue of cars, which were, I suppose, mostly driven by young matrons such as myself on their way to shop or collect young children from school. He yawned and stretched luxuriously, drawing himself inwards and upwards in the process. His whole body was taut with straining, gleaming musculature and his jeans slipped down very low on his lean pelvis. How beautiful he is, I thought, and doesn't he know it. I smiled at the little pantomime and at that moment he caught my watchful eye through the windscreen. He gave me an absurdly exaggerated lascivious grin absolutely dripping with open invitation, and before I could stop myself, I burst out laughing. Well, there was something wonderfully silly about the gesture – his delightful naïveté and his crooked, gappy, discoloured teeth. After a moment's hesitation he grinned, a sheepish, slightly embarrassed grin that said that he knew that I knew that he knew, if you know what I mean. As I drove through the lights he winked at me and as I raised my hand in acknowledgement, my plot was born, just like that.

'Is young Eddie still helping Charlie with his French?'

I snatched the sketch away from Gwen and tore it up. 'Look Gwen,' I began carefully, 'I know what it is that you're not saying that you want me to understand nevertheless, and the answer is no, I'm not having an affair with young Eddie Taverne and yes, he is still helping Charlie with his French. As a matter of fact, I'm expecting him at any minute.'

'Oh, and you want me to go!' Gwen snatched up her things.

'No,' I said casually, 'you can stay as long as you like. He comes to see Charlie, not me.'

'Oh, but go on, Polly . . .' The warm, persuasively intimate tone of voice she could adopt at will was one I always found hard to resist. It had the effect of making me positively *crave* to bare my soul to her. 'He *is* delicious, you must admit . . . and when you remember what an unprepossessing little boy he was . . .'

'Look Gwen, if you're into younger men, I'm sure I can arrange something for you with him.' Her normally pale cheeks flushed a dull shade of aubergine which in itself was interesting because I couldn't recall ever having seen Gwen blush with embarrassment before. I was only teasing her but I wondered if I had unwittingly touched a raw nerve.

'Oh *really*, Polly, I didn't mean anything like that!' she exclaimed self-righteously.

'Didn't you? Actually, I rather thought you did.' Then I laughed lightly to take any malice out of my words. I never quarrelled with Gwen. Something always stopped me. 'Today,' I would tell myself sternly, 'I will show some backbone and have it out with her.' After all, I knew exactly what needed to be said. I had rehearsed it often enough to myself, and to Alan and to Hannah come to that. But there she would be, another, different Gwen, now cold and self-absorbed where earlier she had been warm and funny and caring, and I would find myself feeling grateful for the few precious minutes she so graciously bestowed upon me. I would listen silently for the umpteenth time to the monotonous litany of other people's iniquities against her and I would burst with the desire to shatter her illusions. What always stopped me was my fear of her reaction.

Gwen peered into the biscuit tin and finding that she had finished all the ginger nuts said that she thought she had better go.

'I've got to pick up the boys from Cubs,' she said gloomily

in the sort of voice she normally reserved for picking up her mother-in-law from Watford Junction. I have always thought that Gwen had children because she thought she ought to, being married and all that, and only then discovered that they prevented her from fulfilling herself in more enjoyable ways. However, matters were made worse by the undoubted fact that she loved them. They were always in her way and she was always telling them to clear off. Because she loved them she never stopped feeling guilty about it.

'Has she gone?' Charlie materialized silently at the kitchen door. I nodded. He shifted uneasily from one foot to the other, wiping his inky fingers down his shrunken grey school jersey.

'Is there something you want to say to me?' This was followed by an awkward silence until he said suddenly,

'I bet she's eaten all my ginger nuts again.'

'They're not *your* ginger nuts, they're everybody's.'

'Well I eat most of them.'

'So I've noticed.' I emptied a new packet of Charlie's favourite biscuits into the tin and pushed it towards him along the table. He selected one and nibbled it abstractedly.

'Mum . . .' he said after a while. 'You know my eye?'

'Mmmm.' After Charlie, I probably know his eye better than anyone else. His eye, the one with the squint, was apparent to me, even if it wasn't to anyone else, from the day he was born. In fact, I kept telling people about it. 'There's something wrong with his eyes,' I would say to the doctors and nurses at the maternity hospital, but all they would say was that all babies' eyes wandered a bit at first. 'They'll straighten up when he begins to focus,' they said reassuringly. But they didn't and by the time he was a year old I, for one, had accepted that I was never going to look my son straight in the eye unless I did something about it.

I consulted our family doctor who passed me on to a consultant. After a thorough examination he told me that my suspicions were correct. Charlie did have a squint, or a strabismus as he called it, which sounded to me like a terrible medieval skin disease, in his right eye. 'But that is because he is almost totally blind in that eye,' he finished brusquely.

It's odd, you know, because I just sat there smiling blandly while the consultant, one Mr Brown-Gillies (isn't it ridiculous how many consultants have double-barrelled names), explained precisely what was wrong with Charlie's eye with the strabismus in it. I pretended not to be shocked because I felt that Mr Brown-Gillies was not up to handling emotional mothers. But I was – terribly shocked. I was faint with shock. I couldn't breathe and I couldn't speak with shock. My heart hammered with shock and my knees were weak with shock. My eyes and throat ached with the suppressed desire to cry. It took roughly fifteen seconds and just about as many words for my perfect baby boy to acquire a quite serious handicap, and Mr B-G rabbited calmly on with about as much sensitivity to my condition as a plastic food container. I think if I had fainted or cried he would have been really puzzled.

Charlie had, Mr B-G told me, a rare congenital eye defect and there was nothing he or anyone else could do to restore the sight in that eye. However, he said, he could do something about the squint. He would carry out a small cosmetic operation when Charlie was due to start school. He went on to warn me that the operation, though not a dangerous one, was not always immediately successful.

Charlie's wasn't. Admittedly the squint wasn't quite as bad but it was still bad enough and although Mr B-G seemed satisfied with the results of his endeavour, Charlie wasn't and neither was I.

As one would expect Charlie was unmercifully teased and there was very little I could do to put a stop to it. I spoke to the headmaster, who managed to isolate the worst of the bullies. He spoke to them and then their parents but if anything our efforts had an adverse effect and Charlie was furious with me for interfering. From that time on he became a little stoic. He wouldn't talk about his eye or the bullying that he suffered, and Alan and I watched our happy, outgoing little boy slowly turn into a dour, suspicious child who trusted no one and would look nobody in the eye for fear of ridicule. He also became what we chose to call 'defensively aggressive'. We used to say that if you trod on Charlie's toe he would cut off your foot. He didn't start fights but he generally won them.

'Well, I've been thinking,' Charlie continued, 'and I think I want to see another eye doctor . . . because there's a new boy at school who's had two operations on his eye and he doesn't have a squint any more, and I don't want a squint any more either.' He looked up at me anxiously. But he needn't have looked anxious because I thought it was a jolly good idea and I told him so. To be truthful I had thought of it myself, but because I had been reassured on several occasions by the nurses at the eye hospital that Charlie was in the hands of the Very Best Eye Specialist in the Whole Wide World, I had decided that it would be a bit pointless seeking the advice of a second-rater. After all, what could he do for Charlie that the Best Eye Specialist in the Whole Wide World couldn't? Also I never liked to challenge an educated opinion, which just shows you what a feeble creature I was.

'Tell you what, Charlie,' I said. Charlie looked hopeful. 'I'll speak to Dr Philps about it.'

'Do it now . . . will you? *Please* Mum!'

'I'll ring him tomorrow. It's too late now, his surgery's over.' I pulled him towards me and hugged him fiercely. 'You know we love you very, very much,' I whispered into his small, grimy ear, 'and there's nothing I won't do to try and make things right. But perhaps there really isn't anything anyone can do and I want you to be prepared to hear that.'

'I don't care . . .' He sucked in his breath sharply and shook his head rapidly from side to side. 'I don't care . . . I just want to know for sure one way or the other.' He screwed up his eyes tightly and rubbed them hard with two grubby fists.

'Have a good cry darling, you'll feel much better.' Which is what we did unstintingly until Eddie arrived at the door and Charlie flew up to the bathroom to wash away the shameful evidence of his fall from machismo. I have never told him that crying is unmanly because I don't believe it is. I think therefore that it must be something boys learn through a process of osmosis.

'What's up with Charlie?' The French lesson over, Eddie had taken his customary seat in the corner of the kitchen and was lighting up the first of many strong-smelling French cigarettes.

'I can never remember,' I said, pausing a moment to turn a pair of denim jeans on the ironing board, 'whether jeans should have creases or not.'

'Whose are they?'

'Alan's . . . I think.' I held them up. We looked at them thoughtfully. They were very workmanlike jeans, baggy and large round the waist.

'Yes, they're Alan's.'

'Then the answer's yes,' Eddie said with a little dry smile. 'Why do you iron jeans anyway?' he asked. 'Jeans shouldn't be ironed.' Eddie's jeans fitted so tightly that they didn't need to be ironed and I pointed this out to him. Alan, on the other hand, likes large, comfortable jeans that he can turn round inside of, but he likes them to look tidy.

'Make us a cup of tea, Eddie, I don't want to stop.' He got up obediently and filled the kettle.

It had become Eddie's custom to sit with me in the kitchen for an hour or two after the French lesson on Fridays. He liked the company of older women and I knew there were one or two others dotted about with whom he spent time. Some of us he fancied, like Katya Cox who sunbathed topless on her patio and drank neat vodka at lunchtime, and some of us, like me, were adoptive mothers, though this wasn't always from choice. I think Jenny Southcott, who was divorced and by her own admission randy as hell most of the time, would have preferred to figure in the former category.

Eddie liked to discuss his emotional problems with me. I

think I acquired a sort of guru status for him. I listened while he unloaded and then I would present my analysis at the end. It wasn't something I had deliberately set out to achieve, it was simply the way our friendship developed and I was flattered.

I first met Eddie when he was a pale, unhappy, overweight twelve-year-old at boarding school. Until he was ten he lived with his much-loved divorced mother in a small flat in Harrow. But she died suddenly and he was reclaimed by a father he hardly knew who had remarried years before. His father and step-mother were devoted to each other and their two small daughters and he felt like an interloper. Everyone, he told me, was very pleasant and polite to him but no one tried to get to know him and he gave up trying to get to know them. Boarding school, he said, was almost a relief and when he went up to University he left home finally and never went back. He was sure that nobody noticed his absence.

During his vacations he lived, on and off, with a friend of his mother and to make ends meet he took on several small jobs, one of which was coaching dense small boys in Latin and French.

'I've met this amazing woman,' Eddie said eventually after he had put a cup of tea down beside me on the table. I was relieved that he had forgotten Charlie and his red eyes. He paused to light up yet another cigarette. The kitchen was already beginning to smell like the Paris Métro. 'She's engaged to this meter-reader guy who writes these really incredible poems about sex ... He's been published,' he added in order to impress me with the meter-reader's worth.

Always my main concern for Eddie was that he would sooner or later marry one of his 'amazing' women. He was strongly disposed towards neurotic, self-centred beauties and they latched on to his caring warmth like leeches. Now I'm sure that most men would like to think that they are equipped to handle such women, but the truth is, few are, and Eddie wasn't one of them. However, it took him several years to find this out during which time he was hurt over and over again.

'I'm taking her out on Friday. I thought I'd take her to see *Hiroshima, Mon Amour*, it's showing in Islington. What do you think?'

'What I think isn't important, Eddie. What I want to know is . . . how is it that you're going out with her if she's engaged?'

'Oh, it's an open engagement,' Eddie said blithely. 'He's a really nice guy though. We're mates.'

'When are they getting married?'

He shrugged. 'Dunno . . . they haven't made any plans. I think it's an engagement of convenience myself.'

'What on earth's an engagement of convenience?' Well really, I must be getting old, I thought, because I'm finding the illogical relationships of the young increasingly difficult to fathom.

'Well, it's a kind of protection. You know, if you meet a chick you fancy and you tell her you're already engaged to someone the affair doesn't get heavy and if it does you just say, "Sorry love, I'm engaged . . ."'

'I see, you just want some protection from all those hordes of nubile young things that besiege you all your waking hours!' Eddie gave me a sheepish grin. 'Come on Eddie, it's just a silly affectation, isn't it. Anyway, what's her name, this amazing new woman of yours?'

'From the tone of this conversation Polly I can tell you disapprove of her already.' It was always important to Eddie that I should like his girlfriends and oddly enough I usually did. Unstable and neurotic they might be but they were always clever and amusing and very decorative and I like clever, amusing, decorative people. Who doesn't?

'No, I don't. For heaven's sake, I don't even know her. But you must admit, Eddie, your women do have some outlandish names. I mean, there was Electra and then there was Mercedes, oh, and what about Lorelie . . .?'

'Well this one's no better. In fact it's worse, by your standards.'

'Oh go on, tell me, I promise I won't laugh.'

He sniffed and looked at the floor. 'All right then . . . it's Belle-Amie Paradiso.'

'Good grief! Is that her real name?' Eddie looked up at me accusingly. I presented my studiously serious expression for his scrutiny.

'I don't know if it's her real name,' he replied eventually. 'But it could be . . . she says she was born in Paraguay. She says her mother comes from South American Indian stock and her father is a Portuguese gun-runner.' Gosh, I thought, how romantic, and I remembered those far-off heady days when I told everyone that my paternal grandmother had been a French tart and my grandfather had been killed during the Spanish Civil War. As a matter of fact he was killed during the Spanish Civil War but he was drowned while swimming in the sea off Clacton. 'She's very dark and exotic-looking so it might all be true.'

'Well,' I said, 'at least you're beginning to show signs of healthy scepticism and that can't be bad. I haven't forgotten the time you believed that girl when she said she was a member of the Baader-Meinhof gang. It would have been all right if you hadn't told that man in the disco who turned out to be an off-duty policeman.'

'Need you remind me?' We both began to laugh as we remembered the amazing furore that had followed.

Lizzie's old bike came squeaking up the front path. The door slammed, closely followed by the downstairs cloakroom door. The pattern never varied. She wouldn't use the school lavatories. 'They're filthy, there's never any paper and the doors don't lock properly. What's more, people over five feet five can see over the top and there's an eighteen inch gap at the bottom. I like my privacy.' I understood her feelings perfectly. School lavatories are not designed for pupils. They're designed for easy access by the staff. A locked lavatory door is a clear indication that someone is smoking, or drinking, or fornicating, or glue sniffing, or shooting up, or slashing their wrists. It does not necessarily indicate that someone is expelling their wastes. The business in hand over, Lizzie strode purposefully into the kitchen.

'Now listen, Mum,' she began, then she noticed Eddie. 'Oh, hello Eddie.' She flushed prettily. Well, I found it pretty anyway. It simply irritated Lizzie. 'Is this blushing thing something you grow out of,' she asked me once, 'or do I have to put up with it for the rest of my life?' I told her that it largely depends upon how self-conscious you are and that if you grow out of being self-conscious you usually grow out of blushing. I still blush myself sometimes when I'm caught out in a lie or doing something I'm ashamed of like raiding the fridge in the middle of the night or stealing warm, ripe tomatoes from my friend John Packer's greenhouse when I believe him to be away.

'Hi beautiful.' Despite Lizzie's youth Eddie flirted with her as though she was a grown woman. He simply couldn't resist it. She knew she was being flirted with but she didn't know how to respond. She also had a desperate crush on him which she thought was a secret so we didn't tease her about it. Both her friends Marilyn and Karen had crushes on him too and the three of them, dressed to kill, watched him play cricket at the local cricket club almost every summer weekend. They pretended to me that they were taking the dog for a walk. In the winter they watched him play rugby.

Eddie's presence threw Lizzie into a state of confusion. She looked from one to the other of us, opened her mouth and shut it again and then said, 'Um . . .' We both looked at her expectantly.

'I'm listening,' I said helpfully.

'Oh, yes, well . . . I've just *got* to have a pink leotard.'

'Wow!' Eddie exclaimed, his eyes widening with mock anticipation. 'I'd like to see you in a pink leotard.' He might just as well have said, 'I'd like to see you with no clothes on.' Lizzie blushed furiously again and swung her school bag at him. He dodged but it clipped him sharply on the side of the head and he fell off his stool. Lizzie was horrified.

'Gosh, I'm sorry Eddie,' she cried, rushing round the table in order to help him up but as soon as she realized that she was actually touching his bare arm she drew away from him sharply and hovered over him as he got to his feet.

'Lizzie, love,' I said gently, 'calm down, he deserved it,' and I frowned sternly at Eddie. He was rubbing the side of his head.

'Your mother's right, Lizzie, I deserved it.' He gave her an apologetic smile.

'But you didn't *do* anything. You were only teasing me, I know that. I'm very sorry, I wouldn't ever want to hurt *you*!' The anguish on Lizzie's face touched Eddie and he put his arm round her and gave her a friendly squeeze. She went rigid with embarrassment.

'Eddie, put the kettle on for another cuppa,' I said hastily, 'and you Lizzie, tell me about the pink leotard.'

'You know I've got to have one, I've been telling you for weeks.' She perched on the end of the table and looked at me accusingly.

'I'll look for one tomorrow,' I said.

'You've been saying that for ever.'

Another thing about schools is that they think we parents are made of money. 'I've *got* to have a new pair of rugger boots . . . Mr Jones says so'; 'I need a tin of fruit salad, three eggs, half a pound of sugar, six ounces of plain flour and three milk Flakes'; 'If I don't have an atlas by tomorrow I'm getting a detention'; 'You've *got* to get me a new track suit'; 'I need fifty pence for Miss Burt's retirement present'. It never ends.

'If I don't have a pink leotard by Friday I'm out of the concert. Mrs Benson says they cost fifteen pounds in Lewis's.' I knew very well how important the concert was to Lizzie but at the same time I knew the parlous state of my finances.

'I'll ask your father for the money this evening,' I said.

'It's no use asking him,' Lizzie said scathingly, 'he's always broke.'

Then I remembered my Family Allowance and felt better. 'Don't worry darling, you'll have your leotard tomorrow.' She looked doubtful. 'I promise.'

'Huh, promises promises, always promises,' she muttered drily, draining her cup and sliding down from the table. She sighed. 'I suppose I'd better get on with my homework. Bye,' she said to Eddie. He narrowed his eyes and kissed the air in her direction. Moments later a blast of pop music pierced my ears like hot skewers. Eddie tapped his foot appreciatively and then Jane came in and Eddie was hers for the next half-hour.

Alan stood in the kitchen door and waved his arms about like a manic windmill. Anyone who didn't know would think he was beating back a swarm of invisible bees. What he was actually doing was letting me know how much he disapproved of me sitting in the kitchen with Eddie, smoking and drinking cups of coffee.

'Phew!' he gasped, 'what a fug in here!' And he glanced meaningfully at the ashtray. What he liked best was to find a mountain of stubs. This reinforced his image of me as a lazy, pampered wife with too much time on her hands. 'It's all right for some,' he said dismally and I mouthed it rather cruelly behind his back. Well, 'It's all right for some' is what he always says when people appear to be having fun while he is being virtuously industrious.

I jumped up with a great, if rather belated, show of wifely enthusiasm and planted a dutiful kiss on his four o'clock shadow.

'Had a good day?' I asked brightly. I say the same thing every evening. It would drive me out of my mind to have some woman bleating out the same silly, meaningless question every working day for years and years, but if it irritates Alan he doesn't show it. He generally replies, 'So-so,' and then walks round the house looking for things to chastise me for. It used to drive me wild but over the years I have come to understand that this is quite a common occurrence in any number of households up and down the country and I have learnt to be tolerant. The way I see it, Alan stakes out his territory every evening and each ticking off is a metaphorical pee on a metaphorical gate-post.

'Hi Alan.' Eddie directed a friendly, if slightly dubious, grin at the back of Alan's head.

'Oh . . . hello, Eddie.' What, you here again, he didn't need to say. He frowned very slightly but that frown spoke volumes. 'I disapprove of young men,' it said, 'who have nothing better to do than sit in kitchens all afternoon smoking and drinking coffee with my wife who should also have better things to do.' The fact of the matter is that Alan hates coming home from work to find anyone, other than his wife and children, inhabiting any part of his house. Deep in his traditional heart he longs for a Stepford wife; one who greets him at the door with a full-bodied embrace, his slippers and an iced gin and tonic; who is freshly-laundered and sweet-smelling and who intends to surprise him with something delicious for supper the moment he indicates that he is ready to eat. He would like to see well-scrubbed, industrious children sitting quietly over their homework and he would like each day to end with a Brigitte Bardot movie on the television. I don't know where this fantasy comes from because his childhood home wasn't like that, neither was mine. We don't know anyone with a home like that. We don't even know *of* anyone with a home like that. Yet that is what he wants. Failing that, though, he wants the house free of friends and strangers from 7 p.m. onwards.

'It's little enough to ask,' he said plaintively after Eddie had picked up the hostile vibes and left. 'I don't expect the beds to be made, the house to be clean and tidy or my supper to be in the oven. I don't expect my shirts to be ironed or my socks to be darned or even a new loo roll in the cloakroom.

But I would like to be alone with my family when I get home after work.'

I understood how he felt. He didn't want to be polite and accommodating at a time when he felt hot, tired and irritable. He wanted to draw my attention to the new scratch on the left front bumper of the car, the mess of toys in the hall, the terrible din coming from Lizzie's room, the lawn that won't stop growing, the delays on the Underground and the long hot walk home from the station, and with all that resentment building up inside him he had to make polite small talk with Eddie for a quarter of an hour. I put my arms round him and gave him a friendly hug.

'Don't worry,' I consoled him, 'your dinner's in the oven.'

'Thank God for that.' He sighed with relief and returned my squeeze. Even though I may have forgotten to iron his pink shirt for the following morning and sew a button on his waistcoat, knowing his supper was in the oven, though it might well be warmed-up leftover chicken biriani, re-assured him that he was still loved.

'Do you want to come with me to the sales conference then?' I put down my book and turned over on to my back. This was a long-running debate and always took place in bed. I didn't need to consider the question. I had considered it over and over again for weeks and the gist of my reply never varied.

'Well darling, you know I *really* want to go with you – I shall hate missing it – as you know I love the Lakes. It's just that, as I've already told you on numerous occasions, it's Part Two of my marriage guidance training over those particular three days and I can't miss it, nor can I change the date. I would if I could, you know that.'

'No I don't know that, I don't know that at all.' Alan snapped his book shut and took off his reading specs. 'I happen to think that you don't really want to come with me at all and you're using all this marriage guidance malarky as an excuse. You know you don't really enjoy the sales conference.' He propped himself up on one elbow and took a small yellow pill from a little container on his bedside table.

'Have you got a migraine?'

'Not yet,' he grunted meaningfully, 'but it's brewing,' the implication being that *if* he got a migraine my intransigence would be to blame.

'It's too late to change the date,' I repeated, 'it always was . . .'

'But you always come to the sales conference with me. All the other wives will be there – I'll be the only man without a wife.'

'No you won't. George Small won't have Clarissa with him.'

'That's because they're divorced. Do you want everyone to think I'm divorced?'

'Don't be silly, Alan –'

'But I *need* you. You always help me organize my bit . . .'

'Well, I'm sorry, I just can't this year.' Suddenly, out of the blue, an amazingly intelligent idea popped into my head. 'Look, why don't you take Mrs Thing? She can help you organize your bit and she'll do it far better than me anyway.'

'Mrs Thing?' He looked puzzled.

'You know . . . your secretary. I expect it would be a treat for her and from what you've told me about her she deserves a treat.'

'I don't want to take Mrs Thing, as you call her, I want to take *you*!' Alan closed his eyes and rubbed his forehead violently. 'Oooooof!' he exclaimed and his face creased in agony. 'There,' he announced triumphantly, 'now you'll be sorry.' He lay down abruptly and switched off his light. 'I hope you don't intend to read all night.' Soon, despite his headache, he was breathing steadily and I knew he was asleep. The only thing that stops Alan from getting his requisite seven hours is hunger and I can't remember the last time he went to bed hungry.

Anxiety and guilt keep me awake and I eventually dozed off as the early-morning traffic built up on the road beneath the bedroom window.

Chapter Four

It is thanks to a woman called Joan Schindler that I ever became a marriage guidance counsellor, and I'm sure that wherever she is now she will be amazed to hear that, because I only met her once, briefly, at a small drinks party given by my parents-in-law one Sunday morning maybe seventeen years ago.

I recall that she was full of the dewy-eyed enthusiasm of the fledgling counsellor and she held me spellbound with stories of her training weekends at the Council's residential college in Rugby. One I particularly liked was of two married counsellors, a man and woman, who embarked upon a steamy affair and had to drop out to seek counselling for their own failing marriages.

'What qualifications do you need?' I asked during a quiet moment when her mouth was full of celery cheese dip.

'Well, they don't have to be academic,' she replied, which surprised me because I had always imagined, when I thought about it at all, that counsellors had to be graduates in something relevant like psychology or social studies. 'But there are certain qualities that are common to most of us and if you don't have these then I think it would be difficult to help other people with emotional problems.'

'Such as?' I asked, and Joan pulled a face.

'This is the bit I don't like,' she said, looking uncomfortable, 'because it sounds like bragging.'

'Brag away,' I instructed her.

'Well,' she began reluctantly, 'I suppose most counsellors

are caring, compassionate people. She would be intellectually curious even if she didn't have an "O" Level to her name – some of the required reading is pretty heavy. She needs to be perceptive, and if she's lucky, intuitive. As free from prejudice as possible. It helps if her own background is stable, but it needn't always have been so – a lot of counsellors have quite turbulent histories, may even have been counselled themselves. Actually, I was counselled with my first marriage.' She glanced quickly at husband number two and gave him a small, conciliatory smile. 'It helped me make up my mind to get a divorce, so you see, we're not just marriage menders. A counsellor needs to know herself very well, warts and all, and believe me, by the end of the training she has few illusions left.'

'You make them sound like almost perfect people,' I said when she had finished.

'Yes,' she said thoughtfully, 'I can see that's what it must sound like. But believe me, I have quite a few singularly unattractive faults and prejudices. At least now I *know* I've got them and I'm working on them.'

Some eight years and three children later, I was to be found, together with seven other hopefuls awaiting selection, in a suite of dark, poky rooms in Richmond belonging to the Marriage Guidance Council. Unlike, I would suppose, most other aspiring counsellors, I had absolutely no doubt that I would be selected even though I knew that statistically my chances were no more than even.

There is a stage in one's growth towards maturity when one is, albeit briefly, both arrogant *and* wise. It comes after the stage when one is arrogant and silly and before the point at which one realizes that with maturity comes humility and self-doubt. Anyway, at the time of my selection I was at that first silly, happy stage. As far as I was concerned the Council was jolly lucky I chose them. Well, I could so easily have chosen Citizens' Advice or the Samaritans and they would never have known what they had missed. In my own eyes anyway, I had all the necessary qualities and then some. I knew just the sort of person they were looking for and I was she.

I knew the poor, wilting lily with the migraine didn't stand an earthly unless they decided to give her a second chance, and I felt that the woman who confused incest with celibacy wouldn't fare much better. During her three minute talk on the subject of celibacy she bewildered everyone for a while with her reference to a father having a celibate relationship with his daughter. 'Celibacy,' she told us authoritatively, 'is one of the last taboos.' Thinking about it, she might just have been right at that.

I had to talk about pornography, which I said existed only in the eye of the beholder. I thought at the time that this sounded very clever and I believed it was original. Oddly enough, I don't think I subscribe to that particular school of liberal thought any longer.

Personally I loathed the bossy, patronizing social worker. She knew it all and argued continually with a rather sweet, molish vicar from Somerset who refused to be brow-beaten. I thought it possible that she would be selected because she was so articulate and well-informed. I also felt that she would intimidate the selectors.

The vicar worked very hard at convincing us that despite his calling he was really one of us. He was resolutely honest about himself, though it was clear that self-revelation didn't come naturally to him, and he laughed the loudest at the crude wit of one of the other members of the group. However, interestingly, he wore a dog-collar and once or twice he escaped behind it to avoid giving a straight answer to a difficult question of morality. He put me in mind of a doctor who has been asked by a neurotic, unbalanced patient with a terminal disease if she is going to die. His equivocation eventually began to irritate me.

Herbert was the name of the very tall, unbelievably handsome black probation officer. He was the one with the crude wit who kept the vicar laughing. He was our comedian and a natural show-off. He never stopped changing his position and he reminded me of a large, friendly snake that couldn't get comfortable. He coiled and uncoiled, slithered and twisted, stretched and arched, emphasizing each point he made with graceful, fluid motions of his hands which seemed to have an independent life. He had a soft, sibilant voice with an accent I couldn't identify.

I can't recall much about the other two women. One, I seem to remember, had long, thick, flaxen plaits and wore children's sandals and ankle socks, but all I can recall about the other one is that she cried copiously at one point and I think it had something to do with constipated little girls.

I don't think I was nervous about the day. So far as I can recall I felt excited anticipation once I had been reassured that I wouldn't have to do any sums or spelling tests. I enjoy games of the mind and the emotions and discussions about feelings and how we relate to one another, and this is mostly how we spent the time. By the end of the day I seemed to know those seven other people rather better than I knew some of my closest friends and I felt a sense of loss when we broke up after tea to go our separate ways. I never knew which members of the group, other than myself, were selected although I did once think I saw the vicar leaving the Council's training college in Rugby just as I was arriving. If it was him he had given up wearing his dog-collar.

Alan knew even less about marriage guidance than I did, so when I told him of my intention to become a counsellor he was quite supportive. Not enthusiastic you understand, but he was on my side in a quiet encouraging sort of way. To his friends he said things like 'Well, it'll keep her off the streets,' and to my friends he said, 'Women need an interest outside the home.' I think he was quite proud of me when I was selected because he liked the sound of 'My wife is a marriage guidance counsellor.' So did I, come to that.

In my own eyes anyway I had acquired status almost overnight, and without too much effort I felt that I had become a more interesting person. Dead-eyed men at dinner parties who would normally treat another man's wife with the respect reserved for a plastic sink tidy brightened up perceptibly when I mentioned my new interest, which I did at every opportunity. In my defence I must say that I have noticed this is a common failing in new counsellors.

'Marriage guidance counsellor, eh,' they would say thoughtfully, their eyes gleaming with prurient curiosity. 'I bet you could tell a tale or two.' Nudge nudge, wink wink, know what I mean? I would endeavour to convey with a small, discreet smile that I could indeed tell a tale or two but nothing on earth would persuade me to do so.

Some couples who I suspected might genuinely have a problem or two would tease me in a jocular way. 'You're just the person we need,' they might shout, laughing too loudly while exchanging meaningful glances that they thought I had missed. Sometimes I faced open hostility and scepticism from people who seemed to find it uncomfortable to have me around. These people would confront me, demanding proof that counselling works, which is very difficult because few satisfied clients are willing to stand up and be counted and they tend not to come back years later in order to reassure their counsellor that they are still happy together. I even learnt to accept that certain people, usually men, dismissed me as a 'middle-class, middle-aged, do-gooding busy-body with a dirty mind' to quote the angry husband of one of my early clients.

It didn't take me long to become bored with people's predictable reactions to my new voluntary career and I stopped talking about it to anyone who showed anything other than a genuine, serious interest in it.

Alan's initial support began to wane after a couple of months. Firstly he resented the amount of time I spent counselling. I know he would have felt better about this if I was being paid for my time. He couldn't understand why I put myself through a highly emotional and stressful mill for such nebulous rewards.

'Why do you do it if it causes you such pain?' he would ask after a particularly fraught group session or training weekend. 'What are you getting out of it?' I tried to explain about the pain and the joy of personal growth and the satisfaction I felt when a client made a tiny and positive step towards her eventual goal, whatever it might be. But because he is a man who is not particularly curious about the workings of the mind, he found my growing appetite for knowledge of this type perplexing. I think, without knowing it, he was envious too. 'You behave as though you're privy to some wonderful secret that's denied to the rest of us.' But it was only a secret because he didn't want to share it with me. I would have been very happy to talk to him about my training *and* my clients but he made it plain that he wasn't interested. What I was learning was wonderful but it didn't have to be private. In fact I talked about it every Tuesday with Hannah and Maggie, Tuesday being our day for getting together for a bowl of soup and cheese and biscuits. The drama of my training and my clients became a sort of weekly soap opera and never ceased to hold the attention of my two friends, so much so that Maggie eventually expressed an interest in becoming a counsellor, was duly selected and went through the training a year or two behind me.

Alan, I know, felt threatened by what he felt was my secret knowledge of the workings of his mind. In fact the workings of Alan's mind have always seemed to me to be labyrinthine and mysterious and nothing I have learnt over the years has altered this. Nevertheless I understood how he felt. I think quite a lot of people feel the same when in the presence of a person with an unusual amount of insight into the complex but inexact science of human behaviour. I know I do. I imagine that every twitch of an eyebrow or movement of a hand is of great significance, which is an enormous conceit really when you come to think about it.

The training programme worried Alan. On a practical level it meant that he had to look after the children for three weekends a year and the novelty wore off after the first. But what he found even more difficult to handle was my air of quietly euphoric exhaustion on my return late Sunday evening. I wasn't supposed to be tired, he was. I had been away for the weekend having fun. I was supposed to come home refreshed and ready to make supper and he was supposed to sit down with the papers.

'I don't understand how you can be so tired,' he would eventually burst out, 'when you haven't had to do anything but talk, listen, eat and sleep.' I would shrug as if to say, 'Well I am and that's that,' because it was pointless trying to describe to him the quality of the talking and listening; the tension that built up through those long hours of often painful self-discovery in a group of your peers whose job it was to reveal you to yourself with none of the nasty bits left out; the care one had to take when dealing with other people's innermost feelings; the anxiety that centred on the fear of rejection after a timid, often reluctant confession of sin, or guilt, or failure. Because of the relentless overflow of adrenalin I rarely slept more than an hour or two a night and my already high blood-pressure rocketed, often leaving me weary beyond imagining. By the end of the weekend I was both exhausted and exhilarated.

I rediscovered the incomparable joy of learning new things but this was something I couldn't share with Alan because he disapproved of the nature of the new things I was learning. He was, and still is, suspicious of anything that smacks, to him, of armchair psychology so he had little respect for what he called my 'amateur psychotherapeutics'. What he looked forward to was the day when I found it all as bogus and tiresome as he did. I quickly learnt never to complain about any aspect of marriage guidance because his response was always the same. 'No one's forcing you to do it.' He needed to believe that any complaint I made was the beginning of my disillusionment, and he had no sympathy with or understanding of any of the minor irritations I felt regarding my work. Better not to talk to him about it, I thought, as he finds it all so irksome. But because of this reticence of mine I think I probably failed to prepare him adequately for each new training weekend as it approached over the horizon.

'But it's just not convenient,' he would respond quickly and mindlessly.

'Why not?' I would ask and he would search through his mind frantically for a suitably impressive and convincing reason.

'Well, I thought I'd paint the bathroom,' he might say feebly. Or perhaps, 'You surely realize it's my mother's birthday that week?' And I would reply with something like, 'So who's stopping you from painting the bathroom?' or 'I fail to see how your mother's birthday is relevant . . .'

However, over this latest weekend he did have a genuine, 22 carat gold hurdle to put in my way. I had to admit that the yearly sales conference was a live one. I understood about the wives and the 'instant-divorce-all-expenses-paid' unwritten clause in Alan's contract, but I felt that I had an equally pressing reason for insisting that I should attend my training weekend. It was the second part of the three-part basic training and all three parts were taken by the same group of men and women. If I missed it for any reason whatsoever I would be expected to start my training all over again with a new group at some later date, and the idea of this appalled me. Apart from that, I would begin lagging behind even newer counsellors and I'm nothing if not competitive.

Anyway, our long-running argument was resumed, as I knew it would be, a few weeks later as the weekend in question drew nearer.

'Tell me, Polly,' Alan began, looking at me over the top of his newspaper, 'do many counsellors get divorced?' I assumed that he was reading an article about divorce amongst marriage guidance counsellors.

'Why, does it say something about it in the paper?' I asked.

'No, I was just thinking, that's all.'

'Well, to be truthful, Alan, I really don't know the answer. I would guess that there are fewer divorces because we have access to such a lot of informed help.'

'Hmmm . . . they may not get divorced,' he said, beginning to warm to his theme, 'but I bet there's some unhappy marriages.'

'Oh, why do you bet that, Alan?' I asked sweetly. It was becoming clear to me that Alan was about to voice a very personal and probably quite offensive opinion.

'Well, I imagine all this psychological clap-trap you're into could be quite disruptive.' I snapped my book shut and instead of throwing it at him I put it very carefully on to the coffee table beside my chair.

'I think you're implying that you personally find it disruptive,' I said quietly.

'Well yes, as a matter of fact I do, but it's not only that,' and then he continued reading his paper, making it clear that he didn't intend to pursue the subject any further without some coaxing. I decided not to play.

'Gwen's expecting us early so I'd better go and tidy myself up. It's pike *en croûte* for lunch or something peculiar like that.' At least once a month the Grahams and the Brays got together for Sunday lunch. This Sunday it was the turn of the Brays to entertain the Grahams.

'Oh boy,' Alan muttered petulantly, 'another gastronomic marathon.'

'So what else is it then?' I asked. Alan looked up at me with a puzzled expression on his face. I thought rather spitefully that he looked a little like the pike that Gwen was probably busy croûting right at that moment. 'Why is marriage guidance a threat to family life?' I gave in because I was angry and curious and I knew he wouldn't tell me if I didn't ask.

Alan folded up his paper very carefully and put it on the pile of neatly folded papers at his feet. Then he looked at me with a slightly worried, paternally condescending frown creasing his normally smooth but aggressively protuberant forehead. He sighed deeply, giving me the impression that there was so much to say that he didn't know where to start.

'Okay,' he began, 'I only know how I feel and you're always going on about how important it is to discuss our feelings with each other. I believe you call it "communicating".' I nodded encouragingly. He was quite right. I do go on rather a lot about feelings and discussing them openly so I only have myself to blame when people take me at my word. 'Well,' he continued, 'I feel that you and your new friends in marriage guidance think you are a cut above us mere mortals.' I could see that if what he said was true – that we counsellors *do think* we're a cut above mere mortals – then this could be a very disruptive influence. However, whether it was true or not, and my instant reaction was to deny it vehemently, it was obvious that I made Alan feel as though I thought I was a cut above him.

If I am to be perfectly honest, and although I can't speak for anyone other than myself, with the benefit of hindsight I think I did, in those early days, feel rather superior. But then to my recollection, quite a few embryonic counsellors have manifested signs of *amour-propre* during their early days. Not surprising really when you think about it. Most of us are plucked from our kitchens and the bosoms of our young families and after years of feeling lowly and a bit dim, a little initial self-congratulatory conceit is only to be expected. It doesn't last very long because our training is designed to disabuse us of any delusions of grandeur we might have.

'I'm beginning to feel,' Alan went on, 'that marriage guidance is taking precedence over us ... you and me. For example, I had to take those Italians out to dinner on my own last week because you were counselling that evening.'

I protested loudly. 'But you phoned me in the middle of the day and expected me to cancel all my clients for that evening. I simply can't do that. I have a responsibility towards them!'

'You have a responsibility towards me too!'

'I don't happen to think that my responsibility towards you includes being on call all day and night just in case you need me. But all right, from now on let's agree that I need a few days' notice of your requirements. It would also help if you tried to arrange our joint social engagements with reference to my diary as well as your own. After all, I've had to defer to your diary for years.'

'Well, I can't rearrange the sales conference to suit your diary.' Ah, I thought, now we're getting to it. 'And I need you to be there with me.'

Everything I had said was perfectly fair and logical, but Alan was speaking about feelings and not logic and justice. I knew this and I felt confused and guilty. What he really wants from me on these occasions is my moral support. Simply having me with him helps him relax. He tells me he feels less inhibited and shy in company and he likes to dip into my feminine intuitions and perceptions.

'What do you think old Bloggs really meant when he said . . .' and he listens while I outline what I perceive to be the hidden agenda behind a hostile confrontation between angry men.

'Watch out for young Simmons,' I might say, 'he's not as wet behind the ears as he appears.' I don't mean to make Alan sound impossibly naïve, but he is very trusting and tends to accept a man's own estimation of himself rather too easily. I believe this to be a common male characteristic, whereas I think women have genetically evolved, from necessity, into less trusting and credulous creatures. Mind you, this is only my personal opinion.

But even though I sympathized with the nature of Alan's need for me and even though I was letting him down in a way I felt he wouldn't easily forget, I saw this as a battle of wills that I had to win in order to have some autonomy within my marriage.

'Listen, Alan,' I began reasonably, and I can tell you it is difficult being reasonable with someone who has gone beyond reason. 'Is your sales conference worth wasting nearly a year of my training for? Because that's what it amounts to. Ask yourself, would you do the same for me? I'm damn sure the answer would be no. In fact, have you ever put off anything important to oblige me?' I thought of the times I had attended PTA meetings alone and interviewed teachers; of the times when I had sat alone at home on my birthday or our wedding anniversary. 'Remember how I had to ask them to keep me an extra day in hospital when I had Charlie because you had a business meeting that you refused to alter, and you went off to Italy that time knowing I might have pneumonia –'

'That was different,' he muttered sulkily, 'our livelihood was at stake.'

'Why is it always different and therefore excusable when you do things to me that you don't like me doing to you?' I asked.

'Look, darling –' He stopped and shook his head. 'It's no use, I simply can't argue with you.'

'No, go on,' I insisted.

'Well, I can't just go to the boss and say, "Look here, Jim, it's our wedding anniversary next Friday so you'll have to postpone that meeting in Paris" or "Cancel the lunch with the Japanese tomorrow, Polly's coming out of hospital a day earlier than we expected." Some people may be able to do things like that, but I can't.'

'Well, exactly the same applies to me!' I cried triumphantly. 'I can't say to the organizers of my course, "Sorry, I can't complete my training this time around, and I know it completely mucks up your numbers, but I have to attend my husband's sales conference with him." I mean what'll it be next time, because there's always something? Your nephew's twenty-first perhaps? Or the dog's barmitzvah?'

'I tell you, I can't argue with you,' he said irritably, the implication being that I argue dirty. He always thinks that if I score a point I've only done so by using unfair tactics. 'Anyway, you'd better go and get ready, I want to leave in five minutes.' So for all that we were no nearer to an amicable solution and the weekend was drawing relentlessly closer.

'What do you call a male nun?' We all looked blank. 'A mun!' Mike chortled gleefully and because we were all brimming over with alcoholic *bonhomie* we laughed our heads off. Except Gwen, who had obviously heard it before. 'You've heard about the Irish teachers...' We hadn't. 'They've decided to go on strike during the school holidays.' Again we all laughed while Gwen sat in a brown study at the head of the large oak table, staring abstractedly out at the late afternoon gloom.

Sunday lunch at the Brays' was always an extended meal. Although we rarely started eating much before three, we were expected to arrive around midday in order to consume as much Italian plonk as possible beforehand. Sometimes we would arrive just as the joint was going into the oven and this always worried Alan no end because if he drank too much on an empty stomach he got a migraine. He was reassured if he could smell the meat cooking. We all had a huge cooked breakfast when we were going to lunch at the Brays'.

It was fortunate that Gwen's three boys and our three kids got on well together, although I suppose they all merely tolerated little Jane who not only had the misfortune of being born a girl but was also the youngest. While the adults gossiped and drank and consumed vast quantities of Bombay Mix to keep the pangs of hunger at bay, the six youngsters, virtually unsupervised, played their detailed and complicated games all over the house and garden. I can remember now the sound of their high, excited voices, loud then faint depending on where they were playing. I always had an ear cocked because Jane was often left behind and had to be collected, screaming with rage, from the attic or the dank, dark cellar.

On that particular November Sunday, because it rained monotonously all day, the children were restricted to the house. They were not obliged to sit at table after the main meal was over and they were playing their own particular version of *The Lion, the Witch and the Wardrobe*. Charlie was the lion and his basso profundo roar echoed down the stair-well as we sat on drinking cup after cup of Gwen's delicious proper coffee which gradually turned into tea and was then served with slabs of home-made fruit cake.

'Is this all there is to life?' We all stopped whatever it was that we were doing or saying and looked at Gwen expectantly. I mean, you don't just say 'Is this all there is to life?' and leave it at that. But Gwen did. She sighed, got up from her chair and started banging plates on top of each other in preparation for the washing-up *tour de force* to follow. I followed suit and trailed after her into the kitchen. The men decided that, had there been any sun that day, it would definitely by now be over the yard-arm and Mike, who never mixed the grape with the grain, got out the three star.

'I can't bear it, Polly.' I heard an ominous crack as Gwen slammed a Waterford crystal wine glass into the hot, soapy water. Something like this would normally have sent Gwen into paroxysms of self-mortification. This time she simply took the cracked glass out of the bowl and dropped it casually into the waste bin. 'It came to me last night,' she went on in a dull lifeless voice. 'I don't want to spend the rest of my life being what I am now. I'm a part-time everything and I want to be a full-time something. I would like to be the best in the world at just one thing – I don't care if it's stuffing cushions or stripping pine, I want to be the best at it. I want a paid job with prospects.' She paused. 'And I want to be in love with someone.' I looked up sharply from the task of drying a heavy, cut-glass water jug. I was used to Gwen being discontented. In fact, one of the first things I noticed about her was the discontent in her face. She had a permanently disgruntled look but it wasn't unattractive because she was usually able to turn her discontent into a sort of sour joke which made me feel that she wasn't really serious. I knew she was ambitious too, though Mike usually received the full force of her thwarted ambition and he was a continual disappointment to her. Almost to spite her, I suspect, he took a dilettante approach to his job. He was a natural salesman, some said a genius. He could sell anything to anyone if he was of a mind to, which wasn't often enough to suit Gwen. The secondary thrust of her ambition was directed at her sons. They were, she assured us, in the top 3 per cent according to the educational psychologist who tested their IQ at Gwen's request when they were thought to be slightly backward. However, they were also slightly dyslexic, she said, all three of them, so they had extra coaching every week at vast expense.

Nevertheless, no matter how discontented she appeared or how disillusioned she claimed to be with her life, she had always maintained that her marriage and her love for Mike were the stabilizing forces in it. If it wasn't for Mike, she said to us all, and his unquestioning and undemanding love for her, she would be an absolute mess. She frequently had idle crushes on men which amounted to furtive flirtations and the occasional fumble and I believed then that she actually got between the sheets with the french polisher. 'But I am a passionate woman,' she said by way of excuse, in a suitably passionate voice, 'and I *need* the admiration of other men. They mean nothing to me really and my deep feelings for Mike never change.' That Sunday was, as I remember it, the first time she expressed dissatisfaction with her marriage.

'I don't know if I can spend the rest of my life with Mike,' she said that afternoon, and I was shaken to the very core. 'I've looked ahead into my future and it horrifies me. I want more than this –' she made a sweeping gesture with her hands '– out of life, and I want it now, before I'm too old and it's too late.' A cold shiver ran down my spine. The wind of change seemed to be blowing at my back and I didn't like it. Gwen was my beloved friend despite our differences and petty jealousies. We had planned our lives right down to our joint widowhood in Brighton, our Bath chairs side by side at the end of the pier while we squabbled endlessly over such weighty matters as the merits of cremation over burial and steamed fish over chicken broth.

'Are you serious?'

Gwen cocked her head on one side and looked at me. She was smiling, I remember, and I took this as a good sign. 'Your insecurity's showing, Polly,' she said with a short, hard laugh. Then she added, to my relief, 'No, of course I'm not serious. I'll not leave Mike. But I'm thinking of trying to find a full-time job. I know I can get a nursing job tomorrow, but I thought I'd rather like to train as a health visitor. I'm looking into the possibilities at the moment.'

'But you do love Mike don't you?' I felt like a child needing reassurance from her parents.

'I suppose I do . . . I don't know. What is love? You tell me, you're the marriage guidance counsellor.'

'Well, I've always thought it meant caring for someone more than you care for yourself,' I tried tentatively after some thought.

'Then by your definition I'm not sure I love anyone.'

'Not even the boys?' This was something terrible and new I was learning about Gwen and I was growing angry with her for being honest with me about something I would rather she was dishonest about. Please God, I prayed urgently, make her say she loves the boys more than she loves herself.

'No, I don't think so. I love them, yes, but I don't think I love them in the same way that you love yours. Do you know, when you told me how you felt when yours were born I really envied you because I didn't feel like that at all. I didn't love them when I carried them. In fact, I found the whole business of pregnancy utterly appalling and I wasn't swamped with maternal love when they were placed in my arms. Breast feeding disgusted me. I felt invaded by parasites.' Gwen handed me the enormous meat dish that had recently held her perfect coulibiaca. 'Careful with that,' she instructed me, 'it's very soapy.' She turned round to face me, leant against the sink and lit a cigarette. 'No Polly,' she said after blowing out a thin stream of smoke from the left corner of her mouth in a way that stained one tooth saffron with nicotine, 'I learnt to love the boys the hard way – and I do love them, a great deal – but I felt terribly guilty and unnatural because the feelings I expected to happen didn't. I have always thought that there is something wrong with me, but I can't help being what I am. You can't manufacture feelings to order, can you?' I shook my head slowly in agreement but I felt I had been sandbagged. I couldn't understand how this fundamental truth about Gwen had escaped my notice for so long. I had thought I knew all I needed to know about her but I think in fact that I knew all she thought I needed to know about her and if this was the case, how well *did* I know Gwen?

At that moment, standing in Gwen's kitchen with a damp tea-towel in my hand, my perceptions of her underwent a rapid and uncomfortable change. She was my friend and I loved her, but I didn't feel safe with her any more.

Later that evening Alan fell asleep in front of the television. He is not a man who normally falls asleep in front of the television. He *is* a man who falls asleep when he is bored at dinner parties, though. It has always been a great source of embarrassment to me even though I have managed to persuade my friends that he is simply very tired and not bored at all. Now they watch him fondly as he drifts off, one eye closing before the other which habitually remains slightly open like a cat who can never completely relax its guard.

I watched him as he slipped further and further down in his very own enormous, golden leather chair and I thought how tired and drawn he looked. Thin too, and I remembered that he had only picked at his lunch. Really, I thought, for a man with a healthy appetite he has been eating very little recently and I wondered suddenly if there was something on his mind. I considered the possibility that he was anxious about something and not telling me, but that seemed very unlikely. I told myself reassuringly that he was simply working too hard.

Do I love you more than I love myself? I wondered. The

small-boy pathos of his relaxed, slumbering face was in danger of clouding my judgement. Would I continue to care about you no matter what you did? Would I hand you over to the police if I knew you were a molester of small children? I thought I probably would. Would I stop loving you if you left me for another woman? And again I thought I probably would. Would I die blessing you as you plunged a bread knife into my heart? I thought I probably wouldn't. So, I thought, I guess I love me more than I love you. I thought I ought to tell Gwen immediately. Gwen, I would say, it's all right, you can relax, my definition of love isn't the only one. Then I thought, but I only began to love myself when Alan and I began to love each other. He made me feel lovable. He has always known the black side of me but I have never felt that his love depended upon me keeping my bad bits hidden. So I guess I love him at least as much as I love myself – the two things are, I suppose, indivisible. If he stopped loving me I would stop loving myself. Not much consolation in that for Gwen, I thought. Perhaps I won't ring her after all.

The following Tuesday someone unknown to me removed my purse from my handbag. It must have been on the Tube or walking from Baker Street station to the bus because I still had it when I paid for our tickets at Pinner and I didn't have it any longer when I tried to pay for our bus fares in Marylebone High Street. In fact the greatest loss was in the purse itself. It was a rather splendid natural alligator wallet that Alan had brought me back from a charter trip to Florida to watch the famous Daytona 500 motor race and intrinsically it was of more value than its contents. Indeed, the purse snatcher must have been very disappointed with the three pounds, some loose change, the return halves of two tickets from Pinner and some family photographs.

Charlie and I were making an emergency trip to our dentist, who had at one time practised in Harrow but, having made good, went private and moved to the far end of

Wimpole Street. It was a bit inconvenient but I'd have travelled a lot further for Mr Greene. He was a great believer in preventative dentistry and that counts for a great deal when you have three children.

Charlie had broken a front tooth in the swimming pool. He claimed, when he arrived home, that there was a boy somewhere with half a tooth buried in his heel.

'What were you doing biting this boy's heel?' I asked.

'I wasn't biting his heel, he kicked me in the mouth. I dived in just after him and his heel caught me in the mouth. It wasn't deliberate.' Deliberate or not I was quite unnerved by the sight of Charlie's Nosferatu grin which was doubly compounded by the squint and gave him quite an evil appearance all in all, though Charlie himself wasn't too worried as he rather fancied himself with a broken tooth and he showed it off a bit like a duelling scar. He was not a boy given to grinning until he broke his tooth and then he grinned indiscriminately at everyone until the novelty wore off and he went back to being his normal, truculent, scowling self.

'You've lost your purse, haven't you Mum?' Charlie had been watching me scrabbling about in my bag for a minute or two and it didn't take a genius to know that I was looking for something that probably wasn't there.

'Shut up,' I muttered as I continued to root about in the dark recesses of what a close friend once chose to call my weekend cottage. 'You've got everything in there that you need to set up home,' he had said when, after much searching, I finally withdrew a miniature trowel and fork in order to doctor some sorry-looking house plants in the foyer of a hotel we were all staying at for a weekend break some years ago.

Then I said, 'Yes, I've lost my purse,' and we both panicked as is our style. Charlie, I'm afraid, has inherited my predisposition to over-anxiety.

'What are you going to do?' he asked from between tightly clenched teeth. I looked up hopefully into the wooden face of the conductor and I smiled. When he didn't smile back I knew my runes were cast.

'Um . . .' I began, largely because one usually does begin this sort of conversation with an 'um'. 'I seem to have mislaid my purse.' The conductor raised his eyes to heaven and looked with mock despair at the passengers in the seats behind and in front of us.

'So what do you want me to do about it?' he asked, knowing full well that I didn't expect him personally to do anything about it. I was simply telling him, in my own way, that I wouldn't be able to pay our fares. Charlie was overcome with embarrassment. But then I have always embarrassed Charlie. He is a conservative at heart and most of all he would like me to look and behave like his friend Tim Hocking's mother who bakes on Fridays and blends beautifully into any background with her neat, short hair and her M & S clothes. I look odd, well, odder than Tim Hocking's mother anyway, and I talk too much about all the wrong things to all the wrong people. It never ceases to amaze him that by and large people don't poke fun at me behind my back. If anybody did, mind you, he would flatten them because his embarrassment is a form of pain that he suffers on my behalf – poor old chap.

'Well, what I mean,' I began again, 'is that I don't have any money to pay our fare.' As if he didn't know that already.

'Then you'll just have to get off the bus, won't you?' he proclaimed triumphantly so that everyone could hear and he gave the bell three short rings so that the bus halted abruptly between stops. I felt he had been dying to do that to someone all day and now his spleen was satisfactorily vented.

'No I won't – actually,' I replied very quietly. The conductor, who had been chewing gum in a desultory fashion, stopped chewing and his mouth fell open which was rather disgusting because I could see the lump of grey matter adhering to his upper back molars. He blinked rapidly several times and though he sighed deeply over what he saw as my lack of proper respect, I think he was secretly delighted at the prospect of a break in the dull monotony of his routine. You'll have noticed, no doubt, how people are always saying how the last thing they want is a fight when in fact they are positively lusting for one. I was watching a television programme the other night in which the man being interviewed insisted that he didn't want a confrontation, that he loathed violence, when it must have been clear to everyone watching that confrontation and violence were what he wanted most in the world. He was praying for confrontation and violence with all the fervour of a farmer praying for a dry harvest.

'You can take my name and address,' I continued firmly, 'and I will post our fares, such as they are, to London Transport.' Our journey was quite a short one and our fares couldn't have amounted to more than a few pence.

'How do I know you'll give me your real name and address?' the conductor asked insultingly.

'Do I look the sort of woman who would give you a false name and address in order to swindle the bus company out of a few coppers?' He shrugged eloquently. 'Well, whatever you think,' I said with icy calm, 'I'm not getting off this bus until we have reached our destination and that's that.' He grinned with malevolent satisfaction.

'Then this bus won't move an inch until you do – and that's that.' I think that what we had reached was something called a Mexican stand-off.

By this time the rest of the passengers were becoming decidedly restless and Charlie was nudging my left buttock with a balled-up fist. 'Let's get off, Mum. *Please!*' he whispered frantically.

Of course I knew I would have to get off the bus if only to appease all those other travellers who had no quarrel with the conductor. However, before I was forced to lose what was left of my face, a haughty female voice called from the front of the bus, 'Conductor . . . how much does that poor woman owe you?' He glanced around the bus trying to put a body to the voice. Unable to do so, he addressed the bus at large.

'That, if I may say so madam, is none of your business.'

'Don't be a fool man,' the voice replied sharply, 'I intend to pay her fare.' Oh joy, oh bliss!

'Thank you!' I called out to the disembodied voice. 'Thank you so much.' The conductor glared first at me and then at my benefactress, who had eventually surfaced waving a hand in the air clutching the money for our fares.

'That's not allowed,' the stupid man said, thereby losing what remaining sympathy there was for him amongst his impatient charges.

Obviously such an easy solution to our problem had simply not occurred to anyone earlier because suddenly everyone seemed eager to pay our fares for us. The conductor's impotent rage was balm to my injured pride and even his muttered 'Good riddance' when Charlie and I finally disembarked couldn't dent my renewed faith in the innate goodness of the human race.

Naturally Mr Greene would happily have lent me money for our fares home but unfortunately Charlie reacted very oddly to a new local anaesthetic. The broken tooth was to be left in for the moment: it would either die, in which case Mr Greene would remove it, or it would survive, in which case, at some later date, he would cap it. Meanwhile, however, a cavity was found in one of his remaining milk teeth which Mr Greene thought should be filled.

'I've not seen this before,' Mr Greene remarked with a chuckle as we watched Charlie, who appeared to be very drunk, stagger happily round the surgery after Miss Purchase, the glamorous dental nurse, in order to plant a resounding kiss just beneath her right breast. She looked astonished and flushed prettily. 'I don't remember having thoughts like that when I was eight,' Mr Greene said raising his eyebrows in mock disapproval. I caught hold of a very slippery and determined small boy just before he cannoned unsteadily into a large glass-fronted chrome and metal cabinet that held all Mr Greene's tools of his trade.

'Woooaaah old chap,' I said as Charlie struggled to be free of my restraining arms.

'Wassamatter? Le'me go.' He glared at me with bleary, drunken concentration. I turned to Mr Greene.

'I can't possibly take him home on the train like this,' I said.

'Good heavens, of course you can't. I suggest you wait a while in my recovery room. It shouldn't take long to wear off.'

But an hour later Charlie was still sound asleep on the couch and snoring noisily. However a solution had occurred to me.

'Look,' I said to Miss Purchase when she brought in a cup of coffee for me, 'my husband has the car in town for the day, so if I could ring him, perhaps he can come and pick us up on his way home. He's due to leave the office in about an hour.'

Mrs Rosen answered the phone.

'I'm afraid Alan is out of the office at the moment, Mrs Graham. Can I help?' I explained my predicament briefly. 'Well look, his appointment is just round the corner at Shaft and Webber's and he has to come back to the office to pick up some papers and the car, so why don't I pick you both up in my car and you can wait for him in his office?'

'Oh no, I couldn't put you to all that trouble,' I said, but my protests lacked conviction.

'It's no trouble really. Just give me a quarter of an hour and I'll be with you.'

'That's jolly nice of you,' I said thankfully and I gave her the address. 'Just double park and hoot – I'll be waiting.'

Mrs Rosen arrived in a small, racy, foreign sports car and it was not an easy matter squeezing a sleeping Charlie and me into the passenger seat.

'Well, this is cosy, I must say,' I remarked as Mrs Rosen fumbled beneath my right knee for the gear stick. She laughed.

'It's my son's car actually. It was a present from his father for his twenty-first and I don't approve at all, but mine's in for a service and I must admit I do enjoy driving it from time to time, though I'll never admit that to my son. To be truthful I'd have given an arm and a leg for a car like this at his age.'

'Me too,' I said wistfully. 'Mind you, I'd have given an arm and a leg for any car . . . a scooter even.'

I watched her curiously out of the corner of my eye as she manoeuvred her way adroitly through the mid-afternoon rush-hour traffic.

'It never ceases to surprise me,' she said with a smile, 'that so many people get off work this early.' It was not yet 4 p.m. yet Oxford Street and Regent Street were already packed with commuting businessmen in their Volvos and Granadas.

Sheila Rosen reminded me of a plump, Jewish Anne Bancroft, and I guessed her to be in her late forties. She had a mountain of blue-black hair which she wore in the customary style of the Duchess of Kent and, like Anne Bancroft, she had a humorous, intelligent face which, though it was well-worn and slightly battered, was still the confident, vital face of a woman who knew herself to be attractive and desirable. She wore a lot of cleverly applied exotic make-up and Alan was certainly right on two counts. She clattered and chimed with a hundredweight of heavy gold jewellery and she used a very powerful scent which I tentatively identified as Ma Griffe. She reminded me of the perfumery buyer of a very up-market department store and she didn't look the least bit like a secretary, and even less like one that Scott Fotheringay could afford. Without knowing exactly why, I liked her immediately even though I thought that Alan probably found her just a little intimidating. In her beautifully cut suit she made me feel very down-at-heel and frumpy even though I was wearing my good Jaeger coat and my Russell and Bromley boots.

Having installed me and a very drowsy Charlie in Alan's office, Mrs Rosen brought in a tray of tea that gave off the sweet, fragrant smell of bergamot.

'I hope you like Earl Grey,' she said. 'I know Alan doesn't but it's my favourite so I always keep some in my cupboard. Anyway, Mr Henderson' (Alan's immediate boss) 'likes a cup from time to time and Miss Brothers' (Jim Henderson's very old, crabby secretary who should have been put out to pasture years ago) 'refuses to make it for him because she says it's an affectation.' I assured her that it was my favourite brew too. 'Fine. Now if you don't mind, I have a letter to finish. I know these aren't very exciting magazines,' she handed me one or two trade journals, 'but they're better than nothing and there's a very nice photo of Alan in one of them, with a bunch of Japanese at a trade fair.'

After she had left the room, shutting the door behind her, I slipped the boring old magazines back on the pile (I had already seen the picture of Alan with the Japanese) and sat back with a deep relieved sigh. Charlie mumbled something in his sleep, but other than the very faint clacking of Mrs Rosen's electric typewriter, I was enveloped in a warm, comforting silence.

My mind a contented blank I let my gaze wander round Alan's small, dark but reassuringly familiar office. To begin with everything seemed the same; the family photograph in the corner of his scratched and battered old partner's desk; the surreal pottery pen and pencil holder that Lizzie had made for him one Christmas several years ago; my old portable typewriter that had mysteriously become his, owing, he said, to squatter's rights; the complete set of first edition, uncut library Dickens that was quite valuable and had been the company's wedding present to him on the occasion of his first marriage, and the framed pencil sketch of his first dog, bulldog John. Then I began to notice the changes. The hideous buttercup yellow gloss had gone and the room was now a very pleasing shade of clotted cream; the huge sash window that let in no light because it looked down into the gloomy well of the office block was hung with creamy, French cotton voile sheers and the ghastly strip lighting had disappeared in favour of several strategically-placed pottery table lamps that cast warm glowing circles of light wherever light was needed most.

There was a plant on Alan's desk; a magnificent blue hydrangea in a pretty white lattice-work china pot and I was sitting, I realized, at one end of an unfamiliar small green linen sofa that was definitely spanking-new Habitat. Charlie's head was resting on one of a pair of cream, rough-woven cotton cushions. I had seen similar ones in John Lewis's only recently. There were a couple of tasteful new prints on the wall and his pre-war fake leather swivel chair that had a permanent lean to the left had been replaced by what appeared to me to be a natural leather swivel recliner that reminded me a bit of Mr Greene's dentist chair. In place of the rusting, black metal office hat stand there was a small, neat, white coat cupboard. A large, expensive-looking porcelain bulldog sat importantly on the top of the book-case that housed the complete Dickens. I wondered where it had come from because I knew it hadn't come from home. I wandered over and examined it curiously.

'You'll be noticing the changes I expect.' I spun round clumsily, nearly dropping the ornament. 'I'm sorry if I startled you.' Mrs Rosen stood framed in the doorway.

'You didn't startle me. Well, I suppose you did really.' For some reason I felt guilty standing there with the china dog in my hand – like a child found playing with a precious, forbidden object. I put the dog carefully back on the book-case. 'It looks so like John,' I said as though by way of explanation.

'Yes, I thought that, which is why I gave it to Alan. Somebody gave it to me years ago,' she added hastily. 'I can't think why because I don't much care for dogs – I'm more of a cat person myself.'

'I suppose you're responsible for all this,' I said, glancing round the room as though for the first time.

Mrs Rosen smiled. 'Well, you must admit it needed it. It was such a dark, poky little office, I'm surprised he could work efficiently in it for so long.'

'I've always thought that, but he would never change anything at my suggestion.'

'My dear, I simply bullied him ruthlessly until he gave in for a bit of peace. I expect he's told you I'm a dreadful martinet.' She was making a statement, not fishing.

'No, he has nothing but praise for you actually,' which wasn't quite true. He simply didn't speak about her, but I felt she deserved to think that he did, so I added, 'He says you're the best secretary he's ever had. I think he's very lucky.'

This was followed by a slightly awkward pause and then she said, 'Well, Alan's very pleasant to work for, so we're both suited aren't we? Now,' she continued briskly, 'we'd better get this young man of yours awake and on his feet because his Dad's on his way back to the office.'

'I didn't hear the telephone.'

'No, you wouldn't have done. I phoned him to tell him you're here.'

'That was very kind of you,' I said, surprised.

'Well, it occurred to me that he might decide to leave the car in the office car park and go home by train and that would never do would it?'

I looked at her curiously. 'May I ask you something rather personal?' I asked tentatively.

She cocked her head to one side. 'You can ask, but I can't promise to answer.'

'I know Scott Fotheringay pays peanuts and it's not exactly a glamorous company to work for. You could get a job anywhere.'

'So why am I working here, is that what you're about to ask?' I nodded.

'Well, I don't have any money worries and if I didn't want

to I wouldn't *have* to work – but both my sons are away from home now and I enjoy working. I'd be bored if I wasn't.'

'Yes, I can understand that,' I said, 'but why Scott Fotheringay?'

She looked at me for a long time, frowning slightly as though she was trying to make up her mind about something, then she sighed. 'Sentimental reasons really,' she said quietly. 'I loved my grandfather dearly and he started this company with what funds he was able to bring out of Germany in 1937. Mr Henderson is the son of my grandfather's partner.'

I looked at her in blank amazement. 'I wonder why Alan hasn't told me all this?'

'Probably because he doesn't know, but I would have told him if he'd asked the same question. I didn't intend to keep it a secret.' She leaned over Charlie and shook his shoulder gently.

'What happened to your father?' I asked. Charlie stirred and opened his eyes. He smiled up at Mrs Rosen and she smiled gently back at him.

'He wasn't interested in textiles and the company passed out of the family when my grandfather died . . . Rise and shine, Charlie, your Dad's on his way back to the office.' Charlie rubbed his eyes and stretched sleepily.

'I'm hungry,' he said eyeing the Penguin biscuits on the tray. I handed him one with instructions to keep the wrapper on.

'I can't eat it with the wrapper on, silly,' he giggled and when he caught Mrs Rosen's eye, she smiled with him.

'You know what I mean – I don't want you to get chocolate all over your hands.' I turned back to Mrs Rosen.

'Was your grandfather Scott or Fotheringay?' I asked.

'Neither,' she replied briskly. 'His name was Goldblatt.'

'Then who were Scott and Fotheringay?'

'They didn't exist. At the time Jews were having a difficult time everywhere and my grandfather thought that Scott

Fotheringay sounded true blue and British. He wasn't ashamed of being Jewish,' she added hastily just in case I was jumping to all the wrong conclusions, 'but he was a realistic man and he didn't want to lose what assets he had managed to salvage.'

Then the outer door slammed. Charlie looked up questioningly. 'Is that my Dad?' The door opened and Alan came in.

I always feel slightly shy with Alan when I meet him at the office. He seems strange to me and he treats me in a distant, preoccupied sort of way. He gave me a careless peck on the cheek and ruffled Charlie's hair.

'Hello old chap,' he said to Charlie, 'I hear you've been drunk and disorderly at the dentist.' But before Charlie could reply he had turned to Mrs Rosen. 'I'll sign those letters before I go . . . Oh, and Sheila,' he called after the retreating back of his secretary, 'did Düsseldorf call back?' I thought how masculine and masterful he sounded as he reeled off a list of things for Sheila to see to the following day when he would be in Leeds and I wondered why he rarely sounded like this at home. I reflected that it was probably because I wouldn't tolerate being treated as an employee.

'She's very nice,' I said to Alan as we swung out of Regent's Park and into the long queue of traffic that was slowly threading its way through St John's Wood. 'I like her a lot. She's still quite glamorous considering she must be pushing fifty,' I added in the condescending way a woman of thirty-four refers to older women, or for that matter, a seventeen-year-old speaks of an attractive woman of thirty-four. 'She's sort of motherly too and she obviously looks after you well.' I found it comforting to think of Alan with his migraines and his skew back being cared for by this warm, competent woman. Then I told him the story of her grandfather called Goldblatt.

'Good Lord . . . how extraordinary,' he said when I had finished. 'I wonder why she told you and not me.'

'Apparently you didn't ask the right questions,' I said. 'She says it's not a secret.' But I guessed that Mrs Rosen was not a woman who offered information about herself unless the right buttons were pressed. 'You know, I think you should take her to the sales conference, if only to give her a treat. After all, she organized most of it. It doesn't seem fair to take me.'

'I wonder if the traffic's any better the other way,' he muttered more to himself than to me. 'There's obviously something up at Swiss Cottage.' Slowly he nosed the car into the parallel lane of traffic that was turning off at Lord's Cricket Ground. 'I expect the Westway will be just as bad but at least it speeds up after Acton.'

'Have you got a headache?' I could see lines of stress building up around his eyes and across his forehead.

'Not yet,' he replied shortly.

'So, what do you think?'

'About what?'

'About taking Sheila Rosen with you to the conference?' Alan's face tightened perceptibly and he breathed out sharply through his nose. 'Honestly darling,' I pleaded, 'I don't enjoy going on about it, but we must make a decision soon for everyone's sake.'

'Well, I thought I'd decided,' he snapped, 'but obviously I didn't make the right decision because it didn't coincide with yours.' He glanced at me sharply. 'But all right, I'll take Sheila if it makes you happy. At least she'll be grateful for a super weekend at the Lakes.' Before I could reply there was a plaintive cry from the back seat.

'I want to be sick Dad.' Charlie was sitting bolt upright blinking tearfully with his hand held over his mouth. Alan stopped the car just a few seconds too late and the rest of the journey home was taken up with pacifying Alan, nursing Charlie and cleaning up as best I could with an old copy of the *Daily Mail* and a pair of spare cotton pants I always carry in my handbag in case my period starts at an inconvenient time and in the wrong place. My spare knickers often came in useful in such emergencies.

Chapter Five

Second Opinion Day was at last upon us. Charlie and I had waited two long months for that precious postcard to wing its way from the glass palace on the hill summoning us to our audience with the eye specialist, a Mr Chaudhuri.

'Have I got to go to school today?' Charlie asked. He was in a festive mood, though nervous, and he felt that perhaps some sort of celebratory holiday was in order.

Actually I have always allowed the children an occasional, totally gratuitous day off school and any excuse will do if the time is ripe. It could be that the sun has come out after weeks of rain or there are a few inches of fresh snow on the ground. I might want company on a shopping trip to the West End or perhaps a preferred relation is passing through. Of course we have to make up an acceptable excuse and I realize that some will say that this is reprehensible as it involves them in lies with my connivance. But I'm afraid I feel little guilt because I know what joy it gives them. I would love to have had a day off from time to time when I was at school but this only happened if I had a temperature, which wasn't very often.

'Well,' I began, 'since our appointment is for ten, which means we can expect to be seen nearer twelve, and that makes it almost lunchtime,' Charlie was holding his breath in anticipation, 'it hardly seems worth while going into school for two hours, does it?' He whooped and tore round the house being a Battle of Britain Spitfire, cannoning into Lizzie, who remarked dourly on the unfairness of life.

'Do you wish you had a squint then?' I asked, putting her

bowl of obligatory porridge in front of her. She ladled Golden Syrup over it and then stirred it vigorously until it was a thin, glutinous soup.

'No,' she replied, 'but I'd like the day off.'

'You've had two days off this term and that's quite enough. Anyway, this is Charlie's day.'

'I've got the Curse,' she said hopefully.

'Again!' I exclaimed, pretending to believe her. 'By my reckoning you've had three this month. I think I'd better take you to the doctor.'

She grinned at me sheepishly. 'Well, it was worth a try.' Lizzie, who had only recently begun menstruating, had absolutely trouble-free periods and a perfect twenty-eight-day cycle, but she had seen with what ease other girls at school took days off, sometimes two or three times a month, or were sent home, apparently in great pain, and she felt that her body had betrayed her.

'I want to go to school today because I'm an angel,' Jane said very seriously. Charlie halted abruptly mid Victory Roll.

'I'll tell you what you are,' he shouted truculently, 'you're a big 'ead!' Jane's hands flew to her head and a spoonful of porridge hurtled across the room and landed with a small splat on the fridge door. Before I could get a cloth to it Poppy had licked it off.

'I haven't got a big 'ead, have I Mummy?' Small children are so literal. I remember once telling a sobbing Lizzie that she'd cry her eyes out and for weeks afterwards, every time she cried, she shut her eyes and held them gently in place with the tips of her fingers.

'Charlie means you're being boastful,' I explained. She looked puzzled.

'You're not an angel. Angels are very good and you're not,' Charlie bellowed as he continued his ear-splitting aerial navigation of the house.

Jane ran after him crying, 'I am an angel, I am an angel!'

'Jane darling.' I caught her by the arm as she flew through

the kitchen for the third time. 'I think you're an angel, and that's what matters.'

'But I *am* an angel!' she cried desperately. 'I've been chosen.'

'By whom and what for?' I asked gently.

'By Mrs Yum-yum, for the Navitivity Play, I'm in the Angel Choir.'

Charlie slid into his chair and began spooning cold porridge into his mouth in between gulps of fresh orange juice. I have always felt that he has a digestive system very similar to that of a goat. 'You can't sing for toffee,' Charlie said scathingly. Without being exactly jealous of Jane he had a fine and accurate sense of her various abilities, and singing was not, in his opinion, one of them. Therefore someone had made a grave error choosing her for the Angel Choir and he felt it was his duty to point this out to us.

'For toffees, she'll sing,' I informed Charlie sharply. He opened his mouth to say something more but after looking at my face decided against it.

I turned to Lizzie. 'Now dear, time you were on your bike.' She pushed the half-eaten porridge away from her with relief and gathered up her books from the sideboard.

'You're sure I can't have the day off?' She was pulling on her gloves slowly without looking at me.

'Absolutely.'

'Oh well. Bye then.' I watched her cycle down the path and out into the main road. I waited for the shriek of brakes, which never actually came and to this day seems a miracle to me. The High Road was aptly named the Rat Run by the locals. It appeared to be a country lane with houses on one side and a well-wooded water meadow on the other. It was narrow and winding and very, very dangerous because it was a well-known short-cut. The traffic was always heavy and on several occasions we were nearly mown down by huge lorries mounting the pavement in order to pass each other. I think if we had known more about the High Road we would never have bought number 68.

'Now Jane,' I said, 'get whatever you want to take with you today . . . and *please* put on some matching socks.'

It wasn't until we reached the school gates that I noticed she had put on yet another pair of odd socks. 'Jane, you still have odd socks on!'

She looked at her legs speculatively. 'Well, I defibly changed them.'

'Definitely,' I said. 'The word is "definitely". Say "def-in-ite-ly",' I instructed.

'Why?'

'Then you might remember it next time.' I subjected the offending socks to closer scrutiny. 'Jane, the socks you have on now pair up with the socks you discarded . . . er, took off.'

'Def-in-ite-ly,' she replied slowly and carefully. I beamed at her.

'That's better.' But my attention was distracted from Jane's socks and the pronunciation of the word 'definitely' by a light tapping on the car window. It was Julie, Jane's new and absolutely best friend. Jane screamed 'Julie!' at the top of her voice, as though the coincidence of them meeting outside the school gates was almost too much to bear, and they ran off together plucking at each other's clothes with hysterical joy.

'Don't forget Granny's picking you up today,' I shouted after her. She nodded over her shoulder and waved. And it was at this point that I remembered I had promised Charlie the day off and I had a committee meeting that afternoon.

'Look, Charlie,' I said after we had taken our places in the queue of patients who all had ten o'clock appointments to see Mr Chaudhuri, 'be reasonable. I'm not breaking a promise because I didn't actually promise anything, I simply forgot that I had a committee meeting.' I rummaged about at the magazine table and found an elderly comic for Charlie and a well-worn *National Geographic Magazine* for myself. Charlie ignored the comic and let it slip from his lap on to the floor.

'Pick it up,' I commanded. He considered the matter stonily. 'I said pick it up,' I repeated.

'I was just going to anyway,' he complained as though I should have known of his intention. Then he rolled the comic into a tube and peered through it with his good eye at the people queuing in the area of the huge waiting-room reserved for Mr Chaudhuri's patients.

'Have we got to wait for all these people to go in before us?'

'Everyone, I think, except perhaps that man who has just come in with the little boy. I think he's after us.'

'Then I shouldn't plan on getting to your committee meeting either,' he said with a definite air of triumph. 'We could be here for hours and hours.' I thought he could be right. 'So if we are here for hours and hours there won't be much point in me going in to school will there?' I don't like apparently insoluble problems such as the one I was being presented with, and even more I hate being pressed for a solution while I am still trying to think of one.

'Shut up Charlie a minute, and let me think, there's a good chap.'

I gazed haplessly round at the chattering throng and wondered if I was the only person who hadn't written off the day. The early Christmas decorations gave the place a festive air which seemed to have infected the patients. People had pulled the vinyl chairs into groups and were gossiping amiably over plastic cups of hospital coffee and biscuits while small children zoomed about the highly polished linoleum floor with gaily-coloured toys taken from the crèche in the corner. On the crèche gate there was a large notice that read 'PLEASE DO NOT REMOVE THE TOYS'. There were neither toys nor children inside the crèche, but plenty of both outside it. No one seemed to care and I suppose this was because it was the first week of December and the nearer it gets to Christmas, the less officious official people become.

I turned to look at my neighbours. The couple on my right seemed to be waging a continual war with a small bespectacled boy who was prepared to keep quiet only when his mouth was full of Smarties. On my left a small, thin woman was placidly knitting something that looked like a cross between a loose cover for a small armchair and a hot-air balloon. It hung down over her knees in lurid, fluorescent pink and green stripes and trailed on to the floor where a small girl was holding the tip of it up to her nose and sucking her thumb.

'Bet'chew I'll 'ave this finished before we're called,' she remarked cheerfully as she caught my eye. I laughed. The racing needles halted briefly as she leant towards me confidentially. 'Would you believe our appointment was for ten o'clock *yesterday* morning?' She was childishly delighted by my shocked reaction. 'No dear, I was only joking. But seriously though, it's always the same up 'ere. Gawd knows why they give us all the same time . . . damn stoopid if you ask me.'

'Have you seen Mr Chaudhuri before?' I asked tentatively.

'Bless yer yes . . . been coming up 'ere since she was a baby.' She tapped the child gently on the top of her head and then pulled back some of the long fair hair that was hanging over her tiny, pointed face. 'He's a nice man even though he's a blackie. Well, he's not yer actual blackie, if you know what I mean. I think he's an Indian or a Pakkie. You think he's great don't you luvvie?'

The child looked up at her mother and nodded solemnly and it was then that I noticed her eyes – enormous, shining, liquid orbs, all pupil and no white, like the eyes of an animal that sees only in the dark – matched, yet oddly unmatched. I glanced quickly away. Don't stare Charlie, I pleaded wordlessly. Please don't stare, remember what I've taught you. But he hadn't noticed, busy as he was picking his nose. I slapped his hand.

'Don't do that,' I commanded with unnecessary venom.

'What?'

'Don't pick your nose.'

'I wasn't.' I suppose it must be admitted that there is

absent-minded nose-picking and purposeful nose-picking. On this occasion his was the former. Nothing to be gained, if you know what I mean, but it gave him something to do with his hands. I turned back to the woman and smiled wryly.

'I suppose they all do it,' I said. She was watching me narrowly though.

'One of 'em's glass,' she told me quietly. I nodded.

'Yes, I noticed something.'

'I know yer did, that's why I'm telling yer. People like you always pretend not to notice, but I always know you 'ave, see, so that's why I come right out with it. It sort've clears the air . . . know what I mean?'

'Yes, I do.' Enough people pretended not to notice Charlie's squint for me to understand, at least that.

The woman went on to tell me that cancer had been diagnosed in one of her daughter's eyes shortly after birth and the eye had been removed and replaced with a glass one.

'It's not a bad match really,' she added. 'It's a shame, considering.'

'Considering what?' I hardly dared to ask.

'Well now they think it's the same with the other one don't they.' I felt something dissolving inside me. 'And if it is, they'll 'ave to take that one away too I expect.' I looked at the child quickly but she appeared to be absorbed in a game of her own with an empty Smarties packet that had rolled over from my neighbours on the right. 'Anyway, I think they're going to tell me today.' She told me their tragedy in such a blunt, matter-of-fact way that it was almost possible to believe that she didn't care, but I knew otherwise. I've noticed that people often recount the most terrible tragedies in this way when they don't want you to feel they're looking for sympathy.

'Oh I am really so dreadfully sorry,' I said, which I know sounds inadequate, but she would have been so embarrassed if I had done what I felt like doing, which was hugging that little woman to me and crying with her, if she felt like it.

For me it felt like the right thing to do. It might have been right for her too, but I couldn't risk it.

'So,' she began suddenly and very brightly, 'what's up with your little man then?' Charlie looked up at her and scowled his usual friendly scowl. 'Oh yes,' she said with a chuckle, 'I can see for myself. 'E's got a squint. Well, don't you worry son, he'll soon put that right. I've seen more squints come and go while we've been coming up 'ere than you've 'ad 'ot dinners. Lazy eye is it?' I shook my head.

'No, I wish it was. He's not got much sight in his right eye,' and I told her the story of Mr Brown-Gillies.

'Oh my dear, I am sorry. It must've been an awful shock for you bein' told just like that with no preparation nor nuffin. You wouldn't get that with Mr Chaudhuri – 'e's very sensitive in that way.' How surprising it is, isn't it, that some people (a certain type of person that is) have the happy ability to really care for others in trouble even when they have insurmountable problems of their own.

'Samantha Tuttle for Mr Chaudhuri,' a harsh, tinny, female voice called over the Tannoy. My neighbour looked up brightly.

'That's us dear . . . believe it or not. Well, nice talkin' to yer. Hope everything goes all right.' Mrs Tuttle, as I now knew her to be, pulled the little girl to her feet and gathered up her mysterious knitting. She noticed me looking at it. 'It's supposed to be a tortoise,' she said pulling a face, 'but it's sort've got out of control.' We laughed together.

'I hope things turn out better than you expect,' I called after her as she scuttled off, but I don't think she heard because a pleasant-faced nurse had come to meet her from Mr Chaudhuri's consulting room and they were greeting each other like old friends. It was only afterwards that I realized that although we were probably the same age she had spoken to me as though I was a very much younger woman.

As I had originally predicted, and rather to my surprise because there were far more people to see Mr Chaudhuri than I had anticipated, we were called at about midday. Mr Chaudhuri, a tall, chubby Asian with a badly pock-marked face and beautifully benign, bovine eyes, told us to sit down. Without asking any questions he examined Charlie's eyes.

'This is indeed very interesting,' he said eventually in his clipped, precise English. 'I do not recall having seen such a thing before,' and I knew he didn't mean the squint. 'You know, of course, that the sight in his right eye is damaged beyond repair?' He glanced at me kindly. I nodded. 'But one never knows – one certainly doesn't,' he mused turning to his nurse. 'One day soon we may develop new techniques.'

Charlie's eye defect is a rare one and whenever his eye has been examined (once he got a speck of grit in it and on another occasion he was kicked rather badly during a rugby match) it has attracted a great deal of curiosity. Indeed, it is generally treated as a small, but interesting, phenomenon. Charlie and I don't understand the diagnosis because it is so technical and complicated. I wish we did.

Mr Chaudhuri asked me to recount Charlie's medical history so far as I could and was very puzzled by his colleague, Mr Brown-Gillies' (whom he said he knew only by reputation) acceptance of the status quo. 'It is only correct,' he said when I had finished, 'that I should write to Mr Brown-Gillies, who is, as I'm sure you know, a most eminent ophthalmologist, to inform him that you have come to see me. There may be some very good reason, that I am not immediately aware of, why this young man's eye has been left as it is. In any case I would need to have access to his case notes.' Mr Chaudhuri looked benevolently down at Charlie, who was beginning to wriggle impatiently in the chair. 'But for myself,' he continued. 'I can see no reason for not – getting cracking – as they say,' he sounded amused by his use of the vernacular, 'on making this young man even more handsome than he already is.' The doctor ruffled Charlie's thick, curly hair and Charlie resisted the temptation to pull away in his normal manner.

'Does that mean you can get rid of the squint?' I asked, not even daring to hope.

'Oh yes my good lady, it certainly does.' There was no doubt in his voice. No 'perhaps', or 'I don't want to raise your hopes'. He was certain, and for a doctor to express such certainty, he had to feel it. 'But I must add,' he said, still sounding certain nevertheless, 'that it all rather depends on what Mr Brown-Gillies has to tell me.' I squeezed Charlie's hand and he permitted it without snatching it away. This was a good sign. 'Now, if you will make an appointment at the desk to see me again in about three weeks' time, I will meanwhile write a very good letter to Mr Brown-Gillies.' Mr Chaudhuri beamed happily at us and I felt that he was truly delighted to be able to give us good news.

'What do you think, Mum?' Charlie asked me once we were outside the hospital and walking towards the car-park which was inconveniently situated a very long way away from the Out-Patients Department. 'Do you think it'll be all right with Mr Brown-Gillies? Is there any reason why I have to keep my squint?' I thought resentfully about the eminent, dignified specialist and his adamant insistence over the years that he had done all he could to help Charlie, and I wondered if he was perhaps not quite as competent as the rest of the world believed him to be.

'No, of course there isn't, Charlie,' I told him firmly.

Charlie suddenly ran ahead and leapt into the air to catch a falling dead leaf that was planing gracefully down on the air currents from a branch of an overhanging sycamore.

'You can have a wish if you catch a falling leaf,' he shouted joyfully over his shoulder, 'and I bet you can guess my wish!'

'I bet I can,' I called back laughing. He squeezed his eyes tight shut and held out the dead leaf in front of him like a votive offering. When he had made his wish he tucked the leaf into his pocket and I believe the one I found recently pressed between the pages of a battered old children's annual to be that very same leaf.

'If you don't mind,' he said as he climbed into the car, 'I

think I'll go to school after all. I want to tell everyone the good news.'

'Then we'd better hurry or you'll miss lunch.' Charlie ran into school without looking back and I seized the opportunity to send up a quick prayer of thanks to the Almighty. Then I thought a bit and followed that with a request. 'Please God, let everything be all right. Let Mr Brown-Gillies be understanding and let Mr Chaudhuri be a whizz at squints.' When I felt I'd covered everything, and that included a plea for world peace and His blessing upon all our cats and dogs, dead and alive, I started the car and drove off to meet the ladies of the Committee.

Chapter Six

Three days before the sales conference and part two of my marriage guidance training, Alan came down with something. I knew he was *really* ill because he didn't make much of a fuss. Like so many normally fit people, he actually seems to enjoy the odd bout of minor illness. No one I know can make quite so much of the common cold. One sneeze and he is as excited as a child on the night before Christmas.

'Hear that?' he asks proudly. 'I've *definitely* got one this time.'

'Yes,' I reply, 'like the one you had last week *and* the week before . . .'

If, by some remote chance, it really does turn out to be a cold, *his* cold is the worst cold anyone has ever suffered from. My three weeks of snivelling misery are nothing by comparison.

'You dote know what it's like to have a *real* code,' he snuffles happily. 'I have double codes . . . My codes have codes,' and he tosses yet another man-size tissue carelessly over his shoulder and misses the wastepaper basket by two feet. Poppy, who has a perverted appetite, snaffles it up as though it was a tasty morsel dropped from her master's plate.

'I wish you wouldn't do that with your soiled tissues,' I snap testily, 'they carry all your germs and should be flushed down the loo.'

'I'b too weak to bake the jourdey,' he pleads piteously, 'ad Poppy bust be ibbune.'

'Then you won't feel like anything to eat,' I say, 'being as ill as you are.' He shakes his head and snuggles down under a blanket with a whisky mac to watch the *Dukes of Hazzard*, or more particularly, Daisy's legs.

'Put another log on the fire before you go,' he commands absently.

I have almost finished preparing supper for the rest of us when he summons me to his presence with a little brass bell in the shape of a crinolined lady that he keeps by his side for this purpose.

'I'm not actually hungry,' he reassures me, 'but I think I ought to eat something just to keep up my strength.'

'I'll heat you up some nice bread and milk.' Ma always flushed out malingerers with this threat.

'Don't you think I ought to have something just a little more substantial?' he asks, pretending to be doubtful.

'Such as?'

'Well, Mother always used to give me lightly grilled Dover sole with shrimp sauce followed by chocolate mousse whenever I was ill.' Then he looks at my face and adds hastily, 'But I'll settle for a very small portion of whatever you're having.' Because I haven't catered for him, we all have very small portions of whatever we were having.

However, this time it wasn't one of his phantom colds, neither was it gyppy tummy, which is a condition he claims to have suffered from since he saw active service in Cyprus as a National Service cornet in the now Blues and Royals. This time he looked really ill. His face was butter-coloured and shone with a light surface coating of oily sweat. He was shivering and said he ached all over and had a sore throat and swollen glands. When I took his temperature it registered 101 degrees.

'You've got a dose of flu, my lad,' I told him. 'So up to bed you go and I'll bring you up some Veganin and a jug of iced lemon barley water. I'll ring up Sheila and tell her you won't be in tomorrow.' He looked appalled.

'Don't be daft . . . I've got masses of work to do this evening and I can't possibly miss tomorrow's meeting with

Hans Krebs.' When he is *really* ill, he soldiers on without complaint until he drops.

'Look darling, no one, but no one, in the office will thank you for dumping your flu bug on them.'

'I haven't got flu, and I'll feel much better if you'll just stop fussing.' I watched him doubtfully as he didn't so much sit down in his chair, as fall into it as his legs buckled under him.

'Well then,' I said briskly, 'if you're not ill, you'll feel hungry. It's toad-in-the-hole and roly-poly pudding.'

'Oh goody,' he replied, turning green.

Lizzie, who was the first child to be allowed to eat with us in the evening (Charlie and Jane were still on high teas much to their disgust), placed a heaped plate of food in front of her father and came back into the kitchen.

'Dad looks awful,' she said. We both peered at him through the hatch. He was looking down at his food as though it was a plate of live worms. I shrugged.

'Well, he insists he isn't ill, so we'll just have to be patient and wait until he's delirious or goes into a coma or something.' He ate half a sausage with great difficulty and a spoonful of cabbage and then, claiming that he wasn't hungry because he had been out to lunch, he shut himself away with his papers and his calculator and didn't stir until I poked my head round the door to say good night.

An uncomplaining sick person attracts more sympathy than a complaining one and Alan was so obviously, uncomplainingly ill that I risked my own health by putting my arms round his weary shoulders and laying my cold cheek against his hot and sweaty one.

'I think you should come to bed, my love,' I said gently. He nodded and then trudged up the stairs with all the vigour of a three-toed sloth. I locked up, turned out all the lights and joined him.

By morning, after a sleepless, tossing night of alternate sweats and shivers, Alan was ready to admit defeat.

'Just tell Sheila that I'm a bit off colour,' he whispered

weakly as I dialled his office number, 'but that I'll be in tomorrow. Ask her to ring Hans and cancel our appointment.'

'I'm not surprised,' Sheila said. 'The silly boy's been coming down with something for days, but he just wouldn't give in to it.' I felt slightly ashamed that I hadn't noticed his symptoms earlier like Sheila. 'Tell him not to worry Polly, there's nothing here I can't handle and if he tries to come in tomorrow, tell him he'll find his office locked and the key in my safety deposit box at the bank.' Gosh, I thought, I wish I had a secretary like her.

'I think he's more worried about the sales conference,' I told her.

There was a pause, and then she said, 'Yes, I suppose he would be. Well, if the worst comes to the worst, we'll just have to manage without him because he won't be a help to anyone if he's ill. I'm sure I can manage to cover for him with the help of George Small – after all, I know his presentation backwards,' which is more than I do, I thought with a pang of unworthy envy.

'Sheila says you're not to worry about a thing – everything's in hand, and she says that if you're not fit by Friday, she can manage the sales conference too with George Small's help.'

'Over my dead body,' he growled, and looking at his haggard face, I thought he might not be so wide off the mark at that.

For two days he lay in bed feverishly tossing and turning. At one point he appeared to be hallucinating and complained that the ceiling was about to cave in.

'Can't you see it?' he asked peevishly. 'It's billowing in the wind like a tent.' Apart from the fact that there wasn't a breath of wind that day, the ceiling looked to me to be as rigid as any other healthy ceiling. 'Better call in someone quickly to take a look at it.' He ate nothing, but drank gallons of lemon barley water with regular large doses of Veganin. The doctor was full of sympathy, but said it was simply a nasty bout of flu and there was very little he could do about it.

'It'll just have to work its way through his body,' he told me helpfully. 'And meanwhile give him plenty of fluids and regular doses of those horse pills you're already giving him. He'll feel pretty gruesome for a week or two I'm afraid, but if it's any consolation, there's a lot of it about.' I wondered why doctors think that sufferers feel consoled in the knowledge that there's a lot of it about. Perhaps it reassures people that they are not suffering from something deadly and terminal. Then I wondered if doctors said the same thing about the Black Death.

'Do you feel happier knowing there's a lot of it about?' I asked Alan after the doctor had left.

'Not particularly,' he muttered and I don't suppose he could have cared less if the entire population of the British Isles came down with flu. The only flu he was interested in was his own.

Though he was still extremely weak and looked like a dying man, by Friday he felt sufficiently restored to toy with a small cup of Campbell's consommé with a slice of dry toast. He made one or two private phone calls to the office and then summoned me to his side.

'Shouldn't you be getting ready to leave?' he asked peering at me over his spectacles. If I thought he had forgotten all about my training week-end, I was wrong.

'I'm all ready actually,' I told him, feeling just a shade guilty. A good wife, surely, would have put nothing before the health and welfare of her sick husband. 'Ma's here to look after you and the children and you know she'll spoil you rotten. She's made you some meringues and she says she'll cook you Dover sole with shrimp sauce tonight if you feel up to it.' He smiled wanly and gave my hand a warm squeeze. 'And I want you to promise me that you won't do anything silly, like going to the sales conference. You're not even fit enough to have a bath yet.'

'I promise you I won't go to the conference if I don't feel fit enough, okay?' Since he obviously would not feel fit enough, I left for Rugby an hour later believing that everything was under control in Ma's capable hands.

It was wonderful to see the gang again, though I was disappointed to find that one of our number, a good-looking doctor from Stroud, had dropped out. We were not told officially why this had happened, but rumour had it that he had left his wife to live with an illustrator of children's books. But it was only a rumour. The youngest member of our close-knit group, Charlotte, was heavily pregnant with her second, which was due at any time and caused a little anxiety when she mistook indigestion for labour pains in the bar after supper. Another woman, whose name I'm afraid I forget, was about to have her gall-bladder removed, and she spent a very dismal and uncomfortable two days feeling nauseous and curled up asleep in corners.

Because of my guilt about Alan I found it difficult to concentrate during our Friday evening group session, so after breakfast the following morning, I phoned home.

'How's Alan?' I asked Ma, who always sounded breathlessly distraught over the telephone when looking after my children.

'He's not here,' she told me in an aggrieved, slightly hysterical voice. 'His secretary arrived about half an hour ago in a very posh-looking sports car and whisked him off to that sales conference thing in the Lake District. I told him it was a very silly thing to do . . . he's not looking at all well, but he said that two days by Ullswater wouldn't do him any harm and anyway he was feeling much better.'

'Well, he must be feeling better if that's what he says, because he promised me he wouldn't go to the conference if he wasn't.'

'He looked awful, Polly,' Ma said accusingly. My fault

again, I thought. 'And that nice Mrs Thing took one look at him and told him to go back to bed. But you know Alan. He can be very obstinate once he has made up his mind to something, and he told us both to mind our own business and that was that.'

First I felt angry with Ma for unsettling me with her poor opinion of Alan's health, then I felt angry with Sheila for not having the courage of her convictions and finally I felt angry with Alan for breaking his promise to me.

'I hope he's sick as a parrot,' I muttered venomously to myself as I hurried to room 2B for a case discussion with role-play, which oddly enough I found very relevant to my current situation.

Role-play is a jargon word for play-act and is just one of the many teaching methods used by the Marriage Guidance Council in its training programme. Two or three members of the group assume the roles of counsellor and client or clients and perform in front of the rest of the group. The 'clients' take it upon themselves to be as difficult as possible, while the 'counsellor' tries very hard to impress everyone with her penetrating perceptions. Afterwards the performance is discussed and the poor soul playing the 'counsellor' is left in no doubt that everyone else could have done it better.

It was my turn for the casting couch and I elected, or perhaps I was selected, to play the role of a wife who felt neglected by her husband who she felt was a workaholic and who travelled abroad a lot on business. I was in sympathy with this woman and as a result my performance was very realistic. I gave my 'husband' hell and was very angry with the 'counsellor' for appearing to take his part against me.

'You really got into that role, didn't you Polly?' one of the group remarked, and the 'counsellor' said that she felt she was dealing with a real client. I noticed one or two speculative glances, so I laughed lightly and said that I had always wanted to be an actress, but I don't think anyone was taken in.

I had been home for hours when Sheila eventually deposited Alan on the doorstep, but before I had time to offer her some light refreshment, she had zoomed off into the night.

Although he looked very tired, Alan did at least look a lot better. 'Wonderful little hotel,' he said drowsily as he waited for me to climb into bed beside him. 'Right on the edge of Ullswater and so quiet. The food was so good, I even felt a little peckish myself. Sheila was a brick. Everyone called her my guardian angel. Looked after me like a mother hen – wouldn't let me do a thing for myself and even brought me up hot toddies at night. Can't think why her husband ran off with someone else.' I could have pointed out that good secretaries don't necessarily make good wives, but I didn't because then he would know I felt jealous. 'Did you have a good weekend?' he asked without any real interest.

'Mmmm,' I began. 'It was really amazingly good. But do you remember me telling you about that doctor in the group?' Alan snored softly in reply, so I read a few pages of *Northanger Abbey* before my eyelids began to flicker with fatigue, and then I turned out the light and snuggled up to my sleeping husband.

The reason why the Committee chose to organize *A Midsummer Night's Dream* and not Miranda Cutler's Box Barn Dance was quite simple. My idea wasn't really any better than hers. In fact, a Box Barn Dance would have been very original and great fun. No, what we didn't like was the fact that Miranda had already done most of the groundwork and that the rest of us would have been nothing more than her ciphers. As Gwen said to me privately, 'I have no intention of being a gofer for Miranda Cutler.'

Of course, none of us admitted this when the subject was debated. Well, it would have seemed so petty. But when we talked to each other privately, this is what we thought. Needless to say we put forward several very credible reasons in committee.

The Bloms' Dutch barn, we agreed, was too far away

from the hub of things. And indeed it would have been a wearisome business ferrying everything from base across country to their farm in East Hertfordshire. We also felt, we said, that too much depended upon other people's goodwill towards Bri and Miranda. What, we muttered between ourselves, would happen if Bri fell out with the leader of the Country and Western band who was at that time managing one of Bri's shops. Bri often fell out with his managers and rumour had it (and I must stress that it was only rumour) that this had something to do with Miranda.

Without being invited by the rest of us, Miranda's stage designer friend turned up to a meeting to outline his ideas. However, by the end of the morning we felt that he was just someone else for Bri to fall out with, if Miranda didn't first.

'I'm sorry,' Hannah said eventually, 'but I don't like relying on promises made to us by people not directly involved with the Committee. I think that whatever we choose to do, we must decide here and now to be responsible for everything ourselves.' Hannah was, we felt, voicing the feelings of us all. Miranda simply shrugged, giving a very good impression of a woman who didn't give a damn and I did admire her. But then I have always admired people like her. People who present a detached, self-contained face to the world so that you can never guess what they're feeling. It seems to me such an advantage to be able to keep your feelings hidden whenever you need to.

If the Committee had chosen Miranda's idea I would not have been able to shrug my feelings away with such sang-froid. I'd have made an effort but my actions thereafter would have given me away. I'm ashamed to admit that I would have lost all interest in the enterprise. You see, I don't much like carrying out other people's creative ideas. But I do like other people to carry out mine which I'm told is an Arien characteristic. So it was just as well that I was the only Arien on the Committee or we might have been in trouble. As it was, the others all got on nicely doing what they were told and already we had held a very successful Christmas Craft

Sale which raised a healthy £234.63 towards the expenses of *A Midsummer Night's Dream*.

For a month or more we made things for the sale. Together, in each other's houses, we cut and sewed and stuck and cooked. I designed the house Christmas card that rather unwisely consisted mainly of sparkly things stuck on a stylized Christmas tree. We turned wire hangers into very charming Pierrot pyjama cases. I don't know anyone who keeps their pyjamas in a pyjama case but we sold out of them all the same and I think that was because people thought they would look pretty hanging on the back of a bedroom door. We made dozens of pairs of gypsy-style earrings from a large cache of very small, bright Turkish coins that Hannah had kept because she knew that they would come in useful one day, and we sewed pretty little gingham mob caps to cover Maggie's jars of home-made fruit mincemeat. The Awful B turned out pounds and pounds of peppermint creams that she coloured bright red and green to keep in with the spirit of Christmas, she said. Personally I think she went a bit mad with the colouring and people must have agreed with me because not many were sold. We hid them from B to avoid hurting her feelings.

However, the *pièce de résistance* was definitely Gwen's pastry angels. It was an idea for Christmas decorations that she had picked up from a women's magazine. You make a very stiff dough with flour, salt and a little water and you mould it, like clay, into funny little angels, some praying, some singing, some playing trumpets and some, and this was for the less able, simply standing with their arms outstretched which reminded me of rather inferior child graffiti. You attach a strong loop to some part of the anatomy, usually the head, so that they can be hung, you bake them in a hot oven and then you paint them.

We started modestly enough with conventional cherubim in white nighties, plump and pink (some looked apoplectic), with golden hair and silver wings. But once we had mastered the medium we became more and more ambitious, competing with each other to produce the most outrageous and eccentric members of the Heavenly Host. There were angels in tutus, astronaut angels, French Waitress angels, Bunny angels, cowboy angels, Red Indian angels and angels in drag. Patsy modelled a very funny camp angel with a limp wrist and a poodle tucked under one arm and Gwen produced a fabulous City Gent angel in a bowler hat with a briefcase and a rolled umbrella. I got very spiritual about the whole thing and produced a complete pastry Nativity which was greeted with a lot of suitably reverent awe but not much enthusiasm because nobody recognized it for what it was and it had to be explained to them. Miranda, as you would expect, went over the top. She called hers 'Page Three Angel' but because it was to be a family sale of work we decided that she should be brought out as a private limited edition for adults only. Clever old Miranda built on her success with a limited edition of Kama Sutra angels which rapidly became collectors' items, though I don't imagine they hung from many trees that Christmas.

Buoyed up by our enormous success and by popular demand, we decided our next fund-raising venture would be something a little more sophisticated – a Madeira and Mince Pies Morning – and this was at the top of the agenda for the meeting that afternoon at Hannah's house.

'Polly, you look extremely harassed,' Hannah commented when I arrived half an hour overdue. 'Here, have a sherry.' I took it gratefully and apologized for being late.

'I shouldn't let it worry you,' she said. 'Miranda's not here yet and Gwen phoned to say she'd be late, but at least we have a quorum.'

We discussed the number of tickets already sold and B, as usual, had sold all hers within hours of issue.

'You really are amazing, B,' Hannah remarked warmly. B flushed proudly and said it was nothing really, anyone could sell tickets. I said I couldn't and B looked at me severely.

'It's no use looking at me like that, B,' I said shaking my head. 'I'm quite good at selling people things that I know they want to buy, but I'm hopeless at cold selling. I really dislike having to persuade people to buy something when I am certain they don't want to, or worse still, are buying it to please me.'

B looked puzzled. 'I'm sure I don't know what you're talking about, Polly,' she said. 'I naturally assume people want to buy whatever it is I'm selling or they wouldn't do so, would they. I *never* pressure people to buy things against their will.' Which illustrates one of the differences between B and me. B loves social gatherings such as coffee mornings and garden fêtes and her enthusiasm is infectious, whereas I don't and I tend to sell tickets in an apologetic, craven sort of way. 'I know it's a frightful bore,' I might begin, 'but be a darling and buy a ticket for my sake,' and this puts people right off because they imagine that whatever it is I'm selling tickets for must be awful. B, on the other hand, begins by telling them that she's sorry but they can't have more than five tickets each and she has them begging for ten.

Gwen arrived looking bothered and she was closely followed by Miranda who was unaccountably accompanied by Tiny, her Great Dane. Hannah, for a moment, looked uncharacteristically vicious.

'Who invited *him*?' she muttered as she snatched Snoozy Suzie, her in-season Yorkie bitch, from under the massive backside, just moments before it lowered itself to the ground. 'Do you think you could put Tiny in the car?' she suggested to Miranda after she had thrown Snoozy unceremoniously into the bicycle shed.

'Well, I would,' Miranda replied with a theatrical sigh, 'but he'd tear the car to shreds. He suffers from claustrophobia you know. I had to bring him because he has an appointment with Dog Bodies at four to have his claws clipped. So sorry.' Hannah clenched her teeth and stared hard at her Klitz etching over the fireplace. I guessed she was counting to ten.

Gwen, who is generally cold, even on the warmest day, took up her customary stance in front of the fire with the back of her skirt hitched up. 'I feel that the time for long johns is almost upon us,' she said and she shivered with pleasure as the heat thawed out her haemorrhoids which were particularly troublesome from November through to March.

Miranda, looking like a bunch of sexy chipolata sausages in skin-tight brown leather from top to toe, sank gracefully, if squeakily, into Hannah's black leather Chesterfield. She leant back and shut her eyes, smiling drowsily to herself.

'Mmmmmm,' she murmured in a honey-coated sort of way, 'I've just had a wonderful screw.' As in a child's game of statues, we, each one of us, froze in the middle of whatever we were doing. Gwen had her glass of sherry half-way up to her mouth, which was open to receive it; Hannah was bent double and just about to stoke up the fire; Patsy allowed the match she was holding to light her cigarette to burn her fingers; Maggie was half out of her chair and I was in the middle of blowing my nose. Only B, with hardly a flicker, continued to rummage through her handbag for whatever it was she was looking for.

Miranda half-opened her eyes and surveyed us through her gluey artificial eyelashes with a look of amused condescension or maybe it was contempt. Her shocking lapse into bad taste hung trembling in the air above our heads with all the subtlety of a bandit's belch.

'What was that, dear?' B asked innocently enough, although I have often wondered about that because B has the hearing of a cat and a horror of what she calls 'smutty talk'. But it wasn't a statement that bore repeating and Miranda, recognizing this, shook her head lazily and shut her eyes again.

'She said she's just had a wonderful screw.' Gwen looked triumphantly towards Miranda and smiled one of her coldest and most calculating smiles, and oh my God, Miranda blushed.

'Well, how very nice for you, dear,' B said sweetly and

dismissively. 'Now perhaps we'd better get back to the matter in hand.' We breathed out collectively and there was some contemplative throat-clearing. Gwen winked at me broadly and I winked back and made a mental note to congratulate her later, though I had the feeling that it was B who deserved our thanks.

B said she was pleased to report that all bar six of the hundred tickets I had printed on Charlie's John Bull Printing Set had been sold. 'Polly tells me she still has six tickets left,' B twinkled reproachfully at me from across the room, but leavened it with a tiny smile. 'And perhaps dear you can print a few more. I know I can sell them and it seems a pity not to take advantage of people's seasonal goodwill.'

Hannah was beginning to twitter anxiously. 'Hang on, B,' she said. 'I really do think that a hundred people is a comfortable number in this house, and anyway, we've already ordered the Madeira at cost price. I really can't ask Barney's vintner friend in the City for any more.' I noticed Gwen was beginning to look quite agitated. When she rubbed the end of her nose vigorously with the knuckle of her right forefinger you knew something was about to happen.

'Ahhhh . . . er, now listen,' Gwen began in a quite loud voice. 'Ahh – we um, won't um – actually need any more Madeira actually Hannah. I – I'm – certain we'll have enough.' Hannah shook her head vigorously and said that no, we wouldn't have enough if we invited any more people. We had, she reminded Gwen, worked it out to the nearest glass. Gwen was looking most uncomfortable.

'Yes, I know all that,' she said irritably. 'But I haven't sold all my tickets either.'

B looked over at Gwen and frowned. 'But I thought you said –'

'I know what I said, thank you B, but the truth is, I haven't sold them all. As a matter of fact, I've got them here in my handbag.' She fumbled in her bag and brought out a packet of tickets held together with an elastic band. 'Here you are, B.' Gwen passed the packet to Hannah, and she passed them to B. B took them and started counting them. 'It's all right, they're all there.'

'You're right Gwen, they are all here.' B was regarding Gwen steadily.

'I'm sorry B but I just haven't had time.'

'But Gwen, you haven't sold a single ticket, and you only had ten.' I could see that Gwen was trying to make up her mind about something and when she had, she sighed and clasped her hands in her lap.

'Look, if you must know, I think two pounds a head is far too much for a glass or two of Madeira and a mince pie, especially if it's one of my mince pies.'

'We've got a jolly good raffle, remember,' Patsy Pennant piped up. Patsy was not exactly a ball of fire so I was a bit worried when she volunteered to take on the co-ordination of the raffle, but I shouldn't have been, she was a whizz.

'Yes . . . how're we doing on that front, Patsy?' Hannah asked rather desperately I thought. Patsy, who clearly disliked speaking out, coloured and took a deep breath.

'Well, so far we've been promised a twelve pound oven-ready turkey from Blundell's, a hamper of fruit and vegetables from Walton's, a cut, perm, shampoo and set at Curly's and an intimate candle-lit dinner for two at The Steak House, Harrow-on-the-Hill – the manager's a friend of a mate of mine. I've got several more irons in the fire, though.'

For a moment we forgot Gwen's imminent fall from grace.

'I say, Patsy,' Hannah said warmly, 'that's jolly good.'

'I don't know how you do it . . . Fantastic Patsy . . .' We most of us chimed in with our praise for Patsy's efforts.

'Well done that woman,' B said. In her youth B had been a sergeant in one of the women's services and sometimes her language slipped into that of the parade ground.

'Er, folks . . .' We all turned at the sound of Miranda's lazy drawl. 'Bri and I are donating a VHF stereo car radio and cassette player plus installation costs.' I suppose we all must have looked fairly stunned because Miranda seemed well satisfied with the effect her announcement had had upon us. 'But we think it should be auctioned separately. . . . It'll make more money that way.' Patsy's bright face drooped a bit but she quickly pinned it up again.

'That's smashing, Miranda,' she exclaimed generously. 'And of course you're right. It'll obviously be the star attraction.' How typical of Miranda, I thought. Even little Patsy's minor triumph had to be diminished. Coolly Hannah offered her thanks to Bri and Miranda on behalf of us all.

'So you see, Gwen,' Miranda turned our attention adroitly back to Gwen and the little matter of the unsold tickets, 'the tickets are really cheap at the price.'

'For your friends maybe . . .' Gwen muttered sourly.

'And what's that supposed to mean?'

'You obviously don't mind soaking the same rich friends every time – but I do. Not one of the women on my list has money to throw away and they've already forked out for pyjama cases and pastry angels and Maggie's home-made mincemeat . . .'

'Then why don't you approach some different women?' I was glad it wasn't me at the receiving end of Miranda's insolent stare.

'Because I don't know any different women,' Gwen replied quietly.

'How sad,' Miranda said sympathetically, but there was a mocking glint in her eye. Gwen's eyes narrowed ominously and her rather elegant nostrils flared. She has one of those muscular faces that can assume all those expressions you read about in novels but rarely see. No one, for example, raised an eyebrow to better effect and her tight smile used to send shivers down my spine. A slight but telling flexing of her facial muscles indicated strong disapproval and a twitch of her upper lip, contempt. I, on the other hand, have one of those round, rosy, kindly faces that encourages people who don't know me well to imagine that I am a calm, contented woman and probably a bit dim, and I feel I have to over-react in order to convince people otherwise.

'Now now,' B twittered, 'little birds in their nests . . .'

Gwen glanced at B and her upper lip twitched dangerously. Then she turned her attention back to Miranda and the venom in her eyes was truly memorable. 'Now you listen to me, Miranda Cutler,' she grated. 'Your friends may be rich, dilettante playboys and girls with more money than sense and nothing to do all day but lie around their indoor swimming pools smoking pot in Chesham Bois.' The decadent picture she painted of the Cutler circle of hard-working machine tool manufacturers and garage proprietors living the dolce vita in the Chiltern Hills broke the nervous tension and everyone, including Miranda, burst out laughing. Gwen, looking like the Snow Queen, waited for the laughter to subside and then continued, 'But my friends are mostly ordinary working people trying to make a living and two pounds means the difference between a joint for Sunday lunch or lentil stew.' We all knew this wasn't strictly true, but she said it with such magnificent conviction it might as well have been.

With what pale dignity Gwen drained her sherry glass and gathered up her belongings. She rose slowly to her full height, which on top of her four inch patent-leather court shoes must have been at least six foot two, and surveyed us all with lofty disdain. 'It is obvious to me that I can be of no further use to this Committee,' she said haughtily, and with that she swept out, as they say.

'Oh God,' someone muttered irritably and I think it was Maggie for she had no time for Gwen's regular histrionic scenes. Hannah leapt to her feet and ran out after her. We could hear them arguing outside in the porch and then the front door slammed and Hannah returned looking unusually pink and ruffled.

'Oh honestly,' she said with exasperation, and then, 'Well, somebody say something for heaven's sake.'

'Good riddance is what I say,' is what Miranda did indeed say. 'I mean, she's been obstructive and half-hearted since the beginning and all because she wasn't voted chairman.'

All of which, I have to admit, was more or less true but it wasn't because she wasn't voted chairman. It was because she couldn't devote as much time to the Committee as the rest of us and she felt guilty about it. Recently Gwen had begun working three whole days a week at the Cottage and this left her little enough time to spare for Mike and the boys and the housekeeping. Because the Committee had been her idea in the first place she felt obliged to continue working for it. She often arrived late to meetings and left early. She missed a few altogether and as a result felt out of touch and left out. Ever a perfectionist, she hated giving less than her best.

'Oh why don't you just shut up, Miranda,' I said with some asperity, 'and look to your bloody dog.' With our attention being taken up elsewhere none of us had noticed that Tiny appeared to have fallen madly in love with the drop end of the pretty little Victorian sofa in the bay window and was doing his level best to seduce it. I was about to hypothesize on the possible results of crossing a drop head sofa with a Great Dane when Miranda leapt up with unaccustomed energy and heaved an elegantly shod foot under the dog's working rump.

'Gerroff, you nasty perverted animal!' she shrieked, 'and leave female sofas to male sofas.' Then she looked questioningly at Hannah. 'I suppose it is a female sofa, because I've never been too sure about Tiny's preferences . . .'

Now B gets het up about all sorts of apparently harmless things. She doesn't like 'smutty talk', black stockings with seams, nail varnish, ankle-strap shoes, pierced ears, Olivia Newton-John, leather trousers, Siamese cats, sports cars, Monty Python's dead parrot sketch, Balkan Sobranies, Sunday trading, anything to do with the Roman Catholic religion, cruelty to animals or homosexuality. So you see, in one brief moment Miranda lit three of B's smouldering torches at once.

'*I am disgusted!*' she brayed over our shouts of uncontrollable laughter, her fine contralto voice vibrato with emotion.

'I am appalled . . . and to think I nearly invited Lady Rose to join us.'

More shouts of laughter at the mention of B's beloved Lady Rose.

'My coat please, Hannah - and my frozen prawns from your freezer.'

'Please, B, we'll all calm down in a minute,' Hannah spluttered hysterically.

'No,' B sniffed and tossed her blue-rinsed, prematurely grey, rigidly permed head. 'I'm sorry, dear, for I know it's not your fault.' She looked meaningfully and contemptuously towards Miranda. 'But I have heard enough smutty talk for one day. And you forget, I have to face Basil tonight.' I know B believes in God, but I have a sneaking suspicion that she thinks he looks a lot like her husband, Basil. So, I think, does Basil.

Decisively she zipped up her Morlands sheepskin boots and stepped out. There was a canine howl of pain as her heavy foot landed athwart one of Tiny's massive paws. The dog swung his mighty head round and caught B a savage blow on the back of her knees which promptly buckled under her. She flung her arms in the air looking for support and finding none fell helplessly over the coffee table knocking the sherry bottle, several sherry glasses in various stages of depletion and a full, hot coffee percolator on to Hannah's precious silvery green and pale pink Chinese wash carpet. The dark coffee intermingled attractively with the golden sherry to form the shape of a large, dappled sow with six suckling pigs at her teats. This held my fascinated attention for a full ten seconds before the horror of the accident hit me.

Needless to say the meeting broke up in some confusion. Maggie, a tearful Hannah and I did what we could with the carpet, which wasn't much. The coffee table was a write-off, for B's weight, though not excessive, was enough, when descending rapidly from a height, to crack the table top clean in two.

'Do you think insurance covers things like this?' Maggie asked, trying, no doubt, to look on the bright side, 'or do you think B constitutes what they call an Act of God?'

'I'm sure she'd like to think she was,' I said dismally.

'Do you realize,' Hannah said as she eventually saw me off at the door, 'that we have managed to consume two bottles of Barney's best Amontillado – one way or another?'

'I think we'd better insist on temperance meetings from now on, don't you?' Hannah nodded miserably. 'And we'll have to do something about Gwen.'

'And the Awful B,' Hannah reminded me. 'You know, I'm not sure that this was all such a good idea.'

'We can't call it off now,' I said. 'We'd lose too much face. Anyway,' I said with an effort at cheerfulness, 'I'll see you at the "do" with my forty mince pies and we'll grovel to Gwen and tell B we just can't manage without her . . . you know it'll work.'

'Spare me a thought this evening explaining things to Barney.'

'I think I hate Miranda Cutler,' I snarled.

'Me too . . . Do you think there's a provision in our constitution that allows us to blackball someone like her?' I said I'd give it some thought.

'But let's wait until we've auctioned her wretched VHF car radio, shall we?' Hannah managed a weak smile.

On the way home I had a puncture.

Ma was tight lipped with disapproval by the time I arrived to pick Jane up.

'What sort of time do you call this?' she snapped. 'Really Polly, you never think of anyone else but yourself. You've got a little girl here you know.' Jane was looking at me with the suffering, pious look of a dying Labrador. How she enjoys my disgrace, I thought. She pulled at Ma's skirt.

'Tell her about my tummy-ache, Granny.'

'Yes, Polly. The school couldn't get hold of you.' You lotus-eater you. 'Luckily they have my number and I picked up the poor little mite.' The 'poor little mite' winced delicately for my benefit.

'I can't go to the toilet again.' It was more of a triumphant accusation than a statement of fact.

'I've stewed her some prunes and she's had a spoonful of Syrup of Figs.' Hmmm, prunes and figs – can't fail, I thought.

'I'm really sorry I'm so late Ma, but I had a puncture on the way here.' Ma sniffed.

'Very convenient, I'm sure,' she said, the implication being that I had hammered the four-inch nail into the tyre myself. No point in arguing with her though when she's in that sort of mood. 'And what about the other two. You phoned home of course.' She knew I hadn't. Oh *mea culpa*, what a truly rotten mother I am turning out to be – she knew I would.

'I told them I'd be late,' I countered sulkily.

'And how did Charlie get home if you didn't pick him up?'

'It doesn't hurt him to come home on the bus occasionally Ma. He's got to learn.'

'At eight years old?'

'I was at boarding school at seven,' I reminded her. It was an unfair dig really because by her lights and in those days Ma was only doing what she thought was best for Babs and me, and I still don't know for sure that it wasn't. Babs and I boarded at a charitable institution that was set up during the last century to educate the daughters of dead Freemasons. It was an opportunity for us that Ma couldn't afford to turn down, for when our father died we were left with no money and Ma had to go out to work. I don't remember ever being happy at the school, well, not very often anyway, but I did receive a first class education.

Ma's face went blank as it always did when I brought up the subject of my schooling. She hated having to justify her decision to me and I was very persistent over the years in my pursuit of some indication that she felt remorse for the misery she had inflicted upon me. 'Anyway, I must be off, Ma,' I said quickly before we could get started on the age-old argument. I kissed her lightly on the cheek and pulled an unwilling Jane out of the door. Ma followed us out with Gladys tucked inside her old cardigan.

'I've still got a tummy-ache, Granny,' Jane called back hopefully. She felt cheated, because she thought there was still some mileage to be had from the 'poor little mite' routine. But Ma's attention was elsewhere. An over-excited Gladys was trying to break free from Ma's iron grip in order to hurl herself, or failing that, insults, at the next door's tabby who was preening himself casually on his customary position of strength on top of the coal bunker. Don't waste your energy Gladys, I thought. You're never going to get closer to that cat than you are at this moment.

'I'll pop in tomorrow,' I called from the car, but because she hadn't heard my pledge I knew I wouldn't feel obliged to honour it.

Lizzie looked up from the kitchen table which was spread with the books required for her homework. She was chewing the end of her pencil and frowning thoughtfully.

'How do you say in French "I should have told somebody something"?'

I tried to look intelligent – you know – as though the answer was on the tip of my tongue.

'Of course I'd need to know the context,' I said cagily.

'Well, Monsieur Lepine has just remembered that he didn't lock up his house and he is thinking –'

'Forget it Lizzie, because I don't know,' I admitted.

'I knew you wouldn't.'

'So why did you ask me?'

'Well just sometimes I strike lucky and you remember something useful from your dim and distant school days.' I reminded her of the rather sensitive little poem of mine that they printed in her school magazine. 'Mmmm, I suppose you're still quite good at English. Anyway, I wish you'd stop bragging about that poem – you seem to forget that everyone thinks I wrote it.'

'Mrs Douglas didn't. She put "Good work Mrs Graham" at the bottom of your exercise book.'

'She assumed you helped me, that's all. Anyway,' Lizzie dropped her pencil and studied my face suspiciously, 'where've you been? I've been home for hours.'

'I told you I'd be late.'

'Yes, but not *this* late.' I explained about the puncture and briefly outlined, for her amusement, the events of the day. Just as I was thinking I would risk telling her about Miranda's wonderful screw, Jane returned to the kitchen and asked for something to eat.

'I've been,' she announced. I expressed my relief.

'By the way, where's Charlie?' I asked Lizzie.

'He's gone swimming with Eddie, but they should be back any minute.'

I gave Jane a glass of low-calorie orange squash and a Kit-Kat.

'Well, I suppose I'd better get on with the supper,' I sighed. 'It's not going to make itself.'

Lizzie looked up suddenly. 'That reminds me, Mum. Dad phoned to say he's working late and he'll grab something to eat on the way home. He sounded a bit miffed – said he'd been trying to get you all day.' Lizzie looked at me speculatively. 'He's been working late a lot recently hasn't he?'

I smiled at her teasing innuendo. 'Mmmm, if I didn't know your father I'd be beginning to wonder a bit.'

That's four times in the last ten days, I thought, as I chopped the onions and sweated them with the chopped chicken livers and bacon for the Bolognese sauce. Last time he had a Wimpy and the time before that some Southern Fried Chicken from that place on Russell Hill that appears to be run by a group of druggies suffering from terminal dandruff, endemic impetigo and very probably amoebic dysentery to boot.

Charlie's gruff, cheerful greeting, 'Hi Mum!' rang through the house like the joyful bark of a small terrier. He always sounded pleased to be home no matter where he had been and he would wait expectantly for my response.

I have a friend who lost her son in a cycling accident some years ago. Shortly after Ma's death when I came to understand the nature of grief, we spent an afternoon together just talking about mourning and loss. She was helping me come to terms with my feelings by sharing her experience with me the way some people do who no longer feel inhibited in the face of grief. She told me that more than anything else she missed the thump of his bike as he leant it up against the wall when he came home from school and his shout of 'Hi Mum!' as he came through the door. Now that Charlie drives a car and is away from home more often than he's at home I can feel something of the poignancy of her yearning.

'Cor, something smells good.' Eddie loped into the kitchen and came up behind me sniffing over my shoulder at the sizzling pan.

'Yes, it's funny how frying bacon and onions smell almost better than anything else,' I said.

'What are you cooking?'

'A Bolognese sauce.'

'Mmmm, my favourite,' he breathed. I glanced at him over my shoulder. He looked cold and wet, as though he hadn't bothered to dry himself properly after his swim. His long, fine, almost colourless hair was plastered to his head like damp butter-muslin and his thin angular face, unshaven for probably two days, was red and chapped and he was beginning a nasty cold sore on his upper lip.

'Stay and have some supper with us,' I said impulsively. His face lit up and then dropped just as suddenly.

'What about Alan?' he asked. Having been the victim of Alan's occasional bouts of xenophobia Eddie tended to avoid confrontation whenever possible.

'He's working late and getting something to eat out.'

He still looked doubtful. 'Will he mind?' he said. 'I don't think he approves of me.'

I laughed. 'Of course he won't mind – and he disapproves of anyone who, in his opinion, distracts me from my wifely duties.'

'Go on Eddie, stay,' Charlie pleaded, 'then you can teach me to play poker. You promised.'

'Well, thanks . . . yes, I'd like to. With Midge away' (his landlady and the friend of his late mother) 'I've been living on tins.' Charlie bellowed exuberantly and playfully punched Eddie on the upper arm.

'Right then, both of you, go and dry yourselves off *properly*,' I admonished, 'and get warm in front of the fire.'

After supper when Charlie and Jane were in bed and Lizzie, who found Eddie's close proximity too disturbing, had retired to her room to revise, she said, and listen to some 'decent music', Eddie lounged comfortably back in Alan's chair, slung one long leg over the arm and poured out the last of the bottle of Valpolicello that he had dashed out to buy as his contribution to the feast.

'How're you getting on with your book?' he asked when I eventually joined him after I had tidied up the kitchen.

'It's coming along,' I replied non-committally. We sat in companionable silence for a while listening to the beautiful Mozart piano concerto that poured out of Alan's very superior stereo system. The music lifted me out of myself and I let my shoulders and the tense muscles of my jaw relax.

'What's it about?' Eddie asked suddenly. 'Or don't you want to talk about it?'

'I haven't talked about it to anyone yet.' Which was more or less true, but I felt very tempted to talk to Eddie about it. He waited, watching me lazily over the top of his wine glass.

'Am I in it?' But he laughed to show me that he was only joking. However he continued to regard me steadily and I felt a childish desire to cover my face with my hands to hide the inexplicable confusion I was feeling. He noticed my hesitation and quickly followed up his advantage. 'Come on, tell me what sort of a book it is . . . I mean, is it a spy thriller, or a whodunnit?'

'Good Lord no, it's nothing like that.'

'Then is it a love story?' Although I knew it was impossible, I felt that he had already guessed the content of my book and was having a little fun at my expense.

'Well, yes,' I admitted reluctantly, 'I suppose it is.' I felt myself blushing, but once you've blushed there isn't much you can do about it. You just have to wait for it to subside and hope that no one has noticed.

'I know! You're writing a porno blockbuster under an assumed name!' Clearly the blush hadn't gone unnoticed.

'Hmm . . . I wish it was,' I said ruefully. 'Because I'd like to make pots of money, but I've tried and I'm not very good at it. I find I get embarrassed writing the sexy bits.' Eddie burst out laughing. 'It wasn't lusty enough because I couldn't bring myself to use all those awfully crude words for parts of the body. Actually it sounded a bit like a sex manual by Mrs Beeton.'

Still laughing, Eddie said, 'And you call yourself a marriage guidance counsellor?'

'Yes, well, talking to someone with sexual difficulties isn't quite the same as writing a book aimed specifically at people's private parts.'

Eddie inhaled deeply on his cigarette, blew a perfect smoke ring towards me and regarded me thoughtfully through it.

'It's Mills and Boon then?' he hazarded.

'No, and believe me, I've tried that too. But I'm either too much of a realist or not cynical enough because my characters never behave in the way readers of romantic fiction expect them to.' To escape that unwavering gaze I wandered over to the stereo. 'Would you like the Carpenters or *Tubular Bells*?'

Eddie looked surprised. 'I didn't know you liked Mike Oldfield,' he said, the implication being that he was astonished that I had even heard of him. At that time Mike Oldfield was part of the alternative pop scene and therefore not the sort of musician Eddie would expect me to appreciate. Carefully I put the record on the turntable and dusted it with a little velvet pad. Alan is most particular about such things and I knew he would notice if I didn't.

'It's about an affair between a young man and an older woman.' I spoke my secret for the first time and half hoped that it was still a secret shared only with the stereo. Delicately I lowered the fragile arm on to the record. There was an unpleasant squark as it jumped three rings and I noticed that my hand was shaking.

Pull yourself together woman, I instructed myself briskly. You're behaving like a terrified virgin. You're not about to have an affair with young Eddie, nor do you want one – do you? No, what you're really worried about is that he'll jump to all the wrong conclusions, which will complicate a perfectly innocent and very pleasant friendship. So why did you tell him? Oh shut up and go away!

'Have you ever –' Eddie began.

'I'll make some coffee,' I interrupted quickly. But Eddie followed me out into the kitchen and hovered wordlessly as I went about the business.

'Polly.' I clattered busily about the kitchen making a production number out of two mugs of Nescafé.

'Mmmm?'

'Have you ever had an affair with a younger man? I mean, like, since you've been married?' I was relieved that he couldn't see my face.

'No.' I swallowed hard.

'With any man?'

'No.'

'Have you ever been tempted?'

'No,' I said without hesitation. He must be left in no doubt.

'Oh come on . . . you don't have to stop fancying men just because you're married.'

'I agree with you, but that doesn't mean I want to have affairs with them.' I handed him a steaming mug, picked up mine and, giving Eddie a wide berth, returned to the living-room. Eddie trailed after me. Carefully he put his mug down on the stone hearth and then flopped on to the old alpaca rug in front of the dying fire. He rested his chin on his knees and stared curiously up at me.

'Are you afraid of having an affair? What I mean is, if an opportunity arose and you knew you couldn't possibly be found out – would it make any difference?'

I won't pretend I hadn't thought about this before. From time to time I had imagined what it would be like to have some sort of romantic liaison with some man who has particularly interested me but my imagination had never explored beyond the first exquisite realization that the man in question returned the compliment, which in itself seemed so unlikely that I never bothered to pursue the fantasy any further. There was, for example, the time when I convinced myself that Mike Bray's visits to the library at the same time as myself three Saturday afternoons in a row were no mere coincidence. We struck up a brief intimacy on the strength of our mutual enjoyment of the works of L. P. Hartley, but that is where it began and ended for shortly afterwards the library closed on Saturday afternoons. Then there was Mr George, a melancholy and romantic washing machine service engineer who told me all about his nervous break-down one wintry afternoon and said he was looking for a woman just like me. He found one very similar to me in the next street and then had another sort of break-down when her husband found out.

'No, it wouldn't make any difference,' I said firmly, 'because I'm happy with the way things are and I wouldn't want to jeopardize that.' I felt awkward and embarrassed talking about such personal matters with such a young man and I was certain that neither of us felt as detached and disinterested as we were trying to appear. It is difficult to talk to a strange man about sex and love and things like that without reaching a level of intimacy that is both exciting and at the same time threatening. I have found this to be the case even when I'm counselling. If a third person had walked into that room he would have found us both perfectly relaxed and at ease, but in fact the atmosphere was almost palpably vibrating with unspoken messages. I felt I was walking a delicate, shimmering tight-rope of spun glass. One wrong word, a message misunderstood and my tight-rope would smash and then something unimaginably awful might happen – something ultimately destructive that I wouldn't be able to control.

'But what if you knew Alan was having an affair. Would you still feel the same?' I found Eddie's lean, bony hand fondling Poppy's floppy, black velvet ears unaccountably fascinating.

'I can't say – because he's not.'

Eddie looked up sharply. 'How do you know he's not? I mean, where is he now? He tells you he's working late, but how do you know he's telling the truth?' He smiled mischievously so that I would understand that he was only teasing.

'I know my husband,' I said lightly. 'I'd know if he was having an affair because he'd do something to give himself away.'

Eddie gave a short laugh. 'But Polly, that's what everyone says isn't it? At least, that's what you told me.'

The boy's right, I thought. It *is* what everyone says. An affair is usually the last thing we suspect when our marriages begin to go wrong. We believe that we know our partners so well that we'll notice any deviant behaviour, and usually we do but we put it down to other causes. He's tired; he's having a bad time at the office; he's worried about money; she's not well; it's the time of the month; the children are getting on her nerves; she's bored, she needs an outside interest; that awful divorced friend of hers has been getting at her. It's something I've done or said, or haven't done or said. Indeed, unless one's spouse is an habitual philanderer, an extra-marital affair is quite naturally the last conclusion one jumps to.

'I'll let the dog out.' Eddie leapt up suddenly and opened

the living-room door for Poppy, who was jumping up and down urgently.

'Let her out into the garden, would you. I think she wants a pee.'

With his hand on the door handle Eddie looked back at me over his shoulder. 'Tell me, Polly,' he said, 'do you fancy me?' Then before I could answer, he left the room.

I'll pretend I didn't hear him, I thought. What else can I do? Get up, clear the things away, yawn, and say I feel like an early night. No no, that might be misconstrued. Don't be silly. He didn't say he fancied me, he simply asked if I fancied him. Anyway, he wouldn't would he? Overweight old bat with three children. Call Lizzie quickly, make it a crowd.

'Lizzie!' My voice cracked nervously. 'Lizzie!' I called again.

'Wha'd'y'want?' What did I want?

'Are you busy?' There was a pause.

'Not really . . . I was asleep.' She appeared at the top of the stairs looking like Scott of the Antarctic. She was wearing thick jersey pyjamas, an Aran-knit sweater, Fair Isle slipper socks, an old woollen dressing-gown that had been discarded years ago by Alan, and over all that she hugged a whopping tartan car rug with school-grey mittened fingers.

'You can't be cold . . . That room of yours is like a tropical rain forest!'

Lizzie tutted impatiently. 'Look Mum, what d'y'want? Because I'd like to get back to bed.'

'You didn't say good night.'

She looked at me incredulously. 'Is that all?'

'You didn't say good night to Eddie either.' The look this time was one of blank astonishment.

'If you think I'm coming downstairs looking like this just to say good night to everyone . . .' By this time Eddie was standing behind me at the bottom of the stairs.

'Cor,' he growled expressively, gazing up with mock lust at the bundle of old clothes leaning on the banister.

'Oh God!' Lizzie exclaimed and she stomped furiously back into her room slamming the door twice because the first time it caught on an air pocket and didn't make enough noise.

I continued to look up with an expression of amused fondness on my face because if I turned round I would be nose to nose with Eddie. And I was exquisitely aware of just how close to me he was.

I was saved by the sound of Alan's car swinging into the drive.

'Gosh, is that the time?' I said glancing at the blank space on the wall where the clock should have been. It was away being repaired but I had forgotten. Eddie followed my eyes and gave me a puzzled look. Hastily I looked at the part of my wrist where my watch should have been, only it wasn't because it was on the windowledge behind the kitchen sink.

'Well yes, if that's the time,' he said grinning hugely, 'I'd better be off. It was a smashing meal. Thanks.' He grabbed his denim jacket from the hall stand. 'See you,' he said over his shoulder and he opened the front door just as Alan inserted his key into the lock. They stared at each other for an instant, Eddie awkwardly and Alan with cold curiosity.

'Er, hello and goodbye,' Eddie said with a strained laugh.

'Mmmm, as you say,' Alan replied coolly and he stood back to let Eddie out of the door. I called goodbye to the boy's disappearing back and he waved cheerfully without turning round. I watched him until he had melted into the mist that was swirling up across the road that bounds the water meadows of the River Pinn. It isn't really a river but more a tiny stream that roughly twice a year becomes a raging torrent and breaks its banks. Somewhere, I am told, it runs into the Thames and that makes it seem more important than it really is. I could hear the echo of his footsteps for some time after he had gone from view. I locked and bolted the door and went slowly back into the kitchen.

'What was he doing here?' Alan was standing over the cooker heating his imperative night-time drink of Horlicks, without which, he still assures me, he would be unable to sleep.

'Eating your supper,' I replied shortly. In this case I thought attack was probably the best form of defence.

'Ah, yes, sorry about that, but we've got very behind with the spring price lists . . . Anyway, where were you all day? I rang and rang.' Clearly he had had the same thought. He looked careworn and tired and he was wearing a suit that seemed to render him invisible. A sort of blue-grey-green-brown nondescript tweed job that struck me somehow as being bigger than the man. He simply disappeared inside it. Actually I think it probably *was* a size too large, which would account for the effect. It, together with several other blue-grey-green-brown tweed suits, had been willed to him a year or two before by an uncle who had them tailor-made in Savile Row. He kept one that was in a better condition, and gave the rest to Oxfam. I felt a stab of pity for the man before me so I gave him a warm hug, noticing as I did so how close his bones seemed to the surface of his skin.

'Have you lost some weight?' I asked, standing back from him and looking up into his eyes. He looked away a bit furtively.

'No, I don't think so, but if I have, it's hardly surprising is it, when you think what I've been eating for the past two weeks. I grabbed some Southern Fried Chicken tonight that tasted like cold porridge. I threw most of it away. Still, I've finished the price lists and I've made a start on next month's budget.' There was a sudden angry hiss from the cooker. 'Damn!' he muttered. The milk was boiling over. He turned on the Expelaire.

'I expect Sheila was a help anyway,' I said.

'Mmmm,' he murmured absently as he rubbed hard at the burnt, fatty mess that was quickly congealing on the top of the oven. 'It was jolly decent of her considering she doesn't get paid any overtime.' Gradually he stopped wiping and straightened up, turning round to look at me. 'Did I tell you Sheila was working late with me?' I shook my head. 'No,' he said thoughtfully, 'I didn't think I had. She hadn't volunteered when I spoke to Lizzie.' He gave me an odd, sharply enquiring look. 'How did you know then?' he asked.

'You smell of her scent.' To be truthful, he always smelt of her scent. Everyone who spent any time in her company smelt of her scent. It was one of the hazards of working with her, like working in a restaurant and smelling of cooking, only I suppose stale Ma Griffe was a lot more pleasant than stale food.

'Good Lord . . . Do I? How extraordinary.' He sniffed at the air, and then his sleeves, one after the other, and then he pulled the lapels of his suit up to his nose. 'You're right, I do. Damn woman, she uses that stuff like air freshener. I'll have to speak to her about it. Can't have everyone going home to their wives smelling of Ma Griffe, they're not all as understanding as you.'

'How do you know it's Ma Griffe?' He looked blank, then he frowned and shook his head.

'I don't know . . . you told me I expect.'

'No I didn't.'

'Well, then, she must've done. Hey, what is this? The third degree or something?' I didn't say anything. 'Wait a minute, I remember. She asked me to get her some duty-free on my last trip to Düsseldorf.' He looked comically relieved.

'Well, I'm glad you remembered hers because you forgot my L'Air du Temps.'

'I didn't forget your L'Air du Temps,' he said wearily. 'You know that. They didn't have any. Anyway, I'm going to bed.' He picked up his steaming Horlicks, and putting his free arm round my shoulders, he steered me out of the door.

'D'y'know? You're beginning to sound like a suspicious wife.' He chuckled and laid his cheek against the top of my head and like that we struggled, giggling, side by side and arm in arm, up the stairs that weren't wide enough for the two of us.

While we were getting undressed I told Alan the day's

news. He was quietly pleased, because he never gets hysterically excited over anything, about Charlie's eye. Though naturally he felt obliged to remind me that he had suggested a second opinion years ago. 'Perhaps you'll listen to me next time,' he said, which is what he always says, without fail, when I don't act on something he has said and it turns out that I should have done.

He laughed immoderately at my story of the Committee meeting which I had already embellished with a few nice little touches of my own. Though as usual, his amusement was heavily larded with masculine condescension. Like so many men, Alan likes a good story that involves women making asses of themselves when they step out of the role of good wife. It reassures him to see us as children aping adults. At such times I remind him acidly of the planning meeting he once attended when three of the senior managers lost their tempers.

After hurling vile personal abuse at each other that involved such things as the relative size of certain parts of their anatomy, scatological references of extremely doubtful taste and the sexual habits of their wives and mothers, they began pushing and shoving each other until eventually they fell in a struggling heap on the boardroom shag pile, wrestling and punching each other like teenage hooligans.

I read for a few minutes to allow Alan to settle. He likes to hump about the bed and pummel his pillows madly until he feels reasonably comfortable. Then I turned off the light. Normally I drop off to sleep almost immediately, but that night, despite reciting the Lord's Prayer, the Apostles' Creed *and* the Catechism, I was still wide awake. I had begun the 23rd Psalm when my mind began to wander. And where it wandered was back to my conversation with Eddie – where else? And in particular that challenging bit about Alan working late, or not, as the case may be. I listened to his quiet regular breathing and thought that no one with a guilty secret could sleep as peacefully as that. And anyway, who would he be having an affair with? You need time and opportunity to carry on a successful affair, I thought, and he has neither.

I considered the idea of Sheila but it seemed a preposterous cliché. Would Alan do something as mundane? It seemed unlikely. She's a fantastic secretary though, I reluctantly admitted to myself. The office wife, they're called, and it occurred to me that she was of far more use to him than I was. He didn't need to talk to me about business any more because he talked to her and she understood what he was talking about. She's smart and intelligent and a distinct asset to him at business meetings. She makes coffee exactly the way he likes it and she puts flowers on his desk. But she's so old, I thought, and really not his type at all. Then I remembered Mike Bray's enthusiastic reaction when he had met Alan for a bar lunch and she had been sitting with a friend along the bar.

'She's a cracker,' he had reported back to me in his lustful way and I had simply laughed because the remark was typical of Mike, and anyway, all women were fair game to him. I remember I said, 'I didn't realize she's attractive to men,' and Mike gave me an odd look and said, 'You'd better believe it,' or something like that because that's the way he talks.

Then my poor overworked mind went back to the sales conference and the way Sheila had nursed Alan through a terrible flu bug so that he was able to function and even make his little speech after the dinner on the last night.

'I really couldn't have managed without her,' he had told me and I had felt pleased that I had persuaded him to take her with him instead of me.

The more I thought about it the more anxious I became. You know the way you do, in the wee small hours, when you're unable to sleep. The smallest anxiety becomes monstrous and sick-making, but then in the morning things resume their correct proportions and you wonder what all the fuss was about. Soon I had convinced myself, with ghastly certainty, that Alan was having an affair with Sheila Rosen and that it was all my fault.

'Alan?' I turned over and touched his sleeping back lightly. 'Are you awake?' He shrugged me off irritably and grunted. 'Are you awake?' I repeated in a louder voice. I knew he wasn't, not really, but for the sake of my peace of mind he was going to have to be. I shook him gently. 'I have something very important to ask you.' There was a long pause and then he sighed and turned towards me.

'It'd better be,' he grumbled. 'You know I can't get back to sleep easily.'

'Well, it's important to me anyhow.' He waited. 'Listen . . . I have to know . . .'

'Well, go on then.'

'I know you'll think I'm silly . . . but I'm feeling very anxious about it . . .'

'For heaven's sake, Polly, spit it out.' I took a deep breath.

'AreyouhavinganaffairwithSheilaRosen?' It came out in a garbled rush.

'What?'

'I said,' and I swallowed hard, 'Are. You. Having. An. Affair. With. Sheila. Rosen?' Alan propped himself up on one elbow and studied my face in the sickly orange light from the street lamp outside. 'Because if you are,' I gabbled, 'I have to know . . . you can tell me . . . I won't make a scene because I know it's all my fault.'

'Are you serious?' he asked.

'Deadly.'

'Good God, Polly,' he said wonderingly, 'what on earth's got into you. I just don't believe what I've heard.'

'Well, are you?'

'You're daft, Polly, absolutely daft. Have you been dreaming or something?'

I shook my head. 'ARE YOU?' I shouted.

'Shhhh . . . you'll wake the children. Frankly I don't feel I should have to answer. It's so stupid it's insulting.'

'Humour me then,' I demanded urgently.

'No I am not having an affair with Sheila Rosen, or anyone

else for that matter. Now, can I try and get back to sleep?' At which I burst into tears.

'Give me a cuddle,' I pleaded between sobs.

'You silly old thing,' he said fondly and put his arms around me. I eventually got off to sleep but I had a strange and unsettling dream. I was standing in the concourse of a huge, empty, grimy stone railway station. The walls were covered with large colourful posters but one in particular attracted my attention. It was a picture of a bearded man in military uniform and he was pointing a gun directly at me. Printed underneath were the words 'I'LL GO SHOOT THAT TORTOISE WITH THIS SETTLE GUN'. I knew myself to be the tortoise.

In the morning I asked Alan if he had ever heard of a settle gun, but he hadn't.

Chapter Seven

Poor little Mrs Glynis Shipwrick's under-powered, monotonous voice droned on to the staccato accompaniment of two pneumatic drills with earth-mover percussion. I'd given up trying to hear what she was saying and had taken to looking intelligently concerned and nodding my head thoughtfully from time to time. I knew from experience that by now she would not be saying anything very important. She needed firm steering from me to keep to the point and if she was allowed to wallow self-indulgently she would ramble on about almost anything other than the crumbling marriage she was seeing me to talk about. From the wistful look on her prematurely wizened little face I guessed she was somewhere in the Indian Ocean with her brother and sister-in-law by now. He who had made good in industrial cleansing equipment and could afford world cruises, unlike Barry, her husband, who was happy to remain a milkman, but was poor.

I looked at the clock. Another dreary half-hour to go, I thought, and then I felt my usual stab of compassion for her, because if I, whose job it was *not* to find her boring, found her boring, how much more boring must everyone else find her.

My tutor frequently got angry with me about Glynis. 'If you find her boring,' she would say impatiently, 'then it's up to you to do something about it.' I would then explain that the reason I found her boring was because I couldn't do anything about it. If I could, I pointed out, I wouldn't find her boring.

'She doesn't want anything done about her marital problems,' I would say. 'She simply wants a confidante. A person to chat to about Barry's iniquities.'

'Now come on, Polly,' Aliza would say wearily, 'you *know* that's not your job. And if you believe that's *really* what she wants, then you must bring the case to a close.' And I would explain again how difficult I found this to do.

'She's been coming to me for nearly nine months and she's come to expect things from me. I can't simply say to her, "Shoo, go away, I can't help you."' Then Aliza would tell me that in her opinion I was sentimentally attached to Glynis because she was my first client.

'You're hanging on to her because she's safe. No surprises from our Glynis, eh Polly?' The conversation had varied little over recent months. I had reached the point of doctoring my case notes to keep Aliza happy, though I don't suppose she was ever fooled.

'Mrs Graham . . . er . . . Mrs Graham?' I opened my eyes and found myself staring into Glynis Shipwrick's worried face. 'Are you all right, Mrs Graham?'

I smiled and nodded. 'Yes, of course, I was just considering what you've told me. I feel it might be relevant.' I could hear Aliza's deep voice telling me to admit that I had been dozing and take it from there. 'At least you'll get some movement' she would have pointed out. But it's too late, Aliza, I thought.

I noticed that the drills and diggers had ceased operations and, relatively speaking (because the traffic on the main road outside the marriage guidance offices in Wealdstone never ceased), peace had come to the little room.

'Yes, well, it would be relevant, wouldn't it?' Glynis was looking at me oddly. 'I mean, it's what you've always tried to make me consider.'

'It is? Yes, of course it is.' I cleared my throat and then, to give myself time, I slowly opened a new packet of cigarettes and pretended to search for a lighter in my handbag when I could see it clearly, shining under a woollen glove. 'Mmmmm, I think I'll switch off the fire if you don't mind.

These small rooms overheat so quickly don't they?' I leant over and switched it off and Glynis began shivering immediately. Pavlov's dogs, I thought irritably. Glynis was not a happy woman in temperatures under 65 degrees. She had been conditioned to hot steamy little kitchens all her life and her peace of mind rather depended upon her feeling hot and moist.

'Oh come on, Glynis, it's not cold,' I said reproachfully. 'And when it begins to cool down I'll simply turn the fire on again. Don't worry.'

'I'm not shivering because I'm cold,' she said miserably. 'I'm shivering because of what's happened. I can't stop shivering . . . I shiver all day and all night even though I've taken our Jason back into bed with me. It's my nerves you see.' Depending on the matrimonial bed situation, two-year-old Jason either spent his nights in his cot or snuggled up beside his mother with Barry on the sofa downstairs.

'What *has* happened?' I asked, and then I could have bitten off my tongue because obviously what had happened was what she had been telling me about for the past half-hour. She looked at me accusingly, and quite rightly so, her lower lip trembling and large, unshed tears balancing precariously on the red rims of her lower lids. I watched fascinated as the first one tipped over the edge and raced down her cheek to come to rest on the point of her chin where it hung, a perfect tear, exactly the shape, I thought, of one of my clear glass Christmas tree decorations from Paperchase, until it fell with an almost audible splat on to her plastic patent bag. I pushed the box of tissues across the table towards her.

'You haven't been listening, have you?' Though I continued to meet her gaze, I said nothing. Well, there was nothing to say really. 'Mind you, it doesn't surprise me,' she snivelled and dabbed at her face with the back of her sleeve. 'I know I've got a very boring voice. Barry's always telling me that. "Try an' make your voice go up and down like other people's," he's always saying. He says that some of the things I have to say aren't all that boring, they just sound it because of my boring voice.' Though I felt smitten by guilt, I felt I couldn't argue with Barry on that point. Would it help her if I told her that her voice is boring? I wondered. And if I tell her, what do I suggest she does about it? Take elocution lessons or something? Would her voice be different if she was happy? But then I'd seen her happy, when she believed that things had improved between her and Barry, but even then she sounded as though she was reciting a weekly shopping list.

'As a matter of fact, Glynis,' I said finally, 'I was trying to listen, but found it very difficult over the noise outside. Obviously I missed something very important.' She looked at me suspiciously and then sighed in anticipation of beginning all over again.

'He's left me. Last Sunday.' She waited for some reaction from me, but I was speechless from shock so she continued. 'We had Dad's fiftieth birthday party on the Saturday an' everything was fine. We even made love that night.' She looked sideways at me coyly. 'An' then on Sunday he said he was going to see his Mum an' he didn't come home for his dinner an' I phoned his Mum an' she told me that she hadn't seen him. Then his mate Stan phoned an' said that he wasn't coming home an' then Stan's wife – you remember, my friend Shirley – came on an' said she was coming right over. Anyway Shirley said she was disgusted by it all an' that Stan was no better'n Barry all said an' done. She says that Barry has this "other woman".' She looked beseechingly at me as though I was in a position to deny it all as a filthy rumour. 'You only said he *might* have another woman,' Glynis reminded me. I didn't think I had even gone as far as that, but I did ask her if she had, at any time, suspected that there might be another woman. Glynis, I recall, had dismissed the idea out of hand.

'I wish I'd listened to you now,' she continued. 'Shirley says that everyone else has known for months, but then the wife's always the last to know isn't she?' Somehow she made it sound as though I too had known for months; as though

I was privy to some inside information which I had kept to myself. I suppose I was in a way. I knew Glynis had apparently insurmountable sexual difficulties and I had listened to Barry, through his wife, changing from a bewildered, frustrated man into an indifferent one. He no longer made any demands upon his wife and he spent more and more of his time away from her with his friends, so he told her, at the dairy's social club playing for the darts team. The news that he had defected shouldn't have surprised me, but it did. It didn't fit in with everything I thought I knew about the Shipwrick marriage.

I had come to believe that if anyone left it would be Glynis. Fed up, once and for all, with slobby Barry who picked his pimples and his nose at the same time, who got happily plastered every Saturday night and who made love with his socks on. Unappetizing Barry who snored noisily in front of the telly, splattered his shirt fronts with food and spent his money on girlie magazines. It would be Glynis who would go home to Mum, leaving Barry to exalt in his own midden. But then I have to admit that I never actually met Barry. My fantasy of him, based as it was on the months of listening to Glynis pour out her resentment and bitterness, was of an overweight, complacent chauvinist with dirty habits who treated his wife as he treated his mother, with the same mildly fond detachment, and who initially only got rattled with her on Saturday nights when she complained of a headache and went to bed before *Match of the Day*. I never really considered the possibility of another woman in Barry's life because I couldn't imagine any other woman wanting him.

'Tell me, Glynis,' I asked curiously, 'would you say that Barry was attractive to other women?'

'Well of course he is,' she said looking surprised that I needed to ask such a question. 'I thought you knew.'

'No,' I replied slowly, 'I can't say I ever thought of him in that way. You didn't exactly make it very clear.'

'Oh, didn't I? Well, I know he's put on weight an' he's got

that nasty allergic rash, but he's got a way with him still. You've only got to listen to his stories about all them housewives.' For a moment she sounded quite proud of him as the object of desire for so many lusting ladies.

'So why were you so sure there wasn't another woman?' I asked.

'Well, I'd've known, wouldn't I? There'd've been signs . . .'

'But there were signs . . . lots of them, if you think about it.'

She looked at me blankly. 'How d'you mean?' she asked frowning.

'Well, for a start, he spent lots of his leisure time away from you and you told me that he sometimes stayed away all night.'

'Yes, but he told me, didn't he? That's when he had to travel a long way for a darts match or he didn't want to drive home from Stan's because of the drink. He had darts practice three evenings a week you know.'

'And you believed him?'

'Course I did. Barry isn't a liar.' Her sad eyes flickered away from mine. 'Well, I didn't think he was.'

'But you told me how smart he was when he went out to the club. How he bought new shirts and wore aftershave.'

'Yes, well, he had to look decent when he went to the Sports and Social, didn't he? I mean, his boss was often there.'

'Why didn't you go with him?'

'I told you, I didn't like going. Anyway I had Jason to think about.'

'You could've got a baby-sitter sometimes.'

'I've explained about that too.' Glynis was beginning to sound confused and belligerent. 'I've told you, Jason's a very sensitive child. I can't leave him with just anybody. They wouldn't understand about his funny little ways.' We sat facing each other silently, deep in our own thoughts. I was depressed by my handling of the case. How gullible I had been. A fine counsellor I was turning out to be.

'What are you feeling?' I asked tentatively, the hackneyed counselling phrase sounding almost indecent in the circumstances.

'How d'you mean?'

'Well, do you feel angry, sad? You know.'

She thought about it, picking busily at a piece of dead skin on her upper lip.

'Well,' she began in a businesslike tone of voice, 'what I want to know is, should I cancel our package holiday or not? You see we've booked a camping holiday in Antibes.' She pronounced it 'Antibbies'. 'It was through *Woman's Own* and I don't know whether I ought to tell them what's happened. What do you think?' Practical details like this often cause great concern. I had a client once who knew that her husband was about to leave her and yet she seemed mainly concerned with her son's approaching barmitzvah and the fact that her sister-in-law, whom she loathed, had bought an identical dress to wear for the occasion. I think perhaps it helps to worry about a problem that you feel you can do something about. I remember when Ma died I put enormous amounts of energy into organizing her funeral and answering letters of condolence in order to put off the moment when I would have to think about my life without Ma in it. It's the same sort of thing, isn't it?

'Do you think it's possible that Barry will come back to you?' I asked.

'No . . . and anyway, I wouldn't have him back.'

'So you think you might go on holiday on your own with Jason, or a friend perhaps?'

'No, of course not,' she said as though she thought I didn't understand her problem.

'Then why is there any doubt in your mind?' I felt as though I was thrusting home a spear. Glynis blinked several times and her mouth opened and shut like a fish out of water.

'Well, you know . . . he might . . . something might . . .' She looked down at her handbag which she was clutching fiercely. I watched her knuckles turn white and I waited. The expression on her face, when she eventually looked up at me, was that of a small, hurt child who desperately wanted to be understood and loved.

'I feel awful,' she sobbed. 'I'm sorry for crying, you must think I'm dreadful.' She waited for reassurance.

'No I don't. I think crying is the most natural thing for you to do in the circumstances. I'd be surprised if you didn't.' Gratefully she dissolved into uncontrollable tears.

'I don't understand anything any more ... I know I must've done something wrong but I don't know what. It can't just be the sex thing, can it?' I shook my head because it never is just the sex thing. 'I've told you all those nasty things about him,' she went on, looking hang-dog and ashamed of herself. 'But he's ever so nice really. Well, he used to be – in the beginning. I just want things to go back to how they used to be. Oh I wish I was dead.' She cried copiously without making a sound. Everything ran. Fluid of different consistencies poured from her eyes, her nose and her mouth and she mopped at it ineffectually with tissues which she stuffed into a carrier bag when they were too wet to be of any further use. Her face was swollen and blotchy red. Like me, I thought, you are not a pretty crier, Glynis.

'I'm sorry,' she spluttered helplessly, 'but ... I ... don't ... seem ... able ... to ... stop ...' Without warning my own eyes began to prick. Oh God, I said sternly to myself, don't you start. But the uncomfortable feelings that were slowly welling up inside me overflowed and when I could blink back my tears no longer, I reached out of my chair and put my arms round the small, huddled woman sitting opposite me. At first she was stiff and ungiving. Embarrassed, I guessed, by me, another woman, holding her body. She smelt vaguely of mothballs and mildew. The smell I recognized of a coat that had been hanging in a damp cupboard. Then slowly she relaxed against me with her head heavy upon my shoulder and we sat like that, crying together, until there was a sharp ring on the intercom.

'Damn it!' I flipped the switch irritably.

'Polly?' a tinny voice queried at the other end. 'You've over-run and we need your room.' I looked at the clock. It was 3.15 already and Jane and I were supposed to be meeting Gwen and the boys at the swimming pool at 3.45. I turned to Glynis, who was watching me expectantly.

'I'm sorry love, but our time is well and truly up as you can see.' She nodded miserably. 'Look, if you like you can sit downstairs in the waiting-room until you feel like facing the world. I'll get you a cup of tea.'

'No, it's all right thanks. I've got to collect Jason from my friend.' She looked at me anxiously. 'Do you want to see me next week?'

'Yes,' I replied firmly, 'I do want to see you next week.'

'Oh ... I only wondered ... because now he's gone there's not much you can do about it is there?' But there was hope in her eyes.

'Well, I certainly can't write to him telling him he's got to return to you on pain of death if that's what you mean. But I reckon there's still quite a lot we can do together – things we should have done before as a matter of fact.' The intercom buzzed again. 'All right, all right, I'm coming,' I muttered into it.

I saw Glynis downstairs and out of the door.

'Ta-ra then, see you next week, same time, same place,' she trilled brightly as though we'd just had a pleasant chin-wag over coffee and biscuits. In her mildewed coat she forged her way bravely down the windy street, and I marvelled again at how resilient we women can be; even the most dependent, the most pitiful of us. It didn't make me feel any better, though.

Jane and I joined the queue of pale, skinny, or alternatively tubby, eleven-year-olds, who, having just finished a swimming lesson, were waiting, shivering, shoulders hunched and arms clamped round their bodies, to collect their unwieldy wire baskets of clothes. We, on the other hand, were already beginning to feel uncomfortably hot in the clammy humidity, dressed as we were for the February streets. I was feeling itchy in places I couldn't scratch with modesty and looking at all those bare feet on the slimy, wet floor I could feel an incipient attack of athlete's foot coming on, or maybe it would be verrucas this time.

I have never liked public swimming pools. Though I am not, in the normal way, overly fastidious, Ma instilled in me a healthy, or possibly unhealthy, respect for water-borne germs. It was the regular polio scares of the 1940s and early 1950s that started her off and for years I suffered from the misapprehension that the fearsome disease could only be caught by swimming in public baths during the summer months. This was probably because they closed our pool regularly because of polio and Ma spoke of it as though it was perhaps a shade cleaner than a septic tank.

You must admit it is also very unpleasant to find yourself in close proximity to an emptying bladder. Girls, you know, find it difficult to control this function in water that is heated to blood heat. It is a known fact. When I first learnt this I became mildly obsessed with the idea and couldn't be persuaded into the pool for nearly a year. All I could think of as I sat sweating in the Observers' Gallery watching Charlie having his weekly lesson, was how many bladders were emptying into the water at any one time. Of course I knew this anxiety was irrational, at least I suppose it was, so I kept the fear to myself.

All the children had early attacks of athlete's foot and verrucas and only the week before I had noticed a small boy in the water who had nasty, inflamed scabby spots all over his body. It looked like chicken pox or possibly even impetigo but I didn't dare to make a fuss because I knew that the pool manager, who was himself covered with large scabby spots, though his were clearly those of post-adolescent acne, already regarded me as a bit of a weirdo.

'Hi Polly.' Gwen, Junoesque, with the slightly dented look about her of the chronic fluid retainer, stood beside me, her blue-white flesh clad only in a rather unflattering liver-coloured knitted bikini. 'I'm going to go straight down if you don't mind,' she said. 'The boys'll be in already. See you in a minute.' She slung a large, multi-coloured towel round her shoulders and disappeared down the tiled steps to the pool.

Gwen loved the water. She was a strong swimmer, but not showy if you know what I mean. She could maintain her slow, sedate breaststroke for hours while we hares of the swash-buckling overarm crawl fell exhausted by the wayside, especially those hares amongst us who smoked. I can see her rubber-capped head now, held high above the water, chin up, ploughing its steady furrow up and down the pool undeterred by the flailing arms of small children apparently drowning and the Olympic speed trials going on all round her. She was always very safety-conscious and she would upbraid irresponsible youths who jumped in on top of one another and pushed screaming girls into the deep end. Though I suppose she was a bit of a party-pooper, we all felt safe when we went swimming with Gwen.

Jane found an empty cubicle and called me.

'You take that one darling,' I called back, 'and I'll find another one for myself.' It was worth a try, but as usual her little face fell.

'Can't we share this one, Mummy?' she asked plaintively. I sighed. Jane, always a body-conscious child, hated changing on her own. She worried about people barging in on her unannounced. Unfortunately the cubicles were very small and sharing was a misery for both of us. I would have to squeeze up in a corner while she changed and she would have to climb up and squat on the slatted bench while I changed. Various articles of clothing would fall on to the wet floor and we would become increasingly irritable with one another. However I knew she would refuse to change at all if I insisted on my privacy, so as usual we bundled in together and loathed each other cordially for five minutes.

The din, as we entered the pool, was deafening. It wasn't that full but the acoustics were such that every squeak was magnified into an ear-splitting shriek and the splash of an average twelve-year-old hitting the water at, say five miles per hour from a height of eight feet sounded more like an approaching tidal wave. For a moment I was overwhelmed by a strong desire to retreat into the relative calm of the changing-room. I felt embarrassingly exposed, standing there with nothing between my bare flesh and the wide world full of shapely people but one inadequate piece of brief, revealing clothing. However, the excited tug of Jane's small hand urged me onwards.

Squatting beside her I blew up her armbands. 'Now stay in the shallow end,' I instructed her, 'and don't go wandering off by yourself when I'm not looking.' She nodded solemnly. Even though her feet didn't yet touch the bottom, she despised the children's pool and the little kids in it who splashed happily about with their parents. Once in, she set off across the pool with a very creditable doggy-paddle. In fact, she could probably have managed without the bands, but I couldn't. Like Charlie and myself she was, and still is, very buoyant. Lizzie and Alan, on the other hand, with their long thin sinewy limbs, remind me of nothing more than struggling bundles of kindling faggots in imminent danger of sinking. It was only with continual and hectic movement that they managed to stay afloat. I lie across the water like an air-bed, gently flipping my hands only when I need to change direction.

I dived in and set out on my usual half-length of showy-off crawl before I retired breathless and water-logged to the side. Gwen, approaching, threw me a serene, complacent smile. She drew up mid-stroke, and trod water a few feet away from me.

'All right,' she said in a voice that seemed to boom forth across the length and breadth of the pool, 'so now you've proved to everyone what a fancy swimmer you are, perhaps you can begin to enjoy yourself!' Unable to speak for lack of immediate puff, I narrowed my eyes and flared my nostrils. 'You okay?' Gwen looked mildly anxious.

'Yes. Why?' I spat.

'You look as though you might be in pain.' So much for narrowed eyes and flared nostrils, I thought. 'Where's Charlie?' she asked.

'At home doing his homework, I hope.'

'Oh, I told Rick he'd be here.' Richard, Gwen's number two son, was at the time, and for some considerable time thereafter, Charlie's best buddie. They appeared to have little in common. Charlie's passionate love of sport was not echoed in Rick, who was physically idle to the point of inertia. In fact Rick found most of his friend's sudden and intense enthusiasms faintly absurd, but he was an easy-going boy and he would obligingly swing a cricket bat or kick a football if it made Charlie happy. Rick had inherited his father's dry, urbane sense of humour and had a deft, throw-away style of delivering even the worst jokes that was the envy of many an adult raconteur.

'Mr Chaudhuri said he mustn't swim for at least two months, which means we have at least three weeks to go,' I reminded her. We swam slowly, side by side, until our feet touched the bottom.

'Mummy, Mummy, watch me!' Jane splashed past on the sturdy back of seven-year-old William, Gwen's third and youngest, who should have been a girl in order to please his parents, but who was a rough, tough, squat little fighting machine who already showed the physical signs of the man he would become.

'Be careful Will!' Gwen shouted after him as he thrust his purposeful way through a gaggle of gossiping little girls. Jane squealed with delight as the girls scattered in all directions, heads turned from the churning water, hands held up in self-protection.

'How *is* his eye?' Gwen asked.

'Still very blood-shot,' I managed between gulps. 'But he hasn't got a squint any more. You can imagine how delighted he is. He keeps staring at himself in the mirror. I think he half expects it to revert.'

*

Charlie's operation, when it happened, was very sudden. 'If I do it on the National Health,' Mr Chaudhuri warned me, 'you may have to wait for anything up to a year. I have a long waiting list. However, if I do it privately I can do it immediately.' His motives for telling me this didn't bother me. I knew he was telling me the truth and that was all that mattered.

'How much would that cost?' I asked. His mouth turned down at the corners and he shook his head pessimistically.

'Well, a private room, even only for two nights, isn't cheap. Then there's my fee, my anaesthetist's, my assistant's, nursing fees . . .' The amount seemed staggering and quite beyond our reach but when I spoke to Alan about it he told me that our private health insurance scheme would cover these costs, and knowing this, I was in no doubt.

As I had been instructed, I phoned Mr Chaudhuri at home. His wife answered and spoke to me in the silvery, idiosyncratic English of the home-bound, first generation Asian wife. In the background I could hear the sprightly chatter of small children and I could almost smell the ladoos shining and moist with ghee.

'You will hold on to the telephone for a short time please?' There was laughter in her voice as she called to her husband. When he came to the phone he apologized profusely for being in the middle of his supper and I apologized with equal profusion for interrupting it. We carried on an odd three-cornered conversation for a minute or two. Me with him and he with me and an obstinate small child who seemed intent upon cutting us off. Our conversation expanded further when his wife was called to remove the child. Again he apologized and I reassured him that his household wasn't any different from mine at suppertime.

'If I can obtain the use of an operating theatre and the necessary staff,' he said, 'I can perform the operation this Sunday. Would that suit you?'

'But that's in three days' time.' I felt Charlie, or perhaps it was me, needed a little more time to prepare. After all, it wasn't like sending the television away for repairs.

'Then the following Sunday perhaps?' he suggested. I thought quickly.

'No . . .' I began doubtfully, then more firmly, 'no, I think we'd like to get it over with as soon as possible.'

'Very well.' He sounded happy with my prompt decision and I wondered idly if his fee was already earmarked for a particularly urgent purpose. 'Then I will telephone you with further details when they are known to me.'

The following Saturday evening Charlie was installed in a small room in one of North London's more lugubrious hospitals and at 7 a.m. the next day he went into theatre. If he was nervous he didn't show it but then he had only ever had good experiences of hospitals and doctors and he knew we would shower him with goodies when it was all over. If anything, he seemed excited. I suppose all the discomfort he was about to suffer seemed to him to be worth while. I know the feeling well. I felt it during childbirth.

I must admit I was somewhat bewildered by Mr Chaudhuri's operating team. All Asian, none of them appeared to be employed by the hospital on a regular basis. I had this charming fantasy that they wandered the country, itinerant medics, hiring themselves out as a team on an *ad hoc* basis wherever their services were required, booking operating theatres in the way one might book a squash court, at off-peak times when available. Hence Charlie's early-morning Sunday appointment in the operating theatre of a run-down hospital miles from home. But it was only a fantasy, because the arrangements couldn't have been *that* haphazard, could they?

Later in the morning I returned to the hospital to find Charlie slowly coming out of the anaesthetic. His eye was lightly covered by a lint pad held in place with thin strips of sticking plaster. There were flecks of dried blood on his cheek, his ear lobe and the tip of his nose. I wiped them off gently with a sterile swab that I found in a kidney bowl by his bed. His good eye opened and fluttered blearily at me.

'It's a bag of marbles,' he mumbled. At least, that's what it sounded like.

'What about a bag of marbles, darling?' I asked.

He frowned and looked confused. 'What?'

'You just said . . . oh, never mind.' I stroked the hair back from his forehead. 'How're you feeling?' He concentrated very hard on my question but found it too difficult to answer.

'Have they done it yet?' He tried to touch the covering over his eye but was too weak to lift his arm. His uncovered eye looked at me anxiously.

'The operation's over and everything's fine. I'm told Mr Chaudhuri is very pleased. He'll be in to see you later on.' His eye dropped to the fancy package I held on my lap.

'Is that for me? What is it?' No mucking about with Charlie. I was greatly relieved, I must say, when they grew out of assuming that every visitor to the house would naturally bring them a present. Though I'm not yet sure if Jane has.

'I'm afraid you can't open it yet,' I told him. 'Because you have to stay very still for a bit, and you mustn't cry.'

'I'm not going to cry.' He looked puzzled.

'No, I know, but should you feel like it, you must resist the urge.'

'Okay. I'm thirsty. Can I have a drink?' I poured a little water into a plastic beaker from a large stainless-steel jug.

'Now sip it, don't gulp.' Very carefully I lifted his head from the pillow and held the beaker to his mouth. 'Sip it,' I repeated as he took a large mouthful that dribbled on to his chest.

'But I'm thirsty,' he complained. 'And I'm too hot.' The little room was indeed very hot, and airless too. The radiator was too hot to touch but I couldn't adjust it because the control mechanism appeared to have jammed on 'full'. When I tried to open the window I found that it was bolted at the top but even standing on a chair I couldn't reach the bolt. In the quadrangle outside two nurses were huddled together on a wooden seat sharing a cigarette and drinking coffee from a Thermos flask, their voluminous cloaks drawn round them as meagre protection against the biting East wind. One of them looked up and saw me spreadeagled against the window. She nudged her friend and they both stared. I waved cheerfully just in case they thought I was trying to escape or commit suicide. They waved back and then looked at each other and shrugged.

'Would you come down from there please.' I jumped at the sound of the commanding voice behind me and nearly fell. Feeling foolish I clambered clumsily down and turned to confront the stern-faced West Indian nursing sister who was standing half in, half out of the swing door.

'I'm sorry.' I smiled my very best, appeasing smile. 'I was trying to open the window – it's so hot and airless in here.'

'They're kept bolted during the winter,' she said coldly. 'But you can always adjust the radiator.'

'Er . . . it appears to be faulty.' She tutted and bustled with a crackle of nylon static across the room. She couldn't alter the thermostat either and she looked at me accusingly.

'Someone's been fiddling with this,' she announced and I knew she thought it was me. 'I'll get a man in to look at it.' I thanked her with awful craven profusion which she accepted with a brief nod.

'Tell me, sister,' I asked as she thrust a thermometer into Charlie's mouth, 'what are those two nurses doing sitting outside on such a cold day? They'll catch their death.' She didn't answer me immediately because she was taking Charlie's pulse. After she had shaken the thermometer with a briskly cracking wrist and popped it back into its little container on the wall she joined me at the window and looked out.

'Oh,' she gave a short laugh, 'they're smoking.' I could see that for myself. 'And they're not allowed to smoke in the staff canteen.'

'Isn't there a place for them to have a smoke?'

She sighed. 'We don't encourage smoking here in the hospital, but they're allowed to smoke in the grounds.' The two nurses had been joined by three others and the five of them were squeezed together on the seat looking like a row of smoking magpies. The sister tutted again and turned away from the sight, which obviously displeased her.

'He's a good boy,' she said suddenly and unexpectedly of Charlie, and such were my feelings about her that I was overwhelmed with pleasure and pride at her small concession towards human warmth.

'Did you hear that Charlie?' I asked after she had left. He nodded sleepily. 'Would you like me to open the present for you?'

'No thanks,' he said after some thought, 'half the fun about presents is opening them, so I think I'll wait until I can sit up.' Then he whimpered. 'It hurts . . . It feels as though someone's sticking a needle in my eye.'

'Yes, well, I expect it will hurt just a bit for a while.' He looked miserable enough to cry. 'Look, tell you what, you just relax and I'll read to you. I've found another Percy Westerman in the library. It's called *The Red Pirate*. Have you read that one?' Charlie was not really a reader – still isn't, come to that – but he did enjoy a good PW yarn. He shook his head so I took the book out of my tote bag and began to read. He went to sleep. 'Your Dad'll be coming in to see you this evening,' I whispered before kissing his damp forehead, but I don't think he heard.

'Listen Polly, I've had this great idea.' Gwen lurched towards me as the bullet head of a small boy barrelled into her back. The water churned furiously as Gwen and boy tumbled about trying to regain their balance. The boy scowled at Gwen.

'Piss off!' he growled venomously at her before continuing on his determined way across the pool. Gwen extended a long white arm and plucked him out of the water by the elastic waist of his swimming trunks.

'Say that again, sonny,' she dared him. He looked speculatively at her cold, expressionless face.

'My big bruvver's down there.' He jerked his head towards the deep end.

'Say that again,' Gwen repeated.

'An' me Mum's watchin'.' Gwen's eyes didn't waver from the boy's belligerent face. With that peculiarly male gesture he tossed his long wet hair out of his eyes and rubbed them hard with screwed-up fists. 'Orrigh', m'sorry,' he muttered with obvious reluctance and Gwen, who had been hanging on to his trunks, let go suddenly. The boy pitched face forward into the water. He came up spluttering obscenities, but Gwen was bored with the game and let him go.

'Anyway, as I was saying,' she continued blithely. 'I've had this great idea for a cabaret at the do.' I pulled a face and shook my head. 'For heaven's sake, Polly, you don't know what I have in mind. What do you know about Pyramus and Thisbe?'

'Isn't it the mechanicals' play-within-a-play in *Midsummer Night's Dream*?' She nodded. 'Oh no, you're not suggesting the Committee stages a production are you! Really Gwen, we'd look ridiculous!'

'Not the Committee, no – but what about our children? It's not very long and it really is outrageously funny and I see a certain piquancy about it being staged by children.' Personally I thought it was a brilliant idea. The sort of idea I wish I'd thought of myself in fact. I looked at Gwen admiringly.

'You like it, I can tell,' she said with satisfaction.

'It's smashing,' I replied, my imagination already hooked. 'But what about the others? It's quite an ambitious undertaking. And then you've got to persuade the children. I haven't met a youngster yet who understands Shakespeare, let alone enjoys him.'

'Yes, but this is different. It's pure farce and they can extemporize to their hearts' content – everyone always does with Pyramus and Thisbe. And leave the Committee to me.

I'm sure they'll be very happy if I agree to be responsible for the whole thing.'

Our conversation was cut abruptly short by an urgent shout from William who was jumping up and down on the side looking very distraught. 'Mum! Look!' he screamed frantically, pointing towards the deep end. 'Jane's down there!' Horrified, we both turned to look and I started pushing violently through the throng of splashing bodies.

'Wait Polly!' Gwen called after me. 'You haven't the staying power – I'll get her!' She pushed people out of the way like ninepins and then swam strongly towards my wayward daughter who was jiggling about happily in her armbands directly in the flight path of the busy springboard. A queue of wet, shivering people impatient to dive were shouting at her to move, but either she couldn't hear them or didn't realize that they were shouting at her, for she continued her little game with sublime indifference to the turmoil above her head. The burly youth at the head of the queue was being pushed from behind and I wouldn't have cared to take odds on who would reach her first, Gwen or the boy, who would, when and if he fell, fall on top of her. If he fell sideways she would be swamped but intact. If he fell forward, and this seemed most likely, for his toes were curled tightly over the very tip of the board and he was having difficulty maintaining his balance, Jane could be badly hurt. My heart was pounding and I found I couldn't breathe.

I shrieked at the bath attendant who was idly watching two boys who were in the act of throwing a pretty, squealing girl into the water. Slowly he turned and his eyes swept over the bobbing heads as he tried to locate the source of the unpleasant noise that had interrupted his little entertainment.

Then I saw Eddie running helter-skelter along the side of the pool. He executed a graceful racing dive and ploughed across the pool at vast speed towards Jane who had just realized her predicament and was beginning to panic. As the boy finally fell, back arched and arms outstretched, Eddie reached Jane, lifted her clean out of the water and launched her and himself out from under the shadow of the tumbling boy. He then deposited the trembling child on the side and heaved himself up beside her. By the time Gwen and I had reached them, he had removed her armbands and was drying her with a bright pink towel he had grabbed from one of the benches that lined the walls. Jane was heaving enormous dry sobs every few seconds and looking frightfully woebegone. She was gazing solemnly into Eddie's face with wide, worshipping eyes.

'Eddie rescued me from being drownded, Mummy.'

'Our hero,' Gwen muttered under her breath giving me the knowing look she always gave me when Eddie was around.

Eddie looked up at me frowning. 'What on earth were you doing Polly, letting Jane play in the deep end?' he asked. 'A child of Jane's age was drowned here last month, you must've heard about it.'

'And masterful with it,' Gwen breathed for my ears only. I looked down at Eddie's sleek, brown body as he squatted on his haunches beside Jane and the beauty of it made me catch my breath. Two years before, I thought, he would have been too immature and two years from now he will be beginning to coarsen – at this moment, he is just right and I can't do anything about him. Gwen, watching me, smiled slowly and suggestively. Eddie and Jane, oblivious, were rubbing noses and giggling.

I thanked Eddie, resisting the urge to hug him, which is what I would have done if he had been fully clothed and Gwen hadn't been around, and I thanked Gwen for her valiant effort but she shrugged it off dismissively.

'I wouldn't have reached her in time Polly,' she said, 'but I'm damned sure you wouldn't being as how you're all show and not much substance, so it was worth the try.' I wished she hadn't said that in front of a young man who believed that I had once been captain of the school swimming team. It reminded me forcibly of the time I was found out to be a rabbit on the tennis court by young David Burton who had, on the strength of my claims, chosen me to partner him in the junior mixed doubles.

'Anyway,' I cut in quickly before Gwen could enlarge upon my deficiencies, 'I think it's time I got this young lady home for her tea.' Jane protested loudly. She wanted to stay with Eddie, she said. He would bring her home. 'No, I'm sorry darling, it's home time *now*.'

'Tell you what,' Eddie said to Jane, 'I'll come home with you.' I pointed out to him that he hadn't even had a swim, but he shrugged and said he didn't really feel like swimming any more. 'I'll meet you outside,' he called over his shoulder and he was off, loping round the pool towards the men's changing room.

'Well, who's the lucky one then,' Gwen said with a wistful sigh. 'That young man fancies you, you know.' I frowned and jerked my head towards Jane, who was stamping up and down in a slimy little puddle enthusiastically. Gwen winced and mouthed, 'Sorreeee . . . I forgot.'

'I'll pop round and see you Saturday,' I told Gwen. 'And we can work out some details for your idea.' Gwen suggested that I should come round the next evening because Mike was out at Rotary but I said I couldn't because we were going to a party. Gwen's eyebrows shot up.

'Oh, and which party is it this time the Brays haven't been invited to?' and she was only half-joking.

'Alan's secretary – and you're welcome to take my place if you like. I don't want to go. We've got to go back into town and we probably won't know a soul, but Alan feels we ought to put in an appearance.'

Gwen looked at me thoughtfully. 'Would this be the secretary Mike's always going on about? The one with the boobs and the legs?'

'Well, he's only got one so it must be.' I looked back at Gwen curiously. 'What do you mean, he's always going on about her?'

'Just how gorgeous she is, things like that.'

'She isn't gorgeous at all,' I protested, rather churlishly I must admit, 'that is, unless your tastes run to over-ripe, ageing Cleopatras.'

'All right, all right.' Gwen held up her hands defensively and I noticed that they were shrivelled and discoloured from over-immersion in water.

'So Mike's turned on by over-ripe ageing Cleopatras,' she laughed but a strange expression flashed briefly across her face that I was unable to interpret. I thought later that it might have been alarm. 'Look Polly,' she changed the subject abruptly, 'I'm getting bloody cold just standing here chatting so I'm going to do a couple of lengths with the boys before I call it a day.' She pulled the ear flaps of her strange rubber swimming cap down over her ears and did up the strap under her chin. 'See you Saturday, 'bout three, okay?' I nodded, but I felt a bit guilty for it would be the third Saturday afternoon running that I had abandoned Alan to his car washing without even crumpets for tea unless he toasted them for himself. Poor beast, Gwen would have said, had I told her, in her funny, caring way, and she would have come and toasted some crumpets for him herself.

The party at Sheila Rosen's the next evening got off to a bad start because as I stood in the porch with Alan wondering whether we should ring the bell or walk straight in because the door was ajar, I noticed a large, hitherto undetected grease spot on the pale lavender-blue silk that stretched taut over my bosom.

'Why didn't you tell me?' I hissed at Alan.

'Because I didn't notice it,' he hissed back.

'Well, we'll just have to go straight home,' I announced flatly. 'I mean, it's in a place that draws eyes to it like a magnet and I don't want people staring at my bosom all evening.'

'Don't be silly . . . no one'll notice, and if they do, does it matter?'

What blindly insensitive creatures men can be, don't you agree? I mean, a woman wouldn't say a thing like that, she'd know better. It takes a man to dismiss a grease spot on a bosom so lightly. Just as it takes a man to park a car half a mile from his destination in the pouring rain and during a force 10 gale when his wife has just had her hair done. Only a man would introduce his wife to a bunch of his business colleagues without telling her anyone's name. 'This is my wife,' he says by way of introduction. 'How do, Mrs Gubbins,' they say, and she replies, poor cow, 'How do, Mr Er-Um,' then spends the rest of the evening trying to catch and commit to memory everyone's names as they're bandied about the table. When she gets home, feeling that under the circs she has done a terrific job as company wife, her husband asks her why she kept calling George Soper 'Bill' and Betty Makepeace 'Lillian'. Only a man would tell you that you've got lipstick on your teeth *after* you've been introduced to the Chairman and only a man will remember to tell you that his boss's wife is a vegetarian just as you're about to carve the joint.

'Of course it matters,' I snarled furiously.

'Can't you hold your hand in front of it or something?'

'You surely don't imagine I'm going to spend the entire evening clutching my bosom, do you?'

'Well, keep your coat on then, or drape that scarf thing strategically.' I gave Alan a withering look.

'Oh, hello, is this a private party or can anyone join in?' Startled, we both spun round to face the open door. An immaculately dressed young man was peering out at us questioningly. 'Er . . . I'm Adam Rosen, Sheila's youngest,' he announced extending a limp hand. We both reached to shake it, drew back laughing, reached again and I won.

'I'm Polly Graham and this is my husband Alan.' He turned a dazzling, white smile upon Alan.

'Ah, you're Mother's boss, aren't you. She's always talking about you. Do come in, if that's what you were planning on doing eventually.' We grinned sheepishly at each other as we followed Adam Rosen into the hall. Several people were standing at the improvised bar filling their glasses from a

Waterford crystal punch bowl and there was the usual party hubbub coming from a room that led off the hall. Adam turned to me and seemed to look straight at the offending grease spot. 'I expect you'd like to go upstairs, wouldn't you. It's the first door on the left.' He took Alan's coat and disappeared with it through another door leading off the hall.

In the bedroom to which I had been directed, a clutch of women were closely gathered round the dressing-table gossiping while they prepared themselves for the fray. They looked up as I came in, smiled distantly, and continued their furtive, eager conversation. From the excitement generated I felt it should have been about fornication and adultery but it turned out to be a comparative study of dyslexia from which, it appeared, an assortment of their children suffered. Peering through their heads I was able to pat my wind-blown hair-do into shape and apply a further light dusting of face powder to my shiny nose. It may have been my imagination, but I thought I noticed one or two pairs of eyes focusing on the mirror image of my besmirched bust. After I leave this room, I thought, they will comment to each other on my grease spot and then they will come downstairs and point it out to all their friends.

'Have you come far?' one of them asked politely.

'Pinner actually,' I said, wishing I could have said somewhere smart like Hampstead or Blackheath.

'That's on the Metropolitan Line isn't it?' I smiled and nodded and mumbled something about John Betjeman but nobody picked it up. 'Isn't it near Harrow-on-the-Hill?' I nodded again. 'Because I know some people there. Sarah and Jack Leeming. She's an opera singer.' She lost interest in me when I was forced to admit I didn't know the couple in question and resumed the vitriolic attack on her son's prep school that refused to recognize his disability, which she called 'spatial' I think, though it might have been 'special'.

There was no sign of Alan when I came downstairs, nor Sheila Rosen and her son, so I filled a glass with the warm, cloudy pink, sweet punch and with one hand laid delicately over the grease spot I sidled into the drawing-room.

A few people glanced in my direction but quickly glanced away again to avoid catching my eye, which might have put them in the tedious position of having to make friendly overtures towards me. Edging through the packed room, I looked vainly for a familiar face and was eventually driven to standing on the outside of chatting groups waiting hopefully to be included. But such was their interest in me that I began to wonder if I was invisible. At the most I rated a few vague smiles though one man did volunteer to refill my glass when he refilled the others. However, the group dispersed and I never did get my glass back.

'There she is!' I heard a woman's voice cry over the general clack of conversation. 'Polly, where on earth have you been?' I turned and saw Sheila Rosen pushing through the crowd dragging Alan behind her. 'My dear, we've been looking everywhere for you, haven't we Alan?' She pressed her powdered cheek against both of mine continental style. 'I can see you've been getting to know everyone . . .'

'Well, not exactly,' I murmured, 'but I was trying.' I looked up at Alan. 'As a matter of fact, I was looking for you.' His eyes took on what I call his Wedgie-Benn expression which, on him, indicates exasperation.

'I'm sorry darling,' he said, tossing his head irritably, 'but I had one or two business things I had to clear up with Sheila. We were in the kitchen.'

'Silly me, I didn't think of looking there.' There was an awkward pause and then Sheila took us both by the hand and looked speculatively round the room.

'Now, let me see . . . who would you like to meet . . . I know.' She pulled us along behind her like children. 'Martin – Irene Pettigrew, meet Polly and Alan Graham,' and she clutched Mrs Pettigrew's arm, giggling girlishly. 'You'd better be nice to him Irene, he's my boss.' She turned to us. 'Martin has a chain of lingerie shops and Irene's an accountant.' We regarded each other with polite interest.

'Now I'd better go and check the food.' Sheila squeezed my hand and gave me a warm understanding smile. I was sure she knew exactly how I felt without being told and I warmed towards her as I had done before.

'Can I help?' I asked and I really meant it.

'No my dear, it's time you began enjoying yourself. Anyway, I've got two great sons out there somewhere if I need them.' And with that she left us, trailing behind her a smudgy scent that was part Ma Griffe, part hair lacquer and part, I think, a highly perfumed hand cream that I recognized as a cheap brand one might use regularly in the kitchen after washing up. I found this rather endearing.

'You're a lucky man,' Martin Pettigrew muttered enviously to Alan as he watched Sheila disappear into the mêlée.

'Oh, why's that?' Alan asked innocently. Martin's eyes widened and he gave a short, hard bark of laughter.

'Working with Sheila of course. I never had a better secretary.' Irene Pettigrew sighed and raised her eyes to heaven. Alan glanced at me uneasily.

'You must excuse him,' the woman said jerking her head in his direction with a light, false laugh, 'but he's had the hots for her for years ... haven't you my love?' Martin Pettigrew ignored his wife's dig and sipped his pink drink reflectively. 'Wise Sheila,' she continued, 'left him when he started chasing her round the desk.' I couldn't decide whether they were joking but I laughed anyway so that they would believe that I thought they were. Alan took his cue from me and joined in. The Pettigrews looked at us oddly. They weren't joking and I knew instinctively that theirs was a marriage that had long ago reached the point where awful truths were spoken in public as a means of scoring points off each other. Thankfully, at this point, we were joined by another couple who were obviously close friends. After vague and uncertain introductions and having ascertained that Alan didn't play golf, the two men rudely turned their backs on us and began discussing a forthcoming pro-celebrity golf tournament while the two women appeared to be ecstatic over the other's choice of party frock. Unnoticed and unlamented Alan and I edged away to a quiet corner.

'I don't like parties where I don't know anyone,' I said miserably. 'I wish we hadn't come – I'm sure Sheila didn't expect us to accept. She probably only invited us to be polite.' Alan bridled slightly.

'Well, we did accept,' he said firmly, 'so we might as well make an effort to enjoy ourselves.' He jiggled my elbow in a manner that was supposed to jolly me up a bit. 'Come on, Pol . . . you're usually so good at parties.'

I glanced round the brightly-lit room in the hope that I might spot someone who looked interesting and alone and might want to talk to two other people who were interesting and alone. As far as I could see, all the people who looked interesting were having great fun talking to each other, and to be truthful, they would only have to take one look at us, with our glum, bored faces, to realize that we were probably a lot less interesting than the people they were already talking to. Interesting people at parties very rarely seek out those of us who look glum and bored. I know I don't.

'How about those two over there sitting on the settee? Let's go and cheer them up.' The couple on the settee looked very much as I imagined we must look.

'But they look so glum and bored,' I moaned. Alan looked at me and laughed with genuine amusement.

'And how do you suppose we look?' he asked. I saw his point. 'Come on, girl,' he said and began to push his way through to the couple on the settee. They looked up at us as we approached.

'Hello,' I said, 'you look as though you know as few people here as we do.' The man grinned and stood up.

'If you only know the hostess, then you're right.' He held out his hand. 'I'm Tony Pinder and this is my wife Eva. We're Sheila's new neighbours.' We introduced ourselves. Eva Pinder, I noticed, was looking searchingly at Alan and frowning slightly.

'I'm sorry, but haven't we met?' she asked. 'Your face is

familiar but I don't know where from. In fact, I remarked to Tony that I knew you from somewhere.' Alan studied her smooth, round face and shook his head.

'I'm sure I'd remember if we'd met before,' he said gallantly. She pushed her spectacles up her little, snub nose with a very precise gesture of the middle finger of her right hand. It was an unconscious habit.

'It'll come to me in a minute . . . I never forget a face. Meanwhile darling,' she turned to her husband and proffered her empty glass, 'I'd love another drink.'

'No, let me,' Alan cut in quickly. 'We could all do with a refill.' He collected the glasses. 'Punch for everyone?'

'Er . . . do you mind if I have a whisky and water?' Tony said. 'I've hidden a bottle under the table in the hall. Have some yourself if you like.' He glanced round conspiratorially. 'I can't bear my alcohol adulterated I'm afraid.'

Alan grinned thankfully. 'Nor can I,' he murmured. 'So I'll join you if you don't mind.'

While Alan was gone we exchanged a few personal details. Tony was a dentist who shared a practice with a couple of other chaps in Hammersmith, and Eva, who had just seen their last and youngest daughter into a flat with three other girls, confessed in that humble way we women have that she was 'just a housewife I'm afraid . . .'

'We didn't need the big house in Ealing any more,' Eva confided, 'so we decided to move into something smaller nearer the practice. I love these little terraced houses, but do you know ours cost us more than our great big house in Ealing. Isn't it silly? You pay for the position though.' She looked round the room, which was beginning to clear a little as people went off to help themselves to food. 'I do think Sheila's done this house up beautifully . . . I wish I had a bit of her flair.' For the first time I glanced around, with more than a passing interest, at my surroundings. Yes, I thought, it is lovely. Exotic and vivid like Sheila and a bit over the top. I hadn't realized how many shades of pink there were but Sheila had them all from the flaming pink of a November sunset to the pale, pale pink of Baby's Blush coral in luscious brocades, silks and velvets. To complement her taste for pink she had introduced an unusual shade of lavender blue and a fair amount of gold leaf. It should have looked like a sultan's harem, but in fact the effect was breathtakingly glamorous and expensive.

'Yes,' I agreed with Eva, 'it's beautiful . . . just the sort of house I'd like to have when the children grow up.' Which led, naturally, to talk of my children, so that when Alan returned with the drinks, I was recounting yesterday's episode at the swimming pool. Sheila followed close behind him.

'I'm glad you're getting to know my lovely new neighbours,' she said brightly. 'Of course, Alan,' and she turned to him, 'you've met Eva before.'

'I have?' He looked doubtful.

'Yes. Don't you remember? She called in the other evening to return my *House and Garden* when you were here.' Alan's eyes widened with sudden, desperate recall and Sheila noticed. She studied his face briefly and then glanced at me. Eva Pinder's eyes flickered anxiously round all three of us finishing with a meaningful look towards her husband. Then Sheila sighed.

'Oh Alan, you are a silly boy,' she said, sharing her hopelessness over him with me. 'He's forgotten to tell you, hasn't he?' I cocked my head on one side and looked at her questioningly. 'I gave him some supper the other evening while we were working here on the new range. Well, it seemed silly to be cold, uncomfortable *and* hungry at the warehouse when we could be warm, comfortable and *not* hungry here.' I believed her. What bothered me was why Alan had kept it a secret for I knew he hadn't simply forgotten to tell me.

'Was that the night you had kebabs from the dreadful Greek takeaway in Wembley or was it the fish and chips you threw out of the window in disgust in North Harrow?' I trilled amusingly through gritted teeth. Rotten bad form I know, but understandable surely in the circumstances.

'As a matter of fact it was the night I came in with a raging migraine and went straight to bed and I forgot to tell you in the morning. Didn't I have a wretched migraine that night, Sheila?'

She nodded. 'Yes you did, but really Alan, this is how nasty rumours get started. I'm sorry Polly,' again she gave me her special, warm, understanding smile and I felt reassured, 'but we're working all hours at the moment to get the new range on the road and the Japanese orders sorted out. I hope you don't mind me feeding Alan from time to time. It's better for him than that awful junk he's been eating and it's far too late for him to eat when he gets home.' She looked upset and embarrassed, so though I was still feeling outraged and really not ready to forgive and forget, I decided to appear magnanimous.

'It's very kind of you to look after him the way you do, Sheila,' I said sweetly, keeping my fingers crossed behind me. 'I just hope you get paid overtime, that's all.' Everyone appeared to relax and Alan, who appeared to relax most of all, became overbearingly jovial and appeasing in the way of a guilty man who has unexpectedly received the Royal Pardon minutes before he was due to be executed. He was flatteringly attentive for the rest of the evening, refilling my glass without being asked and usually before it was empty and plying me with overloaded plates of delicious food I couldn't juggle with, let alone eat. But I wasn't to be won over that easily and with him I remained cool and aloof.

Just as we were about to leave, Sheila took my elbow and drew me to one side. 'You probably haven't noticed,' she murmured, 'but you have a large grease spot right in the middle of the bodice of your lovely dress. Take it to the cleaner's first thing in the morning before it has time to set in. Mind you, I have found that ironing grease spots on to brown wrapping paper is very effective.' I am certain she meant to be kind.

Once in the car the atmosphere very quickly dropped from cool to freezing. Alan tried gamely to open up happy little conversations but without success.

'Well, what do you think then?' he asked gaily.

'About what?'

He glanced quickly at me. 'About the party of course.' He knew I usually enjoyed bitchy post-mortems. Normally he would refuse to participate and I would carry on a monologue all the way home.

'Very nice,' I replied shortly.

'The Pettigrews were a bit much weren't they?'

'Were they?' I began to hum loudly along with his favourite Carpenters' tape.

'Awful punch,' he tried again.

'I liked it.' The truth is I have never liked punch. Too sweet and sticky for me, and he knows it. He swallowed audibly and negotiated a tricky bend far too fast. A wheel caught the edge of the kerb and there was a nasty grating sound.

'Damn!' he muttered under his breath.

'Watch it!' I turned to him irritably. 'Do you think you're in a fit state to drive?'

He drew in his breath sharply. 'You know damn well I've hardly drunk anything all evening.'

'Well, just watch it – that's all.' We drove on in silence and for once the music failed to calm my savage (and grease-spotted) breast.

'You didn't forget to tell me about that meal with Sheila, you *failed* to tell me, and that is a different thing altogether,' I said eventually and quite calmly I thought. Alan sighed.

'I told you, I had a migraine . . .'

'Oh, I know you had a migraine, but *if* you remember, when you came in I asked you if you had eaten and you said, "No, but I'm not feeling hungry . . ."'

'Well, I wasn't. I'd just eaten at Sheila's.'

'I know that *now*, but I didn't *then*. *Then* you said that you hadn't eaten, when in fact you had – at Sheila's, so clearly you didn't want me to know. And while we're about it, how many times has this happened? Sheila more or less implied that it wasn't the first time.' Alan took one hand off the steering wheel and squeezed his forehead hard with his thumb and forefinger.

'Look Pol, I've got a headache coming on.'

'Very convenient,' I said acidly. He gave me a piteous, pleading look that would have wrung tears from a glass eye. I, however, remained unmoved.

'Well?' I said, fixing him with my piercingly penetrating Paddington stare.

'Listen,' he said, after a longish pause and staring straight ahead. 'I don't consider that I have anything to hide from you and so I'm not prepared to discuss this matter any further tonight.' And with that he shut up and refused to speak to me for the rest of the journey home. I continued ranting and raving but I might as well have been addressing myself to a block of reinforced concrete for all the good it did me.

A few days later, without warning, my fictional heroine fell in love with my unspeakable anti-hero, Gulley. I mean, all right, he may have been superficially attractive in an Irish tinker sort of way; he may even have had the sort of plausible, raffish charm that sweeps women into bed, but he was not the sort of youth that responsible, mature women such as Caro Stansbury fell in love with and I found her sudden self-indulgence hard to handle.

Gulley was nothing more than a petty thief. Caro was supposed to walk into her living-room while he was bundling the family silver into a battered old hold-all and the brief physical thing they subsequently had together was supposed to act as a catalyst towards the eventual break-up of her steady but hum-drum marriage to perfectly adequate Arthur. But she was not supposed to fall in love with him. In fact she was supposed to discover, only when it was too late, what a truly wonderful man Arthur really was. I was even considering a reconciliation in the final chapter. But now, with Caro limp with love for this wretched boy, all that was out of the question.

When I read back the last couple of chapters I realized what had happened. Gulley, contrary to my plans for him, had been profoundly affected by his affair with Caro and had, in a manner of speaking, found his God, or possibly his Goddess. He became a person that it was perfectly possible to love, and Caro did so. I did feel that if Arthur had spent a little less time at work and a little more time with Caro, things might have been different, but somehow Caro's uncharacteristic behaviour seemed perfectly natural in view of his neglect. Indeed, I felt he almost deserved to be cuckolded, and when I wrote Caro's moving declaration of love to Gulley (which, with hindsight, I realize made more than a fleeting nod in the direction of Elizabeth Barrett Browning), I said out loud to Poppy who was taking an intelligent interest in my work from beneath the kitchen table, 'Well, I'm sorry Poppy, but Arthur damn well deserves what's coming to him.'

Chapter Eight

Let's face it, over the following weeks things got progressively worse. Or maybe, from hardly being aware at all, I had simply become aware of exactly how bad things were. The changes weren't dramatic. It was as though a cloud was passing over the sun and I was feeling the chill. We weren't openly fighting. We weren't even bickering and that's what worried me most, for Alan and I bicker good-naturedly a lot of the time.

Since he was a small boy Alan has nurtured a profound sense of grievance. He is a quiet, temperate man who works harder than most and pays meticulous attention to detail. He is a man of great integrity, usually a gentle man, considerate and polite. People, and that includes me, make the mistake of thinking that because he gets on with the most mundane and unrewarding jobs uncomplainingly, he doesn't need appreciation, but like everyone else, he does. Which explains his sense of grievance. It's true; neither his mother nor his father, nor his brother, nor his various bosses, nor I have ever shown him the appreciation he really deserves.

He's not a hot-shot high-flier because he lacks the killer instinct, but every hot-shot high-flier should have an Alan, for he's the man who tidies up after them. Well, hot-shot high-fliers are prone to getting themselves into dreadful scrapes. Alan is the man who follows through the bright ideas thought up by the hot-shot high-fliers, who rarely have the patience or the staying power to do this for themselves. He is also the man who tidies up after me.

If I'm to be honest, and I do try to be, for what is the

point of inventing an idyllic, fantasy marriage for myself when it must be clear by now that we steer your average creaking ship from one hazard to another with our fingers crossed and a prayer on our lips. The main reason our particular creaking ship hasn't foundered yet is because we had low expectations of ever finishing the voyage (our respective parents gave us three years at the outside), so in a way, things could only get better. We have also developed, over the years, a high degree of mutual tolerance. We have had to, for we are not at all alike. So much unalike in fact that people have often wondered what drew us together. I am intemperate, lazy, self-indulgent and anxious. Of course I am some good things too but it is not for me to list them, though I will admit to being self-aware and intuitive. When we squabble it is because of the differences between us. Fundamentally Alan disapproves of the sort of woman I am, even while he needs the very things in me of which he most disapproves, and my life would disintegrate without the things in Alan which most irritate me. Though we both know this, it doesn't stop us squabbling. It does, however, stop it getting serious.

So when the bickering stopped, I knew something out of the ordinary was happening to us. We stopped laughing too, which was a bad sign. We have always been able to draw a laugh from each other. When he isn't disapproving of my antics and I'm not being irritated by his, we find each other very funny. I never use the word 'love' lightly because it means something different to everyone, but I'm prepared to bet that what we feel for each other is love. Not your mountain-moving, heart-stopping, breath-taking variety, but more the sort of quiet, binding love that you feel, if you're lucky, for your parents, your brothers and sisters and the children that you bear; functional and abiding and uncapricious.

But during those weeks we weren't laughing and we weren't bickering and there didn't seem to be much in the way of conversation between us. Alan seemed to be shut away in a little cocoon and he resented any effort we, the children and I, made to pierce it. He was obviously anxious about something but when I tried to find out what it was, he would reply in an absent, abstracted sort of way, that it was nothing, that he was perfectly all right and would I please stop going on so.

On the rare occasions he came home from the office at a reasonable hour he was irritable and depressed and as much as possible he kept out of our way. He appeared to have lost his appetite. Though he moved his food about his plate he wasn't actually eating very much of it and when, one day, I put my arms round him in a moment of compassion, he moved away quickly, though not before I noticed how bony and thin he felt through his shirt.

'Have you lost some weight?' I asked, looking him straight in the eye.

'No,' he said shortly and that was that. But I knew better.

At night he would slip quickly into bed, present his back to me and switch off his bedside light. On the odd, and getting odder, occasions when I tried to nestle up to him, he would grunt with feigned sleep and draw further over towards his edge of the bed. One night he fell out in an effort to put distance between us. Normally this would have made us laugh, but his cold, indifferent face made me shudder instead.

'My God,' I exclaimed in horrified wonder, 'you can't bear me near you, can you?' He looked at me long and steadily and I felt he was about to tell me something important, but then he must have thought better of it for he sighed, leant over and gave me a quick squeeze.

'Don't talk rubbish, Pol,' he said with a sort of gruff tenderness. 'I'm just so bloody tired and overworked at the moment, I don't have enough energy when I get home to keep my eyes open.' I felt I had briefly pierced his cocoon and that he had really seen me and heard me for the first time in months.

You must be thinking, as I would be if I was you, that I

was a fool, because it was plain as the nose on my face that Alan was having an affair. But you see, despite the evidence, my intuition told me otherwise and I have always trusted my intuition. You know I toyed with the idea. In fact I was more or less ready to cast Sheila Rosen as the 'other woman'. Initially she seemed to be a most unlikely candidate because when Alan looks at other women it is fantasy women of the Sophia Loren and Bo Derek type and Sheila, though striking and charming, had grown-up sons and treated him as one of them. However, I could see that there was something between them, a secret of some sort to which I was not privy, and I was sure that she was the only woman, other than me, whom he saw on a regular basis. Even if he felt inclined to stray, he simply didn't have the time. He was either at work with Sheila, or at home with me.

One morning, when I knew Alan was in Birmingham, I even telephoned Sheila in the office.

'Sheila,' I began after we had dealt with the preliminaries, 'I'm worried about Alan.' The silence that followed seemed endless.

Then she said, 'Oh, why is that?' very calmly, as a good secretary would.

'Well, you must've noticed – he's not eating properly and I'm sure he's lost a lot of weight, though he says he hasn't. He's always exhausted and I think he's depressed about something.'

'Why are you telling me this?' she asked after an even longer silence.

'Well, I thought you might know why he's depressed.'

'He's working very hard,' she suggested.

'I *know* he's working very hard. He always has and it hasn't depressed him before. In fact he's only happy when he's working hard.'

'Then I'm sorry Polly, I really can't help you.' It was as if she was slamming a door on me. I suppose I must have sounded very impatient and waspish. 'Why don't you ask him?' she added.

'Don't you think I have? But he keeps reassuring me that everything's normal and I don't believe him.' I heard her sigh.

'Look my dear, I really don't know what to tell you. Perhaps he'll feel better after his trip to the Far East. I know that's preying on his mind, what with the change of agents and one thing and another. Maybe when he's sorted everything out in Tokyo . . .' she tailed off vaguely, but I felt she knew far more than she was telling me. There were too many unexplained silences followed by half-hearted reassurances. 'I'm really sorry I can't be more help, Polly.'

'Well thanks, anyway,' I said dismally, then I added quickly as I thought of it, 'Please don't tell him I phoned, he wouldn't be best pleased.' She said she wouldn't and, I'm sure without meaning to, rang off while I was still talking, but it diminished me nevertheless. I had expected Sheila to put my mind at rest in some way but instead I felt worse – like a child who has accidentally stumbled upon the edges of an adult secret.

The Sunday before Alan was due to leave for Tokyo my sister Babs and Ma came to lunch. It was customary for them to come to lunch every other Sunday. Babs would motor out from her pretty little end-of-terrace house at the wrong side of the World's End and Ma would walk the half mile from her less pretty maisonette opposite some sprawling, supposedly secret government buildings in Northwood Hills. Of course they weren't secret. I believe they belonged to the Min. of Fish and Ag. or some such department but old myths die hard. Very reluctantly, Gladys would accompany Ma. Being something of an agoraphobe, the little dog hated visiting and most of all she hated visiting us. She bore a grudge against Poppy, who had sat on her once by mistake and broken one of her minuscule hind legs. From that day on, whenever she saw Poppy she peed. In fact, impromptu peeing was Gladys's version of a nervous tic. Raise your voice to her, play with her too exuberantly, drop a saucepan lid or slam a door and she would pee wherever she happened to be standing at the time. I hate to say it, but most of Ma's dogs developed into full-blown neurotics. They were fairly unstable and insecure to start with, for Ma believed in giving a home to mature, unwanted dogs and what a mature, unwanted dog needs most is a lot of tolerant, loving care and attention. I've no doubt that Ma loved her dogs, but she expected from them the same standards of socially acceptable behaviour that she had expected from Babs and me as children. Because the dogs weren't young they found it difficult to absorb Ma's stern training. She was never deliberately cruel to them, but she had unrealistically high expectations of them which they, poor beasts, could never hope to live up to. She believed that she alone understood their funny little ways and she defended herself and her dogs stoutly should we dare to criticize.

With the exception of Babs, we are a family who places great store upon punctuality. 'Punctuality,' Grandma used to say, 'is the courtesy of kings' and what was good enough for kings was good enough for Grandma. Ma, well-trained by her socially ambitious mother, preferred to arrive two hours early rather than five minutes late. As children Babs and I spent many miserable, embarrassing hours on the platforms of main-line stations while people and trains came and went, getting odd looks from porters and ticket collectors as we sat disconsolately on our luggage drinking thick white cups of tea from the trolley and eating cheese rolls. Ma, well aware of our boredom and shame, would attempt to keep our spirits up with sprightly chatter about how exciting it all was and weren't people fun to watch. Gloom was one thing Ma eschewed with all the determination in her strong, blocky little body. She never moaned and she was never, ever gloomy, though God knows she had enough to be gloomy about. I must confess that I enjoyed punishing Ma on such occasions by becoming more and more miserable the harder she tried to amuse me.

'Oh do cheer up, Polly darling,' she would plead eventually

in desperation, 'you're making us all miserable,' which of course was my intention.

However, in my case, Ma's training paid off for I, too, became obsessively punctual, which is maybe just as well, for I married an obsessively punctual man. We have had to school ourselves not to take an invitation for dinner at 8 p.m. as meaning just that. It's a real effort of will to break the training. We force ourselves to sit round corners listening to tapes on the car cassette player until we think the hostess is dressed and the nuts are on the coffee table.

We both disapprove very deeply of Babs's compulsive unpunctuality even though I suspect it is a rebellious reaction to Ma's eccentric time-keeping. The odd thing is that Babs likes to maintain the self-delusion that she is normally a punctual person against whom the fates occasionally conspire. Like most bad time-keepers she has a host of very plausible excuses. She forgets that I've heard them all before, many times. I can't tell you how often a close friend from out of town calls just as she is about to leave home, or her car keys go missing, or her hairdresser runs late, or the chairman of the company requires her presence minutes before she is due to leave the office. The fortnightly Sunday lunchtime traffic snarl-up round the Hangar Lane Gyratory System became a running joke with the family, and this particular Sunday lunchtime was no exception.

It was accepted custom and practice for Babs to prepare a starter at home and bring it with her, so, because she could be anything up to two hours late, lunch was a moveable feast. Alan never got used to this for he is a man whose humours depend on the state of his stomach. Feed him regularly and you have a happy, contented man. He's not greedy. He doesn't need mountains of food to maintain his equilibrium, but he has a metabolism that in my opinion competes with the speed of light and if he is to maintain orbit, he has to be refuelled at regular intervals. The erratic, uncertain timing of Sunday lunch upset his digestion and he became very irascible. Indeed, by the time Babs arrived he would usually be very near the point of spontaneous combustion, as we would all be, though Ma would try valiantly to keep the peace.

'Now you know she's a very busy girl,' she would plead in Babs's defence. 'Please Polly, for my sake, don't get at her when she arrives.'

'But Ma, it's not fair on the rest of us,' I would counter. 'And the more we let her get away with it, the worse she gets.' However, satisfied that I had at least made my point, to please Ma, and because it was after all Sunday, a day set aside for peace and rest, I would try very hard to contain myself when Babs *did* arrive, all pink and flustered and bursting with a selection of excuses from her large repertoire. I think on this occasion I probably frowned with suppressed irritation, for within seconds of her arrival we were squabbling. Babs parried my frown with her usual thrust-and-run-away.

'You can stop looking at me like that, Polly, because it wasn't my fault. Now, how is everyone?' Big hearty beam that dared me to react.

'I wasn't aware I was looking at you in any particular way,' I replied sweetly. 'Sorry.'

'Oh for heaven's sake Polly, don't start . . . I've made a lovely iced lettuce soup, but it really ought to be put in the fridge for a bit.'

Outrage creeping up on me like a London smog, I snarled, 'What's the point in making an iced soup and then bringing it out in your hot car?'

Ma began twittering nervously, 'Now you girls, let's get on with the dishing up.' Ma's desperate appeal fell on deaf ears.

'I'm sorry, but I have no control over the traffic at Hangar Lane.' Babs appealed to the rest of the family for support.

'But if you know the traffic's going to be terrible you should start earlier.'

'I'll have you know it took me nearly two hours to get from Fulham to Pinner.'

'Rubbish! I phoned you an hour ago and you were engaged.'

'Huh . . . checking up on me, were you? Well, it wasn't me speaking on it, so there.'

I smiled a falsely conciliatory smile. 'Look, Babs dear,' I said placatingly, sounding reasonable in order that she might sound unreasonable, 'let's just cool it and dish up that lettuce soup of yours, okay?' Sulkily Babs sloshed pale-green slime into soup bowls.

'Yuck!' Charlie exclaimed, expressing everyone's feelings very vividly. Babs spun round to face him with such force that he backed away from her sharply, straight into Lizzie who was carrying a bowl of soup into the dining-room. It slipped from her hands and smashed on the stone tile floor splattering green gunge over everything and everybody.

'Now look what you've done!' Lizzie screamed tearfully. 'It's all over me!'

'And me!' Jane squeaked. It was at this point that Alan intervened very forcibly.

'For God's sake, aren't we getting any lunch in this house?' he shouted, and strode angrily through the kitchen door, straight on to a puddle of soup which sent him skidding across the floor like a novice ice-skater. The expletives that followed were amongst the most colourful I have ever heard. Ma hastily removed the children from earshot while Babs and I mopped Alan down and cleaned up the kitchen.

We eventually sat down to a ruined lunch at four in the afternoon. The soup had the viscid, gelatinous texture of a neglected goldfish bowl and was as uncontrollable as an egg-white, and my leg of lamb, having 'rested' far too long in a warm oven, was unspeakable. Watching Ma attack her leathery portion put me in mind of Charlie Chaplin in *The Gold Rush* daintily eating his own boot. However, everyone was too cowed by this time to pass comment and a leaden silence hung over us.

Sunday lunches were rarely the success I hoped they would be. In my mind I nurtured a fantasy of domestic tranquillity

– a groaning table, decent wine and a good-natured exchange of news and views. It didn't seem too much to ask, but somehow something always went wrong. Generally speaking it was the exchange of news and views that would get out of hand for we could never agree to disagree amicably. Ma, who was a simple woman, not stupid you understand, but credulous and a bit naïve, would set the ball rolling with her views on current events culled mainly from her favourite tabloid newspaper. Ma had a bewildering array of opinions, often contradictory and always subjective. If it had been any other elderly woman Babs and I would have listened politely and kept our own counsel, but Ma, as family, was fair game.

'You don't *really* believe that, Ma,' one of us would say and Ma, challenged, would bristle like a fighting cock.

'You girls think you know everything,' she would snap, and from then on the fight, becoming embarrassingly personal, would develop along the lines of 'You are . . .', 'I'm not . . .' at which point Alan would cut in in Ma's defence. He was very fond of my mother and secretly shared many of her more outrageous views. I think he also enjoyed provoking my sister and me to the point of imminent hysteria. We were two women he considered too opinionated by half and fighting alongside Ma he felt he had a worthy ally.

Babs's style of argument was proclamatory. Being in a position of some eminence, she had easy access to several horses' mouths. 'I have it on the best authority,' she would announce with an air of finality that could be relied on to send my blood-pressure up several notches, 'for I was speaking with Arnold Gringe, who is, as you must know, chairman of Amnesty International . . .'

'Phooey to Arnold Gringe,' I would counter childishly. 'In my opinion . . .' As a safeguard against being asked to produce my sources I always commenced an argument with my sister with 'in my opinion'. This drove her wild because it is well nigh impossible to argue objectively with someone who makes no secret of the fact that she is arguing subjectively.

That Sunday in late spring, I remember, our squabbling centred round the 'fuss', as Ma would have it, that was being made over one-parent families. A strong, resilient woman herself, who had coped more than adequately with being a single parent on considerably less than what is now called Supplementary Benefit, Ma had very little sympathy with people in the same circumstances as herself who couldn't cope. She was a firm believer in self-help. It was difficult for her to understand that not all single parents were as self-sufficient as she had been. In any case, her way of dealing with the problem was no longer considered acceptable by those in charge of the emotional well-being of the nation's children.

'But Ma,' I began, after she had had her usual carp about people being spoon-fed from the cradle to the grave, 'in those days it was considered okay to send children to boarding school at seven years old and you had Grandma and Grandpa to look after us during the hols. You could take a job without worrying about us.'

'You surely don't imagine I actually enjoyed those years when you were away from home?'

'Neither did we,' Babs muttered under her breath so that only I heard.

'Nowadays,' I continued relentlessly, 'your solution, even supposing everyone could afford it' (Here I should point out to anyone who imagines Ma had the financial resources to send us to a fee-paying school that ours was a charitable institution) 'would only be considered as a last resort. There aren't many people left who still think that it's a good idea to send seven-year-olds to boarding school.'

'I did what I thought was right for you both, and I still do. You were both very lucky, it was a marvellous opportunity.' Babs frowned a warning at me. Opening that particular old wound was just not cricket, but unfortunately I was dogged by an almost obsessive compulsion to do so whenever the opportunity arose. Thus the argument, which had begun as a general discussion, became a hostile confrontation which slid inevitably into an orgy of personal abuse.

'Well, of course Polly, you always were full of self-pity.' In Ma's eyes her two daughters would always be what they had always been. Other people's children grew up and changed, Babs and I were immutable, like larvae in amber.

'Ma, why can't you admit to the possibility that you made a mistake?'

'Oh do shut up, Polly,' Babs cut in, 'you know this gets you nowhere.'

'You're so alike, you and Ma. You can pull me apart limb from limb and I'm expected to sit quietly by and let you but when I retaliate you both scuttle back into your respective holes and batten down the hatches.'

'Ah-ha!' Ma cried triumphantly. 'Now we're to have a demonstration of your persecution mania.' A persecution mania, according to Ma, was yet another thing I had always suffered from, even before I knew what it meant.

'Oh God, Ma, you're so bloody predictable.' A healthy snort of outrage from Ma. During such outbursts Alan and the children usually maintained very low profiles, discretion quite obviously being the better part of valour. However, just occasionally Alan would intercede if the going got too rough.

'Now calm down, Polly, or there'll be tears before tea.' I know he meant to introduce an element of humour into the proceedings but feeling beleaguered I turned on him like a cornered rat.

'And you can keep your nose out of it, you silly little man!' I hissed venomously.

Ma gasped with simulated horror. 'Don't speak to your husband like that!' she commanded in shocked tones. Ma was of the old school. She liked to think she wasn't, but she was. Despite the fact that she had been husbandless for many years and she had worked alongside men until she retired, she regarded them quite simply as superior beings. I have no way of proving it, but I believe that while she was married to our father, though everything points to the fact that she was his equal in most things and his superior in some, she thought of him as her master and I believe she dedicated her short married life to pleasing him and expected very little in return. She was grateful to him for having chosen her, honoured and privileged to be his wife. She spoke of him as one might speak of a saint.

To be truthful, I instantly regretted speaking to Alan so harshly, and if it hadn't been for Ma's ill-judged intervention I would have said sorry almost before the words were out of my mouth; but the implication behind her reproof made a show of remorse unthinkable.

'Oh do pardon my insolence, husband mine,' I said with heavy sarcasm, hanging my head in mock contrition. 'Three Hail Marys before bed tonight.' Babs was looking round the table anxiously. She was not accustomed to the cut and thrust of normal marital disharmony and saw every disagreement as a symptom of imminent break-down.

'*Pas devant les enfants*,' she enunciated impeccably. Ma looked puzzled.

'What, dear?'

'Aunt Babs said "Not in front of the children",' Lizzie informed her grandmother smugly. Jane looked up brightly from her rhubarb crumble hoping to find something unmentionable going on that was not meant to be done in front of her. Family squabbles were two a penny and didn't qualify. Everything seemed depressingly normal so she went back to her pudding.

Still snapping away at each other like angry dogs we reached the coffee stage. Jane, who with the other two had left the table and was watching the end of an old movie on television, came into the dining-room and leant up against me sobbing.

'It's so sad, Mummy, when the old dog dies and the little dog doesn't know he's dead and the man kicks the other dog out with the little dog.'

'But you've only watched the last five minutes,' I pointed out.

'I know, and I'm glad I didn't watch the rest. Oh, and Lizzie says to tell you that Poppy's not here.' Jane's words were followed by a sudden hush.

'You mean . . .' pause for dawning comprehension, 'she's got out again?' Jane looked doubtful.

'I think Lizzie meant that,' she said. Alan shot out of his chair.

'Bloody hell!' he roared and Jane winced. 'Not again! Lizzie! Charlie! Come here!' Two wide-eyed children appeared almost instantly at the dining-room door. You didn't loiter when summoned by an apoplectic father. 'Where's the dog?' he demanded. They looked at one another, each hoping that the other would know the answer.

'How should I know,' Lizzie replied eventually. 'I'm not her keeper.'

'Poppy!' Alan bellowed. Anxiously we waited for her to come bounding into the room. All we heard was the sound of Gladys's sharp little claws on the wooden hall floor. She came scampering towards us in a state of high excitement.

'Ahhh, bless her little heart,' Ma simpered mawkishly, 'you'd tell us where Poppy is if you could, wouldn't you little sweetiepie?'

Poppy was, in her youth, what is known as a 'mitcher', a mitcher being a dog that habitually goes missing and may stay away from home for hours or even days depending upon how the wind blows. When we discovered this unfortunate flaw in her character, we enclosed the garden within a tough, chain-link fence, but Poppy, because she is that intelligent mix of Labrador and Border Collie, quickly learnt to burrow underneath. So we buried more than a foot of the fence underground, whereupon Poppy went into training as a world-class high-jumper. To the top of the chain-link fence we added a couple of feet of chicken wire, yet still she escaped, though we didn't know how. And it was always on a Sunday during lunch. I think the conversation bored her and are you surprised?

'Come out from under the table, Jane,' Alan directed, 'and go and see if she's tormenting next door's goldfish. And you, Charlie,' the child jumped at the sudden command, 'on your bike down to the Cricket Club.' Poppy was a damned good fielder only she insisted upon leaving the game with the ball. The players failed to appreciate this and we received complaints most Sundays. 'Lizzie, you check on the Perry rabbits before we have old man Perry letting off with his pop gun, and Polly, you and Babs go over to the water meadow.' You could tell why Alan had risen to the dizzy heights of Fire Officer in the Blues during his National Service. 'I'll cruise around a bit in the car, and Ma-in-law, you man the phones.' This was an important and responsible job, for very soon reports of sightings would start flooding in. Poppy didn't roam the streets in an orderly fashion like other dogs. She darted about hither and thither, exuberant in her freedom, full of *joie de vivre* and hail-fellow-well-met, chasing boys on bikes, teasing dogs on leads, puncturing footballs, leaping towards cars and darting out of the way at the last moment, pestering innocent picknickers and progressing gradually further and further away from home. Despite her hoydenish behaviour, local people were very fond of her, for she was also an affectionate, humorous dog and when she was spotted trotting along the middle of the High Road or snapping at minnows in the River Pinn, someone would be sure to let us know.

The first call came just as Babs and I were going out of the door.

'She's been sighted!' Ma called after us. 'Trailing a line of clean washing along the end of the Kemps' garden. Mr Kemp says he tried to catch her but all he got for his pains was a handful of dry nappies. He thinks she was making for the Perry rabbits!'

'Oh well, Lizzie'll get her then,' I called back and continued down the drive with my arm linked in Babs's.

'Have you seen Poppy?' I asked young Gerry Kemp, who was poking about in a jam jar full of pond weed. An uncommunicative lad by nature, he shook his head without looking up, but I could feel his eyes following us as we continued along the footpath beside the summer-shallow stream. Old Mr Peckham was tottering towards us preceded by his youthful Jack Russell, Clancy, who was making alarming strangling noises at the end of his choke lead.

'Good afternoon, Mr Peckham,' I began politely.

'If you're looking for that wretched dog of yours,' he interrupted rudely, 'she's digging up the wallflowers in the Walled Garden.' Poppy had lost favour with Mr Peckham when she uprooted a young sapling from his immaculate front garden.

'Oh no, not the Walled Garden!' I wailed. The Walled Garden, together with its charming dove-cote and a tithe barn, was all that remained of what once must have been a fine Tudor mansion. It was tended by several gardeners from the council's Parks Department and was a tranquil refuge from the main road traffic that buzzed round it in all directions like a swarm of angry bees banished from their hive. It was a place where elderly folk came to sit quietly and enjoy the sunshine and all dogs had to be kept on leads.

'Come on Babs.' I quickened my pace a little. 'We'd better hurry before she gets herself arrested.' Two small boys on large bikes cycled past. 'Have you seen a large black and . . .' but they were out of earshot before I had finished my sentence.

I heard someone calling my name. It was Dorothy, my next-door neighbour and friend. She was running towards me followed, at some distance, by lame Leo, the dog that had been sold to her as a German Shepherd and had grown up to be a very ordinary, small black terrier.

'Your mother says that someone has just phoned to say that Poppy is in the primary school playing field being – er – wooed – by a Golden Retriever who belongs to some people called Fasnett and answers to the name of Maltravers.' Dorothy giggled breathlessly.

'But she can't be in two places at once,' I argued, 'and Mr Peckham says he saw her in the Walled Garden.' I hesitated, wondering if it was wise to change direction.

'Look, if you like, I'll walk Leo up to the playing field and that takes me past the Murphy chickens, which is another place Poppy loves to be.' The chickens got over-excited too. I thanked Dorothy, and Babs and I continued on our way.

Babs was unusually silent and I asked her if something was worrying her.

'Well yes,' she said, giving me a side-long look. 'I am a bit worried about something and I've been debating for weeks whether to talk to you about it.' She was silent for a while and I wondered if she was having man trouble or maybe there was a new job in the offing. 'It's Alan,' she said finally and my heart gave an uncomfortable lurch.

'What about him?'

'Oh Polly, come on . . . you're his wife, you must've noticed. All that weight he's lost.' I shrugged. 'And he's so irritable these days and sort of lack-lustre. I can't remember the last time I saw him really laugh, you know, *really* laugh, with gusto, like he used to. When he's not beefing at you he all but ignores you, and the children are just in his way. Perhaps I'm simply imagining it. Am I?'

In the distance I spotted Charlie cycling furiously along the High Road. Cupping my hands, I bellowed at him through them. 'Has she been found yet?' He took both hands off the handle bars and threw them in the air in a Gallic gesture of uncertainty which could have meant that he didn't hear my question or he didn't know the answer to it. In any case he didn't stop.

Bending down I plucked a sorrel leaf and popped it into my mouth. In between meals at school, sorrel and wild rhubarb had been very effective appetite suppressants and I came to relish the sharp, vinegary taste of sorrel. Wild rhubarb, on the other hand, sent my colon into spasm, but it had its uses.

'No, you're not imagining it,' I replied belatedly. We crossed the narrow makeshift bridge over the stream and walked up the wooded incline towards the Walled Garden. 'And don't ask what's the matter with him because I don't know. He refuses to talk about it. In fact he denies there's anything wrong – simply says he's over-worked.'

The small landscaped area known as the Park that surrounded the Walled Garden was bustling with people taking Sunday afternoon constitutionals. Dogs charged in all directions, sniffing round the elderly folk sunning themselves on the wooden seats and chasing children at play. Babs sighed deeply.

'It's hard to imagine you're within ten miles of Piccadilly,' she said rapturously taking several deep breaths of the air that she insisted was fresh. I suppose it was fresher than Fulham but compared to Stornoway, or even Dundee, it was pure poison.

'Can you see Poppy?' I asked. There were several large black dogs prancing about but none of them was Poppy. I saw Ma's friend Mrs Blackmore sitting with an old man in the shade of a yew tree. She waved and beckoned us over. As usual she looked very attractive and smart in a pale dove-grey silk suit, a deep pink shiny straw toque and very high-heeled grey suede shoes that showed off her neat ankles. I always said that Mrs Blackmore was an example to all of us. If I could be just a fraction as well-preserved as her at seventy, I used to say to Ma, I would be satisfied. Ma would grunt non-committally. I think she was a little envious of her friend's still slender good looks and abundant silver hair.

After some polite chit-chat, I asked Mrs Blackmore if she had seen Poppy. She thought for a while and then said, 'Well, I'm almost sure I saw her a while back running wild with a large Golden Retriever. I said to Mr Archibald here, "That's the Graham dog or I'm a Dutchman."'

'Yes,' agreed the old man uncertainly. 'Big black chap making a terrible nuisance of himself. Savage looking beast.' Babs and I exchanged amused glances. 'Should've been on a lead. Don't like dogs myself – smelly boisterous creatures. Dirty habits – more comes out than goes in,' he said graphically. 'Still got a scar where I was bitten by a collie when I was a boy.' He held up his palsied old hand that was grotesquely twisted with arthritis. Politely we peered at the tiny white line on the ball of his thumb. 'Dog had to be put down. My older brother didn't speak to me for a week – it was his dog d'y'see. Anyway he was killed in Flanders.'

'I don't think we're talking about the same dog, dear,' Mrs Blackmore said gently.

'I remember he was called Basil.' It wasn't quite clear whether he was talking about his brother or the collie dog. 'Mother never got over the shock – buried him in the back garden along with Chip the Scottie and a budgerigar. 'Course, he should've been buried in the family plot only they couldn't find a body.' The mysterious processes of the old man's mind turned a tragedy into a comedy – man and dog became one. Mrs Blackmore pulled a wry face and touched her head lightly with a forefinger.

'He's not been quite right since Florrie died,' she murmured softly. 'Two years ago it was. Woke up to find her cold beside him. Been going down-hill ever since, poor old chap. They were devoted. Still, he likes to sit in the sunshine and look at the pretty girls, don't you Percy?'

The old man looked up sharply. 'What's that?'

'I do what I can,' she said in a sad, resigned way.

Babs was stroking a low, overhanging branch of the yew. Though it was as gnarled and twisted as the old man's hands, it was polished as smooth and shining as a piece of abstract wooden sculpture.

'How do you suppose this branch became so smooth?' she asked.

'From generations of people sitting on it and stroking it, I should think,' I said.

'Isn't it incredible when you think that only a few hundred years ago people hunted deer here and maybe even wild boar.' Which was probably true, for a lovely Tudor house in the area was called the Old Shooting Box. However, a latter-day wild boar in the shape of a noisy, smoking, super-charged Mini-Cooper accelerated up the hill with a great deal of revving and double de-clutching and then an ice-cream van chugged into the car-park to the strains of the first few bars of 'Pop Goes the Weasel' and the illusion was shattered.

'Come on,' I said to Babs, who was still lovingly and absent-mindedly stroking the yew branch, 'leave your worry-tree here and help me catch our wild dog before someone gets trigger-happy.'

We peered through the wrought-iron gates of the Walled Garden. The peace within was uncanny.

'Excuse me,' I approached a family who were picknicking on one of the rustic wooden seats, 'have you seen a large, mostly black dog? She has a white bib and two white front paws and a broken nose.' It was like a game of 'the Parson's Cat'. Each time I described her I thought of a further distinguishing characteristic. They stared up at me and then looked round at each other.

'There was one in here a while back, wasn't there Doreen, but I didn't notice if it had a broken nose. I think it had some white bits on it though.' The man looked towards his wife for corroboration. Suddenly a small child popped up from behind the seat like a jack-in-the-box.

'I saw it!' she cried excitedly. 'It was digging a big hole over there.' She pointed towards one of the densely colourful spring flower-beds. 'Daddy shooed it away because dogs aren't allowed in here off the lead – Daddy says so.' I noticed that there were several uprooted wallflowers wilting on the grass. Feeling very guilty I explained to the upturned faces that Poppy had escaped from our garden which was, I assured them, a veritable Colditz.

'Then how did she escape?' the man asked, grinning.

'She built a glider,' I said seriously, taking up the joke, 'out of newspapers, fire kindling and fish glue.' Everyone laughed and the child offered me a partially sucked gobstopper.

'She didn't stay here long,' Doreen, the wife, told us, 'because a big retriever came in and she ran after him.' So, I thought, we would have done better going to the primary school playing field. As soon as we were out of sight of the family, I threw the sticky, partially consumed sweet into a hedge. A dove scurried towards it, pecked it and then eyed it speculatively, wondering, no doubt, whether to swallow it or hatch it.

'How's the "do" coming along?' Babs asked as we retraced our steps along the riverbank.

'Well, it's all organized on paper. We've hired the marquee and a mobile discothèque called Gadzooks which is run on a part-time basis by two enterprising telephone engineers. If everyone who's promised coughs up, we've got a smashing raffle *and* a tombola and I'm currently working on the interior design. I'm thinking in terms of a forest glade with lots of paper flowers and ivy and mossy banks "whereon the wild thyme blows" . . . only that wretched Miranda Cutler keeps interfering.' Babs cocked an eyebrow and gave me a sideways look. I had kept her abreast of the internecine struggles within the Committee and more particularly with my personal battle with Miranda for creative supremacy. I think from her lofty position she thought it all rather childish. 'She keeps sneaking round the other members behind my back trying to persuade them that her idea for Druid mysticism, you know, Stonehenge, runic signs and hazel twigs, is brilliant where mine is simply run-of-the-mill and derivative. My argument is that Druid mysticism is a bit pointless at the beginning of July just before the schools break up.'

'What are you giving us to eat?'

'Well, we're having eat-ins at the moment.' Babs looked puzzled. 'We're trying out recipes on each other,' I explained. 'It's to be a cold buffet but with a bit of a difference. We've more or less decided on a smashing chicken thing with an orange and tarragon sauce that we've called Oberon's Orange Chicken and we tried Maggie's raspberry *crème brûlée* yesterday – she calls it Titania's Temptation. The Committee's divided on Gwen's gazpacho. I like it but some people think it's a bit peppery. She calls it Bottom's Belch because it gives her terrible wind.'

Babs snorted with laughter. 'I see you're sticking pretty closely to the Shakespearian theme,' she said. 'Are you still set on the Pyramus and Thisbe idea?' I nodded. 'Oh God Polly, it's awful. You may all think your kids are captivating, but no one else does. It's a bit like showing your home movies at the Cannes Film Festival.'

'Actually,' I began sniffily, 'it's coming along rather well and it's *very* funny. You've no idea what Gwen's managing to do with some very unpromising material.'

Babs stopped abruptly and turned to face me. 'Yes, I'm sure it's very funny,' she said impatiently. 'But people won't be laughing at Shakespeare, they'll be laughing at your children making fools of themselves. Is that what you want?'

'That's what *you* think. As a matter of fact they'll be laughing because the kids are good, very good. They're delightfully uninhibited and they have no preconceived ideas about how it *ought* to be done. They think it's very funny, so it is very funny. I think you should reserve judgement until you've seen it.' Babs's mouth snapped shut into a tight pucker of disapproval.

Ma met us at the door of number 68 looking strained and worried. 'Two young people have just called at the door to say that Poppy's lying dead in the middle of the cricket pitch.' I felt weak with horror and Babs slumped against me, her face ashen. 'Alan and Charlie have gone to see to her.' Jane came running out of the living-room and threw her arms round my waist.

'Mummy, Mummy, Poppy's dead!' she cried, sobbing noisily. Lizzie, crying silently as is her fashion, followed slowly and as I slipped a free arm round her, she laid a very wet cheek on my shoulder.

'We don't know for sure do we?' I said briskly. 'So let's wait till Daddy gets back.'

'No,' Jane wailed, 'I just know she's dead. I 'spect someone killed her. I 'spect someone gave her poisoned meat like they did in that film about the dog who protected his family from things.'

'Who'd want to kill Poppy?' Lizzie asked quietly. 'The worst thing she's ever done is eat nine sausage rolls all at once. She only plays with people's rabbits and chickens, she doesn't hurt them.' At this point Jane stopped crying and looked at me with pitiful appeal.

'Can we have a new puppy tomorrow, pleeeease Mummy . . . or a kitten like Julie's?'

'Sometimes, Jane,' I said wonderingly, 'you amaze me.' She looked at me doubtfully. Maybe it was a compliment, maybe it wasn't. At a later date, when Babs reminded me of Jane's callousness, I told her of the morning that our father died. I was five years old and had no understanding of the finality of death. However, I was old enough to be aware that I wasn't behaving as people expected me to behave so I gathered the skirt of my cotton frock up to my eyes and pretended to cry. I didn't feel a great sense of loss at the time but from the way people fussed over me I felt I ought to, if only to satisfy them. When I thought I had cried enough I switched off and asked Ma if I could have my father's silver scout badge with the cockade. I didn't see anything odd in my request; after all, he wouldn't want it any more.

Anyway, our grief was all a bit premature, for Alan returned soon after dragging an exhausted, panting dog behind him at the end of a length of washing line.

'She was sound asleep,' he told us and he sounded as if

he'd hoped she was dead. 'Just crashed out in the middle of the cricket pitch. Luckily they were having tea in the club house or there'd've been trouble.' He glared at me accusingly. 'Anyway, that's another Sunday ruined. Honestly, I don't know how you expect me to go on. I never get a moment's peace in this house.'

I bridled. 'Oh and I suppose you think I bribe the dog to ruin your Sundays. "Go on," I say to her, "get lost for the afternoon and there's four lamb chops in it for you."' It was at this point that Alan threw a book at me. He just picked up the nearest book, a copy of the *Good Food Guide* as it happens, and scored a direct hit with it on the side of my head. The force of the blow knocked me sideways, my platform shoe (they were all the rage at the time) turned under my weight as I tried to regain my balance and I fell heavily on my right knee. Tears of humiliation and pain rolled unchecked down my scarlet cheeks. For once, the family Greek chorus was struck dumb.

Alan was the first to recover. He marched towards me with his hand extended. I thought he intended to help me up, but it was his intention only to recover his precious *Good Food Guide*. Aiming a passing kick at my prostrate backside he stormed out of the house and shortly afterwards we heard the car racing down the drive, churning up the gravel as it turned into the High Street.

I suppose if it had happened in a television sit-com, the audience would have screamed with mirth and indeed, in later years, when I recounted the episode at countless dinner parties, I had my audience falling off their chairs and rolling about on the floor – well, it matured with telling. But at the time it didn't seem very funny. I was shocked and bewildered, as indeed were Babs and Ma, by the uncalled-for viciousness of the attack. Over the years I have been far more provocative to less effect. In fact I am normally the one to get physical and I have been known to stalk him round the house with a breadknife in one hand a cut-throat razor in the other.

One either side of me, Babs and Ma heaved me upright and deposited me unceremoniously upon my old Recliner chair, which lurched lop-sidedly to the left as a castor which had been loose for some time finally gave in and spun wildly across the floor into a dark corner. The children hovered round me anxiously, stroking and patting me hesitantly.

'Never mind, Mummy . . . never mind,' they muttered in turn, embarrassment making them shy and uncomfortable. 'Daddy didn't mean it . . . he was angry with the dog really . . .'

'Are you and Daddy going to stay married?' Jane finally asked when she felt I was calm enough to face facts. 'Because if you're not, who will I live with?' Her friend Lucy lived with her mother and saw her father every other weekend. Lucy was well adjusted to the arrangement and enthralled Jane with lurid stories of her two homes and her various permutations of brothers and sisters. At school it gave Lucy added status.

'Don't be silly Jane.' I tried to sound light-hearted. 'Daddy simply lost his temper with the dog and took it out on me because I was the nearest.'

'I was nearer to Daddy than you.'

'Yes, but I'm bigger and stronger than you. Anyway, you know how you throw things at Charlie when you get cross with him,' she nodded doubtfully, 'well, it was just like that. Nothing to worry about. Daddy'll just drive around until he cools down and then he'll come back in time for supper.' Lizzie and Charlie stared at me in mute disbelief. They knew that something quite extraordinary had happened, something that had never happened before, and I could think of nothing to say to them that they would believe and would make them feel better.

'Daddy's very tired and over-worked at the moment,' I pleaded for understanding from those two stone faces.

'He hurt you, Mum,' Charlie mumbled, red-faced. 'He kicked you, I saw him do it.'

'Yes, it was just like the kick you gave Jane the other day

when you really wanted to kick me.' Charlie looked blank. 'You remember, when I took Jane to her dancing class and you wanted to go swimming.'

'I didn't want to kick you.' He looked puzzled. 'I wanted to kick Jane – and I did.'

I have always made the mistake of imagining that children understand far more about psychology than they actually do. I used to think that Lizzie really enjoyed listening to me pontificate on the workings of the human psyche – what motivated people to behave in this or that manner and how to handle the failings of others. Quite recently she told me that most of what I said passed way over her head and the fixed look on her face that I had taken for one of intelligent interest was, in fact, one of polite boredom. She said that she knew I liked to talk about such things so she let me. That particular conversation was quite an eye-opener, I can tell you. Jane, less patient than Lizzie, informed me very early on that she didn't like having 'deep, meaningful chats' with me and that she would rather experience everything for herself and learn by her own mistakes – or words to that effect. I admit I was amazed that she didn't want to take advantage of all my hard-earned wisdom.

'I know you *think* you wanted to kick Jane, darling, but the truth is you were cross with me because I wouldn't take you swimming.'

'I kicked the person I wanted to kick,' Charlie insisted. I shrugged and smiled tolerantly. I can't bear people who shrug and smile tolerantly bang in the middle of an argument, it's so frustrating.

Suddenly Ma, who had been absent-mindedly watching Gladys investigate a huge black beetle that was lying on its back with its legs waving uselessly in the air, turned towards us and clapped her hands briskly. 'Come on you three,' she cried with the sort of false brightness one uses with children in situations such as this, 'let's go round to Mr Khan's before he closes and buy some ice-cream.' I caught her eye and hoped she could see how grateful I felt. The Pakistani family

Khan (an elderly man, his two sons and their wives and his three grandchildren) owned a small corner shop and sub post-office that remained open every day of the week from 8 a.m. until 8 p.m., 365 days of the year.

Jane, who had been slowly insinuating herself on to my lap, slid off, and forgetting the past half-hour, threw herself ecstatically at her grandmother.

'Can I have a Ninety-Nine pleeease Granny, and some Bombay mix and a lickolish chew and can I have some Bendy straws like Julie's?' Ma hugged her affectionately. At certain times Jane's childish insensitivity was a welcome bonus.

'I said we'd buy some ices,' she laughed. 'I didn't say we'd do the weekly shop. Come on you two,' she chivvied, 'one of you fetch Gladys's lead.'

'I want an ice lolly and I'm going on my bike the long way and I'll *still* race you.' Charlie pulled a face at Jane, who stuck her tongue out and blew a very loud raspberry. Reluctantly Lizzie trailed out behind the others. She was old enough to know that Ma was attempting to divert their attention from the recent fracas.

'Will you be all right, Mum?' she asked, still blinking back the tears.

Awkwardly, because my knee was rather painful, I got out of the chair. ''Course I'm all right, my little fleurtleberry. Look!' I did a funny lop-sided dance round the room which, on reflection, must have been reminiscent of the Hunchback of Notre-Dame though I intended to reassure Lizzie that there were no bones broken and that I was full of bounce and vigour. She looked at Babs and shook her head pessimistically.

'That blow on the head's curdled her brains,' she said, then she shouted after Ma, 'Wait for me Granny, we've got some bottles to take back.'

Babs made a pot of tea and brought a cup in to me. She sat down heavily on the sofa, slopping some of hers into the saucer.

'Blast!' she said, carefully tipping it back into the cup, 'now I'll get drops down my front.' For a while we sat silently sipping, then she said, 'Do you want to talk to me about it?' I shook my head. Actually I suppose I did want to talk to someone about it, but not to Babs. Like Ma, she tended to make assumptions about me and my problems based on the frightful teenager she knew best. The one who tormented her, who was self-centred, lazy and manipulative and tried to steal her boyfriends just for the hell of it. I knew I had changed a great deal since those days even if she didn't. Not allowing people to change and mature is a common failing in some of the best regulated families. I have trouble accepting this with my own children. I think I know them better than they know themselves, but I only know the face they choose to turn towards me and because they know that I will continue to love them come what may, that face is not always particularly attractive. But as Ma used to say, 'If you can't let your hair down in your own home, where can you let it down?'

'Do you want to talk to *someone* about it?'

'Mmm.'

'Then why don't you talk to one of those marriage guidance chums of yours?'

'No,' I said emphatically.

'Why ever not – if you believe in the process?'

I won't say it hadn't occurred to me. But something that I can't adequately explain stopped me. I guess I'm the same as everyone else when it comes to admitting that I can't cope with my own problems. Too damn proud. I admit I have problems readily enough, I just don't admit that I can't solve them for myself.

'I do believe in the process,' I assured Babs. 'I just don't have the sort of marital problem that needs *that* sort of help.' It's like being an alcoholic, I thought. No one can help me unless I admit I've got a problem. 'Anyway, I'm not even sure I've got a marital problem.'

'Pshaw!' Babs exploded. 'Your normally loving husband

treats you and the children like unwelcome strangers, he throws a book at you with precious little provocation, kicks your bum for good measure, takes off like a bat out of hell and you're not sure if you have a marital problem? Really, Polly, you, of all people,' and she chuckled as she considered the funny joke (an old chestnut as it happens) of the marriage guidance counsellor with a marriage problem, though I don't find the idea any more absurd than a doctor with flu. Then of course there's the other one of a counsellor running off with her client. Everyone knows someone who knows someone who knows a marriage guidance counsellor who's done that. I'm always being baited with that one at dinner parties.

'Yes, I do know how it must look to you, Babs,' I said, 'but it isn't quite as it appears. Believe it or not, most marriages go through bad patches. In fact, so do most relationships of any duration. I'll tell you, if you and I were married, we'd have been divorced years ago.'

'Then it's just as well we decided against it,' she replied with a giggle and even I had to smile. 'But seriously, though,' she continued, 'you're just going to ignore the problem, and hope it goes away?'

Is Babs right? I wondered. Is that what I'm doing? I thought it probably was. She looked at her watch. 'Crumbs! Look at the time! I've brought a lot of work home this weekend too.' She picked up the two tea-cups and scurried off into the kitchen calling over her shoulder, 'Come on, we'd better get it cleared up in here before Ma gets back or she'll think we've been having fun.'

'The trouble with you, Polly,' Babs began again as she struggled into my rubber gloves. 'Damn it, you've got a hole in these. You're the sort of woman who always has a hole in her rubber gloves, do you know that?'

'Well, if that's the only trouble with me, I suppose I should be thankful.'

Babs tutted impatiently. 'Don't be infantile Polly. No, the trouble with you is that you find it difficult to share Alan's anxieties with him and he knows it. That's why he doesn't tell you things that he thinks will make you anxious. You over-react and get yourself into a terrible state.'

'Did you work that out all by yourself, or did he tell you?' Babs scratched behind her ear, rubbed the end of her nose, hoicked a bra strap back into position and sighed.

'As a matter of fact, he did,' she admitted with apparent reluctance, but I wasn't sure if I believed her. Babs, like a lot of us, myself included, tends to reinforce her arguments by putting words into other people's mouths. I had a friend once who used to impart home truths to her husband through my mouth. 'Polly thinks . . .' she would begin, and out would pop this searing judgement about some aspect of his behaviour towards her and his family. Eventually, fed up to the teeth, I suppose, with being told what a frightful chap I thought he was, he crossed over the road and confronted me on my own doorstep in the middle of the night.

'I wish you'd stop trying to influence my wife against me!' he shouted angrily, while I stood, astonished by his outburst, clutching my dressing-gown about me the other side of the threshold he refused to cross. 'I will hold you entirely responsible if she leaves me,' which she did. I expect he blames me to this day. 'If it hadn't been for that dreadful woman,' I can almost hear him say, 'Gina and I would still be together.' I don't remember ever having passed a critical judgement on Harold. In fact I rather liked him and I considered that he put up with a good deal from his lazy, self-centred wife and their five undisciplined children.

'When did Alan tell you this?' I asked suspiciously.

'Oh, ages ago,' Babs replied airily. 'When he was having all those nasty rows with his father that you didn't know about until they stopped speaking to each other.' I was more than ready to feel betrayed, but Alan was not the confiding type so I remained sceptical. I scowled and sniffed disbelievingly just as Ma came bustling through the door followed by Jane, who was clutching an enormous bag of goodies and looking very pleased with herself.

'The other two are coming home through the meadow,' Ma explained. 'Charlie muttered something about baby frogs under the bridge. Now, I think it's time for a cuppa, don't you?'

Babs glanced at me. 'I've got to be getting back, sorry Ma. I've got a lot of work to do.'

'Oh, just stay for a cup of tea, Babs darling,' Ma pleaded, 'I've not seen anything of you.' But Babs was insistent.

'No Ma, really, I've got to go.'

Ma gave a resigned shrug. 'Oh well, I know how busy you are, dear.' She gave Babs a hug and told her to drive carefully. Her instruction to drive carefully was routine, a talisman if you like, and I know that if she forgot she worried until she knew we had arrived safely at our destination.

I saw Babs out to her car. She opened the driver's window and poked her head out.

'Now listen love, I'm worried about you,' she said very quietly so that Ma, who was standing in the doorway waiting to wave goodbye, couldn't hear. 'I think you ought to talk to someone, so why don't you talk to Gwen. You tell her everything else, so why don't you tell her about this.' I nodded because I had been thinking along those lines myself.

'I think I probably will – if she's got the time to listen. She's been very elusive recently what with her work and the great production.'

Babs shot off in a cloud of exhaust and gravel dust and Ma drew in her breath sharply as she waited for the screech of brakes. When it didn't happen she blew it out with relief.

'Well, we'll have a cuppa anyway,' she said. Jane was watching television so she drew me into the kitchen and sat me down. 'Now Polly, I want to know what this is all about,' she said briskly as she plugged in the kettle. 'It's not good for the children you know, all this violence and shouting.'

'It's not particularly good for me either,' I said sourly.

'Your father and I,' she went on as though I hadn't spoken,

'made it a rule never to disagree in front of you both.' I felt the exasperation building up.

'Let's face it, Ma, you didn't have much of a chance. He was dead by the time I was five.'

'Don't be impertinent,' she snapped and inwardly I smiled. 'Sorry,' I said humbly, 'but look, Ma, let's just not talk about it because we're bound to come to blows. Your way of dealing with feelings just isn't the same as mine.'

Ma's face stiffened. 'Right then, Polly, if that's how you feel, I don't think I'll bother with that cup of tea.' She was on the brink of a sulk. I hoped it wouldn't be a prolonged one because I wasn't feeling in the mood for appeasement and she was due to baby-sit for us the following Thursday.

'Gladys!' she called huffily, 'come on sweetie, it's time for us to go home.' Gladys skidded joyfully across the hall floor and was scooped up and thrust under Ma's arm like a rolled-up swimming towel, then Ma poked her head round the living-room door and bade telly-watching Jane a curt goodbye. Unfortunately her sulks tended to cover everyone even vaguely connected with the person with whom she was displeased.

'I'll give you a lift home,' I offered, kicking myself as she shook her head triumphantly and said,

'No thank you, Polly. I'd rather walk. Oh, and by the way, I'm not sure if I can baby-sit next Thursday after all.' Alan and I intended to have a quiet supper at a local Greek restaurant before he left for the Far East on Friday. 'Evelyn' (Mrs Blackmore) 'has asked me to go on the W.I. theatre outing with her.' I knew Ma had already refused the invitation, so I would just have to sit out her bluff.

'Oh, all right,' I replied lightly, 'I'll make other arrangements.' I wouldn't, of course – Ma would be terribly hurt if I did.

'Goodbye then Polly.' She gave me a cold peck on the cheek. 'And say goodbye to Alan for me – if he returns. I'm not likely to see him again before he leaves.' She knew she would because she knew she would be baby-sitting next Thursday.

'Okay, I'll do that. Bye Ma,' I said walking to the door behind her. Suddenly she turned and stared up into my face intently.

'You be careful, Polly,' she warned. 'You've got a good man there,' and off she went – trip trip trip – small, quick, angry steps down the path and out of the gate without a backward glance.

With the children in bed and the house silent and empty, I gave way to the flood of feelings that had been threatening since Alan stormed out of the house. It is very difficult to remain calm and understanding in the face of another's wrath and frustration, especially when you don't know why they should be feeling that way. If I had known what was troubling him I'm sure I would have felt compassion for him and less self-pity. As it was, I had to pretend the compassion and hide my self-pity for the sake of the rest of the family.

Naturally I was anxious and bitterly hurt, but more than that, I was very, very angry. How dare he humiliate me so thoroughly in front of the children. How dare he frighten them so. How dare he expose our secret troubles to Ma and Babs. After a rage of tears in the back garden where no one could see or hear my sobs and sniffs, and if they did they might think it was one of my hay-fever attacks, I roamed restlessly round the house trying to find something to do that would absorb my jitterbugging concentration. I settled in front of the television only to find that it was showing an evening of sit-com repeats on all channels. I picked up a book but kept re-reading the same paragraph as my mind wandered off course and had to be herded back. It was a boring book anyway and didn't deserve the effort.

Finally I settled down at the kitchen table to do some work on my neglected novel. Something about it had been worrying me for some time and as I sat staring at the exercise book on the top of the pile, I knew what it was. I selected a red felt pen from my roll-top pencil box and ruthlessly scored out the title *Love Walked Right In* and replaced it with *Love Walked Right Out*. Immediately I felt better. I underlined it several times and added a line of exclamation marks for good measure, then I leafed forward to my most recent work.

Caro, having made a superhuman effort to restore her failing marriage, had finally reached the end of her tether with Arthur, who seemed to have gone through a worrying metamorphosis from a wise, understanding, hard-working man who loved Caro enough to care about her unhappiness and was concerned for the state of their marriage into an indifferent, uncaring workaholic who had just announced that they would not be having a summer holiday that year owing to pressure of work. I didn't quite understand why this had happened to Arthur, but somehow the plot seemed to be leading me by the nose and no matter how hard I tried to return to this poor man some of his earlier strengths, he continued on his path to perdition. I picked up my pencil and sat poised for Caro's reaction to his latest iniquity.

'"Right," Caro replied with quiet dignity . . .' The trouble with Caro, I thought, is that she reacts to absolutely everything with quiet dignity. It's time she had a flaming row with Arthur, or told him a few home truths. So, '"Right," Caro replied with icy calm . . .' which wasn't much better than 'quiet dignity', but at least we were heading in the right direction. '"Then I shall simply go on holiday on my own." Arthur shrugged absently without looking up from his computer read-outs and said, "What about the children?"' The trouble was that I kept forgetting that Caro and Arthur had two children and he was quite right to remind me. What can I do with the children? I thought. I can't leave them at home with Arthur, and my plot is ruined if they have to tag along with Caro. Then I had a sudden brainwave.

'"You know very well that my parents are taking them to

North Wales," Caro retorted angrily, "just so that we can go away on our own."

'"Oh yes, so they are," Arthur said. "Well, that'll be nice for you then." Caro was shocked by the indifference of his reply.' So was I for that matter and I decided to punish Arthur there and then.

'"And if I go away on my own," Caro continued remorselessly, "I will have to decide what to do after that." This time Arthur looked up.

'"What do you mean by that cryptic remark?" he asked, raising his eyebrow in a way that infuriated Caro.

'"I mean, I will have to decide whether to stay with you or leave you." There, Caro thought with amazement, I've said it. It's out at last. She found she felt the sort of relief that she had felt when her much-loved father died after suffering for years from a progressively debilitating disease.' Oh Lord, I thought, her father can't have died yet because I've just said that he's taking the children to North Wales. 'Arthur frowned,' I wrote, 'as though he hadn't quite understood her and said . . .'

Exactly what would Arthur say in the circumstances? I wondered. Early Arthur would have hidden his pain beneath his concern for Caro's well-being. He would have understood her restless boredom and would have suggested an Aegean cruise as a palliative. He would have been a totally supportive figure of strength; a port in a storm, and so on. This new emerging Arthur was an unknown quantity. I wasn't sure if he would explode with rage, howl with pain or simply turn on the telly for the Nine O'Clock News. Arthur, I decided, needed a great deal more thought. I would have to decide what was happening to Arthur and why. And then there was Caro, making pronouncements already about leaving him and she hadn't even contacted Marriage Guidance. She was the sort of woman who would go to Marriage Guidance, I was sure of that. But I'd had enough of the Stansburys' muddle for one evening, and anyway, I had a muddle of my own to think about.

I was packing away my author's kit when I heard the unmistakable slither of a guilty car tiptoeing into a garage. This was followed by the slickety-click of a front door being opened and closed by a person who wished to remain undetected and then I heard the soft tread of Alan's feet on the stairs. I threw open the kitchen door and called out, 'Hello?' in the manner of a woman who suspects an intruder.

'Oh, hello,' Alan replied. 'I thought you'd be in bed.' He didn't really because he knew I wouldn't go to bed and leave all the lights on. I simulated surprise.

'I wasn't expecting you back tonight,' I lied.

'So, who *were* you expecting,' he asked with an ironic smile, 'with the porch light left on?' Slowly he came back downstairs. His reluctance to confront me was something almost palpable, like the taste in the air before an electric storm. 'What have you been doing?' he asked, eyeing the mound of exercise books on the table.

'Working on my *magnum opus*,' I replied, gathering up the books and slipping them into my private drawer. 'Only I don't think I'm in the right frame of mind because everyone's behaving very badly.' Alan's face assumed a defensive expression. 'I'm not talking about you – I mean the characters in my book.' He relaxed a little. 'Have you had any supper?' I asked. He shook his head.

'I'm not hungry – thanks.'

'Don't you even want your Horlicks?' He hesitated. 'I'll make it for you . . . if you like.'

'I don't think I need it tonight – I'm very tired – but thanks anyway.' His mouth began working in the way it does when he's thinking about saying something. It doesn't mean that he will necessarily say it, just that he is thinking about saying it.

'Where've you been?' I asked, just to keep him there.

'Oh, driving about, you know. I had a pint with Mike at the King's.'

'I hope you didn't unburden your soul to him. I'd hate

Gwen to know what's up with you before I do.' He sighed deeply and raised his eyes to heaven.

'No, I didn't unburden my soul. We talked about cars mostly if you want to know. Look, Pol,' he began suddenly in a changed voice, 'I'm sorry about – you know – everything. I don't know what got into me. I just saw red and couldn't control myself. But you must admit, you were – all of you, I mean – being absolutely bloody. All that ridiculous bickering and that frightful lunch, and then Poppy taking off. Any other chap would've done the same.' I looked doubtful.

'I think that would depend on his state of mind at the time,' I said.

'It was just the straw that broke the camel's back.'

'Well, that would be fine,' I said drily, 'if only I knew what other burdens the camel was carrying on his back.' Alan's face stiffened. 'Look,' I continued, advancing upon him round the table, 'things aren't all that good between us at the moment. I *know* something's troubling you.' He began to shake his head. 'Don't deny it – I'm not a fool. But if you don't want to, or can't, tell me, just reassure me that it has nothing to do with me.' I put my hands on his shoulders and looked up into his face intently. 'If it's something I've done, or if you're just fed up with me, I have a right to know.' He pulled away from me irritably and started up the stairs again. Then he stopped and turned round.

'All right Polly, I'll tell you this,' he began and my heart leapt. 'I do have some problems that I can't talk to anyone about – not even you – yet. But when everything's sorted out, I promise you'll be the first to know . . . okay?'

'After Sheila Rosen, no doubt,' I mumbled bitterly and then could have bitten off my tongue. 'Sorry . . . sorry,' I cried desperately as his face tightened into an angry mask. 'I didn't mean that. I'm sure you'll tell me all, when you're ready.' But he had turned from me and the moment for reconciliation was past. It made me rather regret having been so conciliatory and apologetic.

Now my head was pounding, so I made myself a cup of tea and took a horse's dose of Veganin. When I eventually turned in, Alan was, or was pretending to be, asleep. I screwed up my pillow in such a way that it supported my neck and eased the tension and surprisingly enough, I was asleep before I had finished the Lord's Prayer.

Chapter Nine

The supermarket trolley was getting depressingly full even though I had worked out that it would be one of those rare, happy weeks when I wouldn't need to buy very much. With Alan away in the Far East and Charlie camping in the Bray boys' treehouse for a day or two, I had felt guardedly optimistic and on the strength of that I had bought myself a badly-needed pair of Dr Scholl's. I hadn't worn them yet and I wondered if they would take them back.

'Mum,' Lizzie said plaintively as I walked determinedly past the Toiletries section. 'I need some Thingies,' the euphemism used in our house for sanitary towels, 'some shampoo and a can of spray deodorant.'

'But I bought you deodorant only last week,' I protested.

'No, it was the week before.'

'All the same.' I gave her a puzzled look. 'Are you using it to kill flies or something? No, not that one,' I commanded as she reached for the largest and most expensive brand.

'But it smells nicer. The other stuff smells like lavatory cleanser and it stings.'

In terms of capital outlay it was undoubtedly cheaper to shop on my own, but over the years a tradition had developed. Every Thursday afternoon, having made suitable arrangements for the other two, who hated shopping unless it was to buy them something, I would pick Lizzie up from school, have a quick cup of tea and a sticky bun at Carlotta's – a quick fix, Lizzie maintained, to keep her from starving to death – and then, having parked in the store's own underground car-park, we would lug our precious, very tough cardboard boxes up into the store and commence the Weekly Shop. Lizzie always moaned and groaned, but she was mortally offended if I didn't take her and from my point of view she was a great help.

'Why don't you try a roll-on? They're much cheaper and this one smells very nice.' I held the little container up to her nose. She pulled a wry face.

'Yuck. It smells like dying flowers, and I don't like roll-ons anyway, they're too wet and slimy.' She grinned ingratiatingly and popped the expensive spray into the trolley.

An electronic chime sounded over the Tannoy and a muffled voice interrupted the canned rendering of a Beatles classic. It sounded like 'Will Staff Nurse Sebag see the Floor Manager' and I used to think that shoppers were in constant need of medical attention and that Staff Nurse Sebag must be rushed off her feet, but I was eventually put straight by Eileen on the check-out who told me that it was 'Will first staff tea-breaks leave the floor now.'

'Polly! Polly!' My name reverberated round the freezer cabinet into which I was upended. Right at the bottom I could see the last packet of chicken livers, but I couldn't quite reach it. Lizzie gave me a dig in the buttocks.

'Mum, I'll get the chicken livers, you talk to Mrs Baines.'

In common with most youngsters, Lizzie didn't like the Awful B. 'She always talks to me as though I'm rather slow and deaf,' she used to complain. 'And I know she disapproves of me.' I had explained that B's apparent disapproval was, in fact, a form of envy. 'It's because you're pretty and bright, and Honour,' B's only child, conceived long after the Baineses had given up hope and often mistaken for their granddaughter, 'is neither.' 'There's nothing wrong with Honour,' Lizzie would argue, 'that isn't caused by having Mrs Baines as a mother.' And indeed, a child would have to be very strong and forceful to resist B's relentlessly single-minded approach to child-rearing. If Honour had ever had any spirit, it had been bullied out of her, and her rather eccentric Angela Brazil appearance and manner were largely due to her mother's admiration of the pre-war public school system. When Honour did eventually rebel, it was absolute and the last I heard of her she was living in a lesbian squat in Islington.

'Listen Polly!' B came bearing down on me at great speed pushing a loaded trolley ahead of her like a battering ram. 'Sorry!' she brayed as she swept past a woman who had been forced to step smartly out of her path. 'But you were in my way!'

'Now listen Polly!' she cried, pinning me against the meat freezer. 'All the tickets are sold but I still have a lot of people who want to come. So I thought we'd issue, say, two or three dozen more tickets. What do you think?'

'But our catering's stretched to the limit with the existing two hundred ticket holders. Apart from that we'd need a bigger marquee and Maggie's garden just won't take it, unless we cut down that row of silver birches.' I was joking of course, but I could see, from the dangerous gleam that came into B's eye, that from her point of view the idea had its merits. 'No, B, don't even *think* it,' I warned with a chuckle.

In order to persuade B back into the fold after that disgraceful episode at Hannah's, we gave her rather more power than was prudent. So that now, as well as being Secretary and Person in Charge of Ticket Sales, she was also Vice-Chairperson in charge of Co-ordination. We had visualized this position as a sort of Minister Without Portfolio, but in effect, it gave B a finger in every pie. It was a decision we had come to regret.

'Excuse me but do you think you could move along a bit?' The speaker was a small, scruffy woman with the face of an exhausted potato under an amazing mop of golden curls. A pasty-faced small boy sucking noisily at a stick of liquorice was clinging to her skirt. I smiled apologetically and tried to shift, only B appeared not to have heard and continued to argue her point in a loud voice.

'I'm sorry, but I refuse to turn away paying customers,'

she bellowed, 'so we'll just have to organize an annexe or something.' I pushed against B's trolley quite forcibly.

'Move along a bit, B, this lady wants to get to the freezer.'

'What?' She glanced from me to the exhausted potato. 'Oh, for heaven's sake,' she said impatiently as though the poor woman had no right to be where she was, but she moved along anyway and with a timid smile at me the little woman began sorting wearily through the packs of frozen New Zealand lamb.

'We can't have an annexe, B, because no one will want to be in it. Ask yourself, would you want to be separated from the mainstream?'

'Well then, it'll just have to be a squash because I'm not turning people away.' I shrugged and wondered what the others would have to say about it. 'Well, I must be off – things to do.' Then she turned to Lizzie and frowned slightly. 'By the way, my dear, I've been meaning to ask you – what *have* you done to your hair? I liked it so much better short, it flattered your little round face.' Lizzie shifted from one foot to the other and frankly scowled. 'Well never mind, I suppose it's the fashion these days, but it gets so lank and dirty don't you think and you do have to be so careful about nits . . .' She beamed at Lizzie with all the charm and humour of a basking shark, patted her maternally on the shoulder and continued on her way.

'Whew!' Lizzie gasped as though she had been holding her breath for five minutes and she glared malevolently at B's broad, square back as it joined one of the check-out queues. 'One day, when I don't have to be polite to the Awful Bs of this world I'll . . .' Just what she would do to the Awful Bs of this world was left open to conjecture because at that point the exhausted potato tapped me hesitantly on the arm.

'I thought it was you, Mrs Graham,' she whispered. The face was, I'll admit, slightly familiar, and I tried to put it into context. 'It's Glynis . . . you remember, Glynis Shipwrick?' She peered at me anxiously.

'Oh, Glynis, I'm sorry, I didn't recognize you. You've changed your hair or something . . .'

Glynis patted her mass of gleaming curls self-consciously. 'It's a wig,' she whispered. 'You see, all my hair come out, well, most of it anyway. The doctor said it was shock but he says it'll grow back again . . .'

I thought of the last time I had seen Glynis. She had been glowing with happiness and, at her insistence, it was to be our last session together. The errant Barry had returned, contrite, and everything was all right, so Glynis had claimed. I had suggested mildly that it might be a good idea if I continued to see her for a bit longer just in case, but she had been adamant.

'It'd just be a waste of your time, Mrs Graham,' she had told me, 'cos everything's fine,' and she didn't want to tempt Providence, I understood that. If I thought there was still something wrong with her marriage, she didn't want to know about it.

'And what about the Other Woman?' I had ventured to ask.

'Barry says it's all over between them. He says it was just a flash in the pan.' She had giggled, I remembered. 'Isn't it a good thing I didn't cancel our holiday?' Eagerly, needing my approval, she told me how Barry had changed. 'And I've changed too,' she added hastily, a sop maybe, for what she might have thought my injured vanity. As she got up to leave she had presented me with a gift-wrapped package. 'Just a small token – you know – just to say thank you an' that,' and a small, sealed envelope. 'I wish it could be more.' There was a five pound note in the envelope to swell the funds of the Marriage Guidance Council. The package contained a box of crystallized fruits and a small bottle of Tweed scent. I was very touched.

'He's left me again you know,' she now said confidingly. 'I rang your office for another appointment but they said I'd have to wait cos you was all booked up.' Lizzie, embarrassed, stood back from us waiting patiently. I handed her my shopping list.

'Nip round, love,' I told her, 'and find what you can.' She took off looking very relieved.

'And are you still waiting?' I asked. Glynis nodded. 'Well, I should have a gap soon.' It sounded so inadequate. 'Look, I'll speak to our appointments secretary and ask her to slip you in somewhere. I'll tell her to drop you a line during the week.'

'He went back to Her, you know,' she began mournfully.

'Yes, well look –' I tried to interrupt. Though I didn't like to sound churlish, the middle of a crowded supermarket was not an ideal venue for a counselling session.

'She's pregnant see, and she says it's his,' she continued regardless. Her eyes narrowed and her mouth puckered as though she was sucking on a lemon. 'But from what I hear about her, it could be anybody's. My friend Shirl – you remember, Stan's wife – he's Barry's friend – well, she says that this woman's been stringing along another bloke but he wouldn't marry her so she come after my Barry again. But I'm not having him back this time.'

'No . . . no . . . quite . . .'

'I went an' saw her an' I told her, I said, "You needn't think I'll take him off your hands again when you're fed up with him cos I won't, see." I told her, I said, "You're breaking up a happy marriage an' you needn't think there'll be anything left for you an' your nipper after I've finished with him cos he's got to look after me an' our Jason."' Glynis paused to take in air. Her grey-white face was mottled with dull purple splodges and her pale, protuberant eyes were darting hither and thither excitedly.

'Well, of course, this is all something –' I began, eager to bring the flow of confidences to an end.

'An' then I took an overdose didn't I – at me Mum's it was, an' this brought on her angina. The doctor called it a cry for help an' he gave me some pills but they made me into a zombie so I stopped taking them, an' then me hair started falling out – bunged up the sink there was so much of it –

so me Dad went out an' bought me this wig.' She pulled at it hard as though it were a hat so that it came to rest just above her eyebrows. 'Feels as though it's coming off all the time,' she said irritably. 'I think it's a size too small. Anyway I've been to see a solicitor an' he's waiting for something about legal aid . . . I don't really understand all about that.'

'No, well . . .' Shoppers were milling about us and I was aware that we were getting a few curious glances.

'Barry wants me to divorce him, but I don't see why I should make it easy for him, so I'm thinking about a legal separation. What do you think?' She looked up at me expectantly.

'Well I . . . I think it would be very wise to wait until . . . Look, when you come and see me again, which could be very soon,' I added hastily as her face dropped, 'we'll talk about it properly.'

'Look, I don't see any point in coming to see you again really because there's nothing you can do now.' Her voice was rising and people were beginning to steer a wide course round us. 'If you could just tell me what you think about a legal separation . . .'

'I don't have any thoughts one way or the other.' There was a hint of desperation in my voice. 'And if I did, I can't just tell you what to do standing here by the meat freezer in a supermarket. It has to be your own decision, you know that, but if you don't want to come and see me again all I can advise you to do is trust your instincts. Do whatever feels right and if you have any doubts whatsoever, don't. Do whatever makes you feel most at peace with yourself and whatever you feel is truly the best thing for Jason. Remember, for his future development, he needs to feel loved by his father and you did tell me that Barry was a loving father whatever else he may have been.' The small boy, who had remained unusually passive during our interchange, perked up at the sound of his name and without warning suddenly pulled away from his mother and darted off in the direction of the confectionery shelves.

'Jason!' Glynis shrieked. 'You come back 'ere.' The child hesitated, looking from his mother to the tempting display of sweeties. 'Don't you touch 'em, do you 'ear,' she cried threateningly, 'or I'll tan the 'ide off of yer!' Out of the corner of my eye I saw Gwen standing in the delicatessen queue. She was watching me with amusement as I hovered uncertainly between Glynis and Jason, who was sidling slowly further and further towards the sweet display, watching his mother all the time with wide, blank eyes as though daring her to carry out her threat, here, in public, in front of a potentially sympathetic audience. Several women were chuckling affectionately as they watched the small boy behaving in a manner typical of small boys. 'Come 'ere you!' Glynis growled menacingly. Then she turned towards me and said in a normal voice, 'Sorry, Mrs Graham, but he's getting to be a proper handful.' I nodded understandingly.

Meanwhile Lizzie, who had temporarily abandoned the trolley, was creeping up behind the child and just as his small hand went out to grab a packet of three chocolate bars, she swept him up into the air and deposited him, kicking and struggling, in front of his mother. We were both unprepared for the swift, sharp blow she delivered to his head with the flat of her hand. The force of the blow jerked him off his feet and he began to scream with rage, pain and ruffled dignity. Glynis didn't seem the least abashed. She simply hooked her hand under one of his chubby little arms and yanked him unceremoniously to his feet. Clearly such hostilities were commonplace between the two of them, for he was immediately pacified with half a Twix Bar that Glynis had to hand.

'He's got to learn,' she said to me by way of explanation. Just what it was he was learning was not immediately obvious. However I felt a sneaking admiration for her sublime indifference to the opinion of others. Many were the times I felt like clouting my offspring in public but had resisted the temptation for fear of what people would think of me. Of course, I always promised myself, and them, that I would deal with the misdemeanour once we got home, but usually I forgot.

An elderly woman passing by with a friend remarked loudly, 'Poor little chap,' and looked accusingly at us.

'Mind your own business,' Glynis said tartly. The woman sniffed and tutted and passed on, muttering to her friend.

Quickly promising Glynis that someone from the office would contact her within the week, while ignoring her repeated protest that further counselling would achieve nothing, I retreated to the relative calm of the delicatessen queue. I was sure I could feel Glynis's doleful eyes boring into my back, but when I looked round she had disappeared.

'What was all that about?' Gwen asked as she nobly sacrificed her place near the head of the queue to join me at the back. I shrugged and told her that Glynis was a woman I knew. Gwen raised an incredulous eyebrow. 'You've got some odd friends, if I may say so.'

'Hmmm, I know,' I agreed thoughtfully, thereby assuring Glynis Shipwrick's anonymity. But the small, unpleasant scene had disturbed me. For some reason I felt responsible for the unhappy change to her fortunes. If I had been more insistent back in the spring about continuing to see her; if I had expressed my doubts more forcefully at the time . . .

'Haven't seen you for ages,' Gwen said casually.

'No, well, we've both been busy. I have tried to phone you several times.' I looked round for Lizzie. She was talking animatedly to a school friend by the fruit and vegetables. 'Actually, I'm badly in need of a friendly ear,' I confided quietly.

Gwen's face registered concern. 'Will I do?' I grinned in relief. 'Well, I must admit I have noticed you've been a bit distant recently, but to tell you the truth, I thought you were a bit off me.'

'Off you? Why should I be off you?'

'Well,' Gwen began with clear reluctance, 'I thought you might be suffering just a teeny-weeny bit from green eyes . . .'

'You mean, you think I envy you for some reason?' Gwen nodded. 'Is there some reason *why* I should be envying you?' I asked suspiciously.

'Well, I suppose I got the feeling that you would like to have produced *Pyramus and Thisbe*, and then there's Eddie...'

'What about Eddie?' I suppose I had registered his absence from the scene but I had assumed that he was studying.

'Well, nothing really, it's just that he's helping me with the production and knowing how you've always regarded him as your property...' She trailed off leaving several things unsaid.

'Good Lord, Gwen,' I remonstrated, 'I envy you a lot of things but *Pyramus and Thisbe* isn't one of them and I'm very pleased that you've got Eddie to help you with the production, you certainly need it.' But having said that, I did feel peculiarly betrayed by his secretive decamp. It was the sort of thing he usually discussed with me first. I wondered why my children hadn't mentioned his presence at rehearsals and supposed that it had something to do with Charlie's lack of enthusiasm for French coaching during the long summer holiday.

'You're right, I do.' Gwen looked relieved. 'So when he offered – said it would be good teaching practice – I accepted. Anyway,' she began on a new note, 'why don't you come over on Saturday after rehearsals and have some lunch with us. You can help me strip the window frames in the attic and we can have a talk.' It was Gwen's habit to ask us over at weekends when Alan was away for any length of time. She reckoned, quite rightly, that weekends were the worst times to be alone with young children.

I protested feebly, 'You won't feel much like feeding all of us after a morning rehearsing all those kids...'

'Oh, it won't be anything fancy, just pizza and salad or something.' I thanked her with genuine pleasure and my spirits lifted now that I had something to look forward to.

As I drove past the bus stop outside the supermarket

I noticed Glynis Shipwrick standing disconsolately in the straggling queue. She was weighed down with carrier bags and Jason was sitting on the kerb sucking an iced lolly. I know I should have stopped to offer her a lift, but instead I accelerated past, carefully not looking in her direction. I simply couldn't face a further twenty minutes of the Shipwrick matrimonial shambles.

'Wasn't that –' Lizzie began.

'Yes it was,' I interrupted tersely.

'Shouldn't you –'

'No, I shouldn't.'

Lizzie glanced at my stony profile and wisely kept quiet.

My dear Polly [the letter from Alan began],

I arrived in Tokyo after a terrible flight at 14.40 hours, eight hours behind schedule would you believe. I think there must have been a Mothers' Union Convention somewhere in the Far East for the plane was full of mothers and babies and young children, all of them hyper-active so I didn't get a wink of sleep and by the end of the flight only one loo was operational. On my return I intend to register a strong complaint with British Airways and I will certainly not fly with them again. [They must have a very fat file of complaining letters from Mr Alan Graham at BA. 'Oh no,' I can hear them say, 'not *him* again,' as they open his neatly typed envelope and read its neatly typed contents.]

Mr Takahashi met me at the airport and we went straight to his office where I had a delayed meeting with Mr Nishino and several other solemn gentlemen of unknown origin. As you can imagine, I wasn't exactly bright eyed and bushy tailed and from the gleam in Mr Nishino's eye I have the feeling that I made more concessions than he had expected. Anyway, at his insistence I joined him and some others for a night on the town and I eventually crawled into bed in the early hours only to find that the hum of the air-conditioning kept me awake until the alarm went off. I had a wretched migraine all morning.

I am writing this on the famous Bullet Train on my way to see Mr Chiya in Osaka. It is the fastest train in the world. It takes three hours to travel 330 miles, which is the distance from Tokyo to Osaka. The day after tomorrow I fly from Osaka to Hong Kong. I will not have time to shop because I have meetings scheduled round the clock. [His way of telling me that he won't have time to buy presents.]

Don't forget to collect my brown brogues from the menders and have you organized with Frater's to pick up the lawn mower? Tell them it is *not* fuel starvation, I've checked. Also tell them that it *must* be back by the weekend after next. Well, it will be next weekend probably by the time you get this letter.

I hope you are sticking to your diet. [A silly promise I always make and don't keep. However he never gives up hoping that the little dumpling he leaves behind him will turn into lean fillet steak while he's away.] And before I forget, *please* try and get round to mending the hole in my cavalry twill trousers. Do you realize I haven't been able to wear them for almost a year?

I've found another unusual elephant for Jane's collection and I bought some more track for Charlie's train-set. [Having bought Charlie a train that was no bigger than a string of sausages on his *first* Far East trip, he found he could only get track for it in one store in Tokyo.] When we touched down in Alaska to stretch our legs I bought Lizzie a polar bear's tooth on a chain.

Give my love to everyone.

Lots of love,

Alan

P.S. I miss you.

There he is, I thought, thousands of miles away from us and surrounded by the strange sights of the Orient and all he can think about are his brown brogues, the lawn mower, his cavalry twill trousers and his flight schedule. With a sigh, I put the letter on the Welsh dresser, gathered up my things and drove over to Gwen's for the second time that morning. Two hours earlier I had delivered Lizzie and Jane for their regular Saturday-morning rehearsal.

Mike met me at the door looking very fetching in a plastic pinny printed with an extremely voluptuous, almost nude female form.

'Thank God you're here. Now I can get on with the lunch,' he said unexpectedly, looking at me hopefully. 'Well,' he said, 'where's the cheese then?'

'What cheese?'

'Oh no,' he wailed. 'Don't tell me you've forgotten it.'

'I haven't forgotten any cheese because no one asked me to bring any.'

'Oh, for heaven's sake . . . didn't Rick ring you?' I shook my head. 'Little toad, he told me he had.'

'Look, I can buzz back to the shops and get you some if you like,' I volunteered.

'No, don't worry. We'll just have to have less topping on the pizza.' I found it hard to imagine Gwen's pizzas with even less topping but Mike had already disappeared back into the kitchen leaving me on the doorstep. 'Don't just stand there,' his disembodied voice echoed round the large, neo-baronial hall. 'Come in and pour yourself a glass of Greasy Dago,' which is the name they gave the huge two-litre bottles of really undrinkable Valpolicella that Mike bought from the Cash'n'Carry.

'Look, can I give you a hand?' I asked, as I glanced round the kitchen at what appeared to be the remains of a chimps' tea party.

'No . . . no,' he replied airily, brandishing a very long, fat cucumber suggestively in my direction. 'I think I'm getting on top of things at last. Why don't you go and snatch a sneak preview of the Royal Shakespeare Junior League next door? You'll find it very,' he paused, searching for the right word, 'very amusing, I think,' he finished carefully.

'Will Gwen mind?'

'Very probably. She's rather touchy about everything these days.'

I stood in the doorway toying with my glass of wine and wondering if I wanted to see my children play-acting enough to brave Gwen's cold disapproval. Yes, I thought, I would like to watch. I'd like to see what progress is being made. The children never talked about the play in my presence but it was obvious from their temporary closeness that they were involved in something they found exciting and seductive. Most children enjoy play-acting once they have been persuaded on to a stage and have relaxed sufficiently to forget their self consciousness, for it really is simply an extension of 'mummies and daddies' and 'cops and robbers'.

Nothing much was expected of me beyond the provision of suitable costumes: a lion outfit for Charlie who was one of three lions – there should, of course, only be one but because three small boys couldn't agree there were three; a flimsy saffron fairy outfit with wings, for Jane was to play Mustard Seed, one of Queen Titania's small attendants. Yes, I know the Fairies aren't on stage during *Pyramus and Thisbe*, but in the end so many children auditioned that the story-line was adapted slightly. Lizzie, as the silent Hermia, simply had to be decorative in a sheet pleated in the style of a Grecian chiton. Charlie had to do a quick change into a peasant's outfit for he had also wangled himself a place in the final clog dance which promised to be both noisy and lively if the thunderous drumming that went on over our heads most evenings was anything to go by.

'Oh go on, Polly,' Mike said, smiling, I suspect, at the wistful expression on my face. 'She won't mind *you*.'

The drawing-room door was ajar and I could hear the squeaky voice of Brian 'Stringy' Pennant, Patsy's tall, stringbean of a boy, proclaiming that he, one Snout by name, presented a wall. I peered in. Stringy was standing centre-stage with his long thin arms outstretched as one crucified. 'And this the cranny is,' he continued. Abruptly his forefinger separated from his middle finger thereby creating the chink through which the doomed lovers protested their love for each other. Stringy peered along his arm to make certain that his hand had obeyed the instructions from his brain. Satisfied, he went on, 'Right and sinister, through which the fearful lovers are to whisper.'

Gwen was sitting on a kitchen stool in a position reminiscent of Rodin's famous Thinker. Eddie stood very close behind her, arms akimbo, with a similarly thoughtful expression on his face. At the back of the area clearly designated as 'stage', children clustered, some sitting, some standing and one busily engaged upon chipping small flakes of paint from a bad oil painting of a Scottish loch whose value lay in its yellow patina of age. On either side, the languid Shakespearian aristos who made up the 'audience' for this play-within-a-play spoke their rather dreary lines.

'Demetrius,' Gwen called, 'do you have any idea what that line actually means?' Demetrius shook his head. 'Well, what you're really saying, in modern terms, is that you've never heard a funnier wall. But actually you're being sarcastic, because you and your sophisticated friends know that walls can't speak. So say that line with a sort of spiteful chuckle. You're laughing at these ignorant yokels. You don't take them seriously. And Stringy, I like the way you let your arms sag from time to time. It's an amusing touch.'

'They're sagging because they're tired, Mrs Bray,' the boy grumbled.

'Precisely. Poor Snout's arms would've been tired too wouldn't they? But you *must* remember to hoick them up again when Pyramus and Thisbe want to whisper through your chink. In fact, Pyramus,' Tom, Hannah's boy, looked up from his script. Hannah had told me that he was having difficulty memorizing his lines. 'Why don't you lift Wall's arms into place once or twice – don't overdo it or it'll stop being funny.' Later on, when Wall and Pyramus acted out their little pantomime, it was so effective that people laughed until they cried. I was forced to reflect that Tom, who was a natural comic, would be a great loss to vaudeville if he fulfilled his ambition and became a marine biologist.

There was a great deal of prurient sniggering amongst the supposedly silent Fairies and Clog Dancers when Pyramus and Thisbe spoke their yearning lines of love through Wall's unsteady chink, which seemed to have stumbled upon the secret of perpetual motion. Eventually Thisbe (Maggie's pimply, pubescent middle son, Jamie, who had been bribed with the firm promise that he could give up the piano) turned on his tormentors furiously and told them that if they didn't shut up he would go home and then where would they be? The barracking ceased immediately, for everyone knew that Jamie was the only chap prepared to play a girl.

At this point Gwen glanced casually in my direction. 'Oh, you're here already Polly,' she said rather disagreeably. 'Well, don't lurk in the doorway like that, come in and sit down quietly, if you can find somewhere to sit.' Eddie's eyes met mine briefly and then darted away. I wondered if it was guilt that I had seen flicker across his face and then decided that it was probably irritation.

I sat down quietly as instructed on the edge of the bay window-seat where I was mostly hidden by a heavy velvet curtain. But Jane, who had been hopping energetically from one foot to the other with a look of frantic concentration on her face, abandoned her post and weaved her way towards me through the mass of restless children.

'I want to go to the toilet,' she whispered.

'Well, you know where it is,' I whispered back.

'Will you tell Gwen where I've gone?' I nodded. 'Don't let anybody else hear, though, will you?' She looked at me anxiously.

'I won't even tell *her* unless she misses you, okay?' She nodded very seriously and then sidled towards the door in a furtive manner that almost guaranteed her maximum attention.

'I know where Jane's going,' a young Fairy chanted in a sing-song voice. Jane threw her a look of undiluted venom before she scuttled out of sight.

Hermia (Lizzie) had struck an abandoned pose on a pile of floor cushions and was pretending to sip something from a neo-Tudor pewter wine goblet. She acknowledged my presence by raising the goblet to me and mouthing 'Cheers'. I looked round for Charlie but he, together with the two other Lions, was not in evidence, though there was a lot of giggling and muttering going on behind the upright piano in the corner.

'Lions!' Gwen thundered. 'Come out from behind there and take up your positions.' The noise behind the piano ceased abruptly and Charlie, together with Rick Bray and Stuart Cutler, came bounding out on all fours. Roaring and growling they pushed their way roughly through the Fairies and Clog Dancers, who gasped collectively and drew back in simulated horror. They crouched beside each other and pawed menacingly at the air while Rick growled in a rough lion-like voice, 'You ladies, you, whose gentle hearts do fear . . .' Everyone then looked expectantly at Charlie who was gazing into the distance with a fixed expression on his face.

'It's you,' Rick stage-whispered, giving Charlie a nudge which nearly knocked him off balance.

'I know, but I think I'm going to –' and Charlie sneezed explosively showering everyone within range. The force of the sneeze flattened him and we all laughed except Gwen who turned and looked helplessly at Eddie.

'Quiet!' Eddie commanded. 'Haven't you got a hanky?' he asked Charlie, who was wiping his nose on his sleeve. Charlie nodded and drew out a filthy, grey square from his jeans pocket. After rubbing his nose energetically, he wiped the floor around him for a radius of two feet. Poor Charlie, I thought. Of all the good genes he could have inherited from me and his maternal grandfather, he has to inherit the hay-fever and asthma gene. He sneezed twice more into his grubby hanky, waited for a fourth which didn't happen and then beamed round at everyone with relief.

'It's all right, that was the last,' he reassured us all. Then his eye caught mine and his face fell. 'What are you doing here?' he asked grumpily.

'Charlie *please*,' Gwen said with patient resignation, 'ignore your mother and get on with it.' Charlie scowled and glared at me accusingly.

'The-smallest-monstrous-mouse-that-creeps-on-floor,' he intoned monotonously.

'Enunciate, Charlie. I am an ordinary member of the audience and I haven't the slightest idea what you have just said.' Gwen looked over at me and shrugged. Charlie repeated the line, endowing each word with a hollow, apocalyptic finality. The third Lion took it from there and the rhythm of the short speech was revived.

Some slight alterations had been made to the text, I noticed, whereby, 'I, one Snug the joiner am' became 'We, three Snugs the joiners are' and thereafter any reference to the Lion was in the plural. Thus 'Well roared Lion' became 'Well roared Lions', etc. This, I learnt later from Gwen, was to avoid any claims to senior status amongst the Lions, who were always trying to upstage each other.

Jane crept back into the drawing-room and I was just in time to pull the back of her skirt out of her knickers before anyone noticed and remarked upon it. This reminded me of the time I had walked through Harrods staff canteen in the same state of *déshabillé* and it was only when I was standing in the queue at the self-service counter that a boy from the Food Hall, who eventually went on to become a buyer, was kind enough to whisper in my ear. From that day forward I was known as 'Red' owing to the colour of my underwear.

As Gwen had predicted the children were quick to grasp the humour of the scene and to milk it to its last drop even if the irony and verbal sophistication of the text escaped them. In fact, the words came a poor second to their totally original slap-stick interpretation of the action. There was a fair amount of ad-libbing amongst the Fairies and the Clog Dancers, who clearly felt they had to justify their presence on stage, and Jane and little Mandy Cutler, who took dancing lessons together with Miss Melrose in St Saviour's Church Hall, had devised, between them, several dainty little fairy-type dances which they executed very seriously before the makeshift thrones of Titania and Oberon. It didn't seem to trouble them that no one took any notice. Indeed, it was all very funny, but I was reminded of Babs's warning that people might well laugh at our children and not with them, and I felt a stab of guilty anxiety.

However, my genuine amusement delighted the cast and they kept casting furtive glances in my direction to make sure that what they thought was funny, I thought was funny too. Lizzie looked a little puzzled by some of my less judicious guffaws and when she accidentally dropped her pewter goblet, which rolled across the stage before coming to rest between Pyramus's feet on the line 'O dainty duck, o dear', she scowled furiously in my direction as I giggled unrestrainedly.

Gwen and Eddie looked at me sharply and Gwen said, 'Oh dear, Lizzie, what a pity you can't do that to order, your mother clearly finds it very funny.'

I shrank further back behind the curtain, but was saved any further mortification by the arrival of Patsy Pennant's husband Jock, who had come to collect Stringy, followed closely by Basil Baines looking for Honour, who made a sturdy but regal Titania.

'Now children,' Gwen called authoritatively as her restless cast began shuffling purposefully towards the door, 'I want everyone word perfect by next Saturday and will you tell your parents that I want all costumes completed and delivered here by next Thursday evening. Pyramus and Thisbe, I'll see you on Wednesday evening at six sharp and speaking aristocrats,

I want you here by seven.' There was a low groan from the speaking aristocrats.

'I don't *need* this,' Gwen muttered as she passed me with Eddie following close on her heels.

'Hi, Ed,' I said blithely. 'Will you have time to coach Charlie next week?'

'Er . . . um,' he managed before Gwen grabbed his arm and swept him out into the hall, which was filling with parents having glasses of wine thrust into their unwilling hands by Mike, who was by this time a little unsteady and very frisky.

'Miranda, my love,' he purred salaciously, 'you are an old man's dream of heaven,' and he patted her leather-clad bottom playfully. 'Wilt thou partake of a glass of red nectar with the old man in question?'

Miranda gave him a tight smile and slid expertly out from under his descending arm. 'Super idea Mike,' she replied over her shoulder as she hastily ushered her two offspring out of the door, 'but I've got to rush.'

Gwen, who had watched this little interchange from between slitty lids, tucked her arm possessively into Eddie's and gave him a deep, meaningful look. Eddie responded in kind and I felt an odd, sharp pang of loss.

Gwen sighed with relief as the door closed behind the last parent with child. Then she turned to me.

'Well, what do you think then?'

'I think it's going to be absolutely smashing.'

'No, *really*.'

'I *really* think it's going to be absolutely smashing.' Gwen frowned thoughtfully and it dawned on me that something more constructive was expected of me. 'It's genuinely funny and it's obvious that most of the kids are enjoying themselves.'

'Which aren't?' she asked sharply.

I thought for a moment and then I said, 'Well, I think the speaking aristocrats are finding it all a bit trying.'

'Mmm, that's what we thought, didn't we Eddie?' He

nodded. 'But there's not much we can do to improve their lot. I know their lines are boring for them, but we can't have them capering about the stage extemporizing all over the place which is what they'd like to be doing. I suppose it wouldn't hurt for them to join in the clog dance at the end . . . some sort of audience participation, if you know what I mean. Give it some thought will you Eddie?'

'I think the Fairies and Clog Dancers are as happy as fleas,' I offered as reassurance.

'Yes, well, it's all right for them. They haven't had any lines to learn and they've been allowed a bit of funny business. This is only the second time I've rehearsed the Fairies so they haven't got bored. Now listen Polly, have you got all your costumes together?' she said, changing the subject abruptly. 'You were having difficulty with Charlie's Lion outfit as I remember.' I told her that I'd decided to pin him into Ma's old beaver lamb coat and that I'd found a very realistic mask in a joke shop in Tottenham Court Road.

'Miranda's made a fantastic papier-mâché mask for Stuart.' Hmm, she would, I thought. 'And she's making one for Rick.'

'Very nice of her,' I said shortly. Gwen shot me a look.

'I would've asked her to make one for Charlie, only they take a long time and time's what we're short of. Actually she's been a great help with the costumes. Designed them all and delivered little sketches to each parent.'

'She didn't deliver any sketches to me.' Gwen looked decidedly sheepish.

'No, well, I've got your sketches here. Didn't think you'd need them knowing how good you are with these things.' I interpreted the look that flashed between Gwen and Eddie as 'I wouldn't have *dared*'.

While Gwen, Eddie and the children were rearranging the furniture in the drawing-room I joined Mike in the kitchen to lend him a hand.

'For God's sake, Mike!' I exclaimed, standing in the doorway and surveying the debris. 'She'll lose her rag when she sees this.' I snatched the broom from his nerveless hands. 'You do something about the surfaces and I'll deal with the floor.' He gazed at me like a woebegone child.

'I dropped the pizza tray and the salad bowl,' he wailed pathetically, 'and the lunch went all over the floor.'

'Shhhh . . . she'll hear.'

'What'll I hear?' Gwen's chuckle reached us moments before Gwen did. I flashed a look at Mike and quite literally saw the colour drain from his cheeks and then we both turned to face the oppressor.

'What on earth?' She took in the parlous state of the room in one glance. All the muscles in her face appeared to contract simultaneously, which had the effect of drawing the soft flesh to the bone until she more closely resembled a mummified corpse than a living, breathing woman. It was a look I had seen before once or twice and it signified cold, hostile rage. 'You sod Mike,' she hissed. 'You bloody sod. What the hell have you been doing for the past two hours?' She looked at him speculatively. 'Though perhaps I needn't ask.'

'Food's all ready,' he slurred miserably as though announcing the death of a loved one. 'Sorry about the mess, first I dropped the tray with the pizzas, too damned hot, then I knocked over the salad bowl.' Gwen glanced at the nearly empty bottles of wine and suddenly I understood Mike's insistence upon everyone having a glass before they left. Gwen could not, with any justification, accuse him of emptying them single-handed.

'Since we obviously can't eat that rubbish,' she indicated the mess with a jerk of her head, 'someone will just have to go down to the chippy.'

'I'll go,' Mike piped up, eager to redeem himself. Gwen raised her eyes to heaven.

'In your state, I'd hesitate before letting you loose with a wheel-barrow. Polly,' she looked at me pleadingly, 'do you think . . .?'

'Of course,' I said hurriedly, thankful for the opportunity of getting out of the house and away from the unpleasant atmosphere for a bit. 'How many are we and what do people want?'

'We're nine,' Mike said firmly.

'Eight,' Eddie corrected him.

'Actually I believe we're eleven,' I said, and Gwen, who had been counting on her fingers, offered the definitive number of ten.

'Just get everyone cod and chips,' she instructed me.

'Well, I would, only Jane is refusing fish at the moment and Lizzie's a vegetarian this week.'

'I'm a vegetarian too,' Eddie muttered apologetically.

'All right,' Gwen said, gritting her teeth, 'seven cod and chips and the fussy ones can forage about in the ruins of the pizzas.'

The children, ever accurate emotional barometers, gathered up their plates of food and disappeared silently into the shadowy recesses of the big, old house. The four adults plodded through their meal in abstracted silence and as soon as he had finished, Eddie jumped to his feet and announced that he had to leave immediately because he had to meet some friends in the King's Road. Gwen nodded glumly as though it was only to be expected in the circumstances.

'I'll ring you,' he mouthed after glancing anxiously at Mike who appeared to be seriously preoccupied with what I guessed was a fishbone lodged between two back teeth. Gwen nodded glumly again. 'See you Mike.' With his finger and thumb still probing round his teeth, Mike looked up and mumbled something incomprehensible.

At the door Eddie turned as though just remembering something. 'Oh, by the way Polly, I'll phone you during the week about Charlie's coaching.' Upon which he preceded Gwen out of the room. She returned some minutes later in a better humour.

*

'So, what's up with you then?' Gwen was half in, half out of one of the small attic dormer windows energetically applying paint stripper to the decrepit wooden frame. She had changed into a pair of paint-spattered white workman's overalls and her hair was tied up, forties style, in a floral cotton scarf. Because there really wasn't anything I could do to help I was sitting on a three-legged milking stool. My knees were drawn up almost to my chin and I was balancing a large mug of coffee on them. It was a mug I had given Gwen one Christmas and it bore the inscription, 'To My Best Friend'. Soon, I knew, the green snout of a ceramic frog would surface above the coffee level. It was one of her possessions that Gwen said she would rescue if the house was on fire.

'Well, it's about Alan really,' I began, not really knowing where to start.

'Hmmm, thought it might be,' Gwen said, giving me a sharp look, and I wondered what messages I had been unconsciously transmitting. Or did she perhaps know something that I didn't? Anyway, with a lot of false starts and back-tracking and deep soul-searching I poured out my doubts while she continued silently with her work. Finally I said, with my heart pounding, all of me yearning for her to laugh and tell me that I was simply over-reacting, 'If I didn't know Alan as well as I do, I'd say there was another woman. Of course,' I continued, doing the laughing myself, 'I know it's really not possible,' I hesitated and Gwen looked across at me expectantly, 'but if it was, I think the woman might be Sheila Rosen, you know, the secretary Mike thinks is very glamorous. If there isn't another woman then I don't know what it is, but there is definitely something wrong.' For a while Gwen didn't say anything, then she swung the leg that was outside the window inside and put down her brush.

'Gosh,' she exclaimed, wincing and rubbing the inside of her thigh. 'That's a really uncomfortable position to sit in for any length of time. It's hard to believe, you know, that you and Alan are having troubles,' she said after I had handed her her mug of coffee. It was probably stone cold but she didn't seem to mind. 'I've always relied on you two to set the rest of us an example. You know, marriages may come and marriages may go, but yours goes on for ever, sort of style. It's very inconsiderate of you to spring this on me at this time – I look to you for reassurance, not uncertainty.' She looked at my face, which I could feel settling into folds of disappointment, and laughed. 'Don't look so woebegone Polly, I'm only pulling your leg. But seriously, you must admit, it's a bit of irony just as you've started Marriage Guidance. Surely it's a case of "physician, heal thyself" or something.'

Well, I must say, that's *very* helpful, I thought, and just the sort of positive, concerned advice I need right now. Bitterly I said, 'Thanks a bunch. I can see I should have come to you a long time ago.'

Gwen looked at me helplessly and said, 'But Polly, I'm sure there's nothing I can advise you to do that you haven't thought of already. I'd say it was time for you both to do a lot of honest communicating, but knowing you, I'm sure you've tried that already.' I nodded. 'And I suppose he refused to talk?'

I nodded again. 'He just keeps telling me that it's all a figment of my highly-strung imagination, which is extremely frustrating when you're a person who trusts her intuitions as much as I do. It's like watching someone kicking around a primed bomb that he keeps insisting is a football.' Gwen laughed at my rather florid metaphor.

'I suppose you could tax Mrs Thing with it. You know, something along the lines of "Keep your filthy hands off my husband or else."'

'I really think I would do something like that if I was certain, but you see, I don't really believe, in my heart of hearts, that they are having an affair.'

Gwen gave me a shrewd, hard look and said, 'Correct me if I'm wrong, but I seem to recall you telling me a few months ago that a lot of your clients refuse to believe that their partner is having an affair even when the evidence is staring them in the face.' The implication behind what she said hit me like a blast of ice-cold air and I gave a perceptible shudder. I could hear myself sounding exactly like Glynis Shipwrick. No, not *my* husband, I'd know if he was playing around . . . and look at Glynis Shipwrick now, I thought. I considered myself as a sad sack in a supermarket, half out of my mind with anxiety and bitterness and wearing a blonde wig to hide my bald patches and I shuddered again.

However, the no doubt unworthy thought did pass through my head that Gwen might want me to believe that Alan was having an affair. I'm not saying that she would have enjoyed my pain, but if your own marriage is showing a few cracks, it's reassuring to know that you're not alone. It's only human.

'Well,' I retorted finally, 'whether he's having an affair or not, he's a troubled man and for my peace of mind I need to know what the trouble is.'

Gwen was watching me speculatively. 'You know,' she began, 'I once suspected Mike of having an affair. Every Saturday, straight after lunch, he used to disappear for hours – to the library, he said – and he'd come home again in time for *Dr Who*.'

'What did you do about it?'

'Well, if you must know,' she replied, looking slightly ashamed, 'I followed him one afternoon.'

'And was he?'

'No.'

'Where was he going to then?'

'The library.' I laughed and she grinned sheepishly.

'What on earth did he find to do at the library every Saturday afternoon?' I asked.

'He changed his library books and read all the magazines and newspapers. It also got him out of doing the gardening. However it all stopped when they decided to close the library at midday on a Saturday.' I remembered the romantic fantasy I had woven round Mike's and my Saturday trysts and smiled to myself.

'Well,' I said, 'that may have been all right for you, but I just can't see myself lurking outside Alan's office in dark glasses and a false moustache with three children in tow.' Our humour, so often in tandem, worked at the image until we were crying with laughter.

'A trench coat and a trilby.'

'How about a Meter Maid?'

'Or a hooker – black leather mini, fish-net stockings, blonde beehive . . .'

'No, I can see too many snags with that one.'

'I've got it!' Gwen shouted triumphantly. 'A pillar-box. Nobody looks twice at a pillar-box!'

'They might look twice at one that moved.'

'Ahhh,' Gwen sighed, defeated at last. Then she perked up. 'Why don't you lurk outside Mrs Thing's house instead?'

'No, it's a quiet residential street. Someone'd be bound to notice me hovering. They'd probably think I was sussing out the joint for a burglary.'

'Not if you were in a Gas Board van.'

'Oh yes, I can just see the Gas Board lending me one of their vans to spy on my husband.'

'I know,' Gwen exclaimed, the light of revelation dawning in her eyes, 'send Mrs Thing an anonymous letter. "If you don't stop having it off with your boss I will tell his wife. Signed A. Well-wisher".' Gwen's crude suggestion brought us both down to earth with a thump.

'But he isn't "having it off", as you put it, with Sheila Rosen, I'm sure he's not,' I pleaded anxiously. I wanted reassurance and that's why it's not a good idea to ask a best friend for help with a marital problem. They want to stay friends with you so they tell you what they think you want to hear.

'Oh God . . . no Polly . . . I was only joking.' See what I

mean? 'We were having a laugh, remember?' But I didn't find any of it very funny any more. Silently I sipped from my mug of cold coffee and Gwen threw her leg astride the window frame again.

'Perhaps he's worried about business,' she suggested casually. 'I think he mentioned something to Mike ages ago about some expected redundancies. Or maybe he's got money worries. Haven't we all,' she added with a light shrug.

'But if that's the case, why can't he talk to me about it? He always used to.' Gwen continued stripping busily and long curly strips of brown gloss paint fell round her like wet hair cuttings. She was frowning and chewing her lower lip contemplatively in a way I recognized. Usually it meant that she had something to say but wasn't sure how to set about saying it. I decided to make it easy for her.

'Go on, say it,' I told her.

'Say what?'

'Whatever it is you want to say but feel you can't because it'll probably hurt me.' She stopped scraping away at the layers of old paint and gazed searchingly at me for a few moments.

'Look, Polly,' she began eventually, 'I know I'm probably the last person you should come to for the sort of help you're looking for – after all, my own marriage isn't exactly a shining example of wedded bliss – and you'll probably scream at me, but if he does have business worries is it possible that he feels he *can't* talk to you about them any more? I mean, you've been very wrapped up in yourself and your own interests since Jane started school. You know, just sometimes you seem to treat Alan as a sort of irritating lodger.' There is another reason why you shouldn't share your marital problems with a best friend. If she tells you what she sees as the truth you tend to question her motives. 'I understand how you feel, I really do. After all those years of feeling like a milch-cow, it's like being reborn. I know, I'm going through the same thing myself. I feel like a powerful engine ticking over in neutral. All it needs is for someone to press the right button and I'll be away.'

'Nobody's suffered because of my interests outside the home,' I protested. 'I'm only doing voluntary work after all. I'd agree with you if I was going out to work every day, but I'm not.' I suppose that was a dig at Gwen who was now working daily at the Cottage on a part-time basis.

'Oh come on, Polly, you're totally immersed in Marriage Guidance. The only difference between you and me is that I'm paid for my work. And when you're not counselling, you're writing your book and when you're not writing your book, you're doing Committee work. I don't care what you say, things change around the house once a woman sees that there's life after child-bearing. You've changed, I've watched you. You're a new woman.'

'Am I?' I looked doubtful because I wasn't sure I felt like one. 'How am I changed?'

'Well, for a start, you've got more self-confidence – you're more assertive. When I first met you, you were always apologizing. You had no self-esteem and the slightest stress sent you off into the most frightful wobble. In those days Alan was the only thing between you and total collapse. You needed propping up all the time, you were so feeble.'

'Huh!' I snorted. 'I'm surprised you condescended to become my friend.'

'So am I, actually. I didn't like the look of you at all, but you were very persistent.' My mouth dropped open and Gwen grinned. 'I'm only joking,' she added, but I didn't believe her.

She was right. I had been persistent. I don't know why I wanted the tall sour-faced woman, who used to stand outside the nursery school with a baby in a push-chair waiting for her oldest son, to be my friend. Standing aloof from the rest of us she looked distinctly unapproachable. Looking back I think it was because she reminded me of a dearly-loved old friend, a woman some years older than myself who had supported me through my tempestuous teens and early twenties only to disappear for ever after a summer holiday in California. I had received a post-card with no return address telling me that she was marrying a metallurgist called J. Howard Braine Jnr, and thereafter it was as though she had never existed.

Despite my fear of rejection, I had plucked up courage, not once, but on several occasions, to approach Gwen and make contact. She had been polite but that was all. Then one snowy February morning I had smiled at her and made some trivial comment about my boots letting in water. But instead of the usual glacial smile in return, she had turned violently towards me as though she was going to say something very angry and had said, instead, 'Look, are you doing anything right now?' I shook my head nervously. 'Well then,' she had continued irritably, 'in that case, you'd better come home with me and have a cup of coffee.' It was more of a command than an invitation, but I had accepted gratefully and indeed, the excitement I had felt was out of all proportion. It didn't take me long to discover that she didn't only look like my erstwhile friend.

'Look,' I said, getting back to the subject in hand, 'you said that perhaps Alan feels he can't talk to me any more about his problems. Well, by the same token, I can't talk to him. Admittedly it isn't problems I want to talk to him about. I want to tell him all about the exciting and exhilarating changes that are taking place in my life. I'd love to talk to him about my Marriage Guidance training but he's just not interested and he doesn't even try to understand what I'm talking about. He believes it's something he's got to put up with until I grow out of it. He treats the Committee as a long-running sit-com but reckons it's safe. He dismisses it all as my do-gooding. Activities to keep the little woman off the streets between ironing his shirts and baking bread. At the moment we're travelling at different speeds on different tracks. He doesn't want to hear how great I feel because he doesn't, and admittedly I don't want to hear how bad he feels because I suspect that what he has to tell me will make me feel bad too.'

'I know what you mean,' Gwen cut in, 'because it sounds exactly like Mike and me. Unfortunately I don't think I'm as motivated as you are to try and put things right.' She slid off the sill on to the floor. 'Can you spare a fag?' she asked, and we lit up and sat puffing in moody silence. We could hear the distant whoops and cries of our children playing in the treehouse and I reflected unhappily that it might not be too long before all the cosy, secure comfort of the past years came to an end.

Suddenly Gwen sighed dramatically. 'And I don't know what to do about Eddie either.' She dropped it into the pool of silence as would any good actress with the best line in the play. I knew what was expected of me but I was not ready to be upstaged so I continued to look absently out of the window as though I hadn't heard. I could feel Gwen's eyes boring into the side of my head like a laser beam. I'll be irreparably brain-damaged, I thought, if she keeps this up much longer. 'I find him very hard to resist,' she continued relentlessly. Ours was a game in which we both knew all the rules. 'And I don't want to hurt him. You may not know this, but he's surprisingly sensitive.' Of course I knew it and she knew I knew it. 'Just supposing we did have an affair, there'd be no future in it but he won't believe this. The trouble is, what I feel is lust, but *he* thinks he's in love. We could simply hit the sack and enjoy ourselves, but he keeps talking about a future which includes rose-covered cottages and babies.'

'Well, you must have given him some encouragement,' I snapped waspishly, unable to contain myself any longer. 'He's not a fool even if he is only twenty.' Gwen smiled the dreamy smile of a woman who knows herself to be desired and I was practically sick on the spot.

'Not really,' she said slowly, shaking her head at the hopelessness of it all. 'It just sort of developed. Of course I could tell he fancied me ages ago – you sense it, don't you. But I've never really been interested in younger men. I think it's a bit undignified.' The barb was pointed. 'I mean, you remember Sheena Watson and her English teacher? God, I can see her now in those frightful pink hot pants with her hair tied up in ribbons. Good thing she couldn't see herself from behind.' I shrugged irritably. I was beginning to find the conversation both distasteful and disturbing. 'But I keep forgetting, you had a thing about him a while back, didn't you?' I knew she'd get round to it eventually and I turned to face her. The sun had sunk below the tall, dark conifers and the light, bright little room was now filled with the watery gloom of early evening. Gwen's face was a featureless white blob that glowed softly in the shadows like a luminous mask.

'I've told you before, Gwen,' I said in a tone of solemn admonishment, 'I like Eddie a great deal and I have always felt compassion for him . . . after all, I remember all that nastiness between his parents, and his mother was a good friend of mine, but I have never had a "thing", as you put it, about him.'

'Oh, I *am* glad to hear that, because it's not what Eddie thinks . . . oh dear,' Gwen pulled the sort of face you pull when you let something slip accidentally, 'perhaps I shouldn't have told you that.'

Thunderstruck, I gaped incredulously at the pale blob which was now, if I was not mistaken, alive with malicious triumph.

'Do you mean to tell me that you and Eddie have discussed what he supposes to be my feelings towards him?'

'We weren't exactly discussing your feelings, but he's very conscious of the fact that he's been neglecting you of late.' Huh, such condescension!

'It's not me he's been neglecting, it's Charlie,' I said furiously, my pride suffering from a severe histamine reaction. 'I pay him to coach my son. It's been *his* choice to lounge about in my kitchen laughing about his amatory successes with his harem of elderly admirers.' Gwen flinched and I knew my jab had gone home, hurray, hurrah! 'Anyway, you've gone on so much about *not* fancying younger men, it's been obvious to everyone that quite the reverse is true. So, if you want to hit the sack with Eddie, or have an affair, or get married and breed, it's all the same to me, only don't expect me to baby-sit when you get bored and want to go back to work, because generally speaking I don't much like other people's babies.' And if that sounds like a miffed woman to you, you'd be right.

I considered Eddie to be my own private fantasy, not my best friend's reality. It was a harmlessly enjoyable pastime thinking about what might have been if things had been different, like if I wasn't married or I was fifteen years younger; and Eddie's flattering attention made up, in some small way, for Alan's recent neglect.

'Well, that's all right then,' Gwen said in a startled voice. 'That's fine. You've made your position very clear.' Too clear, very probably, I thought ruefully. 'I only wanted you to know that I wasn't deliberately poaching on your territory, that's all.' What you wanted me to know, Gwen dear, I thought, is that if I had any designs upon young Eddie, I could forget them because he likes the cut of your jib better than he likes mine.

'Caro reached over Gulley's naked, supine body and picked out a ripe peach from a pile of glowing fruits that were cooking gently in the fierce heat of the midday sun. Her erect nipples grazed through the wiry, golden fleece that lay in damp curls on his sweating, bronzed chest. He stirred and made a small, feral noise at the back of his throat, but his eyes remained closed. If he had awakened, Caro would have been happy for she was ready for him. But she was content to let him sleep while she bit into the soft, white flesh of the warm fruit. Juice oozed down her chin, then dripped on to her chest and trickled down the deep, shadowed valley between her breasts. Almost instantly it dried into a sticky, silvery snail trail. Caro smiled fondly as she remembered another time and another place. Arthur, bending over her hugely pregnant body to lick the juice from an over-ripe pear from one blue-veined, swollen breast. Then she frowned. Arthur, she thought, who would now be . . .'

I wondered what it was that I had decided Arthur would be doing when I abandoned him two weeks earlier. Something tedious and industrious, I thought, knowing Arthur. Like mowing the lawn or planning his itinerary for a business trip to Rotterdam. It wasn't too difficult though to imagine why Caro might be thinking of him fondly and probably a little guiltily at such a time. The fact that he had developed rather rapidly into an out and out prune didn't obscure the fact that he had started his fictitious life as a fine husband and father – the sort of man, in fact, who would take his children to the park on Sunday afternoons and who had found his first encounter with the Desiderata a seminal experience.

Gulley had also become a bit of a headache. His attraction for me depended almost entirely upon his amorality and his rootlessness, and now that he had become something of a born-again Christian with an almost manic obsession with Caro, he was becoming – dare I say it – a bit of a bore. If I was finding him a bore, so, I was sure, would Caro. Yet here she was, in a goat-herd's hut on a Greek island, seriously considering the possibility of chucking up her safe, pure life in Wimbledon for the nomadic ways of her young lover (who, believe it or not, was already toying with the idea of settling down with his mistress in a rented flat in Croydon near to his folks).

Caro had changed in some unexpected ways too. She had cast away her Nanette Newman image like a torn plastic mac, which was unfortunate because her squeaky cleanness was an essential ingredient in the workings of the plot. Her new dashing persona disturbed me, but despite all my best efforts to avoid it, she was now the sort of woman who travelled alone through the Dordogne and read James Joyce over dinner at a table for one. It was all very tiresome and I wondered how other authors coped with the independence of the characters they created.

To be truthful, I was becoming disenchanted with the whole business of writing a book. It was not turning out to be nearly as easy as I had supposed. I had dashed headlong into it, propelled by a sense of urgency that I didn't question at the time, but now, for some reason, was finding difficult to recapture. And I had not bothered to keep notes as I went along. Thus small but important details were overlooked. Charles Linwood, accountant, changed his name to Don and back to Charles again in two chapters and his wife Mary gave birth to a boy in one chapter who turned into a girl a chapter on. Poor Caro aged five years in two chapters and then regressed ten. Summer followed summer, while winter followed spring, and unhappy Arthur, supposedly an orphan since early childhood, suddenly had a very moving scene with his dying mother who talked lovingly of her husband who had been killed at Dunkirk.

'I wish you had known your father,' I reported her as saying with what was almost her last breath, to which Arthur should have replied, 'Oh, but I do Mother,' because I had had the old man crying copiously at his wife's funeral. I would have to correct all these silly mistakes, which would take time and would, in fact, invalidate some of my best prose which was mortifying. And worse still, I was beginning to find the linch-pin of my book, that is to say, the relationship between Caro and Gulley, more and more distasteful. What had seemed to me to be a really original idea that kept me awake at night planning each new daring move now felt tacky and embarrassing. I knew I would be ashamed for my friends to read it. I stopped believing that a woman such as the Caro I had originally envisaged would ever behave with such selfish irresponsibility towards her family. I disapproved of her and I now admit with hindsight that I was probably a bit jealous of her.

As I read the same sun-soaked paragraph over to myself

for the third time I wondered how I had ever imagined Caro into such an unlikely situation. Then an unexpectedly nauseating image abruptly nudged all else from my mind. I saw as clearly as anything Gwen and Eddie, naked as the day they were born, sleepily entwined in the long, warm, sun-dappled meadow behind their isolated pink stone cottage deep in the slumbering countryside and at last I began to understand the nature of the forces within me that had been driving Arthur, Caro and Gulley towards their final dénouement.

Slowly and thoughtfully I picked up the exercise book at the top of the pile and tore it cleanly in two. The others followed, one after the other. There goes Caroline Stansbury, I thought, a silly woman who dreamed of living out her fantasy. And there goes Gulley, chameleon youth for all seasons, and poor Arthur, a victim of circumstance who deserved better, and the neglected kids who were simply half-forgotten props from an abandoned production. By the time I reached Caro and Gulley's peach-strewn love-nest, I was feeling little more than a profound sense of relief. There's much more to writing a novel than meets the eye, I thought just a little regretfully as I looked down at the heap of waste paper in the basket. Perhaps I should begin my writing career with something a little less ambitious – like a short story. I had a heartening feeling there might be money in it, too.

When Eddie eventually phoned, I was very cool.

'Do you know, Charlie's getting along so well with his French,' I lied, 'I don't think he'll be needing any extra coaching. Thanks all the same.'

'Oh, well, okay,' he said, sounding disconcerted. 'But you don't mind if I still drop in on you, do you?'

'No, of course not, but give me a ring first because I'm very tied up at present and I'd hate you to have a wasted journey.'

There was a long silence, and then he said with a cool that

matched mine, 'Right, yes, I'll do that. See you around then.'

'See you around,' I echoed lightly. After a breathless pause, I replaced the receiver with deliberate precision and let out a great sigh that wasn't exactly one of relief but wasn't entirely one of regret either.

Chapter Ten

The fuse on the washing machine blew, mid-cycle. It was full of articles of drip-dry clothing which now lay in a creased bundle in luke-warm, soapy water while I pondered haplessly over the *Reader's Digest Book of Home Repairs*. I know it is the fashion these days to sneer at the *Reader's Digest*, but I cannot imagine how I would have managed without this book during Alan's prolonged trips abroad for, needless to say, things would begin to go wrong as soon as he stepped outside the front door. First a light bulb would go in an inaccessible place, then a bathroom tap would develop a relentlessly irritating drip. A couple of fuses would blow in quick succession and the television would lose its grip on horizontal hold. Invariably a tyre would acquire a slow puncture and unsettling warning lights on the dash-board would start blinking on and off. Someone usually managed to lock themselves inside the downstairs cloakroom and a sash window in the living-room could be relied upon to jam open; this usually in mid-winter when the central heating boiler was having its annual nervous collapse.

I dare say if Alan had been a less handy man about the house I would, from necessity, have acquired the diverse practical skills needed to keep the average house in good working order – I'm not stupid. But I must admit to being the sort of person who lets other people get on with things if they appear to be more capable than me or if they show a desire to do so. It's a form of laziness, I suppose, and it started in early childhood when I discovered, to my surprise, how eager some children were to put up tents, set mouse traps and mow lawns. I figured, even then, that if these activities gave them pleasure, who was I to spoil it for them? I developed into something of a director by nature. I find a job that needs doing and then I direct someone to it who is thrilled to be asked, or if not thrilled, at least willing. Except when Alan is away, this approach to life has always seemed to me to work very satisfactorily.

I had just found the instructions for replacing a fuse when the phone rang. It was Alan.

'Look, Pol,' he began, his voice twanging like a badly tuned electric guitar as it raced across the land masses and oceans that separated us, 'I'm cutting short my trip, so I'll be home the day after tomorrow.'

'Why?' I interrupted, thus cutting myself off completely from what he was saying. The radio telephone is an idiosyncratic device. Because of the few seconds' time lapse it is necessary to remain silent while the person at the other end speaks. The result, if you don't, is a garbled jumble of half-formulated questions and answers and long expectant pauses.

'Did you hear what I said?' Alan asked after just such a pause.

'I missed the last bit. I'm sorry, I interrupted.'

'Oh . . . well, I've decided not to do the South-East Asian leg of the trip.'

'Why not?' I interrupted again and felt like biting off my tongue. I cut back into the conversation as he was saying, '. . . yet exactly what plane I'll be catching, so it'll probably be easier to ring you from Heathrow when I get in.' He didn't sound overjoyed by the prospect of cutting short his trip so I said, to cheer him up,

'I'm *so* happy you're coming home. I've missed you so much.'

'Me too,' he said but I wasn't convinced. 'Anyway,' his distant voice concluded, 'I'd better ring off now as I've got masses to see to before I leave.' Hastily I asked him how to change a fuse. He began to explain but quickly became exasperated by my confusion. 'Oh, for Christ's sake leave it, Pol, until I get home.'

'I can't,' I wailed. 'It's the washing machine and it's full of drip-dry washing.'

'But you've changed fuses before –'

'I know, but this one must be different. I've tried three different fuses and it still won't work.'

'Then it's not the fuse. There's something wrong with the machine.' I must admit, this had not occurred to me and my heart sank. 'Look,' he went on, 'there's a tiny hole at one side of the door. Insert a match into it and the door will open.'

'Are you sure?' Well, it sounded pretty Heath Robinson to me.

'Yes, I'm sure,' he said wearily.

'But what about all the water inside? How do I drain that off first?'

Impatiently, he advised me to read the instruction booklet. 'That's your trouble,' he said, 'it's all trial and error with you. You never read instructions.' Which is true, I never do. I would if instruction booklets were written by English-speaking housewives with no mechanical aptitude instead of Romanian science-fiction writers attending crash courses in English at the Berlitz.

Suddenly there was a bleep and a doodle and a long buzz and we were cut off. I would have rung him back if I'd known where to ring. I knew he wouldn't ring back since we had nothing else to say to one another other than goodbye.

The following day Hannah phoned the Marriage Guidance office with an urgent message for me. I had just completed a totally surreal session with a stately, very black gentleman from an East African state who was under the mistaken impression that the Marriage Guidance Council was a marriage bureau and that I was a candidate for his inspection. Because of cultural and language difficulties it had taken me a full half hour to uncross our wires and when he eventually understood my purpose, he suggested, quite seriously, that I might like to set up a nice little business on the side as a marriage broker. So far as I could understand him, he wanted me to pass on to him the names and addresses of any unhappy ladies I might deem suitable. In essence, it appeared that he was looking for a homely lady of any age, colour or shape to housekeep for him and his seven children in exchange for a marriage certificate and a twenty-four-inch colour television. However, it had to be understood that when he returned to his homeland (he was, he said, an attaché, or something very like that, with his embassy), the good lady would remain here on a very generous pension. He had, he told me proudly, a very large house in Hendon with a swimming pool and a Mercedes Benz motor car. I wondered what had happened to the mother of his children but didn't like to ask.

I had a bit of time before my next client so I put the kettle on for a cup of coffee. 'Anyone else want one?' I asked, and then wondered why I bothered because they always did. I plonked Ellie (our appointments secretary)'s mug, which bore the inscription, in very small script, 'IF YOU CAN READ THIS, YOU'RE DRINKING FROM THE WRONG MUG' down beside her.

'Ta,' she said without looking up from her typing. 'And by the way,' she added, still concentrating on her work, 'your friend Mrs Jackman phoned. Wants to know if you can attend an emergency meeting of the Committee tomorrow morning at her house at ten-thirty a.m. and will you let her know.'

'Can I use the phone?' I asked. 'I'll make it very quick.' Ellie nodded absently as she studied the newly typed letter for errors.

'What's up?' I asked sharpish, when Hannah answered.

'Damn B's gone and sold forty-eight tickets over the top. Had Basil run up the forgeries at the office. She only told me this morning because I was expressing my worries about two hundred being too many for the marquee. Said she couldn't bring herself to turn people away.'

'So she actually went and did it!' I exclaimed wonderingly.

'Do you mean to say she's discussed it with you?' Hannah sounded very indignant.

'No . . . well, not *really*. She simply mentioned that she had run out of tickets and could sell lots more. I think my opinion was being canvassed so I believe I told her that I didn't think it was a good idea, or something like that anyway.' Hannah harumphed. She did – I promise you – she harumphed.

'Well, we've got to decide what to do about it p.d.q. I've organized a meeting for tomorrow morning. Can you be here?' The bell in Reception rang and when Ellie came back into the room it was to tell me that my next client was waiting. Without thinking I told Hannah hurriedly that I would and it was only later, when I was getting into bed, that I remembered about Alan coming into Heathrow.

The children were still pottering about in various stages of undress when I left for the meeting the following morning. Reluctantly Lizzie had agreed to hold the fort until I returned in exchange for a pound (she had beaten me up from 50p) and take-away doner kebabs for lunch.

'If Daddy phones,' I instructed her, 'take a message and ring me at Mrs Jackman's.' Engrossed in a *Woman's Own* article on hormone replacement therapy, she nodded absently. 'And make sure that Charlie cleans his teeth and Jane puts on clean underclothes.' This caught her attention.

'Why can't you do that?' she asked, not unreasonably.

'Because I haven't time to stand over them for the next ten minutes – I'm late already.'

'Well, I can't promise anything,' she warned. 'You know as well as I do that Charlie will say he's brushed his teeth even if he hasn't. Would you believe that he wets his toothbrush and smears toothpaste round the basin in an effort to fool you? I told him he might just as well clean his teeth for all the bother he goes to, but I think it's become a point of honour with him now.'

'Well then, just see to Jane's underwear.'

'If you haven't already removed her dirty ones and put clean ones out, it's too late.' I pulled a face. 'Well, you know Jane, Mum. Changes everything else four times a day and her underclothes only when she has no choice. And please make sure you're home by lunch-time because I'm going round to Karen's this afternoon.'

I called out goodbye to anyone within earshot, whereupon Jane came scampering urgently down the stairs.

'Wait a minute Mummy,' she cried imperiously. She stood on the third to bottom stair so that her eyes met mine. 'How can you go out,' she demanded, 'when Daddy might phone at any time? That's what you said. "He could phone at any time." And when he does, you won't be here, will you? I wouldn't like you not to be here if I was coming home after being away.' She glared at me accusingly.

'It's all right darling – don't worry.' I tried to put my arm round her shoulders but she drew sharply away. Inevitably that irrational guilt that every wife and mother will recognize began its invidious progress from my head to my heart. Call yourself a caring person, it hissed *en route*. Self-centred cow, attending to your own selfish interests when your exhausted husband is coming home after weeks of toil in strange and distant lands – leaving your babies alone in the house, half-naked and hungry . . .

'Honestly Jane,' I pleaded, 'I'll only be gone an hour or two – and if Daddy phones from the airport Lizzie has orders to contact me and I'll come straight home.' The child's cold, grey eyes scrutinized me with a sort of curious speculation. When I stick a pin in this creature, those eyes said, it behaves in a very interesting and entertaining manner. Let's have another go . . .

'I haven't had anything to eat,' she said, still watching me closely, 'and I'm not dressed or anything.'

'Surely you can get yourself a glass of orange juice and some cereal.' Jane sniffed and as I watched her eyes filled with furiously contrived tears of self-pity.

'I can only find odd socks and I haven't any clean knickers and there's a hole under the arm of my Union Jack T-shirt.' This, as every mother will know, is part of a power game called 'Pushing the Old Girl into a Corner'. Jane, I knew, could be coaxed into a tactical submission with a few funny faces and a bit of a tickle but I felt impatient and so disinclined to play.

'Now you're being silly, Jane,' I admonished her sternly. 'You don't need socks, there's some clean knickers in the airing cupboard, I saw them there yesterday, and the hole under the arm of your T-shirt is so small I couldn't get my little finger through it . . . Now bye-bye,' I said firmly, kissing her on the tip of her nose which she rubbed vigorously on the back of her hand.

'You don't love Daddy,' she wailed piteously having one last swipe, 'and you don't love me or you wouldn't leave me with Lizzie. She's horrible to me when you're not here.' There was a strangled sound from the kitchen. 'She is,' Jane insisted. 'She says things like she'll put me in the dustbin and once she said she'd stick red-hot needles up my nostrils.'

'And did she?' I asked conversationally. Jane hesitated. She would like to have shown me some scars, but being an essentially honest child has its draw-backs.

'No,' she said doubtfully, 'but you'll be sorry when she does.'

'Well, you tell me when she does, and I promise I'll be sorry.'

The very picture of a neglected child, shoulders drooping and eyes limpid with unrequited love, with an enormous sigh, Jane turned mournfully away from me. She climbed wearily up the stairs, making exceedingly heavy weather of them, and then waved a limp but brave little hand at me over the banisters. 'You go and enjoy yourself,' the hand said, 'you have fun with your friends while I waste away in rags.'

Lizzie joined me and said with a broad grin, 'You should

put that child on the stage,' and there was real admiration in her voice.

'I would, if I thought the theatre was ready for her,' I said ruefully.

'You shouldn't have a swimming pool,' Hannah was telling Patsy Pennant when I arrived, 'if you can't really afford the overheads.' I knew she was speaking from bitter experience. The Jackmans had blown a Premium Bond windfall on a small pool only two years before and had been regretting it ever since. After the initial blaze of aquatic enthusiasm had worn off it was rarely used. After Barney and Tom had lost interest, Hannah, who is the sort of polite and decorous breast-stroke swimmer who hates to get her hair wet, endeavoured to justify the extravagance with a daily regulation plunge come rain or shine and she issued all her friends with an open invitation. On a really hot day the thought of the cool, clear water was enticing, but the whole procedure was such a fag and took up so much time that I seldom got further than thinking about it. After a while, the second-hand boiler proved to have been a false economy and they were advised to buy a new one. Then the PVC liner developed a terminal leak and had to be replaced just weeks after the guarantee ran out; and just as they thought their troubles were over, the concrete shell cracked owing to hitherto unsuspected subsidence and overnight all the water seeped away into the clay soil and their garden was awash for days. Now it remained, a large, mossy, insect-ridden pit, as a constant monument to their sybaritic folly. When they could afford it, they said, they would have it filled in.

However, the delightful, vine-covered terrace was still a joy with its terracotta tubs of scarlet geraniums and trailing lobelia, its full-grown date palm (a birthday present from Hannah to Barney during the first flush of pool worship) and its white, wrought-iron garden furniture. Indeed, it was a very pleasant place to sit even if there was something rather incongruous about the view. Personally I found the presence of the empty pool oppressive, like an empty stage after the players have all gone home, and I sank into a lethargy during which I wrote a short story in my head about a pool that was haunted by the spectre of a child who had drowned in it.

Because of the delicate nature of our business, no one seemed eager to open the meeting. Even B, who normally enjoyed open confrontation, seemed unusually subdued, and like a child in disgrace, she had seated herself a little way away from the rest of us. Eventually Hannah cleared her throat.

'Well now,' she said in the bright voice of one who has but recently girded her loins, so to speak. 'The first thing on this morning's agenda must be those forty-eight extra people B has sold tickets to.'

'Before you go any further,' B interjected vigorously, 'I feel I must ask for a right to reply.'

'But we haven't accused you of anything yet,' Hannah pointed out reasonably.

'Nevertheless,' B began defensively, 'I think I should be permitted to explain my action before everyone sits down to discuss what to do about it.' She paused briefly for objections. Hannah's face assumed a resigned expression while the rest of us gazed at B impassively.

'I think I should make it clear then,' she resumed in her usual declamatory style, 'that I have absolutely no regrets about what I did. I can see that perhaps I should have consulted the rest of you, but time was running short and I needed to make a quick decision. I did, however, speak to Polly, who raised no valid objections.' Hannah glanced quickly in my direction. I shrugged and raised an eyebrow. 'And I also spoke to Miranda who, I'm sure, will verify that she gave me full support.' Miranda, who was gazing thoughtfully out over the empty pool, appeared not to have heard her name mentioned. Without a break she drew luxuriously on her black Sobranie and exhaled several perfectly formed smoke rings. It was a trick I had been practising unsuccessfully for many years. I knew in a flash that she was the sort of woman who could whistle from between two fingers and throw a ball overarm like a boy and I pondered briefly on the unfair distribution of talents. When it became clear that Miranda's verification was to be withheld, for the time being anyway, B continued.

'I personally don't see forty-eight extra people as a problem and in financial terms we will reap a generous harvest. One more day spent cooking is neither here nor there and we simply pick up the phone to order more wine.'

'What about space?' Maggie cut in. 'Our old tennis court won't take a larger marquee and the one we've hired is only just large enough for two hundred.'

B tutted irritably. 'You know as well as I do Maggie that quite a few people who bought tickets won't attend the function. They were simply donating money to the Fund. People like the Jensons, the Parkes and old Admiral Forbes-Duthie and there are quite a lot more like them.'

'Forty-eight?' I asked in a small, apologetic voice. B shot me a sharp, impatient look and continued as though I hadn't spoken.

'Miranda made the point to me, and I'm prepared to believe her because she has more experience than I do in such matters, that people don't feel that they've enjoyed themselves unless they're squashed together like sardines. Anyway, if we roll the sides of the marquee up, the whole problem becomes academic.'

'And if it rains?' An uncomfortable silence followed my second negative contribution. The weather was something we seemed to have resolved not to discuss but I suppose the possibility of bad weather was always at the back of our minds.

'What a little Job's Comforter you are this morning, Polly.' Miranda casually flicked her ash into one of the geranium pots and turned to me with what must have appeared to everyone else to be a good-humoured smile. I, however, was looking into her eyes. 'Let's just suppose it's *not* going to rain, shall we?' B's gratitude was painful to watch. 'We've no reason to think that it *will* rain. We've had a marvellous summer and the long-range weather forecast is very promising.' To my horror I caught myself hoping it would rain, just to spite Miranda. 'And don't you go praying for rain, Polly Graham, just so that you can say "I told you so."' Mind-reading was obviously another of Miranda's many talents. She chuckled and everyone else joined in.

'All right,' I began waspishly, 'so even supposing the evening is tropical, we only have a week left and speaking for myself, I don't have the time to spend a single day cooking.'

'No one has yet asked you to cook, Polly,' Miranda cut in gently.

'I'm still making those damned paper flowers . . . and incidentally, what happened to all that help I was promised?' The women looked from one to the other with expressions of dismay. It was my idea to turn the marquee into an Athenian copse as a suitable back-cloth for our Shakespearian revelries. Ivy removed from the Bray house walls was to be hung in swathes radiating out from the two tent poles. We had permission to gather bracken from Ruislip woods and thereabouts and I intended to deposit this casually but strategically in large tubs of earth at various points around the floor. The local council had kindly donated the smaller branches of a dying Italian poplar that was due for the chop but I still had to arrange the means whereby these would be transported to Maggie's back garden. However, to add some colour to the décor, for I agreed with Gwen when she said that if I didn't watch out the place might look more like the Blasted Heath, I had undertaken to produce, with, I thought, the help of willing hands, a few hundred multifariously coloured tissue-paper flowers. The willing hands had failed to materialize and now I, with occasional help from members of my family, was spending every spare moment cutting, twisting and sticking. Warehousing was proving difficult too and if you opened the box-room door you were deluged with a soft rustling shower of vivid, exotic and highly improbable paper blooms.

'I'm awfully sorry,' Patsy said in her concerned, anxious way, 'but honestly Polly, I don't remember you asking for any help with paper flowers. What paper flowers are they anyway? I'm sure if you'd asked me for help I'd have offered.' There was a chorus of agreement.

'You *did* offer – all of you.'

'Well look, if you still need some help, Tuesday's free,' Miranda said.

'Well I'm not,' I replied stiffly. 'I have a group session in the morning and I'm counselling all the afternoon.' So there!

Miranda said, 'I see . . .' in the way you might if you thought that a person was biting off more than she could possibly chew and she only had herself to blame if things got out of hand.

I had another problem besides that of paper flower manufacture. Gwen had been very scathing about my industrious efforts to transform Ma's old beaver lamb coat into a lion skin, and admittedly Charlie did look rather weird if you compared him to the other two Gentlemen Jims of the Jungle.

'If I may make a comment,' she had murmured as he shuffled awkwardly on to the 'stage' holding the Tottenham Court Road mask in place with one hand and his long tail in the other. 'He puts me in mind of a little old lady who's about to hold up a sub-post-office.' Charlie heard this and glared balefully at me through the eye-slits.

'I told you it looked stupid,' he had growled in a muffly sort of way. Stuart and Rick meanwhile had to support each other in their mirth and my heart went out to the stolid little figure in the beaver lamb coat. It is time, I thought, to set matters straight and I had pointed out to Gwen that the Lion in *Pyramus and Thisbe* wasn't supposed to look realistic, but like one Snug the Joiner who probably wasn't into papier-mâché and certainly wouldn't have had ready access to a sewing machine and several yards of mustard-coloured nylon fur.

'By that token,' she had retorted sharply, 'he didn't shop at the joke shop in Tottenham Court Road either.' But then she'd added with an apologetic grin, 'But I take your point. I'm afraid Miranda got a bit carried away, but who am I to look a gift lion in the mouth?' Gwen agreed with me that there was a certain sort of rustic charm and distinction about Charlie's Lion that was lacking in the other two, but Charlie, who was not of an age to assert his individuality, insisted upon certain changes to his costume and these turned out to be more time-consuming than I had envisaged.

'So . . .' Hannah broke into the thoughtful silence that had followed my cry from the heart. Others too were beginning to wonder if they could spare the extra time for a further day's cook-in. 'What have we decided?'

'Not a blind thing,' Gwen said tartly, 'and I've taken an early lunch-hour for this meeting, which is nearly up. But before I go I have to say that I can't help with the cook-in unless we do it this Sunday. And don't forget, everyone, that you are expected to attend the dress rehearsal on Saturday morning. The children have got to have an audience at least once before the night.' Gwen left after telling us that she would abide by the majority decision but would like to know what it was anyway.

One by one the remaining members of the Committee stated their reasons for not being able to help with the cooking and B's defiant expression began to disintegrate into one of desperation.

'Look here,' she exclaimed indignantly, 'I can't possibly do it all on my own.'

'Frankly, B,' Hannah began with the merest gleam of satisfaction in her eye, 'you should have thought of that before you sold all those extra tickets.'

'Like all of you,' B went on, 'I have lots of other jobs to finish. I haven't even begun working on my fancy dress yet.'

It had been decided that the Committee members would be more comfortable in simple clothes that didn't hinder us in the execution of our various duties. Gwen's initial suggestion had been Elizabethan noblewomen, but Maggie had pointed out the impracticality of seven women in paniered skirts and huge ruffs jostling about behind the buffet. Someone else thought that court jesters might be humorously appropriate and Miranda designed a diaphanous fairy get-up for us that consisted of a flesh-coloured body stocking and wisps of silk chiffon. We decided that though this might look gorgeously provocative on Miranda, it would not show the rest of us off to our best advantage. Finally, when Hannah came up with the practical idea of serving wenches we were all mightily relieved.

'Just pretty dirndl skirts, off-the-shoulder blouses and mob caps,' she said and I for one was very pleased because that was just the sort of thing that suited me best, looking, as I do, more like a serving wench than a fairy. Unfortunately it turned out to be just the sort of thing that suited Miranda best too. Our collective hearts thudded down to our boots when she pirouetted in front of us. Her 'little dressmaker in Bushey' had really come up trumps this time but you wouldn't have found *her* Elizabethan serving wench in a spit'n'sawdust inn if you spent your life looking. The outfit consisted of a tightly laced satin basque over a sheer lacy blouse, the combination of the two pushing up her small, but no doubt perfect bosom into high relief; a flouncing, red and yellow skirt over masses of frothy petticoats that gave her a hand-span waist; a frilly mob cap that was dotted with fetching little red rose-buds; fish-net tights, for God's sake, and black patent ankle-strap stilettos.

'Good Lord, Miranda,' B had expostulated incredulously, 'you look like a fugitive from the chorus line of *Kiss Me Kate*.' Then she had turned approvingly towards me in my authentic vegetable-dyed hessian and old sheeting and had said, 'Now that's more like it, Polly. "Greasy Joan doth keel the pot" and all that,' but I had wished, more than anything, that I had reminded her of a fugitive from the chorus line of *Kiss Me Kate*.

'Very realistic, Polly,' Miranda had said with an unpleasant smirk. 'Gee, I wish I'd thought of it.'

'. . . And,' B continued, 'I've still got several table-cloths to hem.' We had tie-dyed a collection of old sheets leaf-green and the overall effect was very arboreal although, as usual, because it wasn't her idea, Miranda was very rude about them. She said she thought they looked like scruffy paint rags, and individually perhaps they did, but I was sure that, *en masse*, they would achieve the effect I was after.

'Oh for God's sake, B, I'll do the table-cloths,' Maggie said impatiently.

'And I'll help you with the cooking since everyone else is so *frightfully* busy,' Miranda offered in her sarcastic way.

B's eyes went sticky with gratitude. Ignoring Maggie's generous offer, she cried, her voice trembling with suppressed emotion, 'Oh Miranda, you really are a brick. I don't know how we'd have managed without you.' How unfair of B, I thought, and for some reason I remembered that disgraceful episode at school when Anne Ostler was awarded the singing prize when everyone thought I had it in the bag. She had the voice of a sick parrot. I know, I sat next to her in choir and I used to wonder how on earth she had got through her audition. The fact that she spent the whole of the preceding year dancing sycophantic attention upon the singing teacher, the mannish Miss Bunting, of course had nothing to do with it.

'Oh, I expect you'd've managed,' Miranda said with gentle irony and once again I received the unpleasant impression that she was laughing at us up her sleeve.

A cook-in was arranged and B issued a general invitation to any of us who found ourselves with time weighing heavily upon our hands, to 'come on round and muck in'. She'll be lucky, I thought.

'Now before you go, ladies,' Hannah said loudly over the

sounds of handbags snapping and car-keys clinking, 'I need to know, finally, what kitchen help we have managed to arrange.' None of us wanted to be grounded in the kitchen washing up and those of us with daily helps were instructed to ask them if they would give their services for just one night on a voluntary basis. 'Mrs Grace has volunteered,' Hannah said of her own 'help', 'and she has volunteered Mr Grace for tidying up on Sunday morning.'

Miranda said that her Filipino couple, Conceptua and Jesus, had agreed to put their joint services at our disposal. 'But we'll have to watch Jesus and drink. He's uncontrollable after three pints,' and she smiled a secret smile to herself. I wondered how to handle a chap with a name like Jesus. I rather balked at the idea of shouting, 'I say, Jesus, lend us a hand with these trestle tables,' brought up as I was as a practising Christian. I hoped I wouldn't forget myself and genuflect in his presence.

Maggie told us that her Mrs Bridie would be helping all day Friday but couldn't manage the evening. However, she had offered us her unmarried daughter Trish who was an ambulance driver and owned a Triumph Bonneville motorbike. 'She likes working behind the bar on her evenings off,' Mrs Bridie had told Maggie, 'and she's a good bouncer.'

'Do you really think we'll *need* a bouncer?' Patsy asked tentatively.

'Not really,' Maggie replied, 'but if we did, Trish would be the person to do it. She's built like a tank and looks a bit like Henry Cooper.'

B waited for our merriment to die down and then cleared her throat. 'Um ... I've asked Mrs Walker-Smith,' she began uncertainly. Well, she knew how we felt about Mrs Walker-Smith, 'and she says she's willing to help in the marquee but she doesn't want to work in the kitchen.'

Maggie groaned. B's Mrs Walker-Smith was indeed a bitter pill. The widow of a solicitor's clerk who had fallen under a train on Holborn Station, she was also a crashing snob. This was something we had discovered when she had helped us out with our sherry mornings earlier in the year. 'Of course, I only help Mrs Baines for pin-money,' she had made haste to tell us when it had become clear to her that we expected her to help with the washing-up. 'And Mrs Baines specifically asked me to serve the sherry and the short-bread.' What we didn't need was any more servers, so without a word, Patsy Pennant slipped a pinny over her good black and set to work over the suds. Mrs Walker-Smith, on the other hand, had a smashing time mingling with our guests and regaling them with little anecdotes about her other employer, the Lady Rose Hatt. 'Of course, Lady Rose and I are now inseparable friends,' I heard her telling a group of bored-looking women as I flew past with a plate of short-bread.

'Jolly good, B,' Hannah said briskly, 'and *do* be sure to thank Mrs Walker-Smith for her kind offer, but I really don't think we need to trouble her. You see we only need help in the kitchen.'

B's face fell. 'But I can't tell her that,' she exclaimed in horror, 'she's already made a new dress for the occasion.'

'Well, B, if you've got a spare ticket she can come as a guest,' Hannah suggested innocently.

'But she's quite willing to work in the marquee,' B protested, looking hurt.

'No she isn't,' Miranda cut in sharply, 'she wants to be a guest without paying,' which was what we were all thinking but afraid to say. B looked very troubled.

'She'll walk out,' B warned. 'You know what she's like.' B was terrified of her twice-weekly help. Right from the start Mrs Walker-Smith had made her position clear.

'I don't clean ovens or toilets,' she had said on her first morning, and from then on everything had gone pretty much her way.

'We work side by side,' B used to tell us, but what that meant in practice was that B worked and Mrs Walker-Smith leant on her broom and gossiped.

'Would it matter if she *did* walk out, B?' I said daringly.

'After all, she's about as much use as an ash-tray on a motor-bike.'

B looked appalled. 'If you had a "help" Polly you wouldn't say things like that. They're like gold dust. If Mrs Walker-Smith left it would be almost impossible to find another one and then I'd have to pay her twice as much.' This, we knew, was careful propaganda put out by Mrs Walker-Smith herself. 'You won't find anyone else,' I can imagine her threatening a cowering B, 'who'll clean out your grates for two pounds an hour.' Needless to say, the going rate at the time was £1.50 but B was convinced that there was a conspiracy of rich Americans plotting to kidnap Mrs Walker-Smith. 'You know I hate working for Americans,' the dreadful woman would tell B every few months, 'but I have to look after myself now that Stanley's gone.' Mrs Walker-Smith would get her extra 25p or whatever it was and the American take-over was foiled for a bit longer.

Eventually Hannah took pity on B. 'All right, B, tell her we don't need help serving, but we do need a kitchen supervisor.' What a splendid chairman Hannah is, I thought. No one else would have thought of such a tactful solution. 'Tell her,' Hannah went on, 'that when work's over we'll all join in the fun.'

B looked thoughtful and then she brightened. 'I don't think she could possibly take offence at that, do you?' We all shook our heads vigorously and said firm things like 'Good heavens no,' and 'Why ever should she?'

'It's just that she's such a sensitive woman and I wouldn't want her to feel we were putting on her in any way.'

'Perish the thought,' Maggie muttered to me without apparently opening her mouth.

So, having pardoned B for her sin of omission and having agreed the ways and means of safe-guarding Mrs Walker-Smith's colossal ego, we went our separate ways, agreeing, before we went, to meet for a plenary session on Friday of the following week to iron out any last-minute hitches.

'Not forgetting,' Hannah shouted after us, 'that we are expected at Gwen's tomorrow for the dress rehearsal.'

On the way home I stopped off at the Greek take-away for doner kebabs, and then, for a special treat, I asked Mr Aristophanou to add three of his rosemary- and wine-flavoured sausages for the children and a small container of hummus for myself.

'Today is a celebration?' Mr Aristophanou asked as I guiltily asked for four slices of oozing, sticky baklava.

'In a way,' I replied. 'My husband's coming home from a long business trip abroad.' The elderly Greek chuckled and gave me a broad wink.

'That *is* a reason for celebration,' he smirked suggestively, 'and then afterwards, he can enjoy my wife's baklava, yes?' I didn't tell him that by the time Alan arrived home the baklava would be no more than a pleasant memory. '*Bon appétit!*' he called after me with a friendly leer and I felt the amused, speculative eyes of Mr Aristophanou's full-bosomed, bewhiskered wife follow me across the road and into the car.

The phone was ringing as I came through the door into an empty house. It was Sheila Rosen.

'I've been trying to contact you for the past hour,' she said with the merest hint of impatience.

'I'm sorry,' I replied, feeling not sorry but offended, 'I had an urgent Committee meeting this morning. Lizzie was here to answer the phone.' Or was she? I wondered. The house was as silent as the grave. 'As a matter of fact, I can't imagine where she's got to.'

'Well, never mind,' she said, and I thought, well, you don't have to, do you, she's not *your* daughter. 'I'm just phoning to tell you that Alan's here at the office and he's asked me to tell you that he'll be home for supper.'

'He'll be home for supper,' I repeated stupidly. 'You mean he's gone straight to the office from the airport?'

'Yes, that's what I said, Polly. He's had to come straight in for a very important meeting.' I tried to imagine what sort of meeting could be so important that he had to step straight from a twenty-hour flight into the office, and failed.

'Well, all right,' I said huffily, 'you can tell him you've done your duty.' There was a sharp intake of breath at the other end of the line.

'Don't be too hard on him, Polly. He doesn't like it any more than you do,' Sheila reprimanded me gently.

'Frankly, it comes to something when a chap hasn't got time to ring his wife after being away for three weeks.' There was an awkward pause and I could almost taste Sheila's contemptuous disapproval. For some reason I admit I did feel a bit ashamed of myself. I sounded, even to myself, like one of those selfish, bitter women who believe themselves to be the centre of the universe and treat their husbands accordingly.

'He's been trying to speak to you since he landed,' Sheila said coldly. 'But there's been no reply.'

'No . . . well . . . I'll look into that. Thank you for ringing. Goodbye.'

Glumly I looked at the containers of food on the table. I didn't feel at all hungry and for two pins would have thrown the whole lot down the waste disposal just to spite my irresponsible children. But on reflection that seemed to be a shocking extravagance so I called Poppy, who would surely enjoy the meaty bits, only to find that she was missing too. I said something very rude to myself, which was a luxury I could only afford when the children were out of the house, and then decided I had better go and look for them.

Having made sure they were not in the immediate vicinity, I crossed the road into the meadow. Although there were multitudes of children and dogs swarming about, none of them appeared to be mine. They were not watching the Under 15 cricket practice nor were they buying sweets at Khan's Emporium. Assuming that it was unlikely that all three, plus dog, had been abducted or run over, I returned home to wait for them and to reflect with mounting irritation upon Alan's hurtful neglect. This was the first time Alan had broken with the time-honoured custom of coming straight home from the airport after a long trip abroad. He didn't find it easy to settle back into our normal hum-drum routine after weeks away staying in large, impersonal luxury hotels where he only had to pick up a phone and all his needs were met; where they ironed his under-pants and sewed buttons on his shirts without being asked; where his shoes were cleaned overnight and there were clean towels in the bathroom every day; where he wasn't required to mow lawns and put up shelves in his free time and where his privacy was unbroken for however long he wished it to be. He found the renewed blast of family life disturbing and if we didn't have some sort of private moratorium, he would spend weeks complaining about the service.

I nibbled dismally upon a cold Greek sausage which was unaccountably full of gristly bits that got stuck between my teeth and then I bit into a hot green pepper that had been lurking inside a sodden doner kebab and almost blew off the top of my head. Hot green peppers always give me hiccups; violent, noisy, painful hiccups that leave my digestive system bruised and tender for hours afterwards. I tried drinking ice-cold water from the wrong side of a glass but hiccuped mid-gulp and sprayed a pile of freshly ironed laundry. Then I took a heaped teaspoon of granulated sugar. A single grain went down the wrong way and I coughed and choked for several minutes. That, I thought, will at least have done for the hiccups, but not a bit of it. After a breathlessly hopeful twenty-five seconds, I hiccuped again with such precipitous violence that I struck the back of my head on the corner of an open cupboard door. Things, I thought, while unable to decide whether to cry from the exquisite pain or laugh at the unbelievably ridiculous sequence of events, can only get better – ho ho hum hum!

'*Mum!*' Lizzie's shout carried up from the road outside with disturbing urgency. The gravel path crunched under running feet. '*Mum!*' Recognizing instantly that something was wrong, I leapt to my feet and ran out of the door to meet the children. Charlie reached me first. Breathless and red-faced, he flung himself at me and burst into tears. Lizzie followed dragging a sobbing Jane behind her.

'Poppy's been run over!' she wailed before giving way to tears herself. Instantly the lower half of my body turned to jelly and I slumped down on the doorstep in an ungainly heap – and hiccuped. So much, I thought later, for shock. The children tumbled down on top of me, all needing to be cuddled and restored. It is, as any mother of three or more will know, very difficult to apportion tenderness in equal parts at the same time to everyone and at such times it would be useful to have three heads and six arms.

When things had calmed down a bit I asked Lizzie what had happened. Between sniffs and heaving broken sobs she told me that Poppy had dodged between her legs and run out into the road after the ginger tom from No. 65 when she had answered the door to two women who wanted to talk to her about 'God and things'.

'A red van was passing and Poppy ran straight into it. She made a terrible noise, Mummy.' At the mention of Poppy's terrible noise everyone began crying again. 'The driver stopped his van and lifted Poppy on to the verge. She was all bloody and the skin was hanging off her back legs like –' she gulped for breath, 'like – red flannel knickers with broken elastic. The awful thing was, she struggled to get up and then ran about barking hysterically and wagging her tail as if nothing had happened. People came running out of their houses and tried to catch her but she was like a maniac. In the end Mrs Constantine caught her with a rugby tackle and she wrapped Poppy in a blanket, put her in the back of her car and we all drove to Mr Matthews the vet.' Thank God for Dorothy and her kind heart and presence of mind, I thought. 'Poppy had to have sixty-three stitches,' Lizzie recounted with awe. 'Mr Matthews said it was like stitching a patchwork quilt.'

'Where is Poppy now?'

'Mr Matthews said he wanted to keep her in overnight. He said he'll telephone when Poppy comes round from the anaesthetic.'

'And Mrs Constantine?'

'She's just cleaning up her car – it was an awful mess because Poppy wouldn't stay wrapped in the blanket – and then she says she's coming round.'

I wriggled out from under three sweaty bodies, stood up stiffly and stretched out a hand to heave each one in turn to their feet.

'Where's Daddy?' Jane asked suddenly. 'Is he home yet?' I shook my head and explained that Alan was coming home in time for supper. She looked very disappointed. 'I bet he phoned when there was no one here,' she said, looking at me accusingly. 'I've been worrying about that all the time.'

I hiccuped by way of reply and it was such a funny squawk that despite themselves, the children burst out laughing and couldn't stop giggling for ages.

By the time Dorothy arrived to check on our collective welfare, Mr Matthews had telephoned to say that though Poppy was feeling rather sorry for herself she would be fit enough to come home the following day.

'Oh Dorothy,' I said hugging her gratefully, 'you are a pearl beyond price. Lord knows what would've happened if you hadn't been there to take charge.' Dorothy made a typical gesture of modest dismissal.

'Now Polly,' she said, 'don't be so silly. You'd've done the same for me I'm sure. Anyway,' she went on after scalding her lips on the cup of tea I had poured out, 'I just called round to see if everything was all right. Actually I'd've been round earlier, only when I got home there were two ladies on the doorstep from one of those cranky religious sects waiting to talk to me about the End of the World. I felt I ought to give them five minutes as they had taken the time to call on me.' Which was yet another typically generous Dorothy gesture. I'm afraid you wouldn't catch me asking screw-ball strangers into my living-room to discuss my place in the heavenly scheme of things come the Apocalypse.

*

It was nearly seven when I heard Alan's car turn into the drive. There was a large lasagne browning in the oven and I was energetically shaking the ingredients for a French dressing together in an empty honey jar.

'It's Daddy! It's Daddy!' Jane shrieked excitedly as she tumbled down the stairs and out of the front door. A freshly bathed Charlie followed, wrapped rather stylishly in a towelling loin-cloth, and Lizzie brought up the rear with the dignity that befitted her thirteen years and five months. I let the children get their affectionate and noisy greetings over with and then I stepped slowly out into the warm evening sunshine. Alan was heaving luggage out of the boot of his very dusty car which had just spent three weeks in the open-air long-term car-park at Heathrow and the children were dancing round him like hungry puppies. Even Lizzie, who normally eschewed such youthfully overt signs of enthusiasm, was hopping from one long, thin leg to the other in a fair imitation of an over-stimulated flamingo. With his back towards me, he was unaware of my presence and I was struck by the dispirited droop of his shoulders and the crumpled disarray of his pale-grey, light-weight tropical suit. He looked up at the sound of my footsteps and gave me a wan smile.

'Hello love,' he said wearily, 'it's good to be home.' There was a watchful hesitant look in his grey eyes that I couldn't quite interpret and I knew for certain that he had something important to tell me. I hugged him with a sudden fierce compassion and was appalled to discover he had lost yet more weight. Indeed he seemed fleshless under his creased jacket.

'My God, you're so thin,' I cried in horror.

He stepped back from me sharply and said, 'Nonsense,' in a dismissive fashion and handed me his duty-free bags to carry in.

We are always a little wary of each other during those first few minutes after his return from a long trip abroad. It is as if we are not sure where or how to start. Should I tell him my news first, or should I wait for him to tell me his? Neither of us wants to hear bad news, but we expect to.

'Where's Poppy?' was the first thing he asked. Anyone knowing her would miss her exuberant welcome. Some people who don't like dogs who jump up with muddy paws and tear tights and catch threads in tweed jackets might see it as a blessed relief but for Alan it was a rejection. A communal gasp went up. In our excitement we had forgotten the poor dog and her wounds. I took a deep breath.

'She had an accident this morning,' I told him.

'*What?*'

'Don't panic,' I went on hastily, 'because Mr Matthews says she can come home tomorrow.'

'What do you mean, she had an accident? What sort of accident?' He was giving me his wild-eyed, mad axeman look. It was the onset, I could tell, of the 'I-go-away-and-look-what-happens' period and this would continue until he had made a thorough reconnoitre of his hearth and home. He once told me, by way of an apology for his anal retentive behaviour, that for a while after a long trip abroad he felt excluded from the family circle. He said he liked to imagine that we couldn't manage without him and it always threw him a bit to discover that we could. I understood that, because I once suffered the same feeling of alienation after only a week in Portugal with Babs.

After we had finished explaining the dynamics of Poppy's accident, Alan turned to me and asked suspiciously, 'So where were you when all this happened?'

Lizzie, with her usual sharp insight, saw which way the conversation was drifting and replied quickly for me, 'Mum was at an emergency meeting of the Committee, but I would have been here if you phoned.'

'Well I did, and you weren't,' he said sharply. Patiently Lizzie explained that she would have been if the dog hadn't had an accident. Alan considered the matter and then nodded slowly.

'Well,' he began finally, 'is there anything else I ought to know about before I relax?' It was as if I was a child again, standing in front of Miss Parsons, my house mistress, frantically trying to recall the undiscovered sins I wanted taken into consideration.

'Mummy broke a dinner plate,' Jane piped up helpfully.

'Not a Wedgwood?' Alan exclaimed, his eyes widening in horror.

I shook my head and glared at Jane, but she continued blithely, 'And Charlie pulled his curtain rail down and Lugy's arms have come off,' Lugy being Jane's baby Sacha doll. The doll was the proud possessor of vestigial male genitalia when she christened it Lucy and Charlie was profoundly disturbed on behalf of his entire sex. After considerable heated discussion, Jane was persuaded to compromise with Lugy, which to her sounded acceptably androgynous. 'I'll get her now and you can mend her.'

'Him,' Charlie muttered under his breath, 'mend *him*.' I glanced at Alan and he smiled.

'I'm a little tired right now, Jane darling,' he said, pulling the child towards him and pressing her head against his hip, which was as far as it would reach. 'But I'll do it tomorrow – after all, it's Saturday.'

After supper, and Alan's exotic gifts had been distributed to the accompaniment of squeals of joy, I followed him upstairs and sat down on the bed to chat while he unpacked. He seemed unusually uncommunicative and our conversation developed into a series of questions from me and brief answers from him. Yes, the trip had been fairly successful. Yes, he had taken some good orders. No, my last letter hadn't reached him and yes, Takahashi and his new young wife were thrilled with the antique sterling silver photograph frame I had chosen for them.

'And tell me,' I finally plucked up courage to ask, 'what was the important meeting this afternoon that you just *had* to attend?' A muscle in his jaw twitched. He cleared his throat noisily, sniffed and then drew a handkerchief out of his pocket and blew his nose very noisily.

'Oh, it was just a management meeting,' he said nasally as he pulled and squeezed his nose. 'Sort of forward planning really.' Unsatisfied, I pursued my subject.

'But it must've been a *very* important meeting for you to go straight from the airport . . .'

'Well, yes, it was as a matter of fact. But look, Polly,' Alan swung round to face me, 'I'm absolutely knackered and I just want to sleep for a hundred years, so do you think we can talk about it in the morning? Please?'

He touched my cheek gently and I grasped his hand and pressed my lips to his palm. Usually his homecoming was celebrated with a joyous and revitalizing romp in bed but it was evident that night that nothing could have been further from Alan's mind. On reflection I felt relieved. Without joy and spontaneity love-making is nothing more than a dutiful favour and there was precious little joy or spontaneity around that night. However I felt a stab of tenderness for the flattened, lifeless hulk before me so I said, 'Of course love,' in an accepting sort of way. 'You go to bed and I'll follow you when I've cleared up.' He gave my shoulders a grateful squeeze and planted a dispassionate kiss on the top of my head.

The children in bed and the kitchen restored to its habitual clean but untidy clutter, I sat down in my Recliner to watch the last instalment of an enthralling spy serial that had had me glued to my chair for the past seven weeks at nine o'clock every Friday. Just before the final dénouement, the moment when I would find out, once and for all, who was behind the massive leak of state secrets to the KGB and three particularly grisly murders, the phone rang. On my own I wouldn't have answered it, but I was afraid that the persistent jangle would wake Alan. So, reluctantly, I trailed out into the hall, trying, as I went, to keep the screen in view through the living-room door.

'Hello Polly, this is Jim Henderson. Sorry to disturb you

so late but can I have a word with Alan?' I wondered what Alan's managing director could want at such an hour.

'Can you hold on a minute, Mr Henderson? He's in bed and he's switched off the extension.'

'Oh . . . if he's in bed, don't bother. Just tell him I'll ring him some time tomorrow. Oh, and Polly,' he added mysteriously, 'tell him not to worry, will you? The news is good.' Pondering Jim Henderson's cryptic message I returned to my seat just in time to catch the credits as they rolled across the screen to one of Vivaldi's *Four Seasons*. On Monday, I promised myself (it would have to be Monday because I very much doubted if anyone would be in Granada's public relations department over the weekend), I will ring them up and find out who done it.

The message from Jim Henderson cheered Alan up but he was annoyed that I hadn't woken him.

'He told me not to wake you,' I told him.

'Well you should've anyway. It was probably . . . that is to say . . . it might have been . . . Well,' he finished, 'it must've been important for him to ring at *that* time.'

I eyed him suspiciously. 'Do you know what he wanted?'

'Something to do with next year's budget I expect,' he said, busily pairing off clean socks and putting them away in his sock drawer.

'At nearly ten o'clock on a Friday night!' I exclaimed incredulously. 'When you've just come back from the Far East!'

Alan's eyes slid furtively away from mine. 'Well,' he said quickly, 'better get on with breakfast – got lots to see to today.' He took out of his pocket his little leather-covered notebook and studied his list for the day. 'I've got to collect my grey suit from the cleaner's and my prescription from Boots, check my tyres and oil and wash the car, ring Mother . . .' He glanced at me. 'I don't suppose you remembered to look in on them while I was away.'

'I did, so ya boo sucks to you.' Meeting each other was

not something that my mother-in-law and I enjoyed very much but for Alan's sake and for the sake of the children we maintained contact in a dutiful sort of way. He looked surprised and pleased. He was very fond of his mother and it was his hope that one day she and I would overcome our differences and become friends. He was, I'm afraid, wishing for the moon.

'I've got to collect the lawn mower and then I've got to bloomin' well mow the lawn. It is, as they say, as high as an elephant's eye – and you'd better hurry up and get dressed. Didn't you say something about a dress rehearsal this morning?'

'Oh crumbs!' I yelled, throwing back the bedclothes. 'I'd forgotten all about it. What's the time?' Alan looked at his watch.

'Precisely seventeen minutes past nine.'

'Oh hell's bells and buckets of blood, we're supposed to be at Gwen's by ten!'

'Then you'd better get your skates on, hadn't you? I'll call the children.'

By the time I had washed and dressed, Alan and the children had had their breakfast and were moving about the house gathering their belongings together for their busy morning. I gulped a glass of orange juice and grabbed my handbag.

'We're off, Alan!' I shouted and Charlie made his usual witticism about bad eggs. The two girls groaned but it didn't bother him. He simply pranced about them, holding his nose and shouting, 'Bad eggs, bad eggs!'

'Okay,' Alan said coming slowly and thoughtfully downstairs. 'But I think I'll stick around for a bit . . . one or two things to do here.' But as I shut the front door behind me he was already dialling his first number.

'Stay for lunch,' Gwen commanded after the last member of the cast had been scooped up by his or her mother and directed out of the door. I shook my head and told Gwen about Poppy's accident. 'Anyway, Alan's home,' I added, 'and he'll be a bit miffed if I'm not.'

Gwen raised an eyebrow. 'I thought he was due some time next week?' she said.

'He was, but he decided to cut short his trip.' The eyebrow shot up again. 'I don't know why. He muttered something about the chap he was to see in Singapore being in Australia and Hong Kong being a dead duck, but it all sounded very odd to me.'

'Well, have some coffee anyway,' and while I was still dithering she slid a cup of instant in front of me and sat down heavily with a grunt of relief.

'Whew,' she sighed, 'my back's killing me,' and pressing the palms of her hands hard against the back of her waist, she stretched back against them luxuriously and winced. 'You're so lucky not to have a back.' I agreed with her. Most of the women I knew had back problems, usually dating from childbirth, and they spent a lot of time and often money being pummelled and pulled by strong men with manipulative fingers. From this they gained only temporary relief. Currently in vogue with the 'back brigade' was a brutish Australian horse doctor who operated from seedy rooms in Watford. Rumour had it that he had once been a back-street abortionist but when the market dried up, he turned to backs. It was whispered that one of the ladies had recognized him from her past, which must have been a traumatic experience for all concerned.

'So, what did you think of it?' There was no need to ask what 'it' was, and I was about to launch into a paean of unqualified praise when Eddie sauntered in. He said, 'Hi' to me and as he passed Gwen he rested the tips of his fingers on her shoulder, trailing them down her inner arm. When their hands touched their fingers entwined briefly before he wandered over to the kettle to make himself a cup of coffee. This tender gesture of affection so discomforted me that I forgot what I had been about to say and stared idiotically at Gwen with my mouth hanging open.

'Well,' she said impatiently, 'spit it out.'

'Er . . . um . . .'

'Very lucid,' she commented drily. I managed to pull myself together and told her that it had been an amazing experience.

'Amazingly good?' she asked irritably. 'Or amazingly bad?'

'Amazingly funny, amazingly touching, a lot of class, a lot of style . . . The children actually appeared to be enjoying themselves. I don't know how you managed it.'

'Oh you know – you beat them a little, batter them,' she said with a broad grin. 'A little starvation and sensory deprivation, electric prods . . . nothing too drastic.' She and Eddie exchanged amused glances. 'Do you think everyone feels like you?'

'I should've thought that was evident. It's been *your* morning. This year Pinner, next year the Shakespeare Memorial Theatre.' I couldn't keep the envy out of my voice. Our friendship, though close, did not preclude a certain amount of overt jealousy. We competed in the same areas and both of us were bad losers. Those who knew us found it highly diverting. 'I don't know how you two can be friends,' Hannah used to say, 'you're both so jealous of each other.' But it wasn't altogether a bad thing because it encouraged us to excel. It acted as a catalyst for achievements that were yet to come. However there were occasions when it brought out the worst in both of us and though I can't speak for Gwen, I remember these with shame.

Gwen was looking disgustingly smug so I felt obliged to add that I had thought the Clog Dance a trifle ragged. 'Too much emphasis on Clog, I would say, and not enough on Dance. I was worried about your floor.'

'Yes, I know,' Gwen replied with a thoughtful frown, 'but they love making all that noise.'

'Well, they won't be able to make it on the night.'

'Why not?' Eddie asked.

'We don't have a wooden floor.' The Committee had decided that it couldn't justify the huge expense of a dance floor and we were making do with canvas druggets laid over a thick polyurethane liner. We had been assured that this was perfectly adequate for our needs if we didn't intend to hold the British Ballroom Championships that evening.

'Huh!' Gwen cried, flashing a triumphant smile at Eddie, 'that's what *you* think!'

'Go on then,' I said in a resigned voice, 'surprise me.'

'W-e-l-l,' Gwen began, dragging out the moment, 'I've managed to persuade Mr Grey to lend us the primary school blocks.' She waited for my reaction. The wooden blocks she spoke of could be stacked together like huge, very strong building bricks to form a small stage for the children to perform their school plays and concerts on and I was, indeed, very impressed by her initiative.

'Good on yer, sport,' I said facetiously, doing my impersonation of Charlie's impersonation of Richie Benaud. They both looked puzzled, as well they might. It wasn't a very good impersonation.

'They're hollow,' Gwen went on, 'so the Clog Dance could be deafening.'

'I've suggested we take out separate insurance and wear ear protectors,' Eddie said. A vision flashed before my eyes of 248 Shakespearian characters in ear protectors and I snorted with laughter.

Somewhere in the house a phone rang, and minutes later Mike shambled apologetically into the kitchen.

'Sorry to disturb the think-tank, but Alan says he wants his lunch, Polly.' While Eddie went off to find the children, I whipped round the house collecting their stage clothes, which were distributed at random in every room.

'You'll have Charlie's Lion ready by the night, won't you Polly,' Gwen reminded me as we clambered into the car. 'I must say, I don't quite understand why you've turned the coat upsidedown and put his legs through the sleeves, but I suppose you know what you're doing.' I replied with more confidence than I felt that I had it all in hand and she wasn't to worry. At the same time I made a mental note to dump the whole lot on Ma and let her make some sense of it. It was a convenient fantasy of mine that it flattered Ma to be asked to help out with my numerous sticky situations, but whether she was or she wasn't, she always obliged, bless her.

There were several calls for Alan during the afternoon and he, in turn, made several of his own, first shutting all the doors so that no matter how hard I tried, I heard nothing more informative than a punctuated mumble. It was, however, becoming increasingly clear to me that something fairly momentous was taking place or was about to take place at Scott Fotheringay. But all thought of the Company and its immediate welfare was driven from my mind by a call that Alan received just as I was putting the finishing touches to my 200th paper flower.

Lizzie answered it. 'Who is it?' I called out as I heard the clunk of the receiver on the hall table.

'Some woman for Dad,' she told me as she passed by on her way to call her father in from the garden.

'Well who is she?'

'I don't know,' Lizzie replied impatiently. 'She didn't say her name.'

'Well go and ask. Quickly.'

'Oh Mum,' she whined. I shot her a venomous look. 'Oh, all right.' Lizzie came back and said that the woman's name was Mrs G. de Rose.

'Mrs G. de Rose!' I exclaimed in puzzlement. 'Never heard of her. Are you *sure* that's what she said? You know how bad you are with names.'

'That's what it sounded like, and I'm not going to ask again.'

I shrugged and pulled a face. 'Well, you'd better go and call your father I suppose. He's in the garden tinkering with the mower.'

'Do you know who it is?' Alan asked as he ran his oily hands under the tap. Lizzie sighed a do-I-have-to-go-through-all-of-that-again sigh.

'She says her name's Mrs G. de Rose.'

'I don't know anyone of that name,' he said frowning. 'Are you sure you've got the name right? You know what you are with names.' Lizzie groaned and slammed out of the door. 'Well, I only asked,' he said, aggrieved, as he went towards the phone.

'Hello?' I heard him say in a questioning tone of voice. 'Alan Graham here.' Then I heard him say in a low voice, 'Oh, it's you . . . Look, hang on a minute, this place is like Paddington Station.' Poking his head into the room he said, 'Can't hear over the Expelaire,' and he shut the door of the kitchen with me in it.

I sat very still, holding the paper flower up in front of me like a votive offering. A horrid suspicion, like a transfusion of snake venom, was coursing its way through to my nerve endings and for a brief moment I was quite literally paralysed by my awful imaginings. But that old reliable fight or flight instinct took over and I moved quickly to the kitchen door which I knew from experience never quite closed because of the thick pile of the hall carpet. Very carefully I eased it further open and put my ear to the crack.

'Look, I don't know what's happening,' I heard Alan murmur, 'but if I have to go, I would like you to come with me.' The meaning was unmistakable. He went on, 'But we don't have to worry about it yet because almost anything could happen.' The woman at the other end said something and he replied, 'Yes, I can understand how you feel and if you decide against it, I'll understand. I won't like it, but I'll understand.' I felt as though someone had punched me hard at the base of my spine from behind. My vision blurred and the room slowly began to revolve around me like a carousel starting up. What he was saying seemed damning enough, but that wasn't what disturbed me. It wasn't what he said so much as the way he said it. His was the voice of a persuasive lover, soft and warm and filled with concern. I knew, because the last time I'd heard it, it was addressing me. I put out a hand to steady myself and knocked the letter rack on to the floor from the Welsh dresser. The silence that followed, both sides of the door, was a guilty one.

'Listen,' I heard him say urgently, 'I can't really talk now. It's a bit difficult.' There was a pause, then he said, 'Yes, all right, I'll see you on Monday, and don't make any silly decisions over the weekend, okay?' Her reply made him chuckle and then he said, 'Bye,' and rang off. Quickly but quietly I pushed the door to and returned to paper flower 201. My anxiety was such that I was barely able to breathe, but when Alan came into the kitchen on his way back to his job in the garden I was able to ask in a fairly normal voice who it had been on the phone.

'Oh, it was Sheila Rosen,' he laughed lightly. 'Mrs G. de Rose, I ask you.' A chill swept over me and I felt suddenly nauseous. The bitter taste of bile rose in my throat. The delicate paper petals fell to the floor from my clumsy fingers and I clamped a hand over my mouth.

'You all right?' Alan asked with a slight frown.

'Oh God!' I croaked through my fingers. He peered closely at me with a speculative expression on his face.

'You all right, Polly?' he asked again. I pushed the stool back from the table. It made an ugly scraping noise like chalk on a wet blackboard. Leaping to my feet, I pushed past Alan and fled upstairs to the bathroom where I was explosively sick into the lavatory basin. I continued to retch long after I had emptied my stomach and my ears and eyes were thumping dangerously from my raised blood-pressure. My head felt twice its normal size and I thought my lungs would burst with the effort of drawing breath in between the spasms of dry vomiting. Vaguely I was aware that someone was hammering on the door but if my life had depended upon it, I couldn't have responded.

After a while the initial shock, for that is what it was, subsided and I got up slowly from my knees and ran some cold water into the basin. My face, in the mirror, was the colour of port wine and my lips, by contrast, were opaline. The lack of colour was accentuated by a distinct blue line that appeared to have been added by a fine paint-brush dipped in watery ink. I looked like Jane after one of her temper tantrums. I washed my face and hands and cleaned my teeth and then sat down on the bathroom stool to gather my wits about me.

There was a gentle tap on the door. 'Are you feeling better now?' Alan asked. I couldn't think of a suitable reply. 'Polly? Did you hear me? Are you feeling better?' There was a slight edge of concern in his voice. 'For God's sake stop being silly and answer me, Pol.' I got up and opened the door. He was hovering outside and he looked both anxious and irritated.

'I've been sick,' I stated and because the world was still spinning, I sat down abruptly on the bed. Although it was an unusually warm evening, I was shivering uncontrollably. I always do when I am about to confront an unpleasant situation head-on. Alan sat down beside me and tried to put his arms round my shoulders, but I pushed him roughly away.

'Are you ill or something?' he asked edgily. He's not very good with illness. The symptoms have to be excessive before he believes you're really ill and not malingering, and then he's frustrated by his inability to do anything dramatic to help, so he panics.

'No I'm *not* ill,' I managed to spit out from between my chattering teeth. 'I think I'm in a state of shock.' He raised his eyes to heaven and shook his head.

'Now, what on earth has shocked you?' he asked in the voice he usually uses to humour me.

'Sit down,' I commanded and he did, recognizing, no doubt, that I meant business. 'Now wait there till I get back.' He scowled, but he didn't move.

I swayed unsteadily out on to the landing and called Lizzie. 'Be a dear,' I said when she appeared at the bottom of the stairs, 'and take Charlie and Jane out for a while.'

I expected an argument, but she simply looked up at me and then said, 'All right,' in an expressionless voice. 'Where to and for how long?'

Bless the girl, I thought, and thank God for her sensitivity. 'Take them swimming, and then get them a Wimpy. They won't complain.'

'I'm sure they won't,' she replied with a slight smile. 'Shall I take the money out of your purse?' I nodded. She disappeared and after a great deal of excited running up and down stairs and arguing over towels, she shouted, 'Bye Mum!' and I heard the door slam behind them. The house was suddenly so quiet that I felt sure I could hear the ticking of the time clock on the central heating boiler. Poppy whimpered, but when I went to look at her, she was sound asleep in her basket, her ghastly wound hidden by surplus folds of Labrador. She appeared to have made a remarkable recovery and it was difficult to restrain her natural zest. Our instructions had been to keep her as quiet as possible so that the stitches would hold, but it would have been easier to extinguish a live volcano and indeed, this current prolonged bout of sleep had been induced by a massive dose of doggie tranquillizer. We had been told to use it sparingly, but already the bottle was empty.

I tiptoed back upstairs and stood outside the bedroom with my hand resting on the door handle. Right, now, I addressed myself sternly, you've got no more excuses. The time has come to get everything straight and you've got to be a big, brave girl. I certainly didn't feel big and brave and I had to sit very hard on the bleating infant who was desperately scrabbling her way up from the darkest recesses of my soul. I took several deep breaths and the panic began to subside.

Alan was sitting exactly where I had left him and he was cutting his nails with my delicate Victorian embroidery scissors.

'I wish you wouldn't,' I said querulously.

'Wouldn't what?' He looked up at me in pained surprise.

'Cut your nails with those scissors – they weren't meant for the job.' He sighed and returned them with exaggerated care to the needlework box under my bedside table. I looked with disgust at the parings that lay about him on the floor like fragments of grated Caerphilly cheese.

'Right,' he began briskly, 'now perhaps you'll explain this astonishing melodrama.' I drew in my breath sharply as an enormous shudder attacked my body from the inside out. An unpleasant lump was forming at the back of my throat and I knew I wouldn't be able to hold the tears in check much longer.

'I overheard your telephone call from Sheila Rosen,' I pronounced in solemn, climactic tones, and I waited for the veil of the temple to be rent asunder, or failing that, a gasp of horrified guilt. But he merely sniffed and said, 'I see,' thoughtfully and then waited for me to continue.

'What do you see?' I demanded. Alan shrugged helplessly.

'Well, I see that you've deduced something from what you heard and I'm waiting to hear what it is.'

'I've deduced,' I began, and then had to clear my throat several times to clear my vocal cords of phlegm. 'I've deduced,' I began again, 'that all my suspicions have been justified and that you have been having an affair with . . . no . . . you are in love with,' I corrected myself and felt even worse because being in love with someone is so much worse than having an affair, 'Sheila Rosen!' The difference between all the other times I'd asked this question and this time, was that this time I believed it. Alan drew breath to reply, but I went on quickly. 'And it wasn't *what* you said, though that was incriminating enough, it was the way that you said it. You sounded like a man speaking to a woman for whom he cares a great deal.'

'You're being ridiculous,' Alan began weakly.

'Don't insult my intelligence, Alan.' And I waited, hardly daring to breathe. Please dear God, I implored silently, let him say the right thing. Let me be wrong. But he sat on the edge of the bed looking straight ahead, saying nothing. I saw his silence as a shattering admission of guilt and as it lengthened, so the ball of anxiety in the pit of my stomach grew.

Eventually Alan spoke. 'I really don't know what to say, Pol. The trouble is you're wrong.' He hesitated and then added in a strained, low voice, 'But then again, you're right.' Outside in the sunshine a child shrieked joyously and a dog barked. I wish I hadn't begun this, I thought. I wish I was in a deckchair under the willow instead of in this hot, airless bedroom feeling heart-sick and frightened.

'You mean,' I went on relentlessly, speaking words I didn't want to speak, 'I'm wrong that you're having an affair, but I'm right that you . . .' Bile rose in my throat and though I swallowed hard, the bitter, hot taste remained. 'But I'm right,' I tried again, 'that you . . . you . . . love Sheila Rosen.'

'No, I don't bloody mean that.' Alan mopped his brow with the tail of his jazzy Hawaiian shirt, then stood up abruptly and went over to the large picture window that we hadn't been able to open since the outside of the house had been painted the previous summer. After a lot of heaving and straining, it flew open with such force that I thought the glass had cracked. 'That's better,' he said, 'it's jolly stuffy in here.' Then he started fiddling with the curtains, fussing with the pencil pleats and tidying up the drapes. When he turned round his face was a strained, apprehensive mask and I was shocked.

'Look, Pol,' he said with obvious reluctance, 'it's like this. Scott Fotheringay's being taken over by International Textiles and I don't know if I've still got a job.' I gasped involuntarily and immediately felt faint. 'It's been in the air a long time,' I heard him say through a buzz of dizziness, 'and I've needed to talk to somebody about it . . . and I'm afraid that person's been Sheila.'

Against my will I began to cry. 'But it should've been me,' I sobbed, 'I'm your wife for God's sake, and you should've talked to me about it.' Alan watched me cry with a slightly exasperated expression on his face.

'Few of us knew,' he said, 'and those that did were sworn to secrecy for obvious reasons. But I have to say this, Pol,' I looked up at his blurred figure through my tears, 'even if I could, I wouldn't have told you . . . for your own sake Polly,' he added as if to reassure me. 'Listen, love,' he said gently, and he sat down again beside me and put an arm round my heaving shoulders, 'I worked out long ago that you are far easier to live with if you *don't* know about my troubles, specially when they touch on your own security.' He paused for a deep breath. But when I tried to protest, he continued determinedly. 'You've convinced yourself that you want to know about them because you see it as part of being a Caring Person and a Good Wife, but deep down inside,' he said, shaking his head in resignation, 'you really don't want to know, and you punish me when I make the mistake of telling you. I don't know, Pol, but my problems seem to take you over.' He struggled for the right words. 'You become . . . obsessed, yes, that's the right word . . . and then you do and say impetuous things that we both regret. I mean, like the time you phoned up Jim Henderson and told him to get off my back. I know you thought you were helping, but you weren't. It simply made me look a fool . . .

'Face it, Polly, you can't handle anxiety, you know you can't, and you despise that part of yourself and you take it out on me.'

I heard him. I heard everything he said, and with sudden painful insight, I knew he was right. Moments of blinding self-realization, especially when they are far from flattering and they have been precipitated by another person's perceptions of you, are rarely comfortable, and this was no exception. What a wet lump I am, I thought in deep despair. What a wretchedly weak and self-indulgent wife I've turned out to be.

'So,' I said miserably, 'that's why you've turned to Sheila.'

'But I haven't turned to Sheila!' Alan cried out, angrily thumping his forehead with the heel of his hand, 'well, not in the sense you mean anyway. We're not lovers or anything like that. She's been a good, supportive friend, and yes, I've shared my present worries with her because . . . because . . . she's *not* my wife and she can be objective. I admit we've become closer than a normal boss and his secretary. I think she's a fine woman and I care about what's going to happen to her – to all of us – when the company changes hands, but that's all.'

'So what was that telephone call all about?' I asked truculently.

'Oh Polly,' he said wearily, 'I was simply telling her that if I still have a job, I want her to stay on as my secretary and she was telling me that she didn't think she wanted to stay if I'm moved out to the company's headquarters in Slough . . . and if you think we were saying anything else, I'm sorry.' Suddenly he brightened. 'There is one thing though that should convince you that I'm not having an affair with Sheila Rosen.' I looked up expectantly. 'Mike Bray *is*.'

I wasn't really prepared to believe this. That is to say, I believed he thought he was telling the truth because Alan isn't the sort of man to spread unsubstantiated rumour, but I thought that he'd got his wires crossed in some way. For all Mike's talk and his occasional groping, I didn't think he was even remotely capable of playing the philanderer. Oh, he liked to imply that he was not the tame pussy cat that we all knew and loved, but we all supposed that he would run like hell from a determined predatory woman.

'You see,' Alan explained, 'I saw them coming out of Basil's Brasserie late one afternoon and it was perfectly clear that they hadn't been discussing stock market prices.'

'They might've been,' I countered. 'After all, Mike's a broker and he often gives people advice . . .'

'Polly, they stood at the bottom of the steps with their arms around each other and embraced like lovers before he went off in a taxi. I didn't want to embarrass them so I dodged back into a doorway, but not before Mike saw me. He didn't say anything to Sheila, but he phoned me the next day. We met for a drink and that's when he told me.'

'Is it serious?'

Alan looked at me and shrugged. 'Well, I don't know about Mike,' he said, 'but would you say Sheila is the sort of person who would indulge in a light flirtation with a married man?' I shook my head reluctantly.

Following this amazing news, waves of profound relief swept over me. After months of uncertainty and suspicion I felt as light as air. I felt like laughing and crying and shouting and turning somersaults.

'Oh Alan!' I cried. I threw my arms round him with such exuberance that he over-balanced and we both landed in a heap on the floor. 'I'm *so* sorry . . . I'm such an awful person . . . I don't know how you put up with me . . .'

Laughing, he gently extricated himself from my violent embrace and told me to calm down. Then he took both my hands in his and gazed seriously into my puffy, red-rimmed eyes. Eventually he said, 'Tell me, Polly . . . how's your book coming along?'

'I scrapped it ages ago,' I replied, looking puzzled. I couldn't see what my book had to do with anything.

'Yes, I guessed you had,' he said thoughtfully.

'How did you guess?'

He shrugged and smiled an oddly knowing smile. 'Oh, I don't know . . . I suppose I just haven't seen Eddie around here for a while.' I felt myself blushing and I dropped my eyes quickly in case they gave anything away. 'I read what you wrote, Pol, I'm sorry,' he said, gently touching my cheek with his fingertips. 'And it didn't leave much to my imagination.'

'No,' I murmured, 'I don't suppose it did. But nothing happened, between Eddie and me I mean . . . It was just that you were so . . . absent, and he wasn't. It was all in my mind – a fantasy. Anyway,' I said, looking at him sideways and giving him a wicked grin, 'I can't be having an affair with him, because, you see, Gwen *is*!'

An hour later there was a discreet knock on the door. I shot up in bed.

'Did you lock the door?' I whispered urgently.

'Mmm-mmm,' Alan said drowsily.

'It's me, Mum,' Lizzie said, 'we're back.'

'Oh, fine,' I said. 'Dad and I are just having a little nap.'

There was a pause, followed by some giggling and then Lizzie said, 'No Jane, you *can't* go in because they're having a nap.'

'But I want to tell Mummy something,' Jane protested and the door handle waggled backwards and forwards impatiently. 'Why've they locked the door?' she wailed. 'Mummy, why've you locked me out?'

By this time Alan was fully awake and was sniggering into his pillow. 'Well, go on Polly,' he whispered, 'tell the child why you've locked her out.' I thumped him hard on the back and he shut up.

'We'll be up in a minute, darling,' I called out lightly, 'and then you can tell me.'

'But I want to tell you *now*!' Jane protested. There were sounds of a struggle.

'It's all right, Mum,' Lizzie said breathlessly, 'you go back to ... er ... sleep. I'll deal with this one. Come on, Jane.'

Jane squealed, 'Let go of my arm Lizzie, you're hurting!'

'You can help me make some peppermint creams.'

'Can I add the colours?' Their voices faded down the stairs.

'If you're careful. Nobody ate the navy-blue ones last time.'

Alan got out of bed, stretched, and patting his stomach announced that he was hungry. 'What's for supper?' he asked. It was not something which I had given much thought to that day and in fact I had forgotten to get anything out of the freezer.

'Good,' he said when I told him. 'Because I feel like a large juicy steak with lashings of Béarnaise. If you can get a sitter in a hurry we'll pop into the Steak House while we can still afford it.'

Dorothy, who said that she could just as well watch our television as her own which was on the blink anyway, had just arrived when the phone began ringing. Charlie, who was passing, picked up the receiver and grunted into it in his usual endearing fashion. He is a typically secretive Scorpio and believes that by giving our number out over the phone, he is imparting valuable information to the enemy. It is my opinion that he deliberately disguises his voice too, but he denies this.

'I just don't like phones,' he says as an excuse for his appalling manner. 'They're an intrusion on my privacy. People wouldn't dream of just dropping in on me at any time of the day or night, but it doesn't stop them phoning,' from which you might imagine that people are clamouring for his attention at all times when in fact quite the reverse is true.

'It's for you, Dad!' he bellowed up the stairs and Poppy woke up with an enormous start. Seeing Dorothy, her tried and trusted friend, she remembered her manners and began to clamber unsteadily to her paws.

'Poor old girl,' Dorothy said tenderly as she squatted down beside her. Poppy stretched out and gently licked the tip of her friend's nose and then slumped back into her basket looking dolefully apologetic.

'It's jolly decent of you to sit at such short notice,' I said. 'Doesn't Desmond mind?'

'Good Lord no,' she said with a laugh. 'He's playing with his new hi-fi, and even if he did, I wouldn't like to think of poor Poppy being left in the care of three children,' and she meant it. I smiled to myself. Dorothy's passionate concern for animal welfare sometimes bordered on the absurd.

There was a sudden exuberant whoop from upstairs. Our bedroom door was flung open and Alan, bare-footed and with his shirt tail hanging out of his trousers and his flies undone, came bounding down the stairs two at a time. 'They want me, Polly!' he shouted, swinging off the banister and leaping over Dorothy who was still squatting by Poppy's basket. He put his arms round me, gave me a great bear-hug and let go of me so abruptly that I staggered backwards into the grandfather clock which began to chime for the first time in living memory.

Dorothy stood up with a bemused expression on her face. 'Who wants him?' she asked.

'Who wants you?' I asked.

'International Textiles. That was Jim Henderson. I'm being moved out to Slough as export manager with a decent rise in salary.'

Instantly I was overwhelmed by a marvellous feeling of profound relief. The dismal, grey stone work-house somewhere in the wind- and rain-lashed desolation of the Yorkshire Moors towards which the Graham family was heading fast disappeared in a puff of pink smoke together with cabbage broth, straw mattresses and head lice. I took the house off the market and considered the possibility of a foreign holiday.

'That's fantastic!' I whooped loudly above the cacophony of a crazed dog, a ceaselessly chiming clock and three noisy, excited children who were clamouring to know what was going on. Dorothy simply looked on with a pleased but uncomprehending smile. She did so like happy endings even if she hadn't been following the plot.

'Don't worry Dorothy,' I called back over my shoulder as we spun past her out of the front door. 'Everything will become clear to you in the fullness of time.'

'I'm sure it will, dear,' Dorothy said in her matter-of-fact way, and as the door closed behind us, I heard Charlie explaining to her how I had said they could stay up for the late movie. Little liar.

Chapter Eleven

So where do I go from here? I know where I *want* to go. I want to plunge straight into that final week leading up to the 'do'. For the sake of expediency I would like to pretend that Alan and I sorted out all our problems that very evening and everything was lovely. But the realists amongst you wouldn't believe me, and with my Marriage Guidance hat on, I would be ashamed of myself for misleading you. I owe it to you, and myself, to be honest.

Of course, if you would rather leave Alan and me exactly where we were at the end of the last chapter, released from the emotional pressures of the past months, euphoric with relief and off to enjoy a large, juicy Châteaubriand with Béarnaise at the Harrow Steak House, then that's fine by me. Just stop reading here and resume again on page 305. But if you are at all curious to find out how Alan and I handled the emotional detritus that is the inevitable legacy of such intense turmoil, then read on.

To all intents and purposes I suppose I could say that our life together was safely back on its parallel tracks. Alan settled down in his new position and found the offices in Slough very congenial. Sheila left the company to join a firm nearer her home and Alan was given a third share of a secretary, a pleasant woman called Doreen Blocker who didn't wear scent and made execrable coffee. She was happily married to the warehouse foreman and was a grandmother. I continued with my Marriage Guidance training and later had a short story accepted by *Woman's Own* and began calling myself a writer in secret. I even went so far as to tell a market researcher this, but I felt a bit of a fraud when she got all excited and asked what I had published.

Yet despite this shameless normality, those months of anxiety had left their mark. Oh I know many of you will be thinking that our misunderstanding was but an average hiccup of the sort that comes about in the best regulated marriages. Indeed, those of you who have suffered the agonies of bad marriage and divorce may well think I have over-reacted all along the line. But I don't see it that way. For me, those few wobbly, uncertain months gave the lie to a decade or more of what I saw as a perfectly secure understanding between two people. I was filled with self-doubt. The image I had of myself as a strong, self-aware, perceptive, tolerant earth mother evaporated into thin air and I resumed humiliatingly human proportions. Not a bad thing either, you may say, and you'd be right. But at the time my faith in myself was very shaken.

Not so Alan. With the simplicity that so many men bring to such matters, he felt that now we had sorted out all those irritating little practical misunderstandings – the company take-over, Sheila Rosen, my burgeoning interests outside the home – everything else would take care of itself. He became quickly bored, or maybe he was disturbed, by my sporadic nit-picking at the fundamentals. My recurring need for reassurance puzzled him.

'For heaven's sake, Pol,' he would say with a short bark of laughter that was supposed to conceal his impatience but only succeeded in highlighting it, 'we've been over all that again and again. If the simple truth isn't good enough for you, then I've nothing to add that will make you feel any better.' But I felt that we had left so much unsaid and that somewhere within him he had the few words I needed to hear to make everything all right. The fact that I didn't know what those few words were wasn't important. He just had to say them and I would know.

To be truthful, I knew, without having to be told, that the best healer would be time. There was nothing anyone could do or say that would allay my fears and anxieties overnight. My Aunt Evie's philosophy of life, in the face of dear old Uncle Badger's many harmless little peccadilloes, was 'This too will pass away,' which is, I believe, a quotation from the Bard, and meant, for her anyway, that nothing lasts for ever and it kept her calm, patient and amused every time Uncle Badger's roving eye lit upon yet another rounded rear. I myself adopted this admirable philosophy to combat the rigours of boarding school, but although it helped me accept my continual rejection by Cissie Greenslade's infamous gang of girls who kissed the young gardeners in the fruit store, it also disturbed my peace of mind from time to time for it meant that if bad times always come to an end, eventually, by the same token, so would good times.

So, although to the casual observer our marriage must, at that time, have appeared to be as steadfast as ever, I felt a nagging desire to both understand Alan and in turn be understood by him. I didn't expect that we would spend hours baring our souls to each other in Marriage Guidance mode. That may have been my way, but it wasn't Alan's, and one of the new things I came to understand about him was that very little of any consequence was achieved if we tried to do things *my* way. My feelings are easily accessible. They bubble away on the top of my head and I can describe them to you accurately and articulately on demand. Alan's, on the other hand, are buried deeply within layers of impenetrable self-protection. They are buried so deep in fact, that one could be forgiven for thinking that he doesn't have any. But of course he does. Everyone does. It's just that some of us find it easier to express them than others. Indeed, some of us so enjoy expressing our feelings that we bore the pants off people, we examine them *so* often and *so* minutely. As a counsellor I speak from experience.

Most of the time I guess at Alan's feelings. I say to myself, Alan is this or that sort of a man, so in these particular circumstances, whatever they may be, he should, if he is normal, and he is, feel thus or thus. Then I say to him, 'Is this what you're feeling?' and I outline my assessment of how I think he ought to be feeling. He will think about it for a day or two, and if I'm lucky, he will come back to me with a yes or no, and we might, or we might not, discuss the matter further.

So, sporadically, in jerky, nervous fits and starts, we kept returning to the subject of what had gone wrong between us and why. As you might expect, it was left to me to get things off the ground and I had to choose my times very carefully. Alan, a free man, would simply, but very politely, walk away from me. 'Things to do,' he would mutter as he backed out of the kitchen or took the stairs two at a time. Alan, a captive audience, was a different kettle of fish. Catch him reading in bed or slooshing about in the bath, walking the dog or in the car and he couldn't very well escape a direct onslaught. Even then, it was no easy matter. We work at different speeds and on different levels. So if I worked too fast and covered too much ground too quickly, what should have been a mutual discussion would develop into an accusing monologue delivered by me towards my silent, bored and abstracted husband. However, when I attempted to work at his snail-pace, our dialogue would consist of long, thoughtful silences punctuated by grunts and we would run out of time before anything had been achieved.

However, the picture that eventually emerged from beneath layers upon layers of self-delusion and smug self-satisfaction was of a marriage that was going through a period of quite radical change. It seemed that our hitherto comfortable status quo was in the process of alteration that was largely, though by no means wholly, due to outside influences playing upon me. Although he didn't say so in so many words, I could tell that Alan felt I was reneging on some unwritten contract we entered into at the time of our marriage. He would keep me and our children on condition I house-kept and child-minded. In both those departments he felt I was becoming negligent; which is to say I was not keeping up to his very exacting standards. The fact that I loathed housework and that the children were at school all day was no excuse. He was not totally averse to me having interests outside the house so long as they did not impinge in any way upon what he saw as my primary functions, and of course they did, and they still do. There was, and still is, no compromise between how he thinks I should conduct my life and how I need to conduct it in order to maintain any vestige of self-esteem and independence. Well, that's not strictly accurate. If I could afford to pay a full-time housekeeper from my earnings, Alan would see that as a satisfactory compromise, but I can't, so our frequent discussions on this matter are purely academic.

It didn't take me long to understand that there was absolutely nothing I could do to change, fundamentally, Alan's views on a woman's place in society. He was programmed from birth to hold his convictions and he will continue to hold them until the day he dies. If I was ever to earn more than him he would still maintain that the running of the house was my responsibility. He would help me – he always has – but it is help grudgingly given to a woman who just can't seem to get her act together.

Understanding these things about Alan helped me plan my life. I wanted to remain married to him and I knew that in order to do so any work I undertook would have to be done from home and my voluntary work, which he mistrusted even more, would have to be dealt with while he was away from the house. I have also discovered that he will put up with quite a lot of inconvenience if there is a good meal waiting for him when he gets home from work.

Right now, back into the big top.

It was thought, by all of us, that by Friday everything that could go wrong would have gone wrong. I unearthed an old appointments diary recently and from the jottings in it it's apparent that I, for one, remained in an ever spiralling muddle until the moment our first guests arrived on Saturday evening. For example, I noted my intention to finish hemming some table-cloths on Monday, Tuesday *and* Wednesday. They have become 'damned table-cloths' by Thursday and on Friday they are earmarked for Ma's urgent attention. It is clear I had trouble transporting the Italian poplar branches from the water meadow to Maggie's garden. It seems that a Mr Buckle of the Parks Department was very reluctant to meet me to discuss the matter and cancelled our appointment three times. In the end, I recall, we loaded them up on a trailer hitched on to one of Bri Cutler's Ford Transits and simply stole them. Mr Buckle registered his protest, by which time it was too late for him to do anything about it. I can see I must have worried Ma to death over Charlie's Lion costume and I clearly had second thoughts about my own lack-lustre attire in the light of Miranda's sexy get-up. I can't remember what was wrong with Jane's Mustard Seed costume, but it seems that I contacted the Happy Horace Dress Hire Company in a panic about it.

I made a note to remind members of the Committee that they were expected to help gather bracken from the woods, but I can distinctly recall wandering around with Alan, the children, Poppy who was no help whatsoever, and an old pram that was. At the end of each day there is a pathetic reminder to make yet more paper flowers and there is a note on Friday to collect Jane's boots from Ma, and Lizzie's prescription from Boots. I am reminded to borrow a very long step-ladder and my shopping list for Friday morning clearly indicates that I left an awful lot to do at the last minute. Crêpe paper/glue/fuse wire/string/staples/streamers/Sellotape/marker pens/Blu-tack/drawing pins, etc.

My personal commitments seemed to have suffered somewhat from enforced neglect. I notice that I cancelled all my Marriage Guidance clients that week and I'm pretty certain I forgot about Group on Tuesday morning. I made a brave attempt, according to the diary, to bring my notes up to date for a forthcoming tutorial, but I can't have been very successful, for on Thursday I seem to have rung up my tutor to explain the situation, suggesting that perhaps we might change the date if she felt it was imperative that she should read them. Despite continual reminders, Charlie's hair didn't get cut and neither did Jane get her polio jab, which had to be put off for a fortnight. I sent a letter to Mrs Glynis Shipwrick in hospital. She had attempted suicide again and her mother asked if I would go and see Glynis. Apart from there being nothing laid down in the Marriage Guidance rule book to cover such eventualities, I remember that I just didn't have the time on Thursday to rush across to Northwick Park Hospital. I felt guilty about Glynis. Still do, as a matter of fact. However, I know she survived that particular attempt at self-destruction for I saw her three years later walking along College Road, Harrow. A little boy was running ahead of her and she was wheeling one of those toy-sized baby push-chairs that was inhabited by a very small, very loud baby. She was talking animatedly to an older woman who could have been her mother. My guess is that she either got back together with Barry or she got shot of him and found another. She didn't appear to see me, but you never can tell.

The marquee was erected on Friday. I remember it was a glorious day because Gwen and I got very grimy, hot and sweaty pulling ivy from the walls of Hammer Horror House. So hot, in fact, that after several tankards of Gwen's home-made scrumpy neither of us was capable of climbing the ladder, which seemed to have acquired some extra rungs while we weren't looking.

On the way to Maggie's we picked up Eddie. He slid in behind the driver's seat and then leant forward and blew gently on the back of Gwen's neck. He seized the fingers she fluttered over her shoulder and squeezed them affectionately. Her eyes flickered up to the rear-view mirror, met his, and flickered away again. She was smiling complacently. Uggghhhh!

When we arrived at Maggie's the marquee was already erected and everyone was scuttling about busily engaged upon their various tasks. We shouted greetings as we plodded up the garden, laden, like pack mules, with bundles of poly bags filled with the tools of our trade. Between the three of us, we were to transform the tent, according to my designs, into 'a bank whereon the wild thyme blows'. Luckily others besides myself realized the scale of the task I had set myself, so Gwen and Eddie, who would already be working beside me setting up the little stage, were co-opted on to my team.

Everything we needed was already scattered higgledy-piggledy about the floor of the marquee. There were stacks of tables and chairs that had been lent to us from such various sources as the local bridge club, the Watford Way Community Centre and St Saviour's Church Hall. St Saviour's had also lent us their twelve jumble-sale trestle tables for such things as the buffet, the bar and the tombola. Some wit had piled the primary school blocks one on top of the other until they reached the roof and this set us quite a problem, for the structure was very unsound and when Eddie set a ladder against it and began to climb, it swayed dangerously.

'Well, someone constructed it,' Eddie said, 'so there must be some way of dismantling it.'

'Just pull the bottom one out,' Gwen suggested, 'or push it over.'

'We could damage the blocks.'

'Well, we certainly don't have time to rig up a crane,' Gwen said purposefully, 'and it's not a solid floor.' So we pushed and the blocks tumbled down, clattering and thumping against each other like huge rocks in a landslide.

We worked happily together for the rest of the day. We were visited from time to time by other members of the Committee who brought us up tea and biscuits at regular intervals and stopped to lend a hand, but otherwise we were left alone and slowly my Athenian glade took shape. I wired on the last tissue flower as the sun disappeared behind a row of tall, spindly beeches that had probably started life as a hedge.

'There,' I said with a great sigh of relief. 'What do you think of it?'

In order to see it through fresh eyes we left the marquee and came in again as though we were guests just arriving. We gazed silently and critically at our handiwork and then Gwen said with satisfaction, 'Well, I don't know about you two, but I think we've done Shakespeare proud,' and considering the paucity of the material we had at our disposal, I agreed with her. The transformation was magical.

At one end of the marquee the primary school blocks had been cunningly arranged and disguised to resemble a grassy bank by the strategic use of old potato sacks dyed different shades of green and brown; an old log was covered with green velvet moss and a child's toy red squirrel was peeping out at us in such a way that I felt certain he would take flight if we made too much noise. An old wicker chair, sprayed gold and garlanded with paper flowers, was, Gwen told me, Titania's throne and the paper back-cloth, painted by the children themselves to represent the edge of a forest clearing, filled me with delight. It was of the naïve school with just a hint of Rousseau. In this forest tigerish beasts lurked in the shadows and almost-birds perched on the straight, angular branches of geometric trees. A dragon-faced snake breathed fire at a monstrous dinosaur that I recognized as Charlie's handiwork and a very traditional witch with a pointed black hat and a face like Mr Punch stirred a cauldron that appeared to be full of arms and legs.

'I love that back-cloth so much,' Gwen said, looking at it with a dreamy smile on her face, 'that I'm going to hang it round the stair-well when this is all over.' At that time Gwen covered her walls with her children's paintings believing them to be the purest form of art. I think this is a phase most doting mothers go through when their children are small. My own kitchen was once papered with stick men and women variously labelled 'MUMMY' and 'DADDY', and little square houses of the type you now only see in Scotland. Some trendy friends of ours covered their children's rooms with white lining paper, supplied them with marker pens of many different colours and told them to get on with it.

Initially the effect was quite pleasing. However, as their friends joined in, the graffiti became more and more offensive and eventually the walls were covered with Habitat wallpaper like everyone else's. Their children, trained to express themselves on walls, took to spray cans and have never looked back.

Four trestle tables, covered with old green tie-dyed dust sheets, were lined up along one side of the marquee. The overhang was covered with gold-sprayed bracken that was dotted with silver sequins to look like little drops of sparkling dew. Tomorrow these tables would be groaning with our fairy food. Though slightly wilted, there were still clusters of leaves hanging from the poplar branches and wherever possible we had firmly anchored one to a tent pole so that it hung, like a weeping fig, at about a foot above head level. Some of the branches intertwined overhead and the effect was realistically *al fresco*. The tent poles, covered with ivy, looked like ancient tree trunks and at the base of each we placed heavily disguised buckets of sand in which we planted massed bracken. The bar was decorated to resemble a small, ruined Greek temple. It was covered with white marble-effect Contact and was supported by four plastic Corinthian pillars that were supplied to us by Miranda's interior designer friend. The ivy that appeared to grow up them looked ancient with the dust of centuries. The opposite corner to the bar was left free for the discothèque and in between we decorated two further trestle tables to receive the tombola and the raffle prizes.

The smaller tables at which our guests would sit looked very pretty under their tie-dyed table-cloths and each one had a paper flower posy in the centre arranged round a glass honey jar with a night-light floating inside. We arranged these little tables around the centre of the marquee, which was left free for dancing. Swags of ivy and garlands of paper flowers hung, like Christmas decorations, from the main tent poles to the canvas walls, caught up at regular intervals by brightly-coloured lanterns that were illuminated from the inside by Christmas tree electric candle bulbs.

Of course, in my rose-coloured imagination everything had looked a little less amateur. Things were a little fresher and less creased. In the cold light of day my paper flowers looked rather puny and despite the fact that we had washed away decades of collected grime from the ivy with a garden hose, once it had dried, the illusion of glossy health vanished and the leaves resumed their normal pallid brackish-green. Although I was sure the tie-dyed stuff would look all right under artificial light, in the late afternoon gloom of the marquee it bore a remarkably disturbing resemblance to war-time camouflage. Eddie rather tactlessly remarked that all we needed now was a few tanks and some chaps in flak jackets and we could do a remake of *A Bridge Too Far*. However, not withstanding these few minor short-falls from my very high expectations, I was very pleased with the overall effect.

That evening I received a rather unpleasant surprise. Well, no, that's not strictly true. It wasn't so much an unpleasant surprise, as an amazing development.

When Alan arrived home from work I was in the garden with Ma who was staying with us for a couple of days so that I could be free to help with the 'do'. We were examining an ants' nest that Charlie had uncovered while rearranging a small rockery to accommodate some gun emplacements for the Battle of Balaclava. He was fascinated by the hysterical hordes that came piling out into the daylight.

'Do you know,' Charlie told us, 'that an ant can carry the equivalent of a grand piano in its mandibles.' We told him that this piece of very interesting information was news to us. 'Imagine, Granny, trying to carry a grand piano in your mandibles,' Charlie said wonderingly. The picture of my little mother struggling along the High Street with a grand piano clamped between her jaws was too much for us and we dissolved into fits of giggles.

'*Polly!*' Alan's urgent shout carried out into the garden. '*Where are you, Pol?*' I gave Ma a look that if correctly interpreted meant, 'What have I done *now*?' and went indoors.

'Hello love,' I said, giving him a quick hug to which I felt considerable resistance. 'Had a good day?'

'Listen, Pol,' he said, completely ignoring my greeting, not in order to upset me, but because he is a very single-minded man. 'There's trouble brewing.' He made it sound as if the world was about to tilt on its axis. Mind you, Alan could turn a broken milk bottle into a disaster movie. 'Sheila tells me she's coming to this "thing" tomorrow evening.' He generally referred to the 'do' as 'this thing'. It was supposed to convey to me his feelings of detachment from it. What it actually told me was how much he resented the amount of time I devoted to it.

I shrugged. 'Well,' I said, 'if you don't mind, I don't,' showing how completely indifferent I now felt towards Sheila Rosen. 'But I'd like to know how she got a ticket.'

Alan shook his head impatiently. 'That's not important, although I gather a couple she knows in Moor Park have asked her to go along with them.'

'So? I hope she has a good time,' I said cheerfully, dismissing the subject. 'I've just done a salad for supper because I've not been in long myself.'

'Oh, right,' he replied absently. 'Salad's fine.' I knew then something serious was wrong. Salad wasn't Alan's idea of a proper meal.

Puzzled, I watched him as he wandered over to the drinks cupboard and poured himself a generous measure of vodka, merely passing the tonic bottle over it as a gesture towards moderation. I followed him up the stairs and into the bedroom where he began to change out of his city suit and into a pair of elderly jeans and a favourite burnt umber T-shirt inscribed with the legend 'Rasa Sayang, Penang'.

Then I suddenly made the connection. Of course! Mike and Gwen . . .

'So why's she coming to the "do" tomorrow,' I wanted to know, 'if she knows Mike and Gwen'll be there?'

'To be honest, Polly, I don't think she realizes, and why should she if Mike hasn't mentioned it to her?'

'Then you should've told her,' I said emphatically.

'Perhaps I should've done, but by the time I'd recovered from the shock, she was disappearing into the lift. I only had time to tell her that you and I would be there. In any case, I'm not supposed to know about them, so I could hardly mention in passing that the Brays would be there too, could I?'

'Well,' I said, 'I hope they both behave discreetly when they come face to face, that's all.' Then a thought occurred to me. 'I suppose you could warn Mike and then if he wants to, he can ring Sheila.'

After supper Alan telephoned the Brays only to be told by Gwen that Mike wasn't expected back from Birmingham until late that night, but she asked if she could give him a message.

'No ... er ... no thanks, Gwen,' I heard him say. Then there was a pause, and he said quite desperately I thought, 'No, really, I'm not being secretive ... there's no secret. It's just that it would take too long to explain.' There was another pause and then Alan said with relief, 'Yes, okay, if he gets in early enough get him to ring me. Otherwise, I'll ring back tomorrow morning. Thanks. Bye.' As he was speaking to Gwen I remembered my conversation with her when she had told me that Mike had said he found Sheila very glamorous when he had met her over lunch with Alan. That must have been when it started and that was some time ago. I had an ominous feeling that Mike might be in a reckless mood.

I woke up at five that Saturday morning to the swish-swash of traffic on wet tarmac. It was darker than it should have been and when I peered out of the window I found out why. The sky was an unrelieved, leaden grey and sagged over the chimney pots like a dirty army blanket. Rain lashed down and skidded off the drenched roof tiles. Everything gleamed dully in the orange light of the street lamp. My first reaction was to tear down the curtains, shatter the window and shout blasphemous oaths at God, who was somewhere out there watching me with amused indifference. With difficulty I restrained myself, reasoning that God might appreciate a little self-restraint under such circumstances, and instead turned my impotent rage upon my sleeping husband.

'Wha'? Wha'?' he grunted sleepily as I shook him awake with unnecessary violence.

'It's bloody raining,' I grated.

''S not my fault,' he muttered, which, though true, merely served to enrage me further.

'It's bloody peeing down,' I snarled at him accusingly. 'Unbroken sunshine for weeks, and now *this* – today of all days. *Damn damn damn damn!*'

Alan squinted up at me and sighed patiently. 'You can't do anything about it, Pol,' he said, 'so you might as well come back to bed. Anyway, it'll probably have stopped by the time we get up.'

'It didn't forecast rain.'

'Well it did –' I glared at him '– but not in this area,' he added hastily. I climbed reluctantly back into bed and lay ramrod stiff beside Alan, who was soon snuffling peacefully in his sleep. Lying awake, I listened to the unremitting hiss and drum of torrential rain until 8 a.m. when the phone rang. It was Hannah.

'Council of war,' she said without preamble. 'Maggie's – at nine.'

I swallowed a glass of ice-cold orange juice to revive me, and leaving Ma to prepare breakfast for everyone, I raced through the driving rain to Maggie's. Several early-morning dog-walkers and paper boys narrowly escaped death, but only because I had second thoughts at the last minute, remembering God and Providence and all that.

Apart from Miranda, I was the last to arrive, having the furthest to come. Everyone was sitting in the kitchen in various postures of extreme hopelessness. All the flat surfaces were covered with food in various stages of defrost and mounds of fresh salad ingredients. Some desultory chopping had already started.

'We'll just have to cancel,' Patsy was saying as I arrived. 'We can't possibly carry on in this weather.' Maggie slapped a mug of coffee in front of me and I perched myself on the end of a long pine bench.

'What do you think, Polly?' Hannah asked.

'I think,' I began glumly, 'that I shall burrow deep into the soil, curl up into a small ball and go to sleep.'

'Very helpful contribution to the discussion if I may say so,' Gwen said acidly and B tutted.

'I refuse to be defeated by a little shower,' she said, staring round at each of us in turn as if daring us to contradict her.

'Have you been out there, B?' I asked. 'Because if that's a little shower, I'm the bluebell fairy.'

To be truthful, we all knew that any discussion we might have was purely academic. We were less likely to cancel the 'do' than mow down a crocodile of children with a Sherman tank. We *couldn't* cancel it. It wasn't possible. We didn't have *time* to cancel it, nor could we *afford* to cancel it. The show had to go on and we had to go on with it.

Hannah broke the long and gloomy silence that followed.

'Look, before we make up our minds, let's take a look at the damage,' she said, already beginning to struggle with her unwieldy strait-jacket of a cagoule. Half-heartedly we all followed suit. 'Miranda's following along a little later,' she informed us, although none of us had questioned her absence. 'She said she wants to have a word with someone she thinks might be able to help us.'

'Huh!' I sneered, 'her fancy interior decorator has a direct line to God I expect.' One or two women smiled distantly.

'Well, first of all,' Maggie began, once we had all assembled outside on the waterlogged terrace, 'the path up the garden is virtually impassable.' Muddy water was running down the sloping flag path like a fast-running stream. 'It's very slippery and dangerous,' she continued. 'We can't use it as a route to the marquee, and if it doesn't stop raining and dry up a little, our guests won't be able to use it either – and the grass is like a quagmire.' As though we were following a guide on a tour of a stately home, we followed Maggie up the garden, gingerly hopping from flag-stone to flag-stone as though they were stepping stones across the rapids. The low, grassy bank on either side of the path was being slowly eroded by the fast-flowing water and our way was made treacherous by tufts of grassy mud that had been caught and then held firm by flags that stood slightly higher than the rest. My wellies already looked as though they had been buried up to their ankles in a flooded farmyard.

About twenty yards of neatly clipped lawn lay between the abrupt end of the path and the marquee, which was already sagging heavily beneath small lakes of rain water. Cautiously Maggie stepped out on to deceptively normal-looking lawn and immediately sank up to her ankles. 'See what I mean?' she called over her shoulder. Because we had no choice, we squelched after her towards the relative safety of the large, dripping tent.

As soon as I stepped on to the damp hessian drugget, I knew we had an even more serious problem. Underneath the strips of heavy-weight hessian and the polyurethane lining there was a large amount of standing water and the makeshift covering undulated with every footstep like a massive water bed.

'Jesus!' Gwen exclaimed with considerable feeling. 'Now what?'

'Hello everyone.' Miranda came forward to meet us from the far end of the marquee. 'I've been reconnoitring with my friend Jim here.' She indicated a muscular little man in a bicep-revealing, dazzling white Club Med T-shirt and crutch-hugging jeans who was standing beside her. He flashed us an engaging grin which revealed a gold tooth. I had already noticed the gold nugget hanging round his neck on a thick gold chain, the massive gold identity bracelet and the mounted gold half sovereign pinky ring.

'Hi ladies,' he said cheerfully. 'I'm Randy here's favourite cowboy builder.' He leered towards Miranda in her tightly belted, black ciré raincoat. Gwen and I exchanged superior smiles of disdain, but I couldn't help wishing that I had bothered to put on a little eye shadow before I left that morning, my eyes, when made-up, being my best feature. 'I've had a look around,' Jim went on, 'and I think I can probably do something to help.' Despite myself, my spirits lifted just a shade above absolute zero, for this little man carried about him an air of effortless authority. We watched him as he continued walking round pushing and prodding at everything. Suddenly he grabbed a broom that had been left leaning against one of the tent poles, climbed on to a chair and stabbed violently at the waterlogged roof with the handle. With a great swoosh, the water that had gathered above that particular section crashed down on to the sodden lawn beneath. After several such attacks, the roof regained something of its former shape. Unfortunately Jim's energetic prods brought down a lot of ivy with paper flowers attached and a worrying amount of electrical wiring.

'Don't worry about all that,' he called over to B, who had been standing in the wrong place at the wrong time and was trying to disentangle herself from garlands of fairy lights. 'My lads'll see to it all.' Then he handed me the broom without a glance and took up a central position. 'Now listen, ladies,' he began. He spoke the sort of gentrified cockney that I associated with tough, successful screen villains, and it was somehow very reassuring. Later I remarked to Gwen that if all else failed he could call on the Mob. 'You've got some nasty little problems 'ere. But I'm not a builder for nothin' and I know a thing or two about dryin' things off in an 'urry. So you just get on wiv your chores an' leave it all to yer uncle Jim 'ere.' We perked up visibly and smiled hopefully round at each other. Perhaps, I thought, God was not quite so indifferent to our plight after all. 'I'm goin' off now,' he said, turning to Miranda, 'to get a few of the lads and some equipment,' and with that, he turned smartly on his heel and disappeared through the flap.

'Well!' Hannah exclaimed, and then she said, 'Well!' again in a non-plussed sort of way. 'I suppose we'd better put our trust in Jim and get on with our chores.'

'If you're worrying about his track record,' Miranda said, 'don't. If anyone can help us, Jim can. He's an absolute master of improvisation and if he says he can do something, he generally does it.'

B, I noticed, was looking sloppily tearful and I wasn't at all surprised when she rushed up to Miranda and gushed, 'Oh Miranda, you are an absolute brick, you really are,' and then threw her arms round her in a triumphant footballer's hug. 'Just as we thought all was lost, you, as usual, have come up trumps!' I winced with embarrassment for poor B as Miranda drew back from the fervent embrace with a look of distaste. Miranda just wasn't the sort of person one embraced in an excess of gratitude but B could never understand things like that.

'Thanks Miranda,' Hannah said gruffly and the rest of us followed suit.

'Don't thank me too soon,' Miranda said. 'After all, even he must've had his failures.' That is true, I thought, but despite my ungenerous feelings regarding Miranda, I hoped this wouldn't be one of them.

Later, when Maggie's kitchen was a throbbing, heaving mass of slightly hysterical skivvies, all chopping and mixing, cooking and washing up, Jim returned with three of his lads and a lorry-load of equipment.

'Now, who's boss around here?' he asked, poking his head through the kitchen door.

Hannah looked up and smiled helpfully. 'Well, I'm chairman of the Committee,' she said.

Jim shook his head. 'No . . . no . . . I mean, who knows

all about this house. Where the mains are, things like that.' We all looked at Maggie. 'Do you know where everything is then?' Jim asked. 'I need to know if you've got extension leads and where all your power sockets are – all that sort of stuff,' and he looked at Maggie doubtfully.

'Well, I know where most things are . . . but I think you'd better speak to my husband, he's the handyman around here. He's out in the garage.'

When I went out to the garage to fetch in a tray of plastic containers containing defrosted Oberon's Orange Chicken, Jim and Maggie's husband Richard were in a huddle in one corner muttering about fuses and circuit-breakers. Even though, at the time of which I speak, feminism was still in its infancy, I felt a flicker of resentment at Jim's easy assumption that our 'boss' should be a man because knowing about fuses and circuit-breakers was more important in the general scheme of things than knowing how to mend a zip or knit a jumper.

Although most of the food for the buffet was made in advance and frozen in a selection of freezers belonging to us and our friends, there was still a great deal of work that had to be left until the last minute. We discovered that the orange and tarragon sauce for the main chicken dish didn't freeze, neither did the raspberry creams, once they had been brûléed. The gazpacho, once defrosted, separated and took on the appearance of a curdled pink milk jelly. After some serious thought we decided to heat it up and add some arrowroot in order to thicken it a little. When cold it tasted quite pleasant, though not perhaps quite as we had anticipated. We re-christened it Puck's Pepper Potion with some relief. There had been considerable resistance to Bottom's Belch, but Gwen, who had insisted that it was her invention, had been adamant. However, she refused to acknowledge the revamped creation as one of her own and said we could call it whatever we chose.

Meanwhile Jim, his lads and one or two lurking husbands, who I think had probably come to scoff, knuckled down to the seemingly impossible task of improving conditions for our guests.

'How about a Rain Dance,' Gwen suggested.

'No . . . no!' we all shrieked and I reminded her that a Rain Dance was not for stopping rain but for starting it.

'All right then, how about a Rain, Rain, Go Away Dance,' she said and for the first time that day we found something to laugh about as we embroidered upon the theme of Jim, his lads and our assorted husbands stomping earnestly around in the rain in their wellies and anoraks, waving tomahawks and chanting magical incantations to the water spirits of a suburban garden.

During a well-earned break, Gwen and I donned our rain gear and trudged up the garden to see how the men were coping. They had overcome, as best they could, the problem of the garden path by raising a low platform of planks that rested, two abreast, upon strategically placed breeze blocks. It put me in mind of the walking beam in the gym at school, but as long as I didn't look down I maintained a precarious balance.

'I don't like this,' Gwen muttered, grim-faced. 'And if I don't like it in broad daylight, how am I going to feel about it tonight?' I shuddered as I imagined our guests, in all their glorious plumage, staggering along the narrow gangway with only the flickering light from a few flashlights to illuminate their passage. The twenty-four garden flares that had seemed such a good idea at the time were still in their wrapping, and seemed to us to be a pathetically final memorial to our earlier reckless optimism.

'Do you think Jim could knock up some sort of rope hand-rail?' I said, having in mind the sort of flimsy bamboo bridge one commonly sees connecting one side of a three hundred foot chasm to the other in war movies set in the Malayan jungle. 'I'll ask him,' I added, feeling confident that very little was beyond his capabilities.

As we approached the marquee we were struck by the strange howling sound that was coming from within.

'It sounds like the central heating boiler at the hospital,' Gwen shouted above the din, and she should know I suppose. For myself it sounded like nothing I had ever heard before, but I imagined that the furnaces of hell might sound somewhat similar. We pushed through the flap and were almost blown out again by the blast of hot, moist air that slammed at us with the might of a force ten gale. We stood transfixed by the scene that met our eyes. The whole marquee appeared to be steaming gently like an equatorial swamp in the noonday sun. Everything that was portable had been shifted to one side and the hessian druggets had been lifted and slung over metal scaffolding where they were being subjected to an intensely hot blast of air from what appeared to me to be a huge hairdrier. Three other 'hairdriers' were directing their heat at the soggy, yellowing mulch that had been maturing nicely overnight underneath the floor covering. Later I learnt that the 'hairdriers' were, in fact, industrial driers that are normally used to dry off building sites. Jim saw us and waved cheerfully. Coming over to us, he bellowed, 'If this doesn't work, nothing will,' which seemed to me to be a rather disquieting prognosis. He looked from my anxious face to Gwen's and added, 'Don't worry, ladies, we'll put everything back as it was. 'Course, you'll have to tart up the decorations a bit.' Indeed we will, I thought glumly, as I gazed round at the dripping vegetation and the limp paper flowers. 'Keep yer chin up, luv,' Jim said with a reassuring grin. 'It may look like a tropical rain forest right now but it wouldn't take these buggers long,' and he patted one of the driers affectionately, 'to turn this place into a desert.' Jim agreed to look into the possibility of rope hand-rails along the garden gang-way and then Gwen and I squished our way back to the house.

The monsoon downpour continued unabated throughout the day. But by three o'clock Jim told us that the marquee was as dry as it could possibly be in the circumstances and superficially everything looked more or less normal. Although I didn't care for the feel of the ground underfoot (ominously, our wellies left footprints), the surface, at least, looked dry enough. Everyone joined forces to help revitalize the décor while an army of volunteer helpers loaded the buffet tables with gastronomic artwork and polished glasses at the bar. The discothèque was in place and our two part-time disc jockeys, Garry and Clive, were doing some last-minute adjustments to their 'fully comprehensive lighting system'. Patsy's tombola was a real *tour de force* but when I asked her how she had managed to get so many local shop-keepers to cough up, she winked saucily and said, 'Don't ask,' very mysteriously. As well as another Cutler stereo car radio, we now had a portable colour TV to raffle, a dinner for two at the Bell in Aston Clinton and a year's subscription to a local squash club. All in all things were looking up and despite our earlier gloom, we were beginning to feel quite excited and optimistic. Almost speechless with exhaustion we slumped round Maggie's kitchen table for a final cup of tea.

'Well, I just hope I get my second wind soon,' Hannah said, inhaling deeply on a forbidden cigarette. Barney had promised her that if she gave up smoking for a year, they would spend Christmas with her sister in the USA. If he discovered her smoking this one, seven months of abstinence would go down the drain. 'Because if I don't, I'll be on my back by seven.'

'Second wind nothing,' Gwen growled, 'I'm waiting for my third. And talking of backs,' she said, wincing with the pain of her aching spine, 'I must get home to a long hot bath before I seize up altogether.' Having said that, she gathered her belongings together and left, giving us all a limp wave and a wan smile as she passed the kitchen window. Shortly afterwards I followed and it wasn't until I was climbing into the car that I remembered Gwen and Eddie and Mike and Sheila. Zap zap zap zap! Depressing little squibs exploding one after the other in my tired brain. It was seeing Gwen and Eddie together that reminded me. They were sitting in the front of Eddie's old bone-shaker which spent more time off the road than on it. It was the first time I had seen him all day and I realized that he had come to pick Gwen up and drive her home.

No, Alan told me when I arrived home, he had not been able to get hold of Mike. He had telephoned several times and called round twice so now things would just have to run their course. Unexpectedly, and to my shame, I felt a small thrill of glee at the prospect of a little intrigue. Then my worthy side, the boring bits that I am nevertheless rather proud of, protested self-righteously that Gwen was my best friend and that if it came to it, it would be my duty to protect her from whatever might befall her that evening. Determinedly I put it all behind me while I idled away a blissful half-hour in a Badedas bath and enjoyed the mug of strong tea that Ma brought up to me.

We were in trouble from the start. A few early arrivals reached the marquee in a reasonably dry state, but soon sheer weight of numbers proved too much for the makeshift gangway and it collapsed without warning tumbling several guests into the turgid river of mud beneath. Mrs Lillian Love, who had hired her magnificent Elizabethan farthingale at vast expense from Berman's, went into a state of shock and had to be taken home by her husband. They didn't return. We were able to improvise a toga from a clean sheet for a Julius Caesar, but a chap who claimed to be a modern-dress Shylock made a heck of a fuss and later sent us the cleaning bill for his pin-stripe city suit, which he claimed wittily was his pound of flesh. Though quite a number of far-sighted people arrived in sensible footwear and then changed into party shoes in the marquee, we were obliged to organize several children into a team of boot runners for the less prudent.

There was something undeniably touching about Richard II in a plastic mac and gumboots and Othello cowering under a frilly pink umbrella. Hamlet in an anorak and overshoes is a memory I treasure and my recollection of a large, blonde

Ophelia being carried up the garden by a small green Puck brings to mind Miss Piggy and Kermit the Frog.

By the time the last guests arrived, those first guests who were wearing stiletto heels, and this included Marshall Steerforth who loved any excuse to appear in drag and on this occasion treated us all to a Rocky Horror Lady Macbeth, had already punctured the floor covering, turning it into a colander through which muddy water was beginning to seep. Most people were still milling about, recognizing each other with cries of amazement and cackles of well-will-you-look-at-you laughter, so the fact that they were beginning to sink below water level for the moment entirely escaped them.

The Awful B was the first person to notice the little puddles forming under people's feet and she darted from one Committee member to another in a state of frenzied anxiety crying, 'What'll we do, what'll we do, what'll we do,' like a manic parrot.

'We keep them drinking,' Gwen said to us as we gathered in a small worried knot behind the stage, 'and by the time they're legless they won't care much if they get their feet wet.'

'Oh absolutely right, Gwen,' Miranda chuckled lightly. 'People without legs generally don't worry too much about their feet.' A nervous titter went round the group. Gwen's eyes hardened and the smiles were wiped off our faces. Instructions were issued to those husbands manning the bar to pour generously, and soon, despite their ruined shoes, wet feet and mud-spattered finery, our well-oiled revellers were thronging on to the floor to jiggle and sway to a thoughtfully prepared collection of up-beat, mainstream pop.

'Keep it in a major key,' I instructed Garry and Clive. 'Minor keys are so depressing.' Garry said that wouldn't be easy because most modern pop was written by and for depressed people. However, if we didn't mind a rather repetitive diet he would do his best. So it was that for most of the evening we sashayed about the floor to the music of Abba, the Beatles, the Carpenters, and wonderful, wonderful Glen Miller.

We were serving food to those at the head of the early queue of *cognoscenti* when I became aware that B was, once again, laying eggs. I was on 'Starters' and she was on 'Puddings', but nonetheless I could hear her chuntering away to anyone who was prepared to listen about something that appeared to have gone amiss below stairs. Hannah, as Chairperson, had elected to free-float, as it were, along the tables, helping where help was needed and generally keeping an eye on things, replacing empty dishes when necessary and clearing away gathering debris. As she passed behind me I muttered, 'I think you'd better find out what's up with B. She's all wide-eyed and distraught down the end there.' A few moments later Hannah returned with a story about mutiny breaking out back at base camp, that is to say with the washing-up staff in the kitchen. They were threatening to cast B's terrible Mrs Walker-Smith adrift on a raft with a packet of ship's biscuits and a barrel of water.

'B wants to know if we'll let Mrs Walker-Smith help with the buffet.'

'Oh God!' I cursed and the little woman I was serving blinked apologetically several times. 'I knew we'd have trouble with that frightful person. I expect she's offended everyone with her airs and graces. Why can't B simply tell her to go home?'

'I suggested that,' Hannah whispered, 'but apparently she has no transport and B agreed to drive her at the end of the evening.' Our discussion of the matter was brought to a halt as the lady herself, splendidly clad in chiffon and gold lamé, swayed unsteadily into the marquee and arbitrarily took up her place beside B on the Puddings.

'Bloody woman's been at the booze,' Maggie muttered to me from the side of her mouth and reluctantly I had to admit that she did have the appearance of a woman who was two sheets to the wind. B glanced helplessly down the line. We all glared back ferociously and she looked away in shame. We should have taken the time to deal with the problem then and there but the shuffling queue of hungry people was becoming impatient.

'What is *that*?' a tall, thin, yellow-hosed Malvolio asked sniffily as I handed him a bowl of starter.

'Puck's Pepper Potion,' I replied shortly. He pulled a wry face and looked at it with disgust.

'Looks like cat sick.'

'It's a sort of gazpacho,' I told him with a sigh.

'A sort of *what*?' The queue behind him was beginning to get restless. 'Come on George, move on,' someone called.

'God, you're an ignorant bum George!' someone else shouted good-naturedly.

'It's a cold spicy soup made from peppers and tomatoes.'

'Can't abide cold soup,' he retorted, handing his bowl to the person behind him and moving on. I heard him complaining loudly further along that he liked his chicken roast with sage and onion stuffing and not mixed up in a fruit salad with cream. I suspect he went hungry that night. However, in the main our imaginative dishes were very popular and I was just about to relax a little when Gwen tapped me on the shoulder.

'Do you know who that woman is?' she asked.

'Which woman?'

'The Cleopatra sitting with Mike.' Warning bells went off in my head.

'Surely Mike's on the bar,' I said as I moved along the table gathering up empty dishes for our kitchen helpers to collect and wash.

'I know that's where he *should* be,' she said snapping cleanly through a stick of celery with her sharp, white teeth, 'but he's not. He's sitting over there eating his supper with a very glamorous woman with whom he appears to be on very intimate terms.' I glanced over in the direction Gwen indicated then looked away quickly in embarrassment.

'The woman's Sheila Rosen.' Well, there wasn't much

point in being evasive. 'And Mike has met her once or twice – with Alan. You remember, you told me he had.' Gwen was watching them thoughtfully, which wasn't surprising really because although they appeared to be simply chatting in a friendly fashion, the table-cloth had slipped sideways and Mike's hand was clearly visible, massaging Sheila's thigh in a manner that suggested that they had things other than food on their minds.

'Oh Gwen,' I laughed, 'for heaven's sake – he's just having his usual grope!'

'Mike doesn't grope,' she enunciated slowly and clearly.

'Well, no, of course not – well, not a lot anyway,' and I gave a dismissive little chuckle to hide my confusion. 'But he's like most men given the opportunity.'

'Mike is not like most other men.' Dammit, I thought, how on earth can she have been so blind for so long?

'Well, you're always saying how women fancy him. Perhaps he's just responding to her advances – to be polite.'

Gwen gave me a withering look. 'Go and split them up,' she commanded, 'before anyone else notices.'

I shivered involuntarily before such magnificence but I gritted my teeth and replied bravely, 'Don't be daft, Gwen. I mean, what do you expect me to do? Read them the riot act and tell them to behave themselves?'

Gwen glared at them helplessly, then said, 'Get Alan to do something. After all, she's his responsibility.'

'No she is not,' I stated very firmly, then I explained in a quieter voice that Sheila had come with a group of friends.

'Well, that might make you feel better,' she replied with a malevolent gleam in her eye, 'but where does it leave me?' I suggested that she was over-reacting to what was obviously no more than a casual flirtation and then squelched off in search of Alan. I found him tidying up the wellington boots behind the disco.

'I'm trying to pair them up,' he said peevishly, 'or there'll be the most awful rumpus later on.'

'Very thoughtful of you darling and we'll all be very grateful.' He looked up at me suspiciously. 'And when you've finished, do you think you could try and separate the two love-birds? Gwen's on the war-path.'

'I've tried,' he replied truculently, 'but Mike's already beyond reason. He's really knocking it back . . . and he was rather offensive as a matter of fact.'

'Oh?'

'Yes, more or less accused me of being jealous.'

'Oh . . .'

'Then said something about what was good for the goose was good for the gander and why didn't I ask Eddie to leave his wife alone while I was at it . . .'

'*Oh!*'

'So I've washed my hands of it all and if Gwen wants something done about Sheila, she had better do it herself.'

'But after she's done something about Eddie . . . eh?'

'That's right.' Triumphantly Alan paired off the remaining two overshoes and standing up with an audible creak, he looked at his watch.

'Time I was behind the bar,' he said and disappeared into the crowd after giving me a quick, affectionate hug.

Like the water, the noise level in the marquee was steadily rising. Those who weren't already eating were staggering about with loaded plates looking for somewhere to sit and I noticed that some of the women had already dispensed with their shoes, which was, in the circumstances, a wise move. Shoes abandoned in this way survive to dance another day. Sorry.

I wandered over to the tombola to see how Patsy was managing with her two teenage helpers. The shelves were already almost empty and she looked pink and happy.

'We've made hundreds!' she cried happily. 'And the kids are circulating now with the raffle tickets.' Then she beckoned me closer and whispered, 'Have you noticed Mike Bray?' I nodded.

'Who's the woman, do you know?'

I nodded again. 'She's Alan's secretary,' I replied.

'Well,' Patsy took my elbow and we moved out of earshot, 'I had to go to the loo a while back and Mike and Alan's secretary were huddled together under a golf umbrella behind the garage. He seemed to be pleading with her.' She gave me a direct look. 'Do you know if they've met before?'

'Er . . . yes . . . no . . . well, I think they might've done. I'm not very sure.' Patsy's eyes narrowed, then she smiled knowingly and returned to the tombola to exchange Roy Lubbock's pink ticket for a fluffy, pale-blue toy rabbit. She politely refused his request to exchange it for a packet of white linen hankies.

It has always seemed to me to be a miracle that people still talk about that evening with so much fond affection when I feel we should have offered them their money back. Instead of cries of outrage, our guests treated each new set-back with amused surprise. It was almost as if they believed that everything that went wrong was a happening we staged especially for their entertainment. For example, Mrs Walker-Smith's final and dramatic resignation from the team attracted a boisterous claque of enthusiastic revellers. Fed up by the dreadful woman's eventual refusal to help us in any capacity at all once she had noticed that her 'friend' the Lady Rose Hatt was present, Miranda suggested bluntly to her that she should properly pay for her ticket as had her 'friend'. The result was electric.

'I am not a skivvy,' the woman announced in loud, ringing tones. 'I am the guest of Mrs Basil Baines and I have given up a precious Saturday evening to help raise money for a worthy cause.'

'Please be quiet,' Hannah hissed angrily, taking hold of Mrs Walker-Smith's elbow in order to lead her out of the marquee.

'I will not be quiet!' she shouted, pulling away from Hannah and backing away from us all at the same time. 'I consider I have been treated atrociously. Insulted by those charladies in the kitchen and patronized by you lot.' The majestic sweep of her arms included everyone present. Continuing to back into the centre of the floor, she caught her heel in a hole in the canvas and staggered backwards until she finally lost her balance and fell. In doing so she reached out for support and clutched desperately at a length of trailing ivy that was fastened to a tent pole with fuse wire. Then, in a series of violent jerks as the wires snapped one after the other, Mrs Walker-Smith sank to the ground with a soft wet plop. She lay on her back moaning, 'Oh . . . oh . . . oh!' as the ivy uncoiled and snaked down on top of her, releasing as it fell a shower of paper flowers that settled over her as though on a newly dug grave. Amidst good-natured laughter, we heaved the poor woman up and bundled her out of the marquee.

As you might expect, B was in a frightful state. She knew we were all very angry and she knew our anger was justified, yet despite this, her main fear was that Mrs Walker-Smith would hand in her notice; which was precisely what she did, the very next day, demanding fifty pounds towards the cost of a new dress, a pair of shoes and a hair-do. B paid up like a lamb and within a fortnight had found herself a new help called Doreen Snooks who turned out to be a perfect gem. It's an ill wind, as they say.

While Mrs Walker-Smith was making her undignified exit from the scene, Gwen and Eddie were preparing our young thespians for their grand debut. While chairs and tables were being re-organized to make room for the audience, over-excited children packed behind the stage and overflowed round the sides in order to have words with their parents and to be seen in their costumes. The leads could be seen anxiously muttering their lines to themselves in corners while poor Pyramus, who was as white as a sheet and shivering, nervously sipped from a glass of white wine. Hannah claimed it would give him Dutch courage but I thought it was more likely to make him sick.

'Stage-fright?' I asked. He nodded wordlessly. 'It's a good sign,' I said to reassure him. 'No one ever gave of their best without stage-fright.'

He looked at me piteously. 'Then I'm surprised anyone ever does this for fun,' he whispered miserably. Remembering my own youthful amateur dramatics and those relentless few minutes before the opening curtain, I was able to sympathize.

The entertainment was about to begin when Gwen took me firmly by the elbow and dragged me into a corner away from the others. 'Where's Mike?' she asked in a hoarse voice. I shrugged and glanced round at the colourful crowd of happy, expectant people.

'I expect he's in the audience somewhere,' I lied.

'Well, he's not, and neither is that woman.' We stared at each other wordlessly for a few moments. I knew from the tone of her voice that she expected something from me, but I wasn't sure what. 'This is a bad time for me to go looking for them,' she went on. 'I can't leave Eddie on his own to cope.'

'No, I suppose you can't,' I said carefully. I was beginning to understand where this conversation was leading and I didn't like it one bit.

'So, as a big favour to me, your very best friend, would you be a honey and go and look for them?' She looked at me pleadingly.

'But I want to watch my children perform,' I whined miserably.

'*Please!*' she implored with such intensity that it would have been very unfriendly of me to refuse. So, for the umpteenth time, I struggled back into my wellies, grabbed the communal golf umbrella, accepting with resignation that I was not to see my brood take the audience by storm this time around, and set out into the drenched night to the opening lines of the Prologue.

There was no sign of the love-birds in the garden though I couldn't see very far through the damp shadows under the dripping trees, where they might have been cowering, holding their breaths until I went by, so I made my way down to the house and into the warm hubbub of the cheerful, steaming kitchen where I was greeted by welcoming cries from our small band of kitchen helpers. Washing up was continuing apace and the air was thick with cigarette smoke and brisk chatter. The subject under discussion was Mrs Walker-Smith and from what I heard it was clear she had made herself very unpopular in a short time. 'Lazy cow!' I heard, and 'Bleedin' snob', together with a few other fragrant expletives that don't bear repeating.

'Just going to the loo,' I explained unnecessarily as I edged through the bustling women.

'Well, you'll have a long wait dear,' one of them said. 'There's a terrible long queue.'

'But I thought guests were supposed to use the outside lavatory.'

'So they were dear, but something's gone wrong with the plumbing, so they're having to come indoors.'

I had known this would happen. I had warned them but they wouldn't listen. 'You can't have one loo for two hundred and fifty people,' I told them, but they wouldn't agree on the expense of a Portaloo, so they had only themselves to blame. Unworthily I felt vindicated as I listened to the rumbles of discontent out in the hall.

Trying not to draw attention to myself, I sauntered casually round the house, peering hurriedly into each darkened room.

'You won't find one in there,' someone called from the queue as I looked into the murky gloom of the dining-room.

'What?'

'A loo. You won't find one in there,' the woman repeated.

'I'm not looking for a loo,' I replied politely.

'Oh, I see. Just being nosey are we?' All eyes turned in my direction.

'Well, I can't speak for you, but I'm not,' I retorted acidly.

A few people tittered. 'I'm on the Committee *actually* and I've been sent to look for something ... er ... somebody *actually*. I don't suppose any of you have seen Mike Bray?' People shook their heads and looked blank.

'Wouldn't know him if I had,' someone said and then a woman called Nina who owned a leather shop in Hatch End smirked and said she had seen him a while back walking down the drive with a bottle.

'And he looked a bit unsteady to me, if you know what I mean,' she added with the disapproval the slightly merry feel for the falling-down drunk. I asked if he was alone.

'Yes ... but he was carrying two glasses.' The lavatory flushed and the cloakroom door opened furtively. 'Ooops, my turn,' she cried as a man sidled past the rest of us looking sheepish and apologetic in the way the British generally look when caught coming out of the lavatory. I mean, a Frenchman comes out still doing up his flies and looks positively pleased with himself and an Italian will graciously hold the door open for you and then pinch your bottom for good measure as you go in. But the British behave as though they have been caught out doing something unmentionably disgusting. Odd, isn't it?

My continuing search for Mike and Sheila took me out into the road. I thought I would probably find them in the Bray station wagon, but a feeling of hopelessness settled over me like Pilgrim's burden when I looked up and down the road lined with scores of shining wet cars that all looked the same colour and shape in the depressing light of the orange street lamps. That particular shade must have driven many people mad. It is such a cold, unwelcoming colour that renders everything down to the same shade of mildewed carrot.

When I eventually stumbled upon the Bray car it was empty and looked calculatedly innocent.

'Bugger it!' I said out loud. Then I thought, but of course, they'll be in *her* car, and then I couldn't remember what car she drove. So I began looking for a car with its windows steamed up only to find a great many cars with steamed-up windows.

'Um . . . excuse me,' I said, knocking softly on the window of a shuddering Mini. 'Is Mike Bray in there?' The shuddering stopped abruptly.

'What?' a deep, muffled voice asked.

'Um . . . Are you Mike Bray?'

'No I am not!' the voice replied crossly.

'Sorry.' Further along I stopped by a steamed-up Cortina. 'Hello in there!' I trilled lightly. After a lengthy and rather noisy pause, a window was wound down and a female head popped out.

'What do you want?' she asked me aggressively.

'Oh, sorry, I thought you were someone else,' I said, and quickly passed on. After making the same mistake four times, I was about to admit defeat when I noticed a small Porsche parked away from the other cars and very nearly hidden by an overgrown privet hedge. Then I remembered what car it was that Sheila's son was given by a doting absentee dad for his twenty-first birthday. It was, I noticed, all steamed up.

'Mike, Sheila,' I called softly. 'It's Polly.'

For a while I thought I had been mistaken, but then Mike said, 'Go away Polly,' in a weary, patient voice.

'Nothing would give me greater pleasure,' I assured him, 'but I've been sent to find you by Gwen.'

'Tell her you've found me and I'm asleep in the car.'

'I don't think that'll satisfy her. You see, she knows you're with Sheila.'

There was a hurried, whispered argument inside the car and then Sheila wound down the window and said, 'We're not doing anything reprehensible, Polly. I felt a bit dizzy and we've come out here for a quiet drink,' which is precisely what they appeared to be doing. Well, there wasn't much room to do anything else. 'But you'd better tell Gwen that you've found us.'

'Tell her you found us helping with the washing up or

something.' Mike leant over Sheila and looked up at me through the window.

'No Mike.' Sheila pushed him gently back into his seat. 'Just tell her the truth, Polly. You go back to the festivities. We'll follow you up.' I nodded and as Sheila wound up the window, I turned away and began my sodden journey back up through the torrential rain and mud to the end of Maggie's garden.

A massive roar of laughter greeted me as I approached the marquee. A good sign, I thought, but I hadn't realized that our modest little entertainment was *that* funny. Obviously, I said to myself, the children have really pulled out all the stops this evening, and I took my place at the back of the audience behind a heaving wall of male backs to the immortal lines, 'Asleep my love? What, dead, my dove? O Pyramus, arise . . .' To begin with I could see nothing, but soon I managed to establish a clear view through to the little stage and it didn't take me long to work out that something was badly amiss. I could see Thisbe lying prostrate on the ground sorrowfully declaiming her final tragic lines but there was no sign of a dead Pyramus. Then as my eyes adjusted to the unexpected I realized that half of the 'stage' had sunk at least a foot below the other half and had tilted slightly to the left, and as I watched, Thisbe, who was supposed to fall across Pyramus in her death throes, slithered over the chasm with one snake-like wriggle and fell with a thump on top of Pyramus who resurrected abruptly with a loud, affronted yelp of pain. The audience went wild. Those who didn't know the play probably thought this was meant to happen, and those who did clearly thought that what had happened was a great improvement on the original. The children, always quick to seize an advantage, played outrageously to the gallery from then on. The three Lions, led regrettably by an over-excited Charlie, leapt backwards and forwards across the widening gap roaring and pawing the air with lion-like gestures. Wall stood with one foot on either side and pulled agonized faces at the audience as his legs were pulled further and further apart until he eventually toppled into the chasm with a great whoop of laughter. He was followed by Pyramus and Thisbe and a lot of props and bits of scenery. Caught up in the drama of the situation, those children still remaining on the stage began jumping enthusiastically up and down in an obvious effort to sink it. Gwen was noticeable only by her absence, but two or three members of the Committee who were close to the scene were scrambling about pulling small children to safety off the bucking boxes. I was relieved to see that Jane had escaped into the safety of Alan's arms and both Lizzie and Charlie had managed to reach firm ground, though both were shrieking with laughter at the antics of Honour Baines who was trying to maintain her hitherto Olympian calm on a 'throne' that was being tossed about like a coracle in a storm. Poor B was scampering round shouting instructions at her daughter and making unsuccessful grabs at her feet and the legs of the 'throne', while Basil tried to effect a rescue by clambering on to the slippery, sliding boxes. As Basil crawled towards it, the throne crept further and further towards the edge at the back of what was left of the stage and as he pulled Honour off and into the yawning gap, it toppled backwards, tearing through the beautiful back-cloth and revealing, to everyone's matchless delight, a tearful Gwen clasped protectively in the strong arms of young Eddie. I will remember their horrified faces until the day I die, and so, no doubt, will Mike, who I noticed was standing in the shadows – and he wasn't laughing. Sheila was standing just in front of him, and as I watched he drew her back into the circle of his arms and buried his face in the black mass of her mountainous chignon.

A splendid uproar followed. Far too many well-meaning people dashed forward to help clear the debris and fell over each other in their eagerness to participate. They failed to notice the evil-looking brown fluid that was slowly rising beneath and then over their feet until it was too late and soon our apparently resigned but happy guests were splashing about in the growing puddles like children after a storm.

Others jostled for space on the few remaining dry patches and as a result, things became very intimate indeed, and through all this, exhilarated, hysterical children darted hither and thither like fire-flies, draining glasses of wine and scavenging for food. Booming out over everything came the loud, cheerful strains of 'Seventy Six Trombones', which wouldn't have been my choice in the circumstances but evidently Garry knew what he was doing for I noticed that people were beginning to shuffle round in a sort of military two-step. As I watched, Charlie materialized out of the crowd with a wine bottle in one hand and a French stick in the other. He looked very pleased with himself but then he saw me and the glow faded a little.

'I was very thirsty and hungry,' he protested as I relieved him of the wine bottle. 'You've all had something to eat and drink – we haven't.'

'Find your sisters,' I told him tersely, 'and then go and wait in the kitchen. The mini-bus'll be waiting to deliver you all home.'

'Aw Mum!' he grumbled. 'Why can't we stay? Things are really cool here.'

'You can't stay because this is not a children's party.'

Charlie glanced round at the adults whose party it was and then said, 'You could've fooled me,' then he giggled as a stately Rosalind (I think) who was being propelled round the floor by an even more stately Henry VIII, missed her footing and fell backwards with a mighty splash, bringing Henry down on top of her. Such an event was commonplace now and no one, other than Charlie, gave them more than a passing look.

'Go on,' I said, giving him a gentle push. 'There's plenty of left-overs in the kitchen and you can all help yourselves while you're waiting.' Without further bidding he disappeared like a Will o' the Wisp into the heaving throng and I weaved my way through the dancers towards the end of the marquee where I could see a bedraggled group of Committee members standing in a corner. As I approached, B said something to them and they all turned to look at me.

'And where have you been?' she asked, looking round at the other women for their support. Several strained white faces looked at me accusingly. I hesitated as I met Gwen's wild eyes over their heads.

'Oh, I've been around,' I replied nonchalantly.

'Yes, well, while you've been "around", we've been coping with a major disaster.' B frowned with displeasure. 'I mean, Polly, have you any *idea* what we've been dealing with here?'

'I caught the finale,' I told her wryly, 'and from where I was standing, I would say we had a monumental if unconventional success on our hands.' I looked over my shoulder at the merry throng. 'In fact, I'd say they'll dine out on it for months.'

'I agree with you, Polly,' Miranda cut in. 'I think they believe it was all laid on for their benefit.' She chuckled and looked over at Gwen who was sitting disconsolately on one of the wooden blocks, idly shredding a piece of the torn back-cloth. 'I mean, who will ever forget that last five minutes? I know I won't.' Gwen winced without looking up. Quickly I changed the subject.

'Where are all the children?' I asked.

'You may well ask,' B snapped. 'You were supposed to help Maggie get them changed and ready for their transport home. As it is, Maggie's managing on her own, with a bit of help from dear Eddie.'

'Jolly good,' I said and felt better. B went bright red and pursed her lips savagely.

'We've done most of the tidying up,' she said through gritted teeth.

'Jolly good,' I said again and felt even better. I never could resist a bit of B-baiting.

'Come on everybody!' Hannah suddenly cried, squaring her shoulders and pulling in her stomach. 'Let's get the rest of these blocks out of the way and then we can go out there and enjoy ourselves.' Snapping to like soldiers, everyone other than Gwen started bustling about with renewed vigour.

'Well, there's not much we can do about that,' Miranda remarked as we revealed a large, water-filled crater under two overturned blocks. So we rolled them back in and pinned a large, hastily scrawled notice on one of them. 'KEEP CLEAR — UNEXPLODED BOMB.'

I waited until the rest of the Committee had gone off to enjoy themselves and then I joined Gwen in her moody corner. She looked thoroughly beaten and glum. I gave her shoulder a friendly squeeze and then said, 'I know how you feel, but really, everyone's having enormous fun and the play made everyone laugh even if it wasn't in the way that you intended.' Her eyes swivelled in my direction. 'And I found Mike in the queue for the loo,' I added, keeping my fingers crossed behind my back.

'Oh did you?' she replied dully and turned her gaze back on to the swaying dancers. Then her eyes widened suddenly, like those of a startled cat and she leant forward and peered fixedly into the tattered throng. What has she seen? I wondered. And just then the crowd separated and there, at the centre, I saw Mike and Sheila clasped within each other's arms. Her head was lying lightly on his chest and his cheek was resting yearningly on the soft pillow of her hair. They were moving slowly on the spot in time to the music and it was as if they were alone in an empty room. Then as we watched, spell-bound, the dancers closed ranks and the two love-birds were lost to us. Oh Mike, I thought angrily, you bloody, self-indulgent, drunken silly little boy.

'In the queue for the loo, was he?' Gwen said softly, looking at me, and I was thankful that she couldn't see me blush in the swirling lights of the disco.

'Well he was *then*,' I lied defensively.

'Well he's not *now*,' Gwen said and she slid off the block and looked purposefully into the crowd. I gripped her elbow and held on to it firmly.

'Don't do anything stupid, Gwen,' I pleaded with her. 'After all, you're not in a very strong position yourself, are you?'

'I don't know what you mean,' she said lightly.

'I mean that everyone, including Mike and Sheila, saw you and Eddie just now.'

'Oh *that!*' she said, giving a short harsh cough of contrived laughter. 'Eddie was simply showing me some badly needed sympathy.' My mouth dropped open in astonishment. 'Shut your mouth, Polly,' Gwen commanded with some of her customary vigour. 'You look like a dying codfish.'

'I am simply over-awed by your ability to delude yourself and everyone else.'

'I don't know what you're talking about, Polly.'

'I'm talking about you and Eddie . . . you know . . . what you told me.' Gwen looked at me with bland innocence. 'But I don't know, Polly . . . What *did* I tell you?'

'Come on Gwen.' If there was one thing about Gwen that continually drove me to the point of hysteria, it was her self-delusion. 'This is me you're talking to . . . Good old Polly, your friend to whom all is ultimately revealed.' She shook her head and continued to look puzzled.

'You . . . and Eddie . . . rose-covered cottage . . . babies, etc. etc.?' I watched her closely and was pleased to see the light of comprehension dawning in her eyes.

'Good Lord,' she began slowly, looking at me incredulously. 'You didn't believe all that twaddle did you?'

'As a matter of fact, I did,' I said, beginning to feel slightly foolish.

'Ah, well,' she said, smiling mirthlessly, 'more fool you then. I was just winding you up, Polly. Though I must admit, Eddie's the sort of bloke who inspires day-dreams in respectable matrons, as I believe you've already found out.' She gave me a penetrating look, but furiously I met her eyes and held them. She looked away first.

'You let me believe you were having a torrid affair with that boy,' I accused her heatedly.

'I expect that's what I wanted you to believe at the time.' Gwen tried to pull away from my restraining hand but I held on, digging my nails into her flesh.

'But why?' I demanded to know. Gwen shrugged and had the grace to look a little bit sheepish.

'I think I was jealous. You were so bloody smug and self-satisfied and I wanted to shake you up a bit.'

'Yes, well, the only person you've succeeded in *really* shaking up is Mike, because whatever the truth of the matter, he believes you're involved with Eddie too and frankly, it's hardly surprising. You've been parading that boy in front of Mike for months – I don't see how he could think otherwise.' The noise was building up round us to an almost unbearable level and I found I was having to shout to be heard. The dancers were spreading out and we were being jostled on all sides by vigorous shoulders and bottoms and elbows. I tried to pull Gwen back but she was firmly rooted in the mud. She leant towards me and pushed her face into mine.

'I don't expect you'll believe this, Polly,' she mouthed in such a way that I could lip-read even if I couldn't hear, 'but I've never been unfaithful to Mike. I pretend, just to bring him to heel sometimes.'

'What do you mean, "bring him to heel"?'

'I mean, I know what he is. I'm not such a fool. I know about the groping and the back seats of cars and the one night stands.'

'But you've always insisted that he's true blue and incorruptible.'

'I have my pride!' Gwen cried indignantly. Then she pulled away from me and moved inexorably towards the oblivious couple. I reached out frantically and grasped a handful of cotton blouse, halting her temporarily.

'Don't be an idiot Gwen!' I shouted, just as there was one of those ill-timed lulls in the level of noise surrounding us. People stopped what they were doing and turned to stare and then began to draw away from us in anticipation of yet another spontaneous happening.

'Let go of my blouse Polly,' Gwen said quietly and then, as I clung on, she twitched out of my grasp with a furious shrug of her shoulder. 'Mike!' she called imperiously. He jerked away from Sheila at the sound of his name and then saw Gwen approaching him like an avenging angel.

I stood helplessly wringing my hands on the edge of the expectant crowd and soon I was joined by Miranda Cutler. For a moment she watched with absorbed fascination as Gwen spoke to Mike over the top of Sheila's raven head, and then she said, with obvious relish, 'I wondered how long it would take her to notice what was going on,' and then she chuckled malevolently. 'Who's the woman. Do you know?' she asked me. I shook my head. 'I'd say they've known each other quite a long time, wouldn't you?' By this time Gwen had insinuated herself between Mike and Sheila and was prodding Mike backwards with a stiff, angry finger. He appeared to be resisting. 'Oh goody!' Miranda trilled, 'I think we're in for a bit of good old GBH. What a lark!'

I was about to give Miranda a piece of my mind (the nasty piece) when Hannah came flitting across looking distraught. She was closely followed by B, who was plunging through the puddles like a farmer in a turnip field.

'We must *do* something before there's a scene,' Hannah wailed.

'Let's not,' Miranda drawled lazily, 'and see what happens.' The three of us glared at her with profoundly righteous indignation.

'You really are a quite unspeakable person,' I hissed, making the word 'person' sound like a sobriquet for Jack the Ripper. Miranda looked vaguely startled.

'Yes, you really are,' Hannah echoed bravely. B looked uncomfortable, remembering, no doubt, just how recently she had pinned her colours to the unspeakable person's mast. She always hated to be on the losing side. Miranda smiled a delicately cold little smile and moved away from us with a fastidious toss of her prettily mob-capped little head. I felt certain that I had penetrated her defences at last and then I caught Hannah's eye and we both smiled with satisfaction.

The argument between Gwen and Mike was gaining momentum, and while those of us who knew them both looked concerned, those of us who didn't began to titter with embarrassment. Sheila, who had been hovering anxiously on the sidelines, suddenly moved in and touched Gwen lightly on the arm, no doubt to draw her attention away from Mike. But Gwen was beyond reason and she swung round and knocked Sheila spinning off into the crowd with a mighty swipe of the back of her hand. Mike shouted something at Gwen and tried to move towards Sheila who was being led away by a group of her friends. Without stopping for breath, Gwen swung the same arm back and, clenching her fist, punched Mike fairly and squarely on the jaw. She followed it through with the considerable weight of her whole body and Mike staggered backwards and sat down abruptly in a bucket filled with sand and carefully arranged bracken. He grunted with pain and while he clutched his jaw with one hand, he rubbed his rear with the other. Meanwhile Gwen shuffled and swayed blindly round the clearing they had made for themselves, crying 'Oh' and 'Ah' and clutching her poor broken hand to her bosom as though it was a dying bird. The husbands all dashed in to help Mike to his feet, while Hannah, Maggie, Patsy, B and I rushed to help Gwen.

'And Clint Eastwood makes it look so easy too,' Gwen quipped disconsolately as we escorted her off the floor. 'Now someone's going to have to take me to Casualty because I sure as hell can't drive myself.'

'Come on, Gwen love, I'll take you.' We all looked accusingly at Mike. Poor bugger, I thought. He doesn't deserve all this, and I gave him a covert little smile to show that I understood. Gwen glared balefully at him for a few moments, then her face began to soften.

'Did I do that?' she asked wonderingly. He already had a swelling the size of a small orange on the side of his jaw and it was turning purple as we watched.

'Uh-huh,' he murmured. She looked down at her nerveless hand and then back at Mike's face.

'Well, you can't say you didn't deserve it,' she said defensively and I knew she was as near to tears as I was ever likely to see her.

'Did I?' Mike looked thoughtful for a moment and then said, 'Perhaps I did. But you're no angel yourself. I mean, what was going on backstage I ask myself.' They looked at each other speculatively while the rest of us held our collective breath.

'What about *that woman*?' Gwen asked suspiciously. 'Is it all finished?'

'It never really got started thanks to you,' Mike said, then caught my accusing eye and transmitted an urgent plea for understanding. I nodded faintly and looked away. 'And what about Eddie?' he went on. 'Do I have to put up with him hanging about the place for very much longer?'

Gwen's large eyes widened innocently. 'Oh course not, now that the "do"'s over.'

'That's all right then.' Mike took a few tentative steps towards his defeated-looking wife and she closed the gap and slipped her good hand into his.

'If you're sober, I'll put my boots on and you can drive me up to Casualty because I'm certain I've broken a bone.'

As they left the marquee hand in hand we could hear Gwen concocting the story they would tell the hospital staff to explain their injuries. 'The car skidded and you hit your jaw on the steering wheel and I put my hand out to save myself and squashed it against the dashboard . . .' We looked round at each other and began to giggle.

When I eventually remembered poor Sheila, she had disappeared. Later I learnt from Maggie that Eddie had taken her home, which seemed to me to be oddly appropriate.

By two the wine had run out and most of our guests had left. Just a few intimates remained and they joined in the post-mortem with the rest of us. Despite everything, we were all highly elated. Contrary to our expectations almost everybody claimed to have enjoyed themselves and quite a number of people asked to be put on our 'mailing list' for forthcoming events. Basil Baines obliged us with a rough audit of our accounts and announced cautiously that he thought our net profits would probably be in the region of £1,200, which was far more than we had anticipated.

Then we laughed a lot, for there seemed to be a lot to laugh about, and B worried again about Mrs Walker-Smith and we all told her it was good riddance. Naturally we gossiped a bit about Gwen and Eddie and Mike and Sheila and then suddenly, I was paralysed by a feeling of utterly contented exhaustion. I felt completely at peace with the world and I loved everyone.

'I love you all,' I announced dreamily as I looked round at those tired, shiny faces.

'Oh Lord, she's getting maudlin,' Alan said with a fond chuckle. 'Come on Pol, I think I'd better get you home.' Tenderly he lifted my sore, swollen feet and gently eased them into wellington boots and I remained silent as he put them on the wrong feet. Well, I didn't want to spoil this rare and wonderful gesture. We waved goodbye to those remaining and called out, 'See you in the morning,' and then set off home under our golf umbrella.

'It's stopped raining,' I muttered.

'What?'

'I said, it's stopped raining.' Cautiously Alan poked his head out and looked up at the star-bright velvet sky.

'You're right. It's stopped. Well, what d'you know?' The air, though moist, was fresh and cool and we were drenched in the sweet summer smells that come after rain – honeysuckle, night-scented stock, jasmine and the delicately medicinal scent of balsam poplar.

'If you could bottle this,' Alan said, breathing in deeply, 'you could make a fortune.'

'Look at the stars,' I said. We both stood still and strained upwards towards the cloudless, indigo canopy of twinkling sequins.

'Makes you feel very small and insignificant, doesn't it?' Alan whispered. Suddenly, with an almost audible whoosh, a shooting star shot across the heavens.

'Have a wish,' I told him and I shut my eyes and wished hard that I could lose two stone without having to go on a diet. I suppose I should have wished for world peace or something really worthwhile like that, but I tend towards the belief that world peace is a little ambitious for your average passing star fairy.

'What did you wish for?' Alan asked.

'Oh, you know, the usual,' I replied.

'What's the usual?'

'If I tell you it won't come true,' I said. 'It probably won't anyway, but I live in hope.' I could sense Alan smiling in the darkness.

'Was it the one about world peace?' I said, 'Mmm-mmm' very quietly with my fingers crossed. 'Or was it the one about losing weight without dieting?'

'I'm not telling,' I said sniffily. He chuckled.

'Oh Polly, whatever would I do without you.' Then he slid his hand under my elbow and gently directed me down the slippery path, past the house and out into the road. And what would I do without you, Alan, I wondered, and then I looked down at my funny-looking feet and thought, Well, one thing's for sure. Without you, Alan, I wouldn't be walking like a duck-billed platypus!

The following day we defied the Lord and tidied up.